ALSO BY MEGHAN QUINN

A long TIME COMING

MEGHAN QUINN

Bloom *books*

Published by Bloom Books, an imprint of Sourcebooks
P.O. Box 4410, Naperville, Illinois 60567-4410
(630) 961-3900
sourcebooks.com

Originally published in 2023 by Hot-lanta Publishing, LLC.

Cataloging-in-Publication data is on file with the Library of Congress.

Printed and bound in the United States of America.
LSC 10 9 8 7 6 5 4 3 2 1

PROLOGUE
LIA

"EXCUSE ME," I SAY, BUMPING into a lanky guy in a jam-packed dorm hallway. "Sorry, didn't see you there. I'm all kinds of lost."

"Not a problem," says a deep voice that pulls my gaze up to the tall figure with shaggy-brown hair, dark-rimmed glasses, and a mustache so thick that it almost looks fake. Who knows, maybe it is. "What are you looking for?" he asks while he brings a sixty-four-ounce Slurpee cup to his lips.

"Uh." I glance around, then whisper, "Room 209. But I keep getting turned around because it doesn't seem like there's a room 209."

A smile tugs at his lips. "Scrabble nerd?"

"What?" I ask.

He leans forward and whispers, "It's okay. I'm part of the SSS. Room 209 is hidden for a reason."

SSS = Secret Scrabble Society.

But the first rule about SSS is that you don't talk about it. At least, that's what it said in the invite I received last night. It was a letter delivered to my dorm room. A thick envelope sealed with wax with *SSS* pressed into the red liquid. When I saw the symbol, I quickly locked my door, turned off my lights, and switched on my desk lamp. With bated breath, I delicately opened the envelope and unfolded the sides, revealing the writing on the inside.

I had been handpicked by the SSS to join them tonight. During the grueling three-week tryout process, I played ruthless battles against different members online. After a few losses, a few wins, and two ties, the tryouts were over, and all I had to do was wait. Well, that time has come. I have the invite in hand, and all it says is to show up to room 209 in the Pine Dormitory at 10:23 p.m. sharp, ask no questions, and say nothing. And then I'm to knock with a specific pattern and provide the secret password to get in.

But now that I'm here, lost and confused, I feel like I'm breaking the rules already.

Unfortunately, time is ticking, and I have no idea how to proceed. I don't want to show up late, especially on the first night. But I can't find the room, and…this guy with the 'stache and the Slurpee seems like he knows what he's talking about.

Ugh…but what if this is a test? What if he was planted by the SSS, and I already failed because I mentioned room 209 and Scrabble and… *God*, I'm a failure.

Unsure of how to proceed, I rock on my feet, my hands twisting in front of me as I glance around the hordes of people. What is going on in here anyway? It's a dorm hallway, not a cafeteria. Where are all these people going? I think I need to ditch Slurpee Boy. He knows too much already. And I will not put my position with the SSS in jeopardy. I worked way too hard for an invitation.

"You know, it was nice talking to you, but I think I'll just go look for the room myself. Thanks."

I turn away and head for a dark corridor, only for him to call out, "Not going to find room 209 down there."

I glance over my shoulder to see him sipping on his Slurpee with a smile, his playful eyes intent on my annoyed expression.

"I wasn't actually going that way," I respond with indignance.

"Seemed like you were."

"I was faking you out."

"Were you now?" he asks, that smile growing wider. "Why would you be faking me out?"

I straighten to face him and raise my chin as I say, "Because between your ungodly thick mustache and your shaggy hair, you look like a predator. How can I be sure that you're not attempting to snatch me up?"

His brows raise as he runs his fingers over his mustache. "You know, you're the third person who said I can't rock this mustache. I thought I was looking pretty legit."

The man needs to get a better mirror.

"Your mustache is offensive. I'm pretty sure it would make even the most randy of women go dry." The words fly out of my mouth before I can stop them. Lack of filter—it's my downfall.

I wince as his eyes nearly pop out of their sockets. *Yeah, I was surprised too, buddy.*

"Uh, I don't know—"

Before I can finish telling him I'm not quite sure where in the depths of my being that insult came out of, he grips his stomach, bends forward, and lets out a long, drawn-out laugh, his Slurpee shaking in his hand.

Well, at least he wasn't offended. I've got that going for me.

Either way, I don't have time for this.

Moving past him, I head down the right of the hallway, where I find an unmarked door. Initially, when I was first looking around, I thought this was a utility closet. But paying a little more attention to the door, I think there could be a faint marking of a number on the wall. Maybe… just maybe…it's what I'm looking for.

On a hopeful breath, I knock on the door three times and then kick the footer like I was told just as a tall figure closes in behind me.

"You know, I've never had a girl tell me that I possess the uncanny ability to dehydrate the nether regions of the female race with just my facial hair."

I hold back my smile. "Be glad I'm honest."

The door cracks open, and a single eyeball comes into view. "Password."

"Walla-walla-bing-bang," I answer just as the guy behind me leans forward over my shoulder.

"You missed the *ching-chang* part," he says.

"What? No, I didn't."

"He's right," the eyeball says. "Sorry, no entrance."

"Wait, no," I say as I prevent the eyeball from shutting the door. I pull the invite out from my pocket and say, "I have the invitation...errr, I mean..." *Ugh, stupid, Lia. You're not supposed to show the invitation.* Backpedal. "Actually..." I slip the invite back into my pocket and fold my hands together. "There is no invite, and I have no idea what this door leads to. I just know that I'm supposed to be here at ten twenty-three, and I am, so therefore, I believe I should gain entrance."

"But you forgot the ching-chang," Slurpee Boy says while sucking on his straw.

"There was no ching-chang," I reply with aggravation. "It clearly said, knock three times, kick the footer, and then say, 'Walla-walla-bing-bang.' I know this because I read the, uh...thing twenty-seven times precisely. So either this is not the right door, which perhaps it's not, or you two have not read the instructions yourself, and in which case, I demand to speak to an authoritative human."

"An authoritative human?" Slurpee Boy asks. "Is that a professional term?"

"Dumbing it down for you," I say with snark. "You know, since you have that look."

"What look?" he asks.

"One that's lacking intelligence." Call it my nerves or my irritation, or just the fact that I can't hold anything back, but I just let my insult fly.

Thankfully, that smile of his once again tugs on the corners of his lips right before he says to the eyeball, "She's good, man. Let her in."

"What?" I ask, so utterly confused that I wonder if being part of the SSS is even worth it.

But then the door opens, revealing a very large room, larger than all the other dorm rooms, and it's a haven to all the things I love. Off to the right is a raised bed with a desk underneath that holds three computer screens, speakers, a massive keyboard, as well as a giant mouse and mouse pad that expands the length of the desk...*Lord of the Rings* themed. Hanging on the beige walls are posters, flags, and framed art ranging from *Star Wars* to board games to a large yellow and blue model airplane suspended from the ceiling. To the left is a futon sofa with a coffee table and crates with cushions all along the edges. In the middle, a Scrabble board on a turntable—the fancy kind.

I could totally spend an hour nerding out in this room.

The whole collection of Harry Potter books rests on the bookshelf— and they look like the originals. My mouth salivates.

A framed poster of Adam West as Batman hangs over the sofa, Adam standing tall with a *Kerpow* in comic detail directly behind him.

And under the small television on a flimsy-looking TV stand is what looks to be an original Atari game console. If the owner of this residence owns *Pitfall*, we will be best friends for life.

"Wow, cool room," I say. The fantastic décor speaks to my geeky heart. And the precise organization, from the labeled folders on the bookshelf next to the desk to the stacked shoes on the shoe rack, is next-level.

"Thanks," Slurpee Boy says. "It's mine. I'm also the authoritative person, as you like to call it." He holds his hand out. "Breaker Cane. It's nice to meet you. Maybe as you hang out with us more, you can lower yourself to my lack of intelligence on a more personal level."

My mouth goes dry.

The tips of my ears go hot.

And I feel a wave of sweat crest my upper lip.

Good job, Lia. Really good job.

"Uh, yeah...I didn't really mean—"

"No, no. Don't take it back." He holds up his hand. "I like your brutal and brash honesty. Made me feel alive." He winks.

"Oh, okay. In that case"—I clear my throat—"although your room seems like a dream to explore, you could have tucked the corners of your bed better, not quite 'nurse's corner' tight, your framed picture of Rory Gilmore is crooked, and you have to get rid of the mustache. It's atrocious."

He chuckles and nods while moving his fingers over the bush beneath his nose. "Still trying to perfect the nurse's corner. If you have expertise in this endeavor, then, by all means, present a tutorial. The room I share a wall with plays music loud enough that they force Rory to dance, making her crooked. I've given up. And the mustache, well, I thought it looked good. Seems to me everyone's been lying to me."

"They have been."

"But you don't seem to have that ability...to lie to someone to forsake their feelings."

"Depends on the moment and the person." I look him up and down. "You seemed sturdy enough to handle the truth and also, stressful situations—i.e. not knowing where the room was—snatching any social decorum I might have stored away."

"Well, that can only mean one thing."

Confused, I ask, "What's that?"

"That there is no other choice than to become the greatest friends of all time."

I smirk. "Only if you shave."

"Ehhh, that's something we might have to work out." He rocks on his feet and continues. "Given that you are the only new recruit to the Secret Scrabble Society, you must be Ophelia Fairweather-Fern."

"That would be me. But just call me Lia. My entire name is far too many syllables for anyone to carry around, let alone my first name."

He chuckles. "Your name was a check in the plus column during try-outs. But your brutal use of words we've never even heard of was the real reason you were chosen, especially since we play on a timer."

"That was an added challenge I appreciated. Although the timer star-tled me at first and took a second for me to get used to. That and not being able to see your new letters or the gameboard until your turn started. I had a lot of fun. I'm glad I was chosen."

"It was an easy choice." He sets his Slurpee cup down. "Everyone, this is Lia. Lia, that's Harley, Jarome, Christine, and Imani." From where they're seated at the coffee table, they all raise their hands for a brief hello and then return to the gameboard. "Yeah, they're not really social."

"Well, good thing I didn't come here to socialize." I rub my hands together. "I came to play."

Breaker chuckles and then reaches for his Slurpee again. "Then what are we waiting for? Game on."

I stare Breaker down and then glance at the last two tiles on my shelf.

He has one tile left.

The room has cleared out.

The rest of the SSS has left, claiming early morning classes.

"Your move," he says while purposely running his finger over his mus-tache. I'd dominated this entire game until about three moves ago when he somehow pulled out an eighty-point word, completely shattering my lead.

"I know it's my move."

"Really, because you've been sitting there catatonic for at least five minutes."

"I'm making sure I have the right move."

"Or any move at all." He leans back on the sofa, a smug look painted across his face.

"I *have* a move."

"One that won't win you the game, though, right?" he presses. He knows he has this game. It's evident in his cocky disposition.

"You know, it's not polite to gloat."

"This coming from the girl who was dancing only a few minutes ago because she had a tremendous lead on me."

I slowly look up at him and, in a deadpan voice, say, "It will behoove you to know that I can dish it, but I can't take it."

He lets out a low chuckle as I reluctantly place an *E* after a *W* for a measly five points.

"Nice move." He stares down at his single tile and then lifts it dramatically, only to place an *S* after *huzzah*, giving him thirty-one points. "But not good enough." He leans back again and crosses his leg over his knee. "I win."

I groan and flop backward onto the floor. Staring up at his model airplane, I say, "I had you."

"Never celebrate too early. You never know what can happen at the end of a Scrabble game."

"That's such a cheap move by the way, holding on to an *S* to the very end."

"How did you know I was holding on to it?"

"Because I watched you pick up the tile a while ago and set it to the side."

"Don't tell me you're one of those players. The one who counts the tiles and knows what everyone could possibly have."

"Not to that extent, but I watched you baby that tile and not touch it until now. You saved it on purpose."

"When you're trailing by eighty points, you have to be strategic, and I was. No shame in playing the game."

"I hate to admit it since you won, but it was a good game. I enjoyed the challenge."

"It was a good game. You're going to fit in nicely here." He starts picking up the board, and I lift to help him. "Your application said you're majoring in research and statistics. What's the plan after college?"

"Getting my master's and then becoming a survey research specialist."

He pauses. "That's really specific," Breaker says. "And not a job you hear on a list of what you want to be when you grow up."

"Not so much, but I've always been into surveys. Growing up, I loved filling them out. I spent a great deal of time filling out every survey my parents came across. I loved the idea of someone being able to listen to me and gather information to make a change. And of course, I would make surveys on my own, handwritten ones on construction paper, and pass them around at family gatherings to see how everyone enjoyed themselves. Then I would draw up a report and send out an end-of-the-year letter, showing everyone where we excelled and where we could improve."

Breaker smirks. "And did you find out anything constructive from these family surveys?"

"Yes." I nod as I hand him the last few tiles that need to be picked up. "Whenever my uncle Steve decided to take his pants off after dinner, it always led to him doing the invisible Hula-Hoop on top of the cleared-off dining table—*which no one relished*. I made sure to convey this to the family and Uncle Steve, but unfortunately, I have no control over their behavior. I can only survey what needs to change. Changes are made from within."

"Uncle Steve sounds like a good time."

"He had a mustache…and he's known as the pervert in the family. So yeah, maybe you two would get along."

"Not a pervert," Breaker says while packing up the rest of the game.

"That has yet to be determined."

"Can we make a quick assessment? Because I can assure you, I'm not a pervert." He sets the board game to the side and then leans back on his futon while I press my weight on my hands behind me. I should probably leave. Everyone else has, but for some reason, I feel comfortable here, and I don't want to leave just yet.

"If you wish."

He touches his nose and points at me. "I believe the phrase you're reaching for is, *As you wish*."

"*Princess Bride* fan, are we?"

"What's there not to be a fan of? Revenge, swords, master tales of times before. It's got it all. Not to mention…Fred Savage."

"I actually agree, which puts a check mark in your column of not being a pervert." He fist-pumps to himself, which makes me chuckle. "But that's only one check mark. There are more questions."

"Hit me. Watch me pass with flying colors."

"We shall see about that. Have you ever, since you've donned the mustache, peeped into someone's window, preferably the sex you're attracted to?"

"That would be women, and no."

"Good answer. Next question, have you ever felt the need to walk into the ladies' room because you wanted to take a gander?"

"I've heard there are way more stalls, which I'm jealous of because sometimes I just like to sit and pee. But no, I have not."

My brows pull together. "Sit and pee?"

He shrugs. "I get lazy."

"Okay, seems like more work to sit down and pee, but to each their own. One more question. Have you ever started a club for men with mustaches and purchased mini mustache combs and creams so you can have mustache care parties?"

"Wow, now that sounds like a good fucking time, but no, I have not." He drapes his arms along the back of the futon. "So…have you deduced that I'm not a pervert?"

"Temporarily. I'm putting you on probation."

"That's fair." He places one leg over the other.

"But I do need to ask a few rapid-fire questions, just to double check."

"Hit me."

"Favorite singer or band?"

"Blondie."

"Really?" I ask, surprised.

"Yup." He pops the *P*, looking so relaxed that, in return, he makes me feel comfortable. "Obsessed."

"Okay, good answer. How about favorite candy?"

"Smarties because I'm smart, and I think they make me feel extra clever."

I chuckle. "I guess that's a good reason. Favorite TV show?"

"*Wonder Years*. Hence, the Fred Savage comment earlier. Love him. Second to *Wonder Years* is *Boy Meets World*, as fuck, did I crush on Topanga so goddamn hard. And of course, Cory is my man crush."

"Fan of the Savage brothers?"

"They're my ride or die."

"Makes you seem very relatable."

He drags his finger over his mustache as he says, "Stick around, Lia. You'll see just how relatable a finance major with a penchant to crash his model airplane every time he flies it is."

"I always thought Shawn was whiny."

"Join the club," Breaker says with an eye roll. "Thoughts on Mr. Turner's mullet?"

"Hot," I answer.

"So if I were to, let's say…grow this hair out to be a mullet, what would your thoughts be on that?"

"Pitiful; get your own look."

He chuckles. "Man, you sure know how to bring a man down to his knees."

"Apparently, it's what I do best."

"Apparently, I like that about you, though." He moves his teeth over his lip before saying, "So, Lia, what did you think about tonight? Have fun?"

"I had a lot of fun." Not wanting to sound like too much of a loser, I gently say, "It's been hard meeting people here, you know, people who are on the same level as me. I just recently transferred, so not coming in as a freshman and making friends has been a challenge. Although"—I glance around his room—"I do feel comfortable here, despite these dwellings belonging to a mustache."

"I'm going to take that as a compliment. And meeting new people is hard. Took me a second to figure it all out too. They always say college is where you get to reinvent yourself and find like-minded people. Well, they don't tell you it doesn't happen immediately. I'm a junior now and feel like I've just hit my stride."

"Same. No one seems to like spending countless hours poring over a game of Scrabble or knitting hats for cats."

"Hats for cats?"

"Quite fetching. I sell them to old ladies who think dressing up their cats is fun." I shrug. "Started it for some side cash, but now, I'm invested. But yeah, tonight reminded me that there are like-minded people out there for me, making me feel like myself for the first time in a long time."

His expression softens. "I'm glad, Lia." He strokes the hair under his nose and says, "I bet a lot of you feeling comfortable has to do with the mustache."

"It's not the mustache," I answer with feigned irritation.

He chuckles. "Do you have a boyfriend?" When I eye him skeptically, he holds his hand up. "Not because I'm getting all pervy on you, just genuinely curious."

"I did until he broke up with me and told me I was lame because I started a fan fiction for *Supernatural*. I was into different things than he was, so it was hard to connect. Doesn't seem like I can find many people at all who understand the desire to make Sam and Dean not brothers, but rather...secret lovers."

His eyes widen, and he lowers both legs to the ground as he says, "Hold the fuck on... You're the author of *Lovers, Not Brothers*?"

"Wait." I sit up taller. "You've heard of it?"

"Heard of it?" he nearly shouts and then lowers his body to the ground, so now we're at eye level. "Lia, that shit is addicting. I'm not even gay, but Jesus Christ, their first kiss was the best fucking thing I've ever read. I had actual sweat forming on the back of my neck while Dean slowly rubbed his nose along Sam's jaw, waiting for the cue that Sam was ready. And then...when their mouths collided, I let out a fucking wallop of a cheer. The sexual tension was unnerving."

"And you didn't think it was weird that we know them as brothers in real life?"

"Isn't that what fan fiction is all about? Creating a world that's separate from the original?"

I smile. "You get it."

"Of course I get it. I'm not a moron." He pushes his hand through his shaggy hair. "Christ, you need to write some more. That was some good shit. I'll never forget the scene when Dean is naked, gripping his penis and singing *Eye of the Tiger* to Sam as he closes in." He kisses the tips of his fingers. "Chef's kiss."

Jokingly, I ask, "Are you fanboying over me?"

"Got a problem with that?"

I shake my head, then whisper, "I can't believe you've read it."

"I can't believe you *wrote* it."

And then we stare at each other for a few moments. Silence fills the room, an unspoken truth forming between us—this is the start of something new.

"Breaker?"

"Yeah?"

Shyly, I ask, "Will you be my friend?"

That smile of his I've grown to know tonight widens. "Are you asking me to start a...friendship with you?"

"I believe I am. Is that weird? I mean, we barely know each other. I find your mustache absolutely repulsive, but our commonalities are endless at this point. The fact we can agree that the Winchester brothers being lovers is erotic is unprecedented. I believe that means we need to be friends."

He slowly nods. "I believe it's imperative."

I hold up my hand. "And friends only because that mustache has ruined any sexual feeling I might have toward you."

"I understand. I knew the risks of what could happen if I cultivated facial hair solely along my upper lip." He holds his hand out. "Friends?"

I take his hand in mine. "Friends."

CHAPTER 1
BREAKER

PRESENT DAY...

"GOT SOMEWHERE IMPORTANT TO BE?" JP asks me from across the plane, his eyes fixed on my bouncing leg.

"Just eager to get the hell away from you," I answer, a typical brother response.

"Cute." He lets out a deep sigh. "I hate being away from Kelsey, but the trip to New York was good, right? Setting up our second rent-controlled building feels good."

A few months ago, JP approached me and our other brother, Huxley, about utilizing our fortune for good and offering some rent-controlled buildings in major cities. The buildings would offer a safe, clean, and fresh place to live, providing assistance to those who might need it—like day-care facilities for single parents, financial classes, and access to a market with wholesale food. The point of the project is to help those who need it the most. It's been a successful and rewarding venture.

"It does feel good," I say as I pull my phone from my pocket while the plane taxis to the bunker. I open the text thread I have with Lia, and I shoot her a quick text.

Breaker: Landed. Picking up the goods. You have everything cued up and ready to go?

My phone buzzes right away with a reply.

Lia: I've been ready, just waiting on you.
Breaker: Sorry, poor weather held us up. Be there soon.

"Who are you texting over there?" JP asks, trying to get a look at my phone.

"Lia," I answer.

"Ahhh," he announces with realization heavy in his tone. "That's why you're so eager to get off the plane. You want to go spend time with your girl."

"First of all, she's not my girl; she's my best friend, and if I have to keep saying that to you, I'm going to fucking explode. And secondly, she just got a brand-new glass Yahtzee that we've been dying to play."

"Glass Yahtzee?" JP asks. "That seems like an extremely bad idea. Isn't the point of Yahtzee to shake the dice?"

"Yes, but this presents another level of a challenge: shake the dice without breaking the cup."

JP stares at me, his face devoid of expression. "You're going to slice your hands open. Does this glass Yahtzee come with a warning?"

"Yes, of course. It's a *play at your own risk* situation. And we want to risk it. Don't worry, though. Lia has prepared a hard surface with a blanket. We're being smart."

"Being smart would not be playing glass Yahtzee," he mutters while shaking his head. "Do not call me when you need stitches."

"Not like you would answer the phone if I did."

JP rolls his eyes in a dramatic fashion. "I'm a newlywed, for fuck's sake. Sorry if I want to spend every waking moment with my wife."

"I don't think you actually are sorry," I say just as the plane parks and the flight attendant opens the door and lets down the stairs.

I gather my bag and move past JP to the exit, where I stop suddenly.

Huxley, our older brother, steps out of his car, shuts the door, and leans against it with his arms crossed. Sunglasses cover his eyes, but it doesn't hide the scowl on his forehead or the tension he's wearing under his perfectly tailored suit.

"Uh, JP? Why is Huxley here, looking like he's ready to kill?"

"What?" JP asks as he moves toward the exit as well. He pokes his head out and says, "I don't know. Did he text us?"

Instead of exiting the plane to see what the issue is, we both search through our phones for a text message or email and come up short.

"Nothing," I say.

"Fuck," JP says. "That only means one thing. Whatever he needs to tell us, he doesn't want to be traced."

"What?" I ask. "Dude, you've been watching too many secret operative shows. That is not why he's here in person. Maybe...maybe it's good news. Maybe he has something special to tell us and wants to see our reactions in person."

"How does it feel living in a realm where unicorn crap tastes like strawberry ice cream?" JP gestures toward Huxley. "Look at him, the scowl. He's not here to pet our heads and tell us what good boys we've been. Clearly, we fucked up somehow. Just have to figure out how."

"Will you two get the fuck down here and stop gabbing?" Huxley yells.

"Dude, my balls just shivered," JP says, gripping my shoulder.

"My penis totally just turtled." I step to the side and push JP forward. "You first; you're older. You've experienced more life than me."

"Barely," he says, trying to move me toward the exit first, but I plant my feet on the floor and hold steady. Since JP's been married, I've spent more time at the gym while he's spent more time in Kelsey—with all due respect—so I have a few pounds of muscle over him at the moment.

"Just get out there before he gets even madder." I push at JP. "You know how he hates when we—in his terms—clown around."

"Quit clowning around," Huxley yells.

"See," I whisper-shout.

"Don't push me," JP says, leaning his weight into me, his back to my chest. "You're going to make me tumble down the stairs."

"Oh, good idea. If you tumble down, then there's a good chance you could get injured, and whatever he's here for will be put on a momentary pause while we assess your injuries. That will give us some thinking time. And maybe if you're willing to break a bone, that will grant us at least a few days."

"Oh yeah, let me just throw myself down the stairs."

"That's the spirit," I say while patting him on the back. "Close your eyes. It will be over in a second."

"Jesus Christ," JP mutters before he makes his way down the stairs.

I follow closely. "Oh, I see, going to fall closer to the ground. Smart."

"I'm not going to fall, you idiot."

When we reach the ground, Huxley opens the back car door to his Tesla S and says, "Get in."

I can hear JP gulp as I say, "You sure you don't want to at least fake an injury?"

"I think it's too late, man," he says as he climbs into the car, and I follow.

Once we're in the back, Huxley slams the door, causing JP and me to flinch. When Huxley climbs in the front seat, he doesn't bother to look at us. Instead, he grips the steering wheel and lets out a long, pent-up breath.

A sigh of discontent. Great.

After a few seconds, he turns to face us and says, "Has Taylor been in touch with you?"

"Taylor, as in our lawyer?" JP asks.

"Yes, our lawyer."

We shake our heads. "No, I haven't gotten anything," I say.

"What's going on?" JP asks, his voice growing serious.

"We're being sued for misconduct in the workplace."

"What?" I shout. "By whom?"

Huxley lifts his sunglasses, and his eyes narrow in on me. "Your former employee."

"Uh, excuse me?" I blink a few times. "What the hell for?"

"Let's see, hostile work environment and wrongful termination."

"Wait." I shake my head, trying to get a grip on what he's saying. "Who the hell was this?"

"Gemma Shoemacher."

"Shoemacher?" I ask, eyes wide and disbelief heavy in my tone. "As in the girl who would secretly slip into my office, rearrange my shit, hang up pictures of her relatives, decorate for holidays, and then just leave? The absolute psycho who would corner me in the break room and ask me when my next dentist appointment was so she could watch me get my teeth cleaned? The girl who made me an advent calendar for Christmas and inside each box was homemade thumbnail drawings of me? That girl?"

"Were the drawings good?" JP asks.

"How the fuck is that relevant?" I ask him, losing my temper.

JP shrugs. "Just genuinely curious."

"I mean…watercolor on a small surface is quite difficult, so maybe—"

"Enough about the paintings," Huxley says. "This is fucking serious. Not only has she sued us, but she's also soiling our reputation on social media. She's spreading lies about how we conduct business and how Breaker created a hostile environment for her and berated her in front of fellow employees."

"That's not fucking true," I say. "I was never hostile, even when she 'accidentally' tripped me while I was holding my morning coffee. I've been nothing but kind to that woman, and the reason she was let go was that we found out she was the one going around to everyone's office and stealing their daily to-do lists. She had a whole collection of them filed away in her desk."

"Well, she's spinning a story and attacking our business, and unfortunately, she's getting attention."

"What does that mean?" I ask.

"It means, because she's using the right platforms, she's getting tons of views and now media coverage. This has happened in the past twenty-four hours."

"How the hell does that happen?" JP asks.

Huxley shakes his head. "No fucking clue, but we're fielding calls about it. Lottie said she heard some employees talking about it in the break room before quieting down as she entered. We're losing credibility by the second."

"Because someone is lying," I say, anger heavy in my voice.

"Yes, but the public seems to be clinging to her story. Therefore, we need to take action while Taylor and his team gather evidence for a countersuit. She has no leg to stand on, no evidence, just her word and her friend's who doesn't work for us anymore. But we have security footage, we have the evidence that you've gathered, Breaker, over time, and we have all of her social media posts that have been screen recorded. Defamation will be what takes her down."

"Okay, so…what should we do?" I ask.

"For one, you need to take a step back."

"What?" I roar. "No fucking way. I'm not resigning because someone spreads lies about me. That makes me look guilty, and I'm not guilty. I've been nothing but respectful and professional to that woman."

"I'm not talking about resigning," Huxley says, his jaw growing tight. "We just need you to take…a mandatory vacation. Just so it looks like we're doing the right thing while we investigate her allegations, which means you need to not be in the office."

"That's bullshit—"

"He's right," JP says. "If this was with any other employee, we'd ask them to go on sabbatical while we investigate the allegations. You shouldn't be treated any different."

"But I didn't fucking do anything," I say.

"We know," Huxley says. "But just because we know you're innocent doesn't mean everyone will believe it. We're in sensitive waters here, and we need to make sure we exercise due diligence in the investigation. If we do this right, conduct the investigation correctly, then hopefully it will set a precedent for any future employees who try to do the same."

"I'm afraid to say it," JP adds, "but he's right, man."

I glance back and forth between my brothers, letting their common sense sink in. "Fuck," I mutter as I lean back against the seat and push my hand through my hair.

"It's for the best, Breaker," Huxley says. "And while you're gone, we'll be sure to split up your responsibilities between me and JP."

"Hey now, I didn't agree with that," JP says but then quickly quiets when Huxley gives him a scathing look.

"It won't be for long. Maybe a week or two," Huxley says. "In the meantime, if we have questions, we'll communicate in person. I don't want to leave any sort of paper trail."

"So then what the hell am I supposed to do for the next one to two weeks?" I ask.

"Maybe help Lia with her knitting," JP says. "I know you know how to knit."

I glance at Huxley, and he says, "Knitting might keep you busy."

"Fuck off…both of you," I say right before I exit the car and head straight for mine.

———

"Your food is smelling up the entire elevator," Mrs. Gunderson says as she stands as far away from me as possible, her umbrella tucked under her arm. It barely ever rains in Los Angeles, yet she carries around a large black one every day…just in case.

"Thank you for pointing that out," I say to her as the elevator slows and then beeps, indicating our floor.

"Sarcasm is the devil's tongue," she shoots at me before heading toward her door. I walk in the opposite way and right past my door to the apartment next to mine. "Premarital sex is also the way of the devil," she shouts before walking into her apartment.

"I hate that woman," I mutter as I knock on Lia's door three times, kick the footer, and then say, "Walla-walla-bing-bang."

Lia is quick to open the door, her familiar freckled face easing the tension roaring through my body.

I remember the first time I ran into her in the hallway of my dorm. She was unsure of herself but also so confident that she couldn't help the things flying out of her mouth. Her vibrant red hair and mossy-green eyes under her purple-rimmed glasses stood out, but it was her pure honesty that really drew me to her—unlike anyone I've ever met. And now, I can't go a day without talking to her.

"You didn't say ching-chang," she says with a smirk.

"Ching-chang wasn't a part of it."

She points her finger accusingly at me. "I knew it."

Chuckling, I open my arm that's not holding the food and pull her into a hug. "Missed you."

"Missed you, Pickle," she says, using my nickname that she gave me one night after a misspelled *pickle* during a Scrabble game. "What took you so long? I started to tear apart the dessert I got us."

"You don't want to know." I sigh, and we both walk into her apartment.

I remember the moment she found this place. She'd been looking for about two days and then came across this building in Westwood. She had no idea if they had apartments for rent, but she liked the flowers out front and the Jamba Juice across the street. Lo and behold, when she inquired, there were two apartments right next to each other. She called me immediately and told me I was moving. We've lived here for the past five years.

Whereas my apartment has more windows and open space, Lia's has more character, with exposed brick on almost every wall. And the way the individual apartments wrap around, our bedroom walls buddy up, and our balconies sit across from each other over the atrium in the lobby.

"I do want to know what took so long because glass Yahtzee can only wait so long, and if you're raging, our game is going to end short."

"Who says I'm raging?" I ask as I set the food on her pristine white kitchen countertop. I have the same one, and we try to compete on who can keep theirs whiter. It's so stupid, but fuck, I think she's winning.

"I've known you for a decade, Breaker. Pretty sure I can tell when you're simmering in rage. What's going on?"

Taking a seat on one of her barstools, I rest my arms on the counter. "I don't want to ruin the night. I haven't seen you in over a week, and the last thing I want to do is talk about work." Or lack thereof, thank you, Gemma Shoemacher.

"Yes, and since I haven't seen you in over a week, the last thing I want to do is eat dinner and play a fragile game of Yahtzee with a grump. Now tell me what happened so we can move on and have fun." She sets two plates on the counter and adds, "I've been planning this night for a few days now. Do not ruin it." She threateningly points her finger at me, which I knock away.

"Fine, but we're not harping on it, okay?" I drag my hand over the back of my neck. "I've thought about it enough on the drive over here. I just want to forget it."

"Fine, now spill." She empties out the carton of lo mein and divides it equally on our plates.

"Do you remember that one girl who used to work for me, the one who made me that advent calendar?"

"Remember her? I still have every picture she drew of you in a box in my room. December seventeenth will forever be my favorite. The way she accentuated your nostrils was pure perfection."

My nostrils resembled two giant life rafts on my face, but of course, Lia thought it was the greatest thing she had ever seen.

"Gemma is my hero. Sad she got so crazy and you had to let her go," she adds.

"Yeah, well, she's suing us now."

Lia pauses, smirks, and then shakes her head. "Oh, Gemma, bad, bad move. Don't mess with the Cane brothers and their business." She glances up at me. "What's she attempting to get money out of you for?"

"Claims hostile work environment, berating from me—"

Lia lets out a large guffaw. "Beratement...from *you*?" She points the fork in her hand at me. "That's laughable. I don't think you could hurt a fly if you tried, let alone berate someone in a workplace."

"I know...but she's on some sort of warpath, claiming wrongful termination and all that other bullshit. She's posted it on social media and is now getting press attention because we're Cane Enterprises. Anything to bring us down."

"Yeah, but she's being a total moron because you can't go and make up lies on social media like that; if you're caught, you're effed." She tops our plates off with some General Tso's chicken. "So is Huxley countersuing?"

"How do you know that?"

"Please." She licks the sweet yet spicy sauce off her fork. "I've known you and your family long enough to have witnessed the hard work, dedication, and many hours you've put into building Cane Enterprises. No way in hell is Huxley going to let some stalker—albeit a rather comical one—get away with tarnishing the brand and the business you three have spent so long creating."

"Yes, they're putting together all the evidence they need to present their case. I don't think we're in it for the money, because we don't need it, nor are we in the business of putting people in debt, but Huxley wants to set a precedent. Make sure that people know not to fuck with us."

"Probably smart because this girl has opened the door to the possibility of lawsuits, and if you end this correctly, no one will want to go up against you."

"Yeah, that's the plan."

"So what's the problem? Sure, maybe your ego is slightly tarnished, but when has that ever affected you before? Remember the time in college you were mistaken for the third-best Scrabble player rather than the second? You took that like a champ."

"You're just full of laughs today, aren't you?"

"Just trying to cheer you up." She pulls two Sprites from her fridge and deposits one in front of me, and then she takes the seat next to mine. Our shoulders bump as she gets comfortable. When she picks up her fork with her left hand, bumping into my right, she says, "You took the wrong seat."

"I was preoccupied. Deal with it."

"Are you really going to be grumpy all evening? I was looking forward to a nice night of *will we slice our hands open or will we not*?"

"I'm sorry," I huff while pushing the chicken around my plate. "I didn't mention one thing. The guys said I can't go to work. I have to take time off until they figure this all out."

"So what you're telling me is that you were just granted a vacation, and you're complaining about that, why?"

"Because people will think I'm in trouble or did something wrong when I didn't do anything wrong. I've worked hard to maintain genuine relationships with my employees, and if I'm not there, what will they think of me?"

"I can see why that would bother you," she says. "You do tend to pride yourself on the way you treat people, and this is a slur to your character."

"Exactly. It's really shitty," I say, my voice growing heavy.

"Hey," Lia says, turning toward me. "The people who know you will understand the circumstances. They know you're not some tyrant, running up and down the hallway like a lunatic, yelling at the first person you run into. And the other people, the ones who might believe Gemma, well, they're not people you want around you anyway."

"I know you're right," I say softly. "Just can't seem to wrap my head around all of it."

She pulls me into a hug, and I rest my head against hers. "It will be okay. If anything, Huxley is relentless, and he won't rest until your name is expunged of any wrongdoing."

"I guess so." She releases me, and I let out a low breath. "I'm sorry about all of this. I'm totally bringing down the night."

"It's okay. How about we put glass Yahtzee on hold for now in case you have intermittent episodes of rage? We can't risk the slivers. Want to play cards out on the balcony?"

"Maybe we can watch a show. There's a new documentary called *The King of Kong* that I want to watch."

"Oh, I saw that the other day when I was scrolling through what to watch with Brian," Lia says, talking about her boyfriend. "I suggested it, and he gave me the side-eye. We ended up watching some sports game."

"Some sports game?" I laugh. "Not even sure what sport?"

"A ball was involved."

"Well, that narrows it down."

She chuckles. "Either way, I'd love to watch it. Shall we start it now? Bring our food over to the couch?"

"If you're cool with that."

She tips my chin up and, in a gooey voice, says, "Anything for my pickle."

"Brian would have hated that documentary."

That's because Brian is a douche.

But I keep that comment to myself.

"Yeah, didn't quite scream something Brian would have enjoyed."

Lia shifts and then pokes my stomach. "You going to be okay? You're usually a little more chatty when we watch documentaries."

"Yeah, I was just thinking. I'll be good, though."

"You know, if you need to talk about it, I'm always here."

"I know." I take her hand in mine. "Thanks, Lia."

She gives it a squeeze. "You're welcome. Now get out of here and go to bed. You look like trash."

I smirk. "Can always count on you to deliver the truth." I pull her into a hug and give her a kiss on the top of her head. "Night, Lia."

"Night, Pickle."

I let go and then head to my apartment just as she closes her door. I strip out of my clothes, splash some water on my face, and then brush my teeth. Once I'm ready for bed, I plug my phone in to charge, slip under my covers—naked—and then place my hands behind my head and stare up at the ceiling.

The entire night, I kept wondering why I was so affected by this. I know Huxley will take care of it. I've been getting texts from him all night about how we're going to make sure Gemma doesn't speak another word about me, but even with that reassurance, I still feel...weird.

And I think it comes down to her attack on my character. Gemma attacked the one thing I take great pride in, and that's being a good guy. Between my brothers and me, we all have different personalities.

Huxley is the grump, the domineering one, the take-no-prisoners kind of guy.

JP is the funny one, the easygoing guy, the instigator at times.

And me...well, I'm the levelheaded one, the sounding board, and the good guy.

So having my name slandered with vehement lies is just so fucking painful. I've worked so hard at being above reproach.

Respected.

Trusted.

And someone people could rely on.

For the most part, I've accomplished that, but this...this just makes me think that maybe I didn't.

I scrub my hand down my face just as a light tapping comes from the other side of the wall.

And just like that, a smile spreads across my face.

Reaching up to the wall, I rap my knuckle four times.

Like clockwork, she knocks three.

Four knocks for four letters in love.

Three knocks for three letters in you.

It's something we've done ever since we shared a wall. It's a gentle reminder that even though I'm angry, irritated, or even sad, at least I have Lia, my best friend, the one person who can so easily put a smile on my face. I don't know what I'd do without her.

I don't even want to think about it. Even when things in my life are out of balance, there's one very solid, very predictable constant. Lia.

CHAPTER 2
LIA

"MORNING," BRIAN SAYS THROUGH THE phone. "Just wanted to remind you that we have lunch with my mom this afternoon."

I lift my cup of coffee and say, "Yup, don't worry, I'll be there fifteen minutes early so she doesn't have to comment on how I'm there only five minutes early."

"Be nice," he says.

"I'm…I'm—"

"So did you tell him about us last night?"

I stare down at the engagement ring sitting on my dresser. No, I didn't tell *him*. Brian is not a fan of Breaker's. "Not yet. It wasn't a good time last night."

"Lia, how could it not be a good time to tell your best friend you're engaged?"

"He has some really bad things happening at work right now. Like… inimical circumstances. He found out about it last night. I didn't think it was appropriate to just spring it on him."

"What's going on?"

"Confidential things," I answer because even though Brian is my fiancé, Breaker is my best friend and deserves his privacy, especially regarding his business. "Anyway, I'll tell him soon."

"Okay." He pauses and then says, "You're not avoiding telling him for a reason, are you?"

"What does that mean?" I ask as I move toward my desk. Luckily, I get to work from home since I do contract work for my clients, which means I have my own hours and my own space. I'm not exactly a people person.

"It means I just want to make sure you're happy about being engaged. It's been a week, Lia, and you haven't said anything to him."

"Because he's been out of town. I'm not about to tell him over the phone. It's something I want to do in person."

"Okay…" he says softly, and I can tell he's not happy.

"Brian, I'm going to tell him. I just want it to be a celebration, not something I say in passing or when he's in a bad mood or out of town. He'll be happy for us."

"Are you sure?"

"Why wouldn't he?"

"I don't know. You've just been weird since I proposed."

"Weird, how?" I ask as I take a seat on my desk chair and slowly start to spin around in circles.

"Well, for one, we've only seen each other twice this past week, and I don't know, I would think that since we've been engaged, we'd see each other more. And your texting has been sporadic. That's why I called this morning, because I wanted to make sure you were going to show up for lunch."

"Brian, of course I'd show up."

"I just don't know, Lia. Seems like you don't want to be engaged to me."

"Stop," I say, growing frustrated. "This is all just so…new, okay? I'm taking it one day at a time." I pause as I try to word what's been spinning through my mind over the last seven days. "I may not talk about them as much anymore, but I miss my parents, Brian. They were my world. They should be here with me celebrating. Planning. Being goofy and happy with…*for* me. But…they're not here anymore, and that's just so hard. So if I'm acting strange, it's because I'm feeling…I don't know…sad."

"Oh." He's silent again. "I'm sorry, Lia. I didn't think about it that way. I just assumed, you know, since you're so close with Breaker, that maybe something was going on there."

"Brian," I groan while pressing my hand over my eyes. "I've told you time and time again, nothing is going on with Breaker and me. Please, please don't make this a thing. I don't want to have to keep saying this to you over and over. You should know me well enough that when I say something, I mean it."

"I know, sorry. Fuck, Lia…" He blows out a heavy breath. "It's just been a weird week. I'm sorry."

"It's okay. But hey, I should open my computer and get some work done before lunch."

"Okay. I love you. I'll see you later."

"Love you, too," I answer before hanging up and setting my phone on my desk. I stare at it for a moment, my mind racing.

Brian is right. I have been off. However, I was caught off guard.

I wasn't expecting Brian to propose. We hadn't even talked about it. It felt sort of out of the blue. He took me out on a boat for a sunset cruise, dropped down on one knee, and asked me to marry him. I said yes. It was a beautiful proposal.

The ring is huge.

Bigger than anything I would ever need in my life, and even though it's stunning, it doesn't feel right sitting on my finger. None of it feels right, and I don't know if it's because I'm struggling with my parents not being around for one of the most significant moments of my life or if I'm struggling because even though everything about the proposal was magical, it wasn't quite me, or because I'm struggling to find the words to tell Breaker.

Ever since last year, he and Brian haven't really gotten along. They've been cordial and friendly to each other when we're all in the same room, but the friendship they used to have doesn't quite exist anymore. And it's

Brian's fault, yet he hasn't taken the blame, and I refuse to insert myself in the middle. I tried once, and that exploded in my face because Brian was mad that I was defending Breaker.

But...Breaker didn't do anything wrong.

Brian works in investments. He actually works with some very wealthy clients. One night, we were all having dinner together, and Brian was looking for some...information. He was trying to get some clues as to what was happening with some stocks Breaker and his brothers owned. Valuable shares in renewable energy. It was all sort of...skeezy the way Brian went about it, crossing the lines of insider trading. And when Breaker didn't break and hand over the information Brian was looking for, Brian got angry. It blew up from there.

I've tried my best to smooth it over, but Brian is a prideful man, descending from a family of wealth. He's held to a very high standard by his parents. If he's not climbing the ladder, then he's not worth his parents' time. I think he was trying to land some big scores for his clients to benefit them and prove to his parents he has value.

I could not imagine living a life where you have to prove yourself to your parents day in and day out because their love is conditional at best.

Either way, they don't get along well, and I just don't know what Breaker is going to say when I tell him. I'm not sure if he'll be happy, upset...if he'll try to talk me out of it; I have no clue. And that's mainly because we haven't spoken about Brian much. We kind of just...forget that he's a thing in my life whenever we hang out. It's better that way.

But now...now I don't know what the hell we're going to do.

My phone chirps with a text, and I glance down to read it.

Breaker: Cronuts coming your way. I have a meeting with our lawyer this morning, or else I'd join you.

Smiling, I text him back.

Lia: Cronuts for what?

Breaker: For ruining our night last night. I tried to pull it together, but I couldn't quite get there. Sorry, Lia.

Lia: No need to apologize. What are friends for? Can I get a rain check, though? These glass dice are calling my name.

Breaker: What do you have going on tonight? I'm free.

I give it some thought. Technically, I should probably go hang out with Brian tonight, but I'll see him at lunch, and he *does* want me to tell Breaker, so maybe tonight would be a good idea.

Lia: Bring tacos. See you tonight.

Breaker: You know if I bring tacos, they'll be the pickle-flavored ones.

Lia: Uh, yeah, that's what I expect from you.

Breaker: I've broken you in.

Lia: Like a comfy pair of jeans.

I set my phone back down and smile to myself. As it always has been, texting Breaker—*hanging out with Breaker*—is so damn easy. And he gets that I need cronuts.

Okay, time to get some work done.

———

I hate the dress I'm wearing.

Absolutely hate it.

Brian got it for me maybe a month ago. He told me we were going out for some fun, and he took me shopping. Wanted to celebrate a check he'd just received by buying me some new dresses.

For one, I'm not a huge fan of dresses, especially dresses that conform to every inch of my body, leaving very little room to breathe or walk in.

Also, this dress has flowers all over it, and I'm not against flowers, it's just...these are little flowers, and it reminds me of something a teenager from the nineties would wear. And thirdly, it's short. By God, is it short. The wind blows right up the bottom, giving me Marilyn Monroe vibes with every step.

But Brian bought it for me and asked if I would wear it, so here I am.

"Lia, wow," Brian says as he walks up from behind. "You look stunning."

I turn just in time for him to pull me into a hug, his hand falling to my lower back as he squeezes me.

His signature cologne—fresh and woodsy—surrounds me first, followed by his tight grip, and then the subtle hint of his lips pressed against my cheek.

When I pull away, I smile up at his handsome face.

I remember the first time I met him. I was out having drinks with my friend Tanya, who doesn't get out much because she's a mother of twins. She told me there was a guy who couldn't seem to take his eyes off me, sitting directly behind me. When I turned around to look, Brian was sitting in a booth, beer in hand, his gaze on me. Our eyes locked, and he took that moment to come up to me. He saw that I was hanging out with my friend, so he didn't want to intrude. Instead, he had me put my phone number in his phone so he could text me to get a cup of coffee.

He texted me the next day.

And that was that.

After a year and a half of being together, he's still as handsome as ever.

"You look really good," I say, tugging on the black suit he paired with a dark-blue button-up shirt.

"Thank you." His hand clutches mine, and he says, "You ready for this? Mother is very excited."

Yup. Mother. That's what he calls his mom. It's so formal. When he first used the term, I laughed because I thought it was a joke, but it wasn't. Mother and Father are his parents. To me, they're Mr. and Mrs. Beaver.

Brian Manchester Beaver.

Quite the name.

If I decide to hyphenate his name, I would be Ophelia Fairweather-Fern-Beaver.

Taking the last name Beaver doesn't really scream something I want to do, but I also know that I would insult Brian if I didn't. I don't know. It's a conundrum I'm trying not to think about too much.

I smile up at Brian. "Very ready."

He lifts my hand and kisses the engagement ring I made sure to put on before I left my apartment. "This looks so good on you."

Does it?

Or does it look like I'm opening my own personal attack of misfit toys for the wintertime?

"Come on."

He tugs me toward the doors of The Pier 1905 Club. Situated on the cliffs of Malibu, it's a historic club known only to the rich and famous. The first time I was here, I was so intimidated that I told Brian I wasn't feeling well and bolted early. After the fifth time I met with Brian and his parents here, I grew accustomed to the heavy snobbery in the air. Hence the dress I've squeezed into, the nail polish that miraculously dried before I arrived, and the heels I'm wearing with little straps that cling around my ankles. If Breaker saw me right now, I'm pretty sure he'd barely recognize me.

The gold-plated doors are parted for us by silent doormen, bringing us into the opulent lobby shrouded in light-blue linens and gold and white marble tiles. The theme of the entire club is rich beach. That's all I need to say.

"Mr. Beaver, your mother is expecting you," the host says as we turn toward the dining area.

"She has to get here at least half an hour early," I mutter under my breath.

Brian chuckles. "She always likes to be the first to arrive."

That much is obvious. She wants to be the first to arrive so she can dish out backhanded jabs about time management—despite being fifteen minutes early.

"Right this way," the host says as he guides us through the dining room.

Just like every other time we've met with Mother, we're guided to the back of the dining area and out to the balcony, where Mrs. Beaver always occupies a corner table.

And just like every other time, she sits in a white floppy hat, staring directly at the entrance. In addition to her hands crossed in front of her, her narrowed eyes match her disapproving lips.

I love Brian. So much.

But his mom, pretty sure she's the devil incarnate in a pair of four-inch heels.

When we reach the table, she doesn't bother standing. Instead, Brian bends and places a kiss on her cheek. "Mother, you look beautiful."

"Thank you," she says, her voice dripping with hundred-dollar bills.

You know when someone talks like they're rich—clenched throat, tight lips, disapproving tone in every word? Well, that is Mrs. Beaver, even when she's happy.

When Brian steps to the side, I move forward and offer a curt nod—the way she likes it—and say, "Hello, Mrs. Beaver. It's so nice seeing you today."

Her gaze falls to my shoes first. I thank God I got a pedicure the other day so she doesn't comment about how dry my feet look. Then she works all the way up my dress to my face. With a gentle tug of her lips—that's her way of smiling—she says, "Ophelia, it's nice to see you. Please take a seat. We have much to talk about."

Looks like she approves of the dress because there was no pop of her forehead vein or subtle clamp of her jaw. Finally, I got it right.

Brian pulls out a chair for me, and I sit before picking up my napkin from the table and folding it across my lap.

"It's a beautiful day," I say as Mrs. Beaver lifts my hand and examines my ring.

"Brian, dear, did you get insurance on this?"

"Yes, Mother. As well as a monthly cleaning."

Mrs. Beaver nods in approval. "Good." And then she drops my hand before adjusting the napkin on her lap. "I took the liberty of ordering all of us the salmon salad."

Ugh…salmon. I had it once, and now that's all she orders.

"I didn't want to waste any time looking over a menu. We have a lot to talk about, a lot of planning to do."

"Planning?" I ask, confused.

"Yes, Ophelia. You're an engaged woman now. That means we need to start planning the wedding."

"Oh, so soon?"

Her sharp gaze snaps up to me. "What do you mean, so soon? Ophelia, we only have one month until the end of summer. The club has a spot open on a Saturday night in five weeks, so yes, so soon."

"Wait, you want us to get married in five weeks?" I ask, my eyes nearly bugging out.

Brian's hand slides over my hand in reassurance. "Mother, that does seem rather quick."

Mrs. Beaver now glances toward her son, her steely eyes wilting my fiancé right in his seat. "Brian, do you expect to wait a whole year? The Beavers only get married in the summer. You know this, it's tradition, and since you proposed late, we only have about five weeks to work with."

"What's wrong with waiting a year?" I ask, respectfully. "That will give us time to make sure everything is perfect."

"Brian's niece will be far too tall to be the flower girl a year from now. You must think about the pictures, Ophelia."

Ah, yes, the pictures. Heaven forbid a tall flower girl show up and ruin everything.

"The wedding must be this year and must be in five weeks. That's our only option." She lifts her water glass to her pursed lips, letting us know the decision is final.

"Five weeks, well...I guess we can make it work," Brian says, folding like a cheap lawn chair. "It will be fun, right, Ophelia?" He only uses my full name around his mother, and I hate it because it sounds weird coming from his mouth. The only person I've ever liked using my full name is Breaker because he uses it when it's a special moment, not because his mother forces him.

Mother and son both stare me down. They're waiting for an answer, one that is hard to come up with, given how my throat seems to be squeezing tight on me.

"Uh, sorry." I take a deep breath. "This whole wedding thing is just hard, you know? I thought I'd be doing this with my parents by my side."

"Oh, dear," Mrs. Beaver says as she coldly taps my hand. "That's what you have me for. Now." She snaps her finger behind her, beckoning whatever butler waits in the depths of the wall for her to summon. The butler appears with a thick leather-bound folder and gently places it in front of Mrs. Beaver. "This will be your planning book," she says, turning it toward me. "It has everything in it that needs to be chosen. Of course, given that your parents are no longer with us, I've taken it upon myself to give you a few options for the type of weddings to choose from."

She flips open the folder and pushes it toward me.

"The venue is obviously the club. Our family has had receptions here for years. That will not change."

Great, glad to have a say in that.

"As for the flowers, colors, and theme, there's some leeway in those decisions."

"Leeway?" I ask, my voice coming off more irritated than anything.

Getting married in five weeks is a little much, but being only granted a little leeway? Now that's something I don't know if I'm cool with.

"Yes, well, we do have some very powerful people attending. We need to keep up appearances for that reason alone."

"But what about what Brian and I want?" I ask. "This is our wedding, after all."

Mrs. Beaver's jaw grows tight as she sharpens her smile, turning it into a razor blade, ready to cut down any dream with a smart-witted remark. "Ophelia, you must understand the importance of marrying into the Beaver family. This isn't some ordinary wedding; this is a show of status. This is a way for our family to exhibit the *many* accomplishments we've made to gain the status we have. Every intricate detail will be chosen based on obtaining our place in our circle. I understand you come from humble beginnings, but you will be a Beaver soon, and certain expectations are to be upheld."

Leaning toward me, Brian says, "It's just a party, Ophelia. What does it really matter what kind of flowers are picked out?"

"It matters to me," I say, feeling myself growing emotional. And let me tell you, the Beavers do not do emotions.

"Now, now." Mrs. Beaver pats my hand again. "No need to cause a scene." She flips the folder closed. "I can see you have some thoughts about the wedding, and I don't want to steamroll your special day. How about this...we take it one decision at a time? We can meet, explore options, and you can choose from there."

"That's really kind of you, Mother," Brian says. I almost didn't hear him from how far up his mother's ass he is.

"Well, if anything, I'm an understanding woman," Mrs. Beaver says. "I don't want your bride to be upset with her new family. So what do you say, Ophelia? Think you can manage meetings with me? Make some decisions?"

I swallow down the tightness of my throat and nod my head because what option do I really have? Mrs. Beaver wants the wedding in five weeks. Brian is not going to stand up for us because he's still suckling at the teat of approval, so it seems I don't have any other option than to go along with this plan.

"Yes," I answer. "I think that would be nice."

"Wonderful," Mrs. Beaver says without an ounce of excitement. She snaps her finger again in an instant, and salads are placed in front of us. "Now, let's eat."

She lifts her fork and gently cuts into her salmon while Brian holds my hand and smiles brightly at me.

The things we do for love.

"Thank you again, Lia," Brian says as he walks me up to my apartment. After a prolonged time at the club, we spent another two hours walking around the venue while a wedding planner showed us the spaces. As expected, Mrs. Beaver took the lead. She had her own opinion on the reception and where the cocktail hour needed to be, as well as the dinner. The dance floor would be modest, with just enough room for people to slow dance—according to her, there would be no bumping and grinding at our wedding—and then she pointed out the bride's room where I would be making dress changes.

When I asked how many dresses she planned on me changing into, she said at least three, as if it was the most preposterous question she's ever heard.

Three dresses? How does one person even have the bandwidth to pick three different wedding dresses? Mrs. Beaver pointed out there's the ceremony dress, the reception dress, and then of course the parting dress—the dress I put on just to leave the building. So many useless expenses. By the time we left, it was past five, and I was rushing to get back home.

I took an Uber to the club because Brian always likes to drive me, and as I figured, he wanted to drive me today.

"Thank you for what?" I ask him as I reach my door and turn toward him.

"I know the big wedding thing isn't what you were probably looking for, but it's important to my mother."

"Yeah, I could tell." I press my lips together. Tugging on the lapel of his suit jacket, I say, "Are you sure this is all necessary? Do we really have to have such a grandiose wedding? Maybe we can elope or something?"

He snorts. "Lia, my mother would absolutely kill me. I'm her baby boy, the last one to get married out of her children. She will not allow me to elope."

"You know, Brian," I say in a seductive voice while moving my hand up his chest. "The great thing about being an adult is that you can make your own decisions."

He lightly presses me against my door and smooths his hand up my thigh. "Yes, but when the decision doesn't really bother me, I'm not going to put up a fight about it."

"But don't I matter?" I ask.

He cups my cheek. "Of course you matter, Lia. But I also know that wedding stuff isn't that important to you."

"It should be important to us both, as it's our day."

He brings his lips to mine and presses a few short kisses before pulling away and saying, "We have the rest of our lives to do things the way we want. This is one day, Lia. And it's going to be beautiful; you know my mother wouldn't have it any other way. Trust her, okay? You might feel that what she thinks is perfect."

I sigh just as I hear the elevator ding. I glance over Brian's shoulder just in time to see the elevator doors part and Breaker's face come into view.

Panic rises up, and I quickly pull Brian's attention as I whisper, "Breaker just got here. I'm telling him tonight about the engagement.

Please don't say anything." The words fly out of my mouth so fast that I almost don't understand them myself.

"Tonight?" he asks. "But I thought we could go into your place, and you know…celebrate."

Yeah, that won't be happening. The only time I "celebrate" with Brian in my apartment is when Breaker is out of town. The last thing I need is for my best friend to hear that through the wall we share. Also, weirdly, the only time Brian isn't too tired to "celebrate" is when he's at my place.

"I'm sorry, but I promised we could hang out tonight. I'll make it up to you. I'll bring an overnight bag Friday and spend the whole weekend with you. Okay?"

He grows stiff with irritation and releases me.

"Brian, please, don't be mad."

"No, I get it." He straightens his jacket. "But you're mine this weekend."

"Promise," I say as I loop my hand around the back of his neck and pull him in for a kiss. Of course I intend a peck, but Brian goes in for the kill, adding tongue, making a show of it. When he pulls away, Breaker is standing a few feet away, patiently waiting with our take-out food.

Brian turns and smiles at Breaker. "Good to see you, man. How was New York?"

"Good," Breaker says, looking like the good guy he is, not showing an ounce of how much he dislikes Brian. He's never said it to my face, but I can tell when Breaker enjoys being around someone and when he doesn't. He creates this fake smile, where only the right side of his mouth tilts up. That's the smile Brian gets all the time. "Glad to be back. I prefer the West Coast."

"I don't know. There's something the city has to offer that you just don't get here. Who knows, maybe we'll make our way over to the Big Apple one day, right, Lia?"

Uh, what now?

Breaker's eyes fall to mine, questions in them as to what he means by that, and frankly, I have no clue. Instead of trying to play middleman, I say, "Well, I'll see you this weekend, okay?"

Brian nods and kisses me one more time. "Call me tonight. I want to talk about this weekend and our plans."

"Okay."

"Love you."

"Love you." I wave, and Brian takes off toward the elevator, where he presses the *down* button and sticks his hand in his pocket.

When he's firmly in the elevator, I turn to Breaker, who has his eyebrow raised. "Are you moving to New York?" he asks.

"What?" I nearly shout. "No!" I shake my head. "No. I don't know what he was talking about."

"Are you sure? Because you're looking sort of fidgety right now."

That's because I'm trying to hide the giant ice rink on my finger.

"I'm sure. I think that was just some offhand comment. We're not moving." I turn toward my door, unlock it, and then let us both in.

"Okay, because that would not settle well with me. I mean, I would make the move, but I like it here on the West Coast."

"I do too."

He sets the food down on my kitchen counter and pulls out the to-go boxes while I set my things down. "You look nice, by the way." I feel his eyes on me, and I want to slither away in this dress.

"The dress is not me. Too short."

"It might not be you, but it still looks good. What was the occasion?"

I face him and place my hands behind my back. "Uh, lunch with The Beave."

We came up with the nickname after my first interaction with her. I'm careful when I use it because I don't want to accidentally address Brian's mother as The Beave in front of him. I'm pretty sure that would earn me a hefty scowl, a long lecture, and copious apologies. The man loves his mother. Nothing wrong with that. I just have to be conscious of what not to do.

"Ah...at the club?" Breaker asks in a snooty voice while raising his pinky.

Breaker is a billionaire. He has more than enough money to put the Beavers to shame, yet he doesn't act like he has money. Sure, he might wear the most perfectly tailored suits with the richest fabric, his watches are more like expensive jewelry, and his haircuts cost way more than they should, but he lives modestly in an apartment next to mine because this is what I can afford. He could live in the Flats with his brothers. He could have a beach house out in Malibu, and he could even have a penthouse downtown, but he chose to live here.

"Yes, at the club."

"Get the salmon salad again?"

"Yes, and it was as dreadful as the first, second, third, fourth, and fifth times I've had it."

He chuckles lightly. "Next time, excuse yourself after you order and tell the waitstaff to bring you a burger instead."

I clutch my chest in horror. "And risk the waitstaff being snapped at? No, thank you. I'd rather suffer through the salmon."

"You're a real Joan of Arc, you know that?"

"I try. Okay, I'm going to change real quick because I can't sit comfortably in this without flashing you my underwear."

"Not that I haven't been flashed countless times before."

"By accident! You make me sound like a philandering woman."

"Halloween, five years ago, you wore that maid outfit. I think I saw your underwear more times that night than all the years we've known each other."

"Uh, excuse me, sir. I wore that maid outfit because I lost a bet to you, and that's what you chose. If it was my choice, I would have gone as a piece of toast with melted butter. You know how much I love dressing up as food."

"Yeah, but the maid costume was more fun."

"For you...you pervert."

He rolls his eyes dramatically. "For the last time, it wasn't because I was being pervy. It was because I knew you would hate it."

"Wow, you're such a great best friend."

He smiles broadly. "I know."

Chuckling, I go to my bedroom, where I quickly strip out of the dress and the heels, and trade them out for fluffy black slippers, a pair of cotton shorts, and a murder mystery shirt. I toss my hair up in a bun, then stare down at my engagement ring. Should I wear it out there, or should I tell him first?

I nibble on my bottom lip as I try to figure it out. Five weeks, that's so quick. Like lightning-fast quick, and sure, of course I want to marry Brian, I love him, but five weeks? I'm barely able to wrap my head around the fact I'm getting married.

I tug on the ring and pull it off my finger. I think it's best that I don't go rushing into the kitchen with the ring but rather ease the idea into conversation.

I set my ring on the dresser, then walk back into the kitchen, where Breaker has set up two place settings on the table with drinks and lots of napkins. We're going to need them.

The tacos Breaker gets are from a local food truck around the corner. They make tacos de birria, and they are so good that I would probably get them every night if I didn't have self-control. But because they come with a dipping sauce that the meat was cooked in, we need tons of napkins because things get messy.

"Ugh, they smell so good."

"Yeah, they do, so hurry your ass on over here so I can dig in."

I take a seat across from him. "You could have started without me."

"You know I never do. If anything, I'm a gentleman and will always wait."

"You didn't wait two months ago when I brought over cheesecake."

"Ah, cheesecake."

"Very true. All sweets are your downfall." I pick up a taco, and he does too, and like every other time we've purchased these tacos, we "clink" them as a toast to the meal and then dip them in the sauce. I take a very large bite and chew.

After a few seconds, he asks, "So how was lunch?"

I swallow and answer, "Oh, you know, same old, same old."

He pauses his taco halfway to his mouth, sauce dripping from the crispy grilled tortilla. "Why do I feel like you're hiding something from me?"

"What? Hiding? Ha! No, I don't hide things." I push up my purple-rimmed glasses and chuckle. "Why would I hide something from you? That seems pointless. I tell you everything."

"You're babbling."

"Uh, no, I'm not. I'm defending myself. Because why would I hide something from you?"

He sets his taco down and straightens up. "You're definitely hiding something."

"I don't like your accusatory glare."

"And I don't like that you're prolonging the inevitable of actually telling me what's going on." He nods at me. "Go ahead, spill."

Ugh, he knows me too well. There's no point; he will go all night like this, so I set my taco down and look him in the eyes.

"Something has developed in my life."

"Oh-kay," he drags out.

"Something that will change things a bit."

His brow creases. "You *are* moving to New York, aren't you?"

"Noooooo! I'm not moving, I'm just...changing my relationship status."

His brow rises. "You're breaking up with Brian? Thank—"

"No, he proposed, and we're getting married."

Breaker's mouth falls open right before he says, "Married?"

"In five weeks." I wince.

"Five weeks?" he asks. "Like in...*five weeks*?"

"Yes."

He pushes back, his expression completely shocked. Yeah, I get it. I'm surprised too.

"I know it's coming on quick, but The Beave wants us to get married at the club, and there's an opening, and his family always gets married in the summer, and next year won't work because his niece will be too tall. So yeah, five weeks."

"Wow." He rubs a napkin over his face and tosses it on the table. "That's...a lot of information. Did he just propose today?" His eyes fall to my hand. "Where's the ring? He got you a ring, right?"

"Yeah, it's in my bedroom."

"Why?"

"I didn't want to shock you, and he proposed a week ago. I wanted to tell you in person. Are you mad?" I wince again, my heart beating a mile a minute.

"Why would I be mad?"

"Because, you know, it happened a week ago, and I haven't told you, and I know that Brian isn't really your favorite person."

"But he's your favorite person, so, therefore, I like him," Breaker says, but the lie falls flat. There's just about zero excitement in the inflection of his voice. He swallows, almost as if he's swallowing pain, and says, "Show me the ring."

"You want to see it?" I ask, feeling an awkward tension falling between us.

I know he's not actually happy for me. I know this is all coming out of the blue—just like it did for me. But he's putting on a smile, and he's trying, which only seems to make it feel...worse.

"Yeah, show me your ring."

"Okay." I grab the ring from my room, and then hand it to Breaker once I'm back in the dining area. I don't slip it on my finger but rather just hand it to him.

"Wow, that's nice," he says as he lifts his eyes up to me, probably trying to gauge my reaction. "Put it on."

He hands it back to me, and I slip it on my finger.

"It looks great on you, Lia," he says softly. And there he is, my best friend. He will say just about anything to make sure I feel comfortable, even though he probably knows that I'm anything but comfortable wearing this ring.

"It's different than what I would have picked out," I admit.

"Doesn't make it any less beautiful." He smiles and stands. "Come here."

I stand, and he pulls me into a hug, his strong arms wrapping around me as I rest my head on his chest. I don't know if it's because everything is happening so fast or because he's being so nice, but my emotions get the best of me, and my eyes start to water, so I squeeze him tighter.

"I'm happy for you, Lia." He kisses the top of my head. "Five weeks is quick, but I'm sure it will be great."

My throat tightens, my tears ready to drip down my cheeks. I don't want him to see me crying. I don't like being emotional in front of anyone, let alone Breaker, but it doesn't seem to be something I can stop from happening.

A light sob escapes me, and the moment Breaker hears it, he puts a touch of space between us and bends at the knees to get a look at my face. I swipe my eyes under my glasses, but it's too late.

"Hey," he says quietly. "Why are you crying?"

"I…I think it's all too much for me right now."

"Come here," he says, taking my hand and walking me over to the couch. We both take a seat, facing each other. "Talk to me. What's going on? Do you not want to get married?"

"No, I mean…I do. I just—I wasn't expecting it. Brian and I hadn't ever talked about marriage, so I was caught off guard when he proposed. Then at lunch today, it felt like everything was moving at warp speed. The Beave wants me to wear at least three dresses, which I think is a waste of money. Brian won't stand up to his mom, and the ring is just…wow, it's big, and I always sort of wanted one of those past, present, and future rings with the three diamonds, and then there's you. I was so afraid of telling you because I know Brian is not your favorite person—"

"Let me stop you right there," Breaker says in a calming tone. "You don't need to worry about me or how I feel in any of this, okay? My feelings, my thoughts, my opinions don't matter. All that matters is how you feel and what you want." He squeezes my hand. "So how do you feel?"

"Scared," I admit. "Sad. Not…right. And it's not because I don't love Brian, because I do, but I just think this is all weird. I used to talk about this day with my parents, and they won't be there. Things are happening fast; I don't know. I expected to feel different when I was proposed to."

"Maybe it hasn't sunk in yet," he says. "It might just take you a moment to comprehend what's happening."

"Maybe." I circle my finger over the couch fabric as I stare down. "You're not mad?"

"Lia." He tilts my chin up so I'm forced to look at his crystal-blue eyes. "If I were mad at you, then I wouldn't be a very good friend, now, would I?"

"I guess not."

"This is exciting, okay? Brian proposed, and you're getting married. Let me see a smile."

Tears drip down my cheeks as I attempt a pathetic smile.

He chuckles. "Well, that's just sad."

"I'm trying. I think I was doing okay about the news, just waiting to tell you, but at lunch today, I felt like I was getting steamrolled left and right by The Beave. I know the wedding is important to their family because of their social status, and it's all about keeping up appearances when it comes to them, but I should have a say in all this, shouldn't I?"

"Uh, yes, Lia. This is your wedding. You should have a say in what happens at it."

"I just become a doormat when she's around. It's hard to get my opinion in, you know?"

"It's hard to overcome strong personalities, and I get that. I deal with my brothers every day."

"And I was already steamrolled about the date, and where the reception will be held; I attempted to challenge the decision but fell short. I think I'm going to just end up resenting this whole thing because I'm going to be pushed around, and that's taking the excitement out of it."

"That's understandable. Can you make the decisions without The Beave?"

I give him a look. "That would never happen. She already has appointments made."

"Well then…take me with you," Breaker says, the suggestion making me laugh.

"Come on, Breaker, be serious."

"I'm being serious," he says. "I can go with you. It's not like I have anything going on right now. I have to stay away from work. This might give me something to do to keep me busy." He smirks. "Maybe I can be your wedding planner."

"Oh my God, stop." I push at him.

"Or your maid of honor…ooo, your man of honor. Or, better yet, man in waiting."

"Can you stop being ridiculous?"

His brows tilt down. "Uh, do you have another best friend I don't know about that would take the title of maid of honor?"

I pause and give it some thought. "Uh, not really, no. But I guess I never really thought about it."

"I'm your best friend, correct?"

"You are," I answer.

"And best friends always claim the title of best man or maid of honor, correct?"

"Yessss," I drag out.

"Therefore, by process of elimination, I'm your man of honor, but I believe *man-in-waiting* has a better ring to it, don't you think?"

"You're not being serious, are you?"

"Of course I am," he says with all sincerity. "Listen, Lia. I know this is going to be tough without your parents. Losing them was so hard, and they wouldn't want you to do this alone. I have the time, and even if I didn't, I would make the time for you. I can help. I can be your backup, your wingman, your bodyguard, your bruiser."

"Bodyguard? Do you really think I need protection from The Beave?"

"I've met her before. Her stare alone is terrifying, let alone the manipulation. Trust me, you will need a bodyguard, and I'm your man."

"But what about Brian?"

"What about him?"

"You guys don't get along."

Breaker shifts on the couch and then offers me a smile. "Well, he's going to be your husband. Better late than never to build on that relationship because I won't let any hard feelings or awkward tension with your future husband get between you and me, got it?"

As I listen to him and his words of affirmation, my emotions tighten again, causing more tears to fall.

"What's going on?" he asks, concerned.

"Just…" I look him in the eyes. "I'm so glad I told you. You looked like a pervert with your mustache so many years ago, but I'm lucky to have you in my life."

He lightly chuckles and says, "You know, if you're lucky, I could bring back the mustache for your wedding."

I push at his face. "Don't even think about it."

CHAPTER 3
BREAKER

I PACE AT THE DOOR of JP's house, the morning dew freshly clinging to every blade of grass as the sun just starts to tilt into the sky, warming the temperature for the day.

I got about one hour of sleep last night. One if I'm lucky.

Once I calmed Lia down and we finished our tacos, we played a few rounds of glass Yahtzee, but neither one of us was paying attention. I think both of our minds were somewhere else. We called it a night, and when I went to bed, she knocked on the wall, I knocked back...and then I didn't go to sleep.

My mind kept whirling over and over again.

She's engaged...to Brian.

When she said she was going to have a relationship status change, I really thought she was going to break up with him. And fuck, I almost said, *THANK GOD!* Could you imagine if I let that fly? She cut me off right before I could. And sure, were they kissing in the hallway when I arrived? Yes, but body language is telling, and, at the moment, Brian was the one leaning into her while Lia had a slight lean away. That kiss was all him.

But lo and behold, it's not a breakup in their future, it's a wedding, and that makes me...well, fuck, it makes me feel weird.

Because it's Brian. The guy makes her happy, but he doesn't get her. He doesn't know Lia like I do. If he did, he wouldn't have gotten that engagement ring for her, one that I'm pretty sure you can see from Mars because it's so big. Either he would have asked me, the best friend, or he would have known. Never in a million years would I have picked that ring out for her or pressured her to get married in five weeks, only a year and a half after her parents passed away.

Yup, Brian met her a week after their funeral. Lia's parents were both in a tragic helicopter accident late at night. Her mom was killed on impact. Her dad had a chance, but he coded and passed away during surgery. Two weeks later, Brian picked her up in a bar. She was raw, sad, and needed comfort, and she found it in Brian.

But she still has a hard time dealing with the loss of her parents, and I don't think he's considered that. All he cares about is checking off the requirements his mother sets up for him.

Have a successful job.

Buy a nice house.

Get engaged to an acceptable woman.

Have a fancy wedding.

Deliver grandchildren.

He's on a trajectory, and I'm not sure if Lia is on the same one.

But who am I to say something to her?

I pull on my hair just as the door opens. JP is in a pair of shorts and nothing else. His hair is a mess, and he looks ready to murder me.

I pick up the box of donuts that I set on the stoop and say, "I brought breakfast."

"Dude." He rubs his eye. "Just because you can't go to work doesn't mean you need to bother me."

"This isn't about work. I need to talk to you."

"Is it about the psycho who made you a pair of boxers from tweed fabric?"

"It was burlap, and no. This is about Lia."

"Lia?" he asks, perking up now, a smile crossing over his face. He takes in my fidgety stance, the bags under my eyes, and then…"Oh shit, you finally realized you love her."

My face falls flat.

"I'm going to fucking kick you in the dick with that shit," I say as I rear back my leg, and JP quickly jolts out of the way. "It has nothing to do with my *platonic* feelings toward her. Got it?"

"Sure." He just smiles again and pushes the door open. "I hope there's a cronut in there. I've been craving one."

"There is," I say. "But you're not going to get it if you're a dick to me."

"Dude, you're the one at my house. I can treat you however I fucking want."

At the top of the stairs, Kelsey calls down while dressed in a robe, her hair rumpled as well. "Who is it?"

"Breaker," JP says. "He needs to talk about Lia."

I glance up just in time to see a smile cross over Kelsey's face. Before she can say anything, I cut her off. "No, I don't have fucking feelings for her. This is different."

Her smile falters. "Oh, okay. Let me put my hair up, and I'll be right down. Want me to call Lottie over so you have another girl's opinion?"

I'm about to say no when I give it a second thought. Having another girl's opinion might not hurt, and since Lottie and Huxley live right across the street from JP and Kelsey, it works out.

"Sure, tell her I brought donuts."

"She'll be over here in minutes, I'm sure."

Kelsey takes off toward the bedroom while JP and I go to the kitchen, where JP starts making a pot of coffee.

"You know, it doesn't shock me that you came to my house rather than Huxley's."

"After walking in on Huxley and Lottie fucking against a wall, I learned my lesson. Can't get the vision of his clenched ass out of my head."

"Kelsey and I fuck against walls."

"I'm well aware. The only difference is if I walk in on you and Kelsey, you'll just laugh about it. Huxley gives me the silent treatment for a week and then a lecture about privacy between a husband and wife."

"He still is rather uptight, isn't he?" JP asks. "You would think after marrying Lottie, he might loosen up a touch, but he really can't seem to let the stick out."

"At this point, the stick is a permanent resident."

JP chuckles while he turns on his coffee maker and starts making a large pot for everyone. He also sets out all the essentials for the espresso maker in case people decide on that as well.

"Want me to grab plates?" I ask.

"Yeah, it would be nice if you made yourself useful."

"Just a simple yes would suffice," I reply just as Kelsey walks into the kitchen. She's changed into a pair of shorts and one of JP's shirts. There's no doubt she probably wasn't wearing anything under that robe.

"Lottie will be over in a second. I said *donuts*, and she ran. Not sure about Huxley, I heard him groan in displeasure when Lottie hopped out of bed." Not surprising, Huxley is very possessive over Lottie. Then again, JP is also very possessive over Kelsey.

Me…well, I haven't had anyone I care enough about in my life to be possessive over. Watching my brothers find girls and marry them, you would think that it would make me jealous, make me want to go off and find someone for myself, but I'm content. I don't want to press to find love just because everyone else is. The way I see it, when that one special person comes into my life, I'll know it, and I'll never want to let her go.

The front door flies open and through the large entryway, Lottie's voice echoes, "Donuts, get in my mouth!"

I look over my shoulder just in time to see Lottie charge in wearing a tank top and bike shorts. Her hair is a mess as well. Trailing behind her is a not-so-happy-looking Huxley.

"Why the hell are we gathering so early this morning?" Huxley asks as he walks up to me and rests his hand on the island. "Is this about the job? I'm not getting into it with you. You can't be around while the team conducts a thorough investigation."

"It's not about the job," I say.

"It's about Lia," JP coos like a goddamn schoolgirl. I quickly direct a scowl in his direction, causing him to hold up his hands. "I didn't say anything about you liking her."

"No cooing either."

"Christ, sensitive much?"

"What's going on with Lia?" Lottie asks, her mouth full of a jelly donut.

"Well, since you're all here, might as well tell you that Lia is engaged."

"Aw, really?" Kelsey asks, clapping.

"Engaged? Wow, that's great," Lottie says.

"To Brian?" JP asks.

"The douche?" Huxley adds.

"Wait, why is he a douche?" Kelsey asks. "Do we not like him?"

"The boys don't like anyone," Lottie says, taking another bite.

"No, we don't like him," JP says and then turns to me. "How do you feel about it?"

"Not great," I answer while taking a seat at the island and placing my head in my hands. JP sets a cup of coffee in front of me, but I don't even bother touching it. "He doesn't deserve her. He's not good enough. And you should have seen the ring he got her. It doesn't have one ounce of Lia in it. It's as if he went to the most expensive and gaudy ring shop, said, 'Give me the most expensive ring you have,' and then bought it. And worst of all, The Beave wants the wedding in five weeks."

"Five weeks?" JP asks. "Jesus, that's quick, although our wedding was quick too." He smirks at Kelsey. "But that was to accommodate Kazoo's schedule."

"Yes, planning a wedding around a pigeon has always been a dream of mine."

JP pulls Kelsey into his chest and kisses her neck. "You loved everything about our wedding."

"I did."

Pulling the attention back to me, I say, "And last night, when she told me, she cried."

"Happy tears?" Lottie asks.

I shake my head. "No, sad tears, nervous tears, unhappy tears. There wasn't excitement in her voice, and she kept asking me if I was mad. Why the hell would I be mad?"

JP and Huxley exchange looks while the girls look away.

"What?" I ask, seeing that some sort of secret conversation is happening between all of them that I don't know about.

JP is the one to talk first. "Dude, don't you think that a little part of Lia thinks maybe, just maybe, you would have made a move on her at one point?"

"What?" I shake my head. "No. We've never thought of each other that way. This has nothing to do with our relationship."

"Does she know you don't like Brian?" Lottie asks.

"I've never said I don't like him, but she's aware we don't get along."

"Maybe that's why she's asking if you're mad," Kelsey says. "You two are so close that maybe she's looking for your approval."

"But I don't approve of him. That's the problem. He's not right for her, and I don't know what I should do about it."

"Nothing," Huxley says, commanding the room with his deep voice. "Absolutely nothing. If you get between her and Brian, you're just going to ruin your relationship with her."

"So what, I just let her marry the douche?"

"Yes," Huxley says.

I blow out a heavy breath. "But—"

"There is no *but*," Huxley says. "She has lost enough in her life. The last thing she needs is for you to make things complicated for her."

"So am I just supposed to act as her man of honor and smile and say yes to everything she picks?"

"Wait." Lottie slaps her hand on the table. "You're going to be her maid of honor? God, why do I find that the most precious thing ever?"

"That's really cute," Kelsey adds. "And yes, you should. If you don't want to hurt her, only help, then you smile and be supportive. Also, quick question, who is The Beave?"

"Brian's mom. Mrs. Beaver, we call her The Beave—not to her face. Think of Emily Gilmore but snobbier."

"Ooo, brutal," Lottie says.

"She's already been giving Lia a hard time. That's why the wedding is in five weeks, because of The Beave's demands. Brian's mom has been taking over everything, and last night when she was crying, I told her I would help her out, be there for her, but fuck, I didn't get one ounce of sleep last night."

Lottie leans forward and whispers, "Are you sure you don't have feelings for her?"

"I don't!" I shout, only to garner a look of death from Huxley for yelling at his wife. Quieting my voice, I say, "I don't. I think I'm worried about what will happen when she marries Brian. She won't be my neighbor anymore, that's for sure, and I doubt she'll be able to hang out with me as much, and if she does, it will involve Brian. I don't know. I feel like I'm losing her, and I'm going to lose her quickly."

"What if you talk to Brian?" JP asks.

"That's a good idea," Kelsey piggybacks. "It seems as though the big problem is with him because, let's be honest, this isn't about picking out flowers that Lia likes. No matter what, you're going to make sure you help her in any way possible. This seems like you need to fix things with Brian to feel comfortable with Lia moving forward. Because she loves him and said yes to the proposal, which means she wants to move forward. She might be struggling because her best friend and soon-to-be husband don't get along."

"Great point," Lottie says as she picks up another donut. "Fix things with Brian, and I bet it all works out."

"But I can't stand being in the same room as him," I reply.

"Looks like you're going to have to learn." JP smiles.

———————

I glance down at my watch and then swirl my glass of water in my hand. Fucking ten minutes late, I already can't stand the guy, and now he's going to pull this shit?

After I left Kelsey and JP's house, I drove back to my place and went for a run. I wasn't ready to commit to their suggestion, but after the run, I realized they were probably right. If I want to put Lia at ease and make things less awkward for me, maybe I need to give Brian a chance. So I sent him a text, asking him what he was doing for lunch and if he wanted to meet.

He was eager with his text back and told me the time and place. Now that I'm here, I feel like I was set up because the fucker hasn't even texted that he was going to be late.

I pull my phone out of my pocket and find a text from Lia.

Lia: I have to meet with The Beave at a church, the church she wants me and Brian to get married at. Please tell me you can go with me.

A church? I'm not sure Lia has been to a church...ever.

Breaker: I'm there. Got your back.
Lia: Thanks, Pickle.

Breaker: Maybe I can be your Pickle of Honor.

Lia: Don't even tease me. You know I'll have a shirt made that says that.

Breaker: I would wear it with pride.

"Hey, man," I hear Brian say, his footsteps approaching. "Sorry about the wait. I was closing a conversation with a client who wants to invest in bitcoin." He lends out his hand. "How are you?"

I pocket my phone and give him a solid shake. "Doing good," I say just before Brian takes a seat across from me at the booth I secured for us ten minutes ago.

"I heard about the lawsuit." Great opener, way to bring up a sore subject. What a douche. And of course, he's heard about the lawsuit. I wouldn't be surprised if he had something to do with it. He's always been jealous that I've been more successful than him. "Hostile work environment?" Brian shakes his head. "I don't believe it one bit." Well, at least he has the wherewithal to recognize right from wrong in this case, or at least pretend he does.

"Yeah, can't really talk about it for legal reasons, but thanks for the support." Wouldn't talk to him about it anyway. Not going to willingly hand him fodder to hurt me with somehow.

"Aw, sure, yeah. I get it. I'm sure your team is handling things."

"Like they always do." I smile just as the server comes up to our table. We put in a quick order of sodas as well as two steak salads, and then she takes off.

"So," Brian starts. "Lia told me she told you about the big news." *Unfortunately.*

"Yeah, congrats, dude," I say, feeling so fucking awkward that I actually despise myself at the moment. The fakeness is making me feel icky. "You already know this, but you're going to marry the best girl out there."

"I do know it. I'm really fucking lucky and so glad she said yes. When I proposed, there was a bit of a pause in her answer, and I thought she was going to say no. But I chalked it up to a hitch in her breath from excitement before she said yes."

Huh, interesting.

Bet there was a pause for a reason.

In my hopes of hopes, it's because deep down she knows…the guy is not meant for her.

"The ring is amazing, too," I say, even though I don't mean it. The ring is an abomination.

"Thanks. When I saw it, I immediately thought of Lia."

Not sure how, but whatever.

"So five weeks? That's pretty quick," I say.

"My mom is pressing it to be five weeks. There's a reason behind it. Lia must have told you she was apprehensive about the timeline."

"Yup," I say, not wanting to speak for Lia but also wanting to stand up for her.

"Yeah, it's quick for me too, but the reason is all there. I'm just glad you'll help her through it. Lia said now that you have time off with the investigation, you can go to the appointments with her. My mother can be strong-willed, so it will be good that you're there to help Lia. Just wish I could, but I'm totally slammed at work."

"I'm sure." I rub my hand over my jaw. It's time to be the bigger man. I mean, I'm the better man of course. "So since you guys are going to be married soon, I thought it would be good if we got together and, I don't know…just talked. Maybe get some grievances off our chest that we might have and start on a clean slate. I feel like there's been some tension between us. Or have I been reading the situation wrong?"

"Nah, things have been weird," he admits. "I think it was after that chatter about the stocks. Things went downhill from there."

Well, hell, I didn't expect him to be so honest and upfront. Got to give the man credit for that.

"Yeah." I twist my glass on the table, the condensation collecting on the wood. "That was when things got weird."

He leans back against his booth seat and undoes the buttons of his jacket. "I'll be honest. I felt intimidated by your friendship with Lia and of course your success with your brothers, and I went about it in all the wrong ways. I'm sorry about that."

Huh...

This is, well, this is not what I anticipated. I expected him to maybe place blame on me, or say nothing was wrong, or even pick a fight, but this...yeah, I don't know how to handle such honesty.

I grip the back of my neck. "Thank you for the apology. That, uh, that means a lot, man."

"Yeah, I should have done it a while ago; maybe things wouldn't have been so awkward between us and we could have hung out more, but pride is a funny thing."

"I get that. I probably should have approached you earlier too."

"Why are you approaching me now? Besides the wedding coming in close."

I shrug. "Just thought that maybe it would be best for everyone. I think Lia sensed the tension between us, and she's already stressed, so I didn't want to stress her out even more. I thought if I could remove a stressor for her, it might ease her mind." I want to say *ease her apprehension*, but fuck would that open a door I don't want to walk through with Brian.

"Thoughtful," he says with an edge. Now that was the kind of tone I was expecting, not the happy-go-lucky guy I was just talking to. In seconds, I watch his posture stiffen, his expression grow hard, and the smooth edges of his jaw become jagged.

Sound the alarm...the man is on alert and ready to strike.

And here I thought he was going to be mature.

Mentally rubs hands This is what I was waiting for.

Keeping an easy-breezy tone, I say, "And with you guys getting married, I don't want to lose her. I know things will change because she will be your wife, and I'm going to respect that. I won't be able to drop in all the time as I do now, and I know our friend dates will be few and far between. I just don't want any awkwardness to get between us."

Brian nods. "I can understand that."

It's all he says.

He doesn't reassure me.

He doesn't offer up a plan that could solve my anxieties over losing Lia.

Just a simple understanding. My suspicions were correct. Once they get married, it's going to be hell on earth to hang out with Lia. And let's be honest. If I were in his shoes, I wouldn't want the best friend to crowd my marriage either. Especially if I was marrying Lia—*which would be weird*—but I wouldn't let him near her.

Our drinks and salads are delivered at the same time, and as we set our napkins on our laps and pose our forks, I can't help but wonder why he's so defensive about my relationship with Lia. We've never, and I mean *never*, given him a reason for concern. So why the fuck does he hate me so much?

"You know, I've always admired your friendship with Lia." He looks up at me. "That's all it's ever been, right?"

Jesus…

Okay, so that's why he hates me.

"Yes," I say, looking him dead in the eyes. "She's my best friend, that's it, nothing more. You don't need to worry about anything other than us just being friends."

He slowly nods. "Well, if that's the case, I'm supposed to have Lia all to myself this weekend, but I would love to go out on a double date with you."

"Oh, that would be cool, but I'm not seeing anyone at the moment, so your double date would sort of be a third-wheel situation."

"I'm aware of your dating status. That's why I have the perfect person for you."

Errrr...what?

"You have someone for me to go out on a date with?"

Brian nods. "Yeah. Her name is Birdy. She is my buddy's sister, and she's been having a hard time finding a genuine guy. He was telling me about it last night, and I thought, you know, I might have the perfect person for her. And since, you know, you don't have any romantic feelings for anyone else, this might be the perfect chance to meet someone new."

Any romantic feelings for anyone else? That's a specific way to say that. I feel like this is a test.

This isn't an act of goodwill or a way to get closer to me on a friend level. This is a test, and if I fail, he won't believe me when I say nothing is going on between Lia and me. This is him trying to see if an ounce of romance exists between his fiancée and me.

"A double date." I smile up at him. "Sounds like fun."

Can you hear the lies dropping off my tongue? No one, and I mean NO ONE, likes to be set up, let alone on a double date where you get to be stared at the entire time by an established couple.

If you're looking to spend your evening in horror, that's the way to do it.

But I would do anything for Lia, so...it looks like I'm a double dater now.

"Great." Brian beams, his rabid expression vanishing. "I'll set everything up and have Lia relay the info to you."

"Sounds great," I say as I take a bite of my salad.

Go be friends with Brian.

Get to know him better.

Clear the air...

Yeah, Kelsey and Lottie can go to hell with their advice.

Lia: Uh, earth to Pickle, earth to Pickle, are you there?

Breaker: I don't want to hear it.

Lia: A DOUBLE DATE?? Who are you and what did you do with my best friend?

Breaker: Maybe I left him back in New York.

Lia: Do I need to borrow your private jet to fly myself back and see if I can find him?

Breaker: Not sure the greatest SWAT team out there could find him at this point.

Lia: I can't believe you said yes to a double date. Frankly, I'm a little disappointed in you. You don't conform to social engagements.

Breaker: But Brian asked, and I felt obligated to say yes. Who knows, maybe this girl will be the love of my life.

Lia: Birdy and Breaker, it does have a nice ring to it.

Breaker: We clearly would need to name all of our children with B names.

Lia: Bertha, Bernard, and Barabbas...Auntie Lia is coming for those snuggles.

Breaker: Watch out, Barabbas is still wetting his pants when you squeeze him too hard.

Lia: I thought Birdy took him to the pediatrician to see what the squeeze pee was all about.

Breaker: Weak urethra, just going to have to give him time. Squeeze gently.

Lia: Barabbas is getting a head pat. Bertha and Bernard will be squeezed.

Breaker: Don't you DARE treat Barabbas differently. He's human like the rest of us.

Lia: You're right...you're right, that was wrong of me. I'll just squeeze gently and wear old shoes.

Breaker: Now there's a good aunt.

Lia: For the record, Birdy is a blond, and blonds aren't your favorite. So curb your displeasure.

Breaker: A blond? Huh, maybe this one I'll like.

Lia: Only time will tell. Seriously, though, you're good with this? I can cancel with Brian.

Breaker: No, it's good. Seriously. Might be nice. I haven't been out on a date in…well, a long time.

Lia: I've never seen you out on a date. This is sort of exciting. I get to see how Breaker puts on the moves.

Breaker: Please don't stare at me the entire time, watching my every move and smirking behind your napkin.

Lia: The urge to do just that is sitting very heavily on my chest because the joy I would reap from that is so overwhelming that my cup would be full for weeks. But I understand such behavior will cause you to sweat, and no one likes a sweaty pickle.

Breaker: Your concern for me feels so genuine. Thank you.

Lia: Anytime. So do you know what you're going to wear?

Breaker: Can we not do this, please?

Lia: Umm, great suggestion, but no. Brian setting you up with Birdy is probably one of the best things to ever happen to me.

Breaker: More than your engagement?

Lia: Don't tell Brian…but maybe.

Breaker: I always knew you were a different breed, but this really proves it. I'm going to bed.

Lia: But I'm not done teasing you and testing your patience.

Breaker: At least you're honest about it. Good night.

I raise my hand to the wall and knock four times.

She knocks three, and for the second night in a row…I don't get much sleep at all.

CHAPTER 4
LIA

"TODAY IS THE DAY!" I singsong as I make my way through Breaker's apartment to his bedroom, where the curtains are drawn and he's still in bed. Just a lump of a human sprawled across his mattress. "Good morning!"

"Grrrrrrr," he growls into his pillow.

"Time to rise and shine," I say while I fling open his curtains, flooding his room with the brilliantly bright California sun. "It's date day."

"Which is not until tonight, so why are you bothering me now?" he groans while placing his pillow over his head.

I turn to face him and spot part of his ass cheek hanging out for the world to see. "My God!" I say, covering my eyes. "Your butt is showing."

"That's what you get for walking in on me. You know I sleep naked." He adjusts his blankets.

"How would I know that?"

"You're my best friend. You should know everything about me." His voice is muffled by the pillow, but I can still understand him. "Like I know that if I were to remove this pillow, I would find you in a pair of bike shorts, some random Zelda shirt, and your hair clipped up because you can't have it touching your neck so early in the morning." He moves the pillow to the side to get a look at me, and when he sees he's right, he smirks and puts the pillow back.

"That was a lucky guess."

"Not a guess." He pokes his head. "All knowledge up here. Let me guess: You also ordered breakfast to lessen the blow of waking me up, and it will be here in five minutes. You ordered pancakes because you've been craving them. Still, you didn't get them from your favorite place because you know I prefer the breakfast burrito from Salty's. Hence, you caved and ordered from there despite them not having the maple-walnut syrup you love so much."

"You know, it's unflattering to be a know-it-all."

His chest rumbles with a laugh. "Not trying to flatter you, so no problem there." On a loud sigh, he raises his hands above his head and says, "Toss me my shorts."

I walk over to his dresser, where a pair of shorts are folded, and I hand them to him. He slips them under the bed, and I watch him shimmy into them without showing off any skin. He then flips the covers off him and sits on the edge of the bed. His hand presses into his eye as he attempts to wake himself up.

I just stand there and stare.

Breaker is a far cry from the man I once met.

In that dorm hallway, he was tall, lanky, and had enough shaggy hair on the top of his head to be mistaken for a Yorkshire terrier. Now, well, not so lanky anymore. Broad shoulders with sinew wrapping around them, flowing down his biceps, which are thick but not in a bodybuilder way. He's strong, fit, with enormous pecs and a pair of abs that quite frankly I'm jealous of. And his hair is no longer shaggy, more like perfectly cut to look messy, but it really isn't. And instead of his pasty white complexion from being inside nonstop studying, he is a beautiful bronze from running outside with his shirt off.

I've never truly ogled my best friend, but...I can admit he has a really nice body.

Like...really nice.

"This burrito better be good," he says as he stands, completely missing the fact that I just checked him out. Thank God for that. He works his way toward the bathroom, where he shuts the door. I leave him to his business and head out to the kitchen to start a pot of coffee for us. He always carries the dark chocolate raspberry coffee that I love. He says he can't taste the flavor, only smell it, but I can taste all the raspberry goodness; it's why it's my favorite.

"I can smell the raspberry from here," Breaker says as he stands at the doorway of his kitchen, scratching his chest, a lopsided grin playing at his lips.

My eyes travel down his chest, to the V in his hips that is shown off by his low-hanging shorts.

Okay...really, *really* nice body.

Not sure if he's kicked up his workout routine lately or what, but he's uh...he's looking good.

I turn away and hide the slight blush of my cheeks as I say, "It's potent because I haven't unleashed it in a while."

"When was the last time you had breakfast here?" he asks as he takes a seat on the counter.

"I don't know; we've been doing dinners more lately."

"Yeah, because you spend a lot of weekend nights over at Brian's, and I'm usually rushing around in the morning on weekdays looking to get to work. I don't have time for casual breakfasts."

I turn to face him and lean against the counter. "Well, now that you're on sabbatical, you have all the time in the world."

"Maybe this time will give me a moment to get to know...Birdy." He wiggles his eyebrows, making me laugh.

"You know, I cyberstalked her last night."

"Did you really? What did you come up with?"

"Wouldn't you like to know?"

"Yeah, I would." He nods at me. "Come on, spill. Tell me what I'm getting myself into tonight."

I grab my phone from the counter, and while the coffee brews, I show Breaker the screenshots I took last night for this very purpose—to share with him.

"Okay, first of all, she's really pretty."

"Looks aren't everything, but that's a bonus. Let me see." I show him a picture of her in a skintight light pink dress with a sunset behind her. Her hair is long and curled, and she's holding a champagne glass. Surprisingly, I see his eyes widen. "Wow, okay, yeah. She's beautiful."

I pause and say, "But she's a blonde."

"Yeah, think I can get over that." He smirks at me. "What else do you have?"

Feeling weird because I didn't think he would have that kind of reaction, I go back to the screenshots on my phone. I don't know, I knew he was going to think she was pretty because it's obvious, but his reaction suggests he's actually interested.

Why is that a bad thing in my head?

It shouldn't be.

I guess this whole situation is just weird, is all. Breaker doesn't date that much. He's taken girls out, had one-night stands, but an actual girlfriend, not really.

"So, uh, she really likes baseball. She loves the Chicago Rebels. Not sure who they are, but she has some fan page dedicated to a player's butt."

"Which means she's a butt person. That bodes well for me, as I have a nice ass."

"Do you?"

"Oh please," he scoffs. "You know I do, and don't even try to deny it. What else do you have on her?"

Not that I've looked, but he does. An annoyingly nice butt.

"She likes…get this…romantic comedies."

"What's wrong with that?"

I study him, truly study him. "Breaker, they're so cliché."

"For a reason," he says. "They bring joy to people. I know Kelsey and Lottie are obsessed with them. They've changed my mind. I can see the appeal. Something about having hope at the end of a story, knowing that it's all going to end well, makes you feel all warm and cozy inside."

I set my phone down, cross my arms over my chest, and ask, "What have you done with my best friend? You hate romantic comedies."

He hops off the counter and says, "People can change, Lia. It's okay. The world won't fall apart." He smirks and then pulls me into a hug. "Are you jealous I'm going out with this girl tonight?"

"What?" I pull away. "Why on earth would I be jealous?"

He lets me go just as a knock sounds on the door. The food is here.

"Because you're supposed to be the only woman in my life, right?"

"Well, yes. Of course."

He laughs and presses a quick kiss to my head before grabbing the food. "Don't worry, Lia, you'll always be my best friend." He turns toward me and then adds, "But you can't offer me benefits, and a guy has needs." His smirk makes me believe he's joking.

I push at his bare chest. "Ew, gross. Don't be that guy."

"Lia, I've always been that guy, but you just don't see it because you'd give me shit."

He sets the food out on the table, and I say, "So you think you'll like her? Go out with her?" I lean in and whisper, "Have sex?"

"Jumping the gun a bit, but I'm open. And I mean, she's really pretty. Who knows, maybe I'll be taking her as my date to your wedding. Maybe she'll catch the bouquet, maybe I'll catch the garter, and we'll have a whirlwind romance where Bertha, Bernard, and Barabbas aren't just a thought but a reality."

"All because of Brian. Could you imagine?"

"Honestly, I can't, but I'm just going with the flow at this point."

"And why exactly?" I ask, popping open the container to my pancakes.

He looks up at me from where he's unfolding his burrito from the foil.

"Because I want to make sure you're happy, Lia. I know how stressed you are about all of this, and if I can ease some of that stress, then I'm going to do that for you."

"You don't have to ease the stress by going out with Birdy."

"It's one date, and it's more for Brian than anything."

I eye him suspiciously. "And when have you ever started doing things for Brian?"

"Since he's going to be your husband and…and I don't want to lose you," he says quietly.

I pause, my head tilting to the side. Is he serious? When I study him for a moment and take in the way his shoulders curve inward and the dip in his posture, I can tell he is. "What? Breaker, you're not going to lose me."

He sets his burrito down and faces me. "Lia, we have to be real about this. In five weeks, things are really going to change. You're no longer going to live next to me. You're going to be occupied with your new life, and sure, I know you won't forget me, but I don't want there to be any reason for there to be distance between us other than actual distance. I don't want to give Brian a reason to put a wedge between us."

"I wouldn't let him," I say.

"I know, but if I don't get along with him, that could hurt your marriage. There could be resentment, so yeah, I'm going to do something for him. Sure, because I know if I do this little thing for him, I won't run the risk of not getting to hang out with you." Breaker's busy, so we don't get to see each other daily. But so far, since I've been going out with Brian, there hasn't been much disruption to how much time we spend with each other. But the idea that we won't just be able to walk a few steps out our front doors to see each other is startling.

"Do you really think life will change that much? I mean…you could always move close." I smile. "Your brothers live across the street. That could be us."

He tilts his head to the side. "Are you…asking me to follow you?"

His teasing tone causes me to roll my eyes. I pick up the syrup that came with my pancakes and drench them. "Not if you're going to be obnoxious about it, but yes, it doesn't have to be a straight cutoff when I get married. Brian understands our relationship, and who knows, if things work out with Birdy, maybe we can continue to go on double dates. And on those double dates, we can annoy them with our history by talking about all the college fun we had while they just sit there and stare at us."

"And when you say *college fun*, you really mean all the nerdy and embarrassing things we still do today."

I place a bite of pancakes in my mouth. "Precisely."

———————

"Lia, you ready?" Breaker asks, knocking on the door.

I check myself one more time in the mirror and make sure everything is in place.

Let's be real for a second. I'm not one who often goes all out when it comes to gussying up. I prefer minimal makeup because I don't like how it cakes on my glasses. I don't curl my hair often, and if I have a choice between jean shorts and a dress, I always choose jean shorts, but tonight, I felt the need to…spice it up.

I know what you're thinking. It's because Birdy is so pretty, right?

Well, you would be wrong. Birdy has nothing to do with this. I thought I would try to match the level of gorgeousness of my ring.

I know you don't believe me, but that's the reason, the ring. Not Birdy and her beautiful long blond hair or her long black eyelashes or the fact that she has such a nice pair of boobs that mine look like corn nuts in comparison.

This is all about the ring.

I smooth my hand down my purple tube dress, which just so happens to match my glasses. It also accentuates my curves—what little curves I have. I spent an hour curling my hair, and then I brushed out the curls because that was what the girl on the YouTube tutorial told me to do, and she was right. It's made my hair all wavy and pretty. And my makeup, well, I made sure to highlight my eyes with mascara and then put on a subtle lipstick that wouldn't clash with my dress, more accentuate it.

I'm pretty sure Brian is not going to recognize me. Maybe this is a good thing, spice things up before we get married and show him exactly what he's hitching himself to.

Clutch in hand, I open my front door and nearly choke on my own saliva as Breaker comes into view.

This is…this is not the Breaker I know, who wears junky old Jack Skellington T-shirts and backward hats because he's too lazy to worry about his hair.

This is a different Breaker.

Sophisticated.

Date Breaker.

Wearing a pin-striped gray suit and deep black button-up with the top few buttons undone, he looks so freaking good, like he belongs in a magazine. His pants are tight around his thighs but loosen up around his calves and ankles where the fabric stops. He's wearing loafers with no socks, and his hair is styled to the side in a messy way, giving him a sultry look that I wasn't expecting. And that tan chest, peeking out through the buttons of his shirt, so easily reveals the slightest hint of corded muscle that identifies him as a man who spends a great deal of time in the gym.

His suit fits him like a glove, not an inch to spare of fabric.

Handsome.

Sexy.

Arousing.

All the adjectives that come to mind.

"Wow, Lia," he says, taking me in and pulling on the back of his neck. "Shit, you look really good."

I'm snapped back to reality as I glance down at my dress and black high heels and then back up at him. "Oh, thank you. I, uh, I thought I would match the fanciness of my ring." I hold it out to show him as if he hasn't seen it before. "See? Fancy. And I'm fancy. We're all fancy."

His brow creases. "You okay?"

"Yes, great. Thank you. Just telling you I'm fancy."

He chuckles. "All right, well, glad we established that." He holds his arm out for me. "Ready to go?"

"Yeah, of course. So ready. Never been more ready. Just the most ready, so let's get this show on the road."

"You're being weird," he says as I lock up and then walk arm in arm with him toward the elevator.

Maybe because you look really good.

And smell nice.

And have a sense of suaveness circling you that I wasn't prepared to see.

"No, I'm not. Can't a friend just tell another friend how fancy they feel? Is that a crime?"

"Not that I'm aware of, but I can google it if you want me to."

I take a deep breath and step onto the elevator with him. His cologne's so heavy that it makes me feel dizzy in an odd, perplexing way.

I've never seen him like this because he's always been secretive about who he takes out, how he dates, and everything about his sexual life. Whenever I've asked before, he's been blasé about it, not diving too deep, never showing emotion or interest in the topic. But seeing him like this, it's all so different.

"Why have you always been secretive?" I nearly shout.

"Err, what?" he asks, letting go of my arm and facing me as we descend to the main lobby of our apartment complex.

"With dating, you've never talked about it. You've never told me anything about the women you see. Why is that?"

"Where is this coming from?" he asks as the elevator doors part. Breaker's car is waiting out front, the valet with key in hand.

I motion to his suit. "This is…this is not the Breaker I'm used to. I don't see you dress like this, all suave and, you know…handsome." I gulp.

And that stupid smirk of his appears as he says, "Yeah, well, I never see you like this either." He motions to me and says, "All dressed up and… beautiful. Normally, I hang out with the troll lady who lives next door and has a penchant for eating green olives straight from the jar."

My eyes widen, and I push him to the side, causing him to laugh. "I'm not a troll lady." Now the part about the olives, that's true.

"Your matted hair the other day told me otherwise." He tips the valet and then opens the door for me, but when I get in, he doesn't shut the door right away. He rests his hands on the roof and says, "I don't talk about it much because there isn't much to talk about. And I'm not the type of guy who runs around to his friends, telling them about the pussy I scored the night before. But if you so desire, I can start doing that."

"Do you score a lot?"

"More than you're probably aware, but since you're curious, I've gone through a bit of a drought as of recently. Just haven't had time. I think the last woman I was with, if you must know, is your friend Charise, the one you hooked me up with for Huxley's wedding."

"Wait, seriously?" I ask. "You hooked up with Charise?"

"A few times." He winks and then shuts the door on me, leaving me in a state of bewilderment.

When he climbs into his side of the car, I ask, "A few times? Like… more than once?"

"That's usually what *a few times* means." He puts the car in drive and pulls away from the apartment building.

"But she never said anything to me. You never said anything to me. How am I supposed to know you're hooking up with my friend? Did anything come of it?"

"Triplets, actually. Not humans, puppies. She has custody, but I have visitation rights."

"I'm being serious, Breaker." I push at his shoulder, causing him to laugh.

"Nah, it was just sex. Neither of us was looking for anything serious, plus there was no connection other than a carnal one." He wiggles his eyebrows.

"Ew, don't say *carnal*." I fold my arms and sink into my seat while Breaker drives us toward downtown, where Brian made a reservation. "So you're just out there dating, having a good time, and not telling me about it?"

"Why would I tell you? Just so you can push me and say *ew*?" he asks in a teasing tone.

"Well, yeah."

He chuckles. "Thanks, but I think I'll pass."

"So tonight, are you going to be all...touchy-feely and Date Breaker?"

"If you're staring me down the whole time, then no. Not sure I can put on the moves when your judgmental glare is directed my way."

"Judgmental? Nothing about me is judgmental."

"Ha!" He guffaws. "Lia, you were judging Birdy earlier today when you saw that she likes romantic comedies."

"Uh, you used to make fun of them until apparently recently, thanks to your sisters-in-law. The question really is, do I even know you at all, Breaker?"

"You tell me." He grips the steering wheel so he's only using one hand while the other falls to the armrest, and for a moment, I think about him driving Birdy around. Would he place his hand on her thigh? Would he lace their fingers together? Would he bring their connection to his lips and place a gentle kiss to her perfectly lotioned knuckles? I couldn't imagine Breaker doing any of this; then again, it's because I've never seen that side of him. Out of all the years we've known each other, I've never observed him with a woman. "Name my biggest fear."

"We don't need to do this," I say on a sigh.

"Yes, we do." He pokes my leg. "Come on, what's my biggest fear? And you're the only one who knows this."

"House fire where you can't get your signed *Lord of the Rings* memorabilia out of the house fast enough, and you lose it."

He winces and pats his heart. "Still gets me just thinking about it. My turn, you ask me a question about you."

"Why are we doing this?"

"To prove to you that we know each other better than any other person and that will never change. So go ahead, ask me a question."

"Fine. What is my least favorite childhood memory?"

"The day you got your period. You were at a friend's house for a sleepover and got it in the middle of the night on the sleeping bag you borrowed from your friend. She made you feel bad because you stained it, and then you had to wait for your mom to pick you up. Courtney is a real bitch who I hope burns in hell."

That makes me smile. "She didn't have to torment me about the stain, that's for sure."

"Yeah, well, hopefully, karma has repaid her in the form of a corn on the bottom of her foot. That shit is painful."

"One could only hope."

"Okay, what is my least favorite childhood memory?" he asks.

That's easy. I remember the day we talked about it. It was our senior year in college. We went to a frat party but ended up chatting on the porch the whole night. We both had a few drinks, but nothing that would impair our cognitive behavior. He leaned back on his hands and told me all about the day he lost his dad.

"When your dad passed away," I answer softly. "And how you wish you told him you loved him more than you did. How you regret not saying that to him enough. I remember that like it was yesterday because I clung to that and always told my parents I loved them after that."

He slowly nods. "And you're the only person who knows that. I never told my brothers. I never told another soul. So I might not talk about the menial things like the girls I take out or hook up with because it has no value to our friendship. But the important things? Those are the things I tell you about, and that's what should matter the most."

"Why are you trying to make me emotional?"

"I'm not trying to make you emotional." He reaches across the console and grabs my hand. "I'm just trying to tell you that no matter what happens, you will always know me best, and there's a reason for that. You're my best friend, Lia. Nothing can come between that. I won't let it happen. Hence us driving downtown to go on a double date."

"You're a really good guy, you know that, Breaker?"

"I try." His grin stretches from ear to ear. "Now, let me show you a new song that I've been simping over."

"Oh my God, do not say *simping*. You cannot pull it off."

"Says who?" he asks with feigned insult.

"Says me."

"And who made you the authority?"

"I did."

"Ehh, that's fair." He casually shrugs.

I laugh as he cues up his new favorite song. Breaker is right. Nothing can come between us.

Nothing at all.

CHAPTER 5
BREAKER

BIRDY'S PICTURE DID NOT DO her justice.

Not even a little.

She's stunning.

And sweet. I almost half expected her to be beautiful but stuck up in some way. Or lacking personality. That's not the case at all. She seems very down-to-earth and shy. At least that's what I picked up while we were waiting to be seated.

When we arrived at the restaurant, Brian was already here, talking on his phone, but the moment we stepped up, he got off the phone and pulled Lia into a big hug while telling her how beautiful she looked. And he's right. I don't want to say this because it will sound corny, but when she opened the door to her apartment, she took my breath away. I've always considered Lia gorgeous, but seeing her in that dress, yeah, she looks really fucking good. But I quickly tamped down that initial reaction to her appearance because it would do me no good. I realized that back in college after I saw her dressed up for the first time for a date. I was so taken aback that I started to crush on her.

And I quickly realized what a bad idea that was, given how much I cherished our friendship, so I tucked away those feelings, and I've been able to block them out. Every so often, they appear, but I know better. Tonight is no exception. Whereas Birdy is stunning, you can tell she does a lot to her appearance. On the other hand, Lia's just naturally beautiful with her deep mossy-green eyes and adorable freckles.

Once Brian stopped kissing Lia—quite uncomfortable to witness—Birdy stepped up, looking all shy. Brian introduced us, and we spoke for a few moments before we were directed to our seats.

Now that we're at a table, four chairs around a square setting, Birdy sits on one side of me and Lia on the other.

"Have you been here before?" Brian asks.

"I don't believe I have," I answer. "What about you, Birdy?"

She shakes her head. "No, it's probably the fanciest place I've been."

"Well, the wagyu is magnificent if you like steak," Brian says, staring down at his menu. "And please, feel free to get whatever you like. Dinner is on me."

"Oh, that's not necessary," I say as Brian looks up from his menu.

His jaw grows tight with a smile. "This was my idea. Therefore, I'll be treating everyone."

You can see it in his eyes. The insecurity. He knows how much I'm worth—it's easy to look up—yet he feels the need to prove he can keep up. There is nothing to prove and no competition. Therefore, I just leave it in his hands. If he wants to pay for my dinner, by all means, he can pay for it.

"Well, thank you. That's really kind of you, Brian," I say, feeling my professional side come out, and I can see Lia chuckling behind her menu from the corner of my eye. She always makes fun of my professional side. She thinks it's hilarious when I drop the sarcasm and am on my best behavior. She says it's like witnessing children visiting their grandparents. They're always on their best behavior, minding their manners, and never saying anything that would ruffle anyone's feathers.

After the server takes our order, I decide to get to know Birdy better. By the way, she ordered a salad with dressing on the side, no croutons, no onions, and no cheese. So basically, just lettuce and meat. Doesn't she know that the croutons are the best part?

"So where are you from?" I ask her.

"Originally Tennessee, but I've lived in Los Angeles for the past ten years. I went to school here and loved it so much I decided to stay."

"Hard to leave California once you live here. Did you study marketing in school?"

She nods and pushes her hair behind her ear. "I did. And my master's. I've always been good at spinning a good story to sell something."

I shake my head. "It takes a creative mind to be in your field. When my brothers and I first started building our business, we had to work on our marketing, and Huxley, my eldest brother, thought it would be smart to give me the job of branding." I lift my water glass up to my lips. "Let's just say that didn't go over well."

"Oh, come on," Lia chimes in. "I really liked the logo you created."

"Don't even bring it up," I say as I move my hand over my face.

"Oh goodness," Birdy says. "I have to see this now. Do you have a picture?"

"I do," Lia replies while taking her phone out of her clutch. "I have a folder in my phone of all of the embarrassing things Breaker has done over the years. It comes in handy when I need to ground him."

"Which is not often," I say, trying to make sure Birdy knows I'm not some egomaniac.

"Often enough to have a folder." Lia flips through her phone and then turns the screen toward Birdy. "So he combined an *H* for Huxley, a *J* for JP, and a *B* for him, all together with a *C* as well."

Birdy cringes. "It looks like a bunch of crumpled-up letters."

Lia laughs. "He was going for simple."

"To my defense, I had no right being in charge of this. I never said I had any design experience, and it was poor judgment on my brothers' part, putting me in charge of this task. But I was smart enough to suck at it, which made us spend the money to get it done professionally."

"Smart," Birdy says. "Always leave it to the professionals." The server comes up to our table with the bottle of wine that Brian ordered, and while he samples it to make sure it's what he's looking for, I ask Birdy if she has any siblings.

"Just a brother. But he's ten years older than me, so we've never been super close. Not like best friends, but we do look out for each other. But friends, probably not like you and your brothers, I assume. You must be close to work together."

"Very close, sometimes obnoxiously close. We get into each other's business way too much. When I'm the one who isn't needing help or hasn't done something stupid, I enjoy watching the drama unfold."

"Would you say you're in charge of mediation in your family?"

"I am," I say in surprise as I turn more toward her. Brian must have approved the wine because the server starts filling up the wineglasses. "Does it seem like I would be the mediating type?"

"You're very calm. You have this air about you that makes me think that you like to keep the peace."

"I do," I answer. "Don't care much for drama."

"Pffft," Lia says next to me.

I glance over my shoulder. "Care to weigh in?"

"Uh, senior year, the second semester during the Scrabble championships, you were *living* for the drama. You were part of the drama. Flirting with two girls from the same team, creating an uproar when they found out…in the middle of the game."

"That's not drama, Lia. That's called strategic Scrabble play." I tap the side of my temple. "Mental fortitude is a key component to winning championships, and if you can mess with your opponent in any way to throw off that mental fortitude, then you have to. So yeah, I took one for the team and flirted with two women." I turn to Birdy and add, "I don't ever do that in real life, just need to put that out there."

She smiles softly. "Doesn't seem like you would be that kind of guy."

"Hey, Lia, why don't we go stand out on the balcony while the food cooks, give these two some time alone to chat?" Brian says with a nauseating wink.

"Oh, sure, yeah," Lia says while she lifts from her chair and joins Brian. I can tell from the stiffness in her response and the hesitation in her step, the last thing she wants to do is give Birdy and me space. No, she wants to be a voyeur, watching and listening to every second of this interaction.

If the roles were reversed, I would be the same way.

"They're so cute together," Birdy says.

"Yeah, they are," I reply, even though it feels like a lie coming out of my mouth.

"So you met Lia in college?" Birdy asks.

"Yeah, we were part of a secret Scrabble group, and she was very impressive with her spelling skills. After her first night, we sort of bonded over all things that interested us, and we've been best friends since."

"That's so cool. What were some of the things you bonded over?"

"Uhh." I look off to the side and then lean a little closer. "If I tell you, it might deter you from wanting to stick around on this date because Lia and I don't usually like mainstream popular things."

"Try me." She brings her wine up to her pink-painted lips. "I might surprise you."

"Okay." I rub my hands together and turn toward her. "I have a deep obsession with *Lord of the Rings*. I read the books when I was younger, became quickly obsessed, and haven't looked back since. I've dressed up as Gandalf for Halloween far too many times for me to count. I enjoy building model airplanes and flying them. I find it incredibly soothing. I'm an avid board gamer. I will try any game at least once. I prefer the ones where I go on a quest. Sports don't really interest me. I'll watch them, but I'm not a die-hard fan. I've been known to enjoy a comic book from time to time, but nothing mainstream like Marvel or DC. There's this one series of comic books about Sherlock Holmes that I really enjoy reading. I'm toeing the line of becoming a Disney adult. I'm an annual

ticket holder, attend the Halloween party every year, and have a sick obsession with *The Nightmare before Christmas* as well as *Mulan*. The montage where she becomes a 'man' gives me chills every time. And my favorite movie is *The Thin Man*. There's a whole series of them, and in the late fall, there's an old movie theater downtown that puts on a marathon of them. Lia and I go every year."

Birdy sips her wine and pauses for a moment. After a few seconds, she finally says, "A hot nerd, I think I can get on board with that."

I let out a chuckle and lift my glass to hers, where we clink them and sip.

"What do you think, man?" Brian asks. "She's great, isn't she?"

Birdy excused herself to the bathroom after her plate of salad was taken away by the server. I shamelessly watched her walk away with a pretty hefty sway to her hips that I appreciated.

"Yeah, she's pretty awesome," I say as I pat my mouth with my cloth napkin and then set it on the table. "Seems like we have some differences when it comes to interests, but she did say she enjoys hiking, which is a plus."

Lia has been quiet for a while. Well, most of the dinner, actually. Brian has been talking to her about work while Birdy and I have been conversing.

"Did you tell her that you like bird-watching when you hike?" Lia asks.

"Uh, skipped out on the part where I mention my binoculars, bucket hat, and notebook."

Brian laughs. "I bet that's a sight to behold."

"Not many people get to see that side of me for that reason."

"I don't know. I think the bucket hat looks good," Lia says, her eyes flashing toward me.

Brian shifts in his chair and clears his throat. "So would I be safe to assume that you'll be driving Birdy home tonight?"

"If she needs a ride, sure," I answer.

"Will you be asking her out again?" Lia asks softly.

I shrug. "I don't know. Maybe. She seems cool, and getting to know her without an audience who likes to share embarrassing pictures might be helpful."

"But those are the best pic—"

"Well, don't let us keep you," Brian says just as Birdy approaches. I don't fail to notice how he cut Lia off, or how she slinks back in her chair from the abrupt interruption. Brian stands from his chair and buttons up his suit jacket. "I've already taken care of the bill. Lia and I are going to head out as it's a bit of a drive to Malibu."

"Yeah, of course," I say as I stand as well. Way to make this incredibly awkward with a blunt goodbye. There was no interlude, just a short-snipped *we're leaving*. Wanting to make sure Lia is okay, I turn to her and pull her into a hug. "You good?" I ask softly. She nods against my shoulder, so I take that as her answer and say, "Have a good weekend."

"Okay. Thanks," she says softly, her voice sounding strange. I'm about to ask her if she's sure everything is okay, but I think twice of it, not wanting to spark any questioning from Brian.

So I release Lia and say, "Text me about next week and your appointments. You know I'll be at all of them."

"I will." She smiles as Brian comes around and places his hand on her lower back.

He lends out his hand and offers me a shake. "Good seeing you, Breaker. Have fun; the night is still early. Maybe take Birdy out for dessert."

No pressure. Jesus.

"Sure, thanks again for dinner." They both take off, and I turn to Birdy. She's standing there, unsure of what to do, with her clutch tight in her hand. "So." I stick my hands in my pockets. "Uh…when I go on hikes, it's more for bird-watching." She laughs. "Just want to put that out there before I ask if you want to get dessert."

"Bird-watching, huh? Seems like a good time. Don't know much about birds, but I don't mind learning."

"If that's the case, would you like to go for dessert?"

"I would love it." Birdy loops her arm through mine, and we walk out of the restaurant together.

"Okay, this cheesecake is amazing," Birdy says as she takes another bite. "The raspberry swirl should be illegal."

"I told you it was good," I say as I take another bite. "And you doubted me."

"I didn't doubt you. I was just thrown off. I wasn't expecting to grab dessert from a food truck."

"I live off food trucks," I say while taking another bite. "Near where we live is a taco truck that makes the best fucking tacos with dipping sauce. Lia and I try to limit ourselves, but it doesn't help that they're parked right around the corner."

"Do you and Lia eat dinner together often?" Birdy asks.

"Uh, not really. Maybe like twice a week. Whenever she's not with Brian."

"I wish I lived near my friends. It would make it easier to hang out."

"It is convenient."

She picks at a piece of cheesecake and says, "I think I'm overstepping when I ask this, but I guess I'm just curious. Have you and Lia ever been... romantic?"

I shake my head. "Nah, we're just friends. Never even thought about it. I guess it's an honest question to ask when you see two people of the opposite sex hanging out as much as we do. My brothers always ask me despite me giving them the same answer."

"I'm sorry if that was inappropriate. I was put through the wringer with my last relationship, so I guess I just want to be up front and honest, not that this is a relationship or that you want to ask me out again, but just in case, I like to cover everything."

"I get that. I've, uh, I've never really been in anything serious, nor do I date much."

"Oh, really?" she asks. "I guess that was stupid of me to assume otherwise."

"No, not stupid. We did go on a double date, so your assumption is valid."

She sets her fork down and crosses one leg over the other. "So why don't you date much, Breaker? You seem like a pretty levelheaded guy. Sweet. Kind. Thoughtful. Why aren't you putting yourself out there?"

"Going deep tonight, are we?" I joke. "Well, I guess I just haven't found the person I want to spend more time with. It's not that I'm against dating, but I just haven't clicked with someone enough to spend more time, if that makes sense. And with my busy schedule, I haven't really put the feelers out there either."

She nods. "I can understand that." She glances to the side and says, "And I guess you're not that lonely because you have Lia."

Very true. Lia keeps me fully occupied when I need it.

"Yeah," I answer softly.

"So what happens after she gets married? Do you think you two will hang out as much? And I ask that not in a mean way, just trying to understand."

"Don't worry about insulting me or anything like that. I get the curiosity. And we talked about it a little today, said we could find a house near each other, still hang out." I twist my lips to the side. "I don't know. I'm not sure how much we will see each other, though. I know we'll never forget about each other, but I do know our dinner dates will probably become few and far between."

"I can only imagine they would because married life is different," Birdy states, confirming my fears.

"It is." I bite down on my lip. What does that mean for me? I can tell you what that means. It looks like I'm going to be a whole bunch of lonely soon. "Shit, Birdy, looks like I need to start dating."

She laughs and pats my hand. "Well, when you're ready."

I look up at her and smile. "Maybe I could be ready. What do you think? Would you want to do this again? Maybe not with such a sad ending talking about my pathetic life?"

"It's not pathetic at all. I actually think it's sweet. My mom always told me that true friendships are hard to find, but they are the most important things to hang on to. What you have with Lia is so special. You want to hang on to that."

"I do. But I think you're right. Married life will be different, and I might not be lonely now when I have her, but that will change after she's married. It's about time I put myself out there." I take Birdy's hand in mine. "Would you like to go on a second date with me? Maybe a hike? I can show you some birds."

She smiles brightly. "I would love that."

———————

Beep.

Beep.

Beep.

I grumble under my breath and peel my eyes open as I glance at my phone that is lit up.

Who the hell is texting me?

With blurry eyes, I bring the phone closer to my face and note the time. 1:15 a.m. This better be fucking important.

I glance at the sender and see that it's from Lia. I rub my eyes a few times and then swipe on her text to read it.

Lia: Hey, you up?

Lia: You never texted me after your date.

Lia: Are you still with her?

Groaning, I get comfortable on my side, and I text her back.

Breaker: You know, this is a conversation that could be had in the morning.

Lia: Oh, you are awake. Look at that.

Breaker: Because of you.

Lia: Oops *charmingly smiles*

Breaker: *Rejects the charming smile*

Lia: Don't be mad, I couldn't sleep, and I was curious. So...how did it go with Birdy?

Breaker: Are we really doing this right now?

Lia: Yes.

I groan again and text her back.

Breaker: Good. She's pretty cool. We have few obvious things in common, but she was super nice, sweet, and pretty of course.

Lia: Of course. Did you invite her back to your place?

Breaker: Seriously? No. I barely know her.

Lia: As if that has prevented you before.

Breaker: This is different.

Lia: How is this different?

Breaker: Because I'm trying something new.

Lia: Something new? Tell me more...

Breaker: I thought I would try to date her.

Lia: Wait...seriously? But you don't date.

Breaker: Yeah, I know, but with you getting married soon and your time being consumed with your soon-to-be husband, I figured I should maybe find someone to, you know...be compatible with.

There isn't a response.

For a few minutes, and I wonder if I said something wrong or if she fell asleep until my phone rings in my hand. Seeing her name scroll across the screen, I pick up and put my phone on speaker so I can rest it against my pillow and talk.

"Hello?"

In a hushed voice, she asks, "Are you trying to replace me?"

"What? No. Why would you say that?"

"That last text, it sounds like you're trying to find a replacement."

"Lia, come on, you know I'm not trying to replace you. You could never be replaced, but let's be honest, as much as we like to believe things won't change, they will. Brian will be your top priority once you're married, and you can't let anything get in the way. Which means I'm going to have some free time. I don't want to be sitting around in my apartment by myself all the time, so maybe it's time I go out and find someone."

"You won't be alone. We're going to live next to each other, remember?"

"Still, Brian won't want me over all the time, Lia. Face it, things are changing, and that's okay. We knew the time would come."

"But...I don't want things to change," she says softly. "I like things the way they are." *God, so do I. I liked it when I had full access to my brothers too, but that ship has sailed.* It's life, I guess. But I can't ignore this opportunity. I swallow hard and then say, "So then why did you say yes to his proposal?"

She's quiet, and I know it's a question I don't think she knows how to truly answer other than the generic statement.

"Because I love him."

But are you in love with him? I want to ask her that so bad, but I also don't want to cause drama. I don't want her second-guessing herself. If she says she loves him, then I need to believe that.

"Well, then, this is what happens when you fall in love, Lia. Things change."

She's silent again and then says, "But Birdy? She doesn't seem like a person you would go out with."

"Why do you say that?"

"Well…" I can hear her take a deep breath. "You don't have a lot in common. She seems like the popular-girl type, and you're more on the interesting scale."

"Interesting?" I laugh. "Please describe that for me."

"You just have different interests that don't match up."

"And you and Brian have interests that match up?" I ask before I can stop myself. "Last time I checked, he thinks it's lame that you and I freak out over a new board game."

"He said that once."

"Once is enough."

"What are you saying? Do you not want me marrying him?"

No, I would prefer that you didn't.

"I didn't say that." I drag my hand over my face. "I'm just trying to say that sometimes interests don't match up, and that's okay. Look at you and Brian. You don't have everything in common, but your relationship still works. Look, I've only met Birdy once, so I'm not going to suggest that I've met my future wife or anything. But what's the harm in finding out if we're compatible? Maybe those different interests won't be a deal-breaker like they're not with you and Brian. There's only one way to find out."

"So does that mean you're going out with her again?"

"Yeah, we're going on a hike next weekend. I'm going to teach her about birds. Who knows, maybe she'll become a fanatic like me."

"What's with the Cane brothers and their birds?"

"Hey, JP likes pigeons because he feels guilty about them not being loved, but he couldn't care less about other feathered friends."

"Please, for the love of God, don't call them *feathered friends.*"

"Well, if I don't try to put myself out there and date, they very much might be my only friends, and although the solitude of being the crazy bird man sounds charming, I don't think I'm ready for that title just yet."

"I can see it, your poncho, a bucket hat. A cane."

"Please…please don't envision that."

She chuckles and then sighs. "I'm sorry, Breaker."

"Sorry for what?" I ask.

"Well, for one, waking you up. And also for giving you a hard time about Birdy. I guess I'm just stressed with the many rapid changes. I was comfortable, content, and now my life feels like a whirlwind of change, and it's all happening at a frightening pace."

"You know you have the choice to slow it down."

"By disappointing others."

"Yes, but it's for the sake of your mental health," I reply. "Don't try to please others just for the sake of it."

"I know you're right, Breaker. I know you are, but I just don't have it in me to disappoint others. Brian is so sensitive. I think if I postponed, he'd think it had to do with him, and I don't want him thinking that. I just need to take this one step at a time."

"Okay, but just so you know, if you want to try to slow this down, you just let me know, and I'll step in and help."

"I know, and I love you for that. Just promise me you will be here every step of the way."

"I promise."

"Thank you."

CHAPTER 6
LIA

"WELL, IT'S NICE," BREAKER SAYS as we step out of his car and stare up at the rather ornate and grand stone church right in front of us. On an almost vacant street in the heart of Los Angeles is a Catholic church with a tall spire reaching up into the sky and an arched entrance that feels more intimidating than welcoming.

I glance up at the grandiose building and say, "There are gargoyles on the edge of the roof. That doesn't really scream wedding vibes."

Breaker puts his arm around me. "Not really, but the reason gargoyles were carved into buildings in the first place was to ward off evil spirits from entering, so…if you look at it that way, then maybe it's a good thing. There will be no evil spirits lurking in your marriage."

I glance up at his freshly shaved face—he usually keeps some scruff on it but chose to go clean today. "Are you going to put a positive spin on everything?"

"I will until you tell me you absolutely hate it. At that point, I will jump the positivity ship, but you need to give it a fair shot first. Who knows, maybe the inside of the chapel really captivates you."

"I'm not religious, Breaker."

"You don't need to be religious to appreciate the sanctity of divine architecture. Think about what it took for people to build this building back in the day. All the intricate carvings and details you don't see in today's modern aesthetic."

"Correct me if I'm wrong, but no Chipotle has gargoyles or intricate carvings, and I still very much enjoy walking into their establishments."

"Because you're a whore for salty lime chips, just like Lottie."

"How do you know that?" I chuckle.

"That's where Huxley and Lottie were on their first official date, if that's what you want to call it. It's where they went over the terms of their fake fiancé contract. Honestly, saying it out loud really doesn't sound real. Anyway, she took home the chips that Huxley bought when he really wanted them. He bitched about it for days."

"You guys are billionaires. You can buy your own Chipotle and turn it into a chip factory for your own personal pleasure. Why was he bitching about someone taking his chips?"

"It's the principle of the thing," he says just as The Beave steps out of a black sedan parked a few feet away.

The Beave is something else. Lanky legs always on a minimum of four-inch heels, she always wears an unflattering resting bitch face, accompanied by a nude-colored lip. She mimics the royal family by always wearing a jacket that you can't quite tell is a dress or is actually a jacket—even in the California heat—and she pairs it with a hat when she's outdoors. The only time she doesn't wear a hat is when she's sitting down for a meal. She reminds me of Yzma from *The Emperor's New Groove*, but minus the grayish purple skin, saggy tits that touch her belly button, and adherent henchman who cooks a mean spinach puff.

"Ophelia, hello," she says rather coldly and then turns to Breaker, a smile playing at her lips. "Mr. Cane, what a treat for you to join us today." She holds out her skeleton-thin hand, and Breaker takes it and offers her a simple shake.

"Please, Breaker is just fine, and I couldn't miss an opportunity to be the perfect maid of honor for my girl." He gives me a squeeze.

"Maid of honor?" The Beave asks, glancing at me. "I wasn't aware that you would be having a man on your side of the altar."

I hold back my smirk. The Beave wasn't expecting a wrench in her plans this early in the morning, I bet. There's no doubt she's a traditionalist and requires the traditional setting of a wedding. The bride has women on her side; the groom has men. Well, welcome to the modern century because that's not how we'll work.

"Breaker is my best friend. I wouldn't have it any other way."

"Well, maybe we can consider—"

"It won't be any other way," Breaker says, cutting in, subverting my authority.

The shitty thing about this situation is that even though this is my wedding, The Beave is not going to listen to anyone other than herself. The only person, and I mean ONLY person, who could overturn her decision is Breaker. Not me, not her son, no one else, only Breaker, and that's because she values Breaker more than her son and me. The only reason is because of how thick Breaker's wallet is.

"I see." The Beave straightens up. "Well, then, I guess I will make a note of that." She then looks him up and down and says, "You know, Breaker, I heard the news about your former employee."

Classic.

God, she's like clockwork. I saw her mentioning that from a mile away.

Breaker cuts her off at the knees, and now she's trying to do the same, trying to even the playing field. Little does she know the reason the Cane brothers are so successful is because they see right through social climbers and don't let them tear them down.

And from the confidence in Breaker's expression, I know he sees right through The Beave.

"Tragic, isn't it?" Breaker asks. "That a girl with so little self-worth spreads lies to grab attention? Our lawyers are handling it. There will be an apology once we present the required evidence of the former employee's inappropriate behavior in the workplace. Then again, I shouldn't be saying anything because of how confidential it is."

"Ah, understandable."

"But thank you for your concern. I'm doing quite fine."

She offers an even smile and then gestures toward the church. "Now, I believe we have a church to view and a priest to meet." She turns, and with her assistant, who appears at her side, she starts up the steep stone stairs that lead to the red-door entrance.

Hanging back for a moment, I cling on to Breaker's arm and say, "I'm so sorry she brought that up."

"Don't apologize for her. She's disgustingly transparent. I knew she was going to bring up the lawsuit, and shutting her down was easy."

"I know, but still, she shouldn't have said anything."

"Lia, I'm fine."

"Okay." I clutch him tighter. "I'm going to need your help making our way up these stairs. These shoes Brian bought me are a touch too big."

Breaker glances down at my shoes, examining them. "I was wondering where the hell you got those."

"You don't like them?" I ask as I turn my feet to the side. This whole outfit screams Brian. A fluffy red mini skirt with a black tank top and black four-inch heels that I would never, ever wear, I feel more like a newborn clown than the sophisticated lady about to marry the very sought-after Brian Beaver.

"They're nice, just not you."

"What makes you think that? The gold buckle on the toe or the fact that I look like I'm a newbie trying to walk on circus stilts?"

"Maybe a touch of both." He chuckles.

"Well, at least The Beave didn't say anything disapproving."

We head up the stairs, Breaker helping me the whole time. "Way to find the positive. Now, let's just focus on whether we like this church."

"I'm going to say no."

"Do you have a second venue where you want to get married? A counteroffer?" Breaker asks as we make our way up the stairs.

"I do, actually, but I know The Beave is going to hate it."

"Then that means it's perfect," Breaker says as we reach the door and step into the opulent church.

The entrance opens into a large cathedral space with natural wood beams crisscrossing against the vaulted ceiling. Rows and rows of pews face the altar while a red velvet carpet stretches along the candlelit aisle. The altar is intricately carved with the same natural wood as the beams while also draped in linens and an arrangement of flowers that seems rather extravagant for a midsummer mass.

Leaning toward Breaker, I whisper, "I'm surprised the lit candles aren't a fire hazard."

"And those candleholders don't look too sturdy."

"Isn't it just divine?" The Beave asks in awe. "We won't be able to fit everyone into the pews, but we will live stream the wedding to those waiting at the club for you to arrive."

I blink a few times while I glance at the *many* pews. "How many people do you plan on inviting?" I ask.

"Ophelia, I emailed you the guest list." She snaps her fingers, and her assistant appears at her side with a box. The Beave opens the box and pulls out the crown of a veil. "Now, let's see this on."

"Hold on, what guest list?"

The Beave ignores me and slips the veil on top of my head, digging the clip deep into my scalp until I'm almost positive she drew blood.

"I sent it to you, Ophelia. Honestly, do we need to talk about organization?" She removes the rest of the veil from the garment box, dragging the tulle fabric out in piles. Jesus, how long is this thing? And why did she put it on my head?

"I guess I didn't see it. I was sort of busy this weekend."

Busy with Brian, her son.

"Well, if you took the time to worry about the upcoming nuptials, you would have seen I have a little over two thousand invites going out." She gestures toward the aisle. "Now, please, walk down the aisle so I can see how this veil looks."

I blink, completely oblivious to what's happening to me. "Two...two thousand?" I ask, my mouth going dry. "Like two thousand people?"

"More like four to five. There are couples and families." She gestures for me to walk again, but I stand still.

"Oh my God," I say, my armpits starting to sweat. "That's...that's too many people. Can the club even hold that many people?"

"Of course not," she says, waving her hand at me. "That's why we have secured the private beach as well. It's all about appearances, even if people won't be able to see everything. Now, if you'll please..." She motions down the aisle.

I turn to Breaker, my heart racing, my eyes pleading for help. "Did you hear that?" I say through clenched teeth, the veil tangling up in my legs. "Two *thousand* people, Breaker."

Luckily, Breaker senses my panic. "That seems like a lot," Breaker says. "Has Brian gone over the list?"

The Beave dismisses him with her hand. "Brian has better things to do than bother with wedding details."

"But...it's the start of his marriage. Don't you think he should be a little interested?" Breaker asks.

Her head snaps toward Breaker. "He's interested enough, but a guest list is menial. You should know the importance of his high-level job. I can't be bothering him with these questions. That's why I'm in charge. Now, Ophelia, walk down the aisle so I can see if the veil is right for you."

"Yeah, but that's a lot of people, Mrs. Beaver," Breaker continues as I try to straighten the veil out. I kick at it with my feet while the assistant—not sure of her name—attempts to help as well. "Lia doesn't do well in big crowds. Unless you want a bride passing out at the altar, I think you need to pare down."

The Beave turns toward me and says, "That's not true, is it?"

Not proven, but I could see it being a possibility, so I go with it. "I have weak knees," I answer while tilting the crown of the veil. "Where did this veil come from?"

"It was mine from when I married. Please don't kick at it with your hooves. It's a precious heirloom."

"Oh…" I smile. "It's lovely. You can really smell the history." Very… musty. "Anywho, can't say that a passed-out bride at the altar will result in cherished wedding memories. If I pass out, it's going to embarrass Brian."

Anything that might harm, embarrass, or taint her son, The Beave is going to want nothing to do with it.

"I wasn't aware that you're a risk at the altar." She glances down the aisle. "If you pass out, that would ruin the entire ceremony."

No one likes a fainty bride.

"Yeah, and what if I hit my head on one of the pews?" I ask. "A cracked head leads to blood, and I don't think guests will want it to be a gory wedding. Especially if I wear this heirloom veil. Not sure blood comes out easily from fabric like this. Perchance, do you know the length of it?"

"Fifty feet," The Beave answers absentmindedly.

Fifty feet, dear God, who needs a veil that long? She's not even royalty.

Cutting in, Breaker says, "White dress, blood, and gore don't really say *high-class wedding*. Not to mention, she bleeds easily. We're talking pools of blood."

"Iron deficiency anemia," I say, nodding my head.

"Well." The Beave turns her nose up. "Perhaps I'll speak with my doctor and get him to prescribe you some Xanax for the day to avoid any way of you passing out."

Of course she would have a pharmaceutical solution.

"Uh, that won't work," I say, glancing up at Breaker, looking for help.

"Yeah," he says, picking up on my plea. "That won't work because… uh…well, she's a puker."

The Beave recoils in disgust. I don't blame her. Didn't see that coming.

"Pardon me?" she asks.

Breaker nods, going with it. "Yup, a serious puker this one." He points his thumb at me. "Any sort of medication that curbs her anxiety, she just pukes right up. And not just a little. It's projectile. I remember a time in college when she took some calming meds—can't quite remember what it was—but she took some before her final exam in data statistics and mechanics because she was so nervous. After the first ten minutes of dry heaving, she started throwing up all over her exam and the poor girl in front of her. It was a disaster. Since then, she's stayed as far away from the medication as she can. I don't think risking Xanax on the day is worth it, so I believe we should just cut down the guest list. How about you send it to me?" Breaker suggests. "Since I'm so immersed in who to rub elbows with, I'll be able to pick who will be insulted and who doesn't matter when it comes to being there."

Puking during an exam? We couldn't have found a less disgusting image to plant in my future mother-in-law's head?

I glance over at The Beave, ready to see absolute disgust on her face. Instead, she has the lightest of smirks; like if I didn't know her, I wouldn't be able to tell, but there it is, plain as day, her often imprisoned joy.

"Oh," The Beave says, clasping her hands in front of her. "You're attuned to the social ladder?"

"Of course. How do you think I became a billionaire?" Breaker asks with a wink, and I know, deep in my bones, that it absolutely pained him to say that. If you should know one thing about Breaker, it's that he is not one to flaunt his money, ever, so for him to mention he's a billionaire in front of The Beave, that just goes to show that he's being the best friend that I need at this moment.

"Well, that would be lovely then. I will take you up on your generous offer," The Beave says before turning and heading down the aisle. I guess that's it. Fine by me.

Pinching his side, I joke, "Dropping the billionaire title just like that?"

He chuckles under his breath and whispers, "Got her to send me the list, didn't it? We can look it over together. Bring your red pen."

"I'll bring multiple. There will be a slashing. The gore might not happen at the wedding, but it sure as hell will happen over the guest list."

The Beave turns on her heel and says, "Now, are you Catholic, Ophelia?"

"Uh, that would be a no." I itch the spot where the veil clip is digging into my scalp.

The Beave's brows crease. "I believe Brian told me you were."

I shake my head. "Nope, not a Catholic. I actually don't really have a religion at all."

"How could you not have a religion?" she asks in disgust. "Who on earth do you thank for everything in your life before you go to bed?"

"Uh…my parents?" I ask.

She sneers. "Well, that just won't do." She snaps her finger to her assistant and says, "Phone." Her assistant quickly offers The Beave her phone, and I watch as she taps away on it. She lifts it up to her ear, and while she waits, I feel her gaze look me up and down, her perusal purely judgmental and meant to put me in my place. "Father Joseph, yes, it's Mrs. Beaver, how are you? Good. I have a slight problem. Brian's fiancée just informed me she's not Catholic. Yes, I know…" She pauses. "Uh-huh. Well, what if I offer a large donation to the parish?" Her lips tug at the side. "Yes, very large."

Is she bribing the priest? Good God. Isn't there something terribly wrong about that? Doesn't that grant you a fresh ticket to hell—if you believe in that?

"That's great. Thank you." She hangs up and hands her phone back to her assistant. "Problem diverted. Father Joseph will take care of it."

"What does that mean?" I ask.

"Best not ask questions, Ophelia. You've already done enough with your lack of faith."

Isn't she precious?

"Don't Brian and Lia have to take pre-cana classes?" Breaker asks. "And isn't that required to be done six months before the wedding?"

"Like I said, best we do not probe with questions. What needs to be done will be done, so let's drop it." That sounds very…godlike. She gestures to the altar. "Now, if you would please walk down the aisle so I can see how the veil looks in this space. We have asked for the walls to be repainted before the wedding a bright white as well as for the carpet to be replaced since it's quite dingy, but this is the example of opulence we expect when it comes to wedding pictures. Of course, your dress will have a minimum of a twelve-foot train so it can descend the stairs along with the veil."

On unsteady feet, I start walking down the aisle. "Twelve feet?" I ask. "That seems like a lot of fabric."

"Lovely observation, dear." She watches me as I slowly, and I mean slowly, take one step at a time. She gestures toward my glasses. "Did Brian talk to you about laser eye surgery? We can't have you wearing glasses on the wedding day."

I pause as my hand rises to my purple glasses. "Why not?"

"Glasses glare in pictures. Do you really think I want pictures of my son marrying a woman who looks like she has one eye because of the glare? No. Plus, he doesn't care for your glasses anyway. He called them childish. I believe he was going to talk to you about LASIK surgery. I have a doctor who can get you in this week." She snaps her finger again. "Book an appointment for Ophelia to go visit with Dr. Rosenblad."

"I don't want LASIK surgery. It freaks me out," I say.

"Ophelia"—The Beave pins me with a glare—"there is a time and a place to act like a child or act like an adult. Please remember your age." She brushes past us and heads down the aisle while calling out to her assistant to take notes on flower arrangement placement.

I just stand there, stunned.

Brian said my glasses were childish?

I thought he always liked them. I didn't think there was anything that he didn't like about me. But knowing that he doesn't like them, that… wow, that hurts.

Insecurity quickly chokes me as my throat grows tight with embarrassment.

"Hey," Breaker whispers as he slips his arm around me. When I don't look at him right away, he tugs on me and forces me to meet his eyes. "Your glasses are fucking awesome," he says quietly, his mouth close to my ear. "Besides your heart, your honesty, and your sauciness, your glasses are one of my favorite things about you."

"Breaker." I shake my head, but then he grips my chin, holding me still.

"Not only are they a direct depiction of your personality, but they make the beautiful light-green flecks in your eyes stand out even more. It's already sometimes impossible to look away from them, but when they're highlighted so exquisitely, you can't help but be captivated."

I glance away, but he forces me to look at him again. "I'm so embarrassed," I say.

"The only people in this scenario who should be embarrassed are The Beave for saying such a demeaning thing to you and Brian for even thinking that your glasses are unflattering." His thumb caresses my cheek, and he quietly adds, "You're gorgeous, Lia. The glasses accentuate just how gorgeous you are."

"Th-thank you," I say as his words penetrate the sorrow swirling around me.

I glance up at him, expecting a reassuring smile, but instead, I'm greeted by a deep gaze of seriousness. And for a moment, we stand there, staring at each other, his sweet compliment resting between us.

He's told me I'm beautiful before.

He's even told me I look hot.

But it's always felt like what a best friend would say.

But this moment, it feels entirely different.

I want to dive deeper into his statement.

I want to see if there is more emotion behind it or if I'm the one who is only feeling this way, but just as I open my mouth, his phone rings in his pocket, freeing us both from the trance we were in.

"Uh, I'm going to grab this," he says awkwardly. "Excuse me." He blinks a few times, almost as if he's trying to get his head on straight, and then pulls his phone out and answers it. "Uh, hey, Birdy." Birdy? She's calling him? "No, it's okay. What's going on?" He glances at me and then says, "No, I don't think I have any plans tonight."

Um, I thought we were going over the guest list, but then again, I don't think we planned a time for that.

"Yeah, sure, sounds fun. I'll meet you there. Text me the info. Yup, see you then. Bye." He hangs up the phone and sticks it in his pocket. "Sorry about that."

"Seeing Birdy tonight?" I ask as I awkwardly adjust the large veil at my side.

"Seems like it," he says and then turns to me with a smile. "Shall we blow The Beave over with your ceremony suggestion?"

"Sure," I say, feeling weird that he changed the subject so quickly.

"And what would that suggestion be?" He holds up his finger in a jovial way. "Hold on, let me guess." He taps his chin and says, "Uh, it has to be somewhere unique because that's who you are, but also something quaint and old-school." He snaps his finger. "The old courthouse."

"I would love that, but you know it can't even fit one hundred people."

"Good thing we're paring down the guest list then." He wiggles his brows.

"There's no way she would go for that, and if I'm going to suggest something, I might as well suggest something that would make her think that she came up with it."

"Okay, I'm listening," he says as he folds his arms.

I tug on the veil, attempting to pull it off, but The Beave shouts, "You're not done with that, Ophelia. I'm still processing how it will look."

I roll my eyes at Breaker and then shove the clip back on my head. "Well, as much as I hate the club for obvious reasons, they have a beautiful garden out back that would be perfect for the ceremony. People could watch from the balcony of the club, from the lawn, or from chairs in front of the altar."

He nods. "It's not exactly you, but just you enough. Want me to suggest it?"

"I hate to say it would be better coming from you, but I think that's the truth."

"Don't worry; I've got this." He puts his arm around me and guides me down the aisle toward The Beave. The whole time, my mind is racing about my glasses, about Breaker's warm voice telling me how much he loves them, about his date with Birdy, and about this damn veil. It all makes me so nauseated. "Mrs. Beaver," he calls out.

"Yes?" She turns her spindle-like body to us.

"You know, I was thinking, the reception will be at the club, right?" Breaker says so casually that if I didn't know him, it might be disturbing to see how quickly he can turn on the charm.

"That's correct," she says, folding her hands together.

"Beautiful choice, by the way. I went there for a wedding a year or so ago, and it was breathtaking." God, I hate when he gets like this, all proper. It's not the man I know. But it's his business persona, and it's why he's gotten where he has, because he can charm like no other, just like JP. Huxley, on the other hand…well, he's the hammer. Huxley has a tough time being charming. To him, things are black and white. There is no gray…well, besides Lottie.

"It is picturesque." The Beave studies Breaker. I can sense her wanting to know where he's going with this.

"And because it's so picturesque, it makes me think, although this church is beautiful, it pales in comparison to what the club has to offer. I was just there the other day, having a meeting with Clinton Mars. Do you know him?"

Ha!

Of course The Beave knows Clinton Mars. Everyone does. He's one of the wealthiest men in America. He created a little piece of hardware that goes in every phone, and he's made so much money off it, he basically sneezes hundred-dollar bills now.

Leave it to Breaker to drop the right name to make The Beave weak in the knees. This is why he's my best friend, my man of honor.

"Yes, of course. Clinton is a wonderfully sharp and intelligent man. I was lucky to meet him a few months ago," The Beave says, her eyes sparkling.

"Well, we took a stroll through the gardens during our meeting, and he raved about how they were so beautiful and what a perfect setting they would be for a wedding. He was actually thinking about having his daughter get married there."

"Really?" she says, her mind racing now. You know the phrase *keeping up with the Joneses*? Yeah, The Beave lives her life by that.

"Yup, and I thought…he was right. The gardens are breathtaking, beautifully landscaped with the ocean in the background, just spectacular."

The Beave slowly nods her head. "You know, the flowers will be in full bloom in five weeks." She snaps her finger, and her assistant appears by her side. "Get the club on the phone at once. I need to make arrangements." She then turns to us. "Now the gardens would be magnificent, but I worry about your ability to walk in heels in the grass."

"Oh, don't worry about it at all," I say, not wanting her to find an excuse not to use the gardens. "I'm quite astute with heels."

"Very astute," Breaker says.

"The most astute," I add, which, of course, causes The Beave to give me a look of derision. "Uh…just watch. I'll strut up and down this carpet." I flop the length of the veil behind me, and with the utmost concentration, I walk down the aisle, pretending to hold a bouquet. My sweaty feet slip against the surface of my heels, but I keep them in place as I make it down to the altar.

Thank Jesus, I made it.

"Walk back," The Beave says, her voice unconvinced that she believes I can execute walking in heels.

God, she's such a freaking pill.

Shoulders set back, hands poised in front of me, I put one foot in front of the other and head back down the aisle.

Eat your heart out, Beave.

You can make me feel like shit about my glasses.

You can take away my right to choose my own wedding.

But I refuse to allow you to make me feel like I can't walk in freaking heels.

"See," I say as I hold my hands out, approaching her. "Not a problem at…" On my last step, my foot slips out of my shoe, throwing me off my balance. "Oh shit," I cry out just as I reach for the closest thing near me…

A candleholder.

I clutch it tightly.

"Whoa, buddy," I say on a shaky breath. "That was a close one." I chuckle just as I glance up at the candle as it shakily rocks in place.

"Uh, Lia," Breaker says as he steps forward.

But it's too late.

It all happens in slow motion as the candle tips over and falls to the ground. My eyes travel with it, watching as it falls right on top of the gathered fabric of the veil.

My breath catches in my chest.

My eyes widen.

And in seconds, the veil bursts into a fury of flames.

"Oh my God!" I shout. "Oh my God, I'm on fire. I'm on FIRE!" I toss the candlestick to the side, and with one heel on and one heel off, I fly down the aisle, running away from the flames...as they chase after me.

"The veil!" The Beave screeches.

"You're on fire," Breaker cries.

"Put it out, put it out, put it out," I scream.

"Jesus Christ," Breaker shouts. "Roll, Lia, roll!"

"Roll where?" I shout back as I circle the altar, the flaming veil moving closer and closer to my head. "Dear Jesus, don't set my hair on fire. Please, for the love of your father, don't set it on fire."

"An heirloom," The Beave says right before she collapses into a pew.

"Roll, for fuck's sake!"

I drop to the ground and roll, tucking my knees in so I'm not caught up in the pews. "Is it out?" I yell. "Am I still burning?" I glance over my shoulder and see the flames chasing after me. "Ahhhhh! Breaker, it's coming to get me. Save my soul...save it!" I continue to roll as I see smoke lift into the air. "What's that smell? Is that my hair? Breaker, help—"

Splash.

Water douses me, soaking me to my bone while putting the fire out at the same time.

I glance up to see Breaker holding a very large metal bowl, his chest heaving, horror in his eyes.

"Is it...is it out?"

He swallows hard and nods. "Yeah, it's out."

I lay flat on the ground, wet and horrified, as I let out a deep breath. "Where did you get the water?"

He glances down at the empty bowl and winces. "Uh...I believe I just blessed you hard with holy water."

I shake my head. "Baptism by fire just took on a whole new meaning," I say as I hear The Beave mumbling some sort of prayer in the background. I swallow hard. "Consider me converted."

———————

"She hates me," I say as Breaker opens the door to the stationery store.

After I gently gave The Beave back her ruined heirloom veil, I told her I was going to change clothes before our next meeting to pick invitations. Breaker whisked me away, and instead of discussing what just happened, we sat in silence as we drove along the palm tree–lined streets of Los Angeles.

Breaker scratches his cheek as he says, "I think *hate* is a strong word."

"Breaker, I set her precious heirloom veil on fire."

"Not on purpose. I think that's something we need to stress. You did not set the veil on fire on purpose."

"I'm sure she sees it that way." I glance toward the back of the shop, where I see The Beave with her assistant at a table, looking over what seems to be different textures of paper. "How do I even approach her? Do I apologize again? Do I just leave the decisions up to her?"

Breaker pulls me to the side and whispers, "It was an accident. Was it embarrassing? Yes, but it was an accident. She will respect you more if you head to this next meeting with your head held high and not constantly apologizing. You said what you needed to say, so move on. Okay?"

I nod. "You're right. Just…move on."

"That's the spirit." He straightens and puts his hand on my back, guiding me to the table where The Beave is sitting.

As we approach, she glances up and says, "Ophelia, I wasn't sure you would show up, given your appearance when we left the church, but it seems like you can clean up appropriately."

I tack on a smile as I say, "Wasn't too difficult." I can sense she's looking for me to crumple, and I want to. I desperately want to fall to her feet and apologize over and over again, but Breaker is right. She will respect me if I don't. "So what are we looking at?"

"Paper density and weight," The Beave says. "Really, it's not necessary that you're here."

"It is," I say as I take a seat next to her, and Breaker takes a seat next to me. "These are my wedding invites, after all. Plus, paper is fun." I pick up a stack and flip my finger through the thick pieces of paper. "Do you know what I love about paper?"

"I'm sure you have some well-thought-out opinion that I can't *wait* to hear," The Beave says with a heavy dose of condemnation.

I can see we're still angry about the veil, and I'm sure she's looking to cut me down, but like Breaker said, don't buckle. Hold strong.

"I do, actually," I say. "Paper is a journey—"

"Uh, Lia, I need to speak to you for a second," Breaker says, standing abruptly.

I glance up at him, confused. "What?"

"I need to talk to you." His eyes grow wide. "Now."

Sensing the urgency, I excuse myself from the table and head to a corner where Breaker turns his back from The Beave and traps me between the walls and a collection of watercolor pens for sale.

"What's going on?" I ask.

"Just saving you before you make yourself look like a fool."

"What do you mean?"

"Paper is a journey?" he asks. "Where exactly were you going with that?"

"Well, if you let me finish, you would have seen that I was going pretty far with it. I had an entire diatribe about how it opens humans to new worlds."

"Yeah, let's keep the philosophical talk to a minimum. The Beave is not going to want to hear it. She's on edge. Just keep the talking to a minimum. Okay?"

I glance over Breaker's shoulder and catch a glimpse of the deep, menacing scowl she's sporting as she flips through templates. Huh, maybe he's right.

"Okay, yeah. Maybe she doesn't want to know how paper is a journey."

"I can bet my balls on the fact that she doesn't want to hear it." He pats my shoulder. "Deep breaths. Don't ramble for no reason. It shows weakness. Pick out an invite with confidence."

"I can do that." I nod. "Thanks."

"You're welcome."

We head back to the table, and like the gentleman he is, Breaker holds out my chair for me, and I take a seat. The Beave glances up and asks, "Everything okay?"

"Yes, quite good. Thank you." I let out a deep breath, and as Breaker takes a seat, I say, "Funny how paper is made, right? I watched this documentary—"

Breaker pops right back up from his seat and says, "Lia, another word."

Reluctantly, I follow him back to the corner, where I whisper, "What did I do now?"

"How about we try this?" he says, with one hand on my shoulder. "You don't talk at all."

"So just sit there in silence with her?"

"Yes."

"You know I can't do that. I don't like silence. I can hear people breathing. It makes me uncomfortable."

"I know, but your chatting won't do anything to this situation besides make it worse. So just focus on picking an invite and try not to say much."

"That seems so cold."

"This is a cold situation," Breaker says. "After you burned her heirloom veil in effigy, this is no longer a lovey-dovey time. This is war, and if you don't want to be pushed around, you're going to have to hold your head high, shut the fuck up, and pick out what you want." I go to respond, and he adds, "You know how you are so perplexed by the way Huxley can not say a word but get everything he wants? It's because he's silent, and people buckle under the silence. Don't buckle. Make her buckle."

"You're right. Be like Huxley; make her buckle."

"Precisely. Okay, ready to go back there?" I nod. "And no talk about paper journeys and the mechanics of how it's made."

"My lips are sealed," I say.

"Good."

We head back to the table, and once again, Breaker holds out my chair for me. "Excuse me, I have to use the restroom. I'll be right back," he says right before heading to the back toward the restroom sign.

Okay.

Focus, Lia.

You are quiet. You are strong. You are not buckling.

Without saying a word, I pick up a folder and start flipping through it. Every so often, I can feel Beave's eyes on me, but I continue to look through template after template. All of them are far too fancy to even consider. I don't want something super stuffy. It can be pretty, but gold filigree seems a bit much.

Lifting my head, I ask the owner, "Do you happen to have anything that isn't as fancy?"

"Excuse me?" The Beave asks. "What do you mean *not so fancy?*"

Do I answer?

I was told to be quiet.

Would Huxley answer?

Or would he just stare?

I think he would just stare.

So that's what I do. I stare at her.

"Ophelia, I asked you a question."

I know, but I'm supposed to just stare, so…that's what I do, as sweat creeps up my neck, because this staring thing is hard.

The Beave must pick up on what I'm doing because she folds her hands in front of her and stares back.

Oh God!

It's a stare-off.

Breaker did not prepare me for this.

Why did he choose this moment to go to the bathroom? He had a chance when we went back to the apartment to change. This is poor peeing management on his end, leaving me here like this, all alone with a teaspoon of confidence in what I'm doing.

And boy, is she good.

Really fucking good.

Those beady eyes stare back at me. She recognizes it's a showdown, and if I know this woman like I think I do, she won't back down. Huxley might be the king of not talking, but man, oh man, it looks like The Beave can run a master class on it.

Just look at the way her eyes remain steady.

Not a twitch.

Not a fidget.

Meanwhile, over here, I'm a party of one, heading straight into the fiery pits of hell as I attempt to hold steady. But I'm wilting.

I can feel it.

There's too much silence.

It's killing me.

I'm going to break.

I'm going to snap.

I'm going to...

"Paper was invented by the Chinese back in 100 BC," I blurt, feeling an overwhelming sense of relief. "And now, one single pine tree can create over eighty thousand sheets of paper. Can you believe that? Wow, what a dedication to the journey of paper, which is of course, quite the tale in and of itself, but I won't bore you with that other than to say that paper really can transport us from world to world, and sure, some people might say it's the author who is transporting us, the words are just on the paper, but you can't print words without paper. Although I guess you can read electronically, ehh... Either way, I think paper is a journey, and don't you think we should appreciate that journey? I mean, look at this piece of paper," I say as I pick up a thick card stock. "Where do you think it came from? What part of the world did this traverse? For all we know, this used to be part of a tree that once housed a sloth or maybe a gibbon. And to know that it was a house at one point and is now going to offer its—for lack of a better term—body to us so we can invite people to the start of a new journey in life…do you see the full circle here? Just marvelous." I pick up a pile of paper and run my fingers through it. "All marvel—ouch." I chuckle and then shake out my hand. "The paper didn't like me stroking it like that. Bit me right on the finger." I shake my hand again, but this time, a line of red dots splatters across the paper and right across The Beave's face.

Oh.

My.

God.

I glance down at my finger and immediately feel faint as I see blood pooling.

"Dear God, I've done it now," I say as I sway, holding my finger up.

"What the hell?" Breaker yells as The Beave just sits there in a shocked, catatonic state. "Jesus, Lia. Can we get some tissues?" He holds my finger up and then wraps his arm around my shoulder to keep me from falling. "What happened?" he asks.

I glance up at him and whisper, "I buckled."

———————

"How are you feeling?" Breaker asks as he sits across from me in his car.

"How do you think I'm feeling?" I ask as I set down my yogurt drink.

"Besides embarrassed, humiliated, and regretful, I want to know how you're doing physically."

"Fine." I stare up at Brian's office building. "Do you think she already called him and told him?"

"Can't be sure," Breaker says. "But from the way she wiped your blood off her face with vehement swipes, I'm going to say yes."

"Then it's official. I can't show my face near her ever again."

"You're going to have to, and don't worry, I will be there with you."

I shake my head. "I should just go back to my apartment, drown in my sorrows."

"Is that what you want to do?" Breaker asks.

I press my lips together and stare down at my linked hands. "No. I want to talk to Brian."

"Then I think you need to go talk to him." Breaker takes my hand in his. "I can go up there with you."

"No, that would be a bad idea." I undo my seat belt and open the door. "I can and should do this on my own." I glance up at Breaker. "Thank you for everything today, despite you leaving to pee at the worst time ever."

"I've already noted that I'm to pee before I ever leave you alone with The Beave again."

"Good." I hop out of his car and say, "I'll see you later."

"Good luck."

I wave goodbye and head into Brian's office building. After the blood was cleaned and Breaker offered to pay for all damages to the bloodied paper, The Beave roughly showed me her three choices, and instead of putting up a fight, I went with her favorite. It's an invitation anyway, not like my actual wedding dress. She offered me a curt goodbye and took off.

Breaker took me to grab something to eat to help with my anemia; then I asked him to drive me here because not only do I want to clear the air about what happened at the church…and the paper shop, but I also need to talk to him about how he spoke so negatively about my glasses. Because despite the distractions from the day, that has stuck in my mind.

"Hello, Miss Fairweather-Fern, how are you?" Brian's assistant, Beverly, says as I approach.

"I'm good; how are you, Beverly?"

"Just lovely. Congratulations on the engagement. Brian has been talking nonstop about it."

I smile kindly. "Thank you. We're very excited." The lie slips off my tongue with ease. Not so much excited as I'm nervous. Hopefully, excitement comes soon. "Uh, is Brian available? I know I came unannounced, but I hoped I could talk for a moment."

"He always wants to see you," Beverly says. "I believe he's just working right now, not on the phone."

"Okay, thank you."

I wave to Beverly and make my way toward his office. She's always been so kind to me. In her fifties, she is as efficient as they come, detailed, and never lets anything slip, ever. I remember when Brian first hired her, his mother was furious. Said he needed someone younger, not that she should have a say in it. Still, Brian's intuition has paid off because Beverly has been such a tremendous help to him in getting all his work done throughout the day.

Plus, she's nice to me, so bonus.

I knock on his door, then push open the frosty glass, poking my head in.

He looks up from his desk, and when he spots me, his face completely lights up with a smile.

"Lia," he says as he stands. "What a great surprise." He walks over to me, takes my hand, and pulls me into his office while shutting the door behind me. Before I know what's happening, he has his hands on my cheeks and tilts my head as his lips land on mine. I place my hands on his chest for balance while he kisses me deeply like we haven't seen each other in days. Not sure if his mother has talked to him yet. Not sure I would receive the same welcome. "I'm so glad you're here," he says between kisses.

I move my mouth along with his, sink into his hold, and let all the stress and concerns fall to the side as I allow myself to be right here, at this moment.

After a few more seconds, he groans and pulls away, his eyes looking heady and his breath labored. "Okay, things are going to get out of hand if I keep kissing you." He smiles and strokes his thumb over my cheek. "Why am I so lucky to see you this afternoon?"

God, he's being so sweet, I almost feel bad about bringing this up, but if I don't, it's going to thoroughly bother me, which will turn into resenting him, and I don't want to resent him.

"Have you spoken to your mom yet?"

"No, I've been busy. She's called twice, though. Why?"

"Uh, I went to look at the church with your mom this morning."

He pulls me toward his desk, and he takes a seat on the edge while pulling me between his legs. "How was it? Beautiful, right?"

"Very," I answer. "But I think we might change it to the gardens at the club."

"Oh wow, that would be...that would be perfect." He smiles so lovingly that I question myself and what his mother said earlier.

"I think so." I want to tell him it's thanks to Breaker but decide that's probably a sore subject. The last thing I want to do is make him mad or defensive, especially when I'm about to have this conversation with him. "But something happened when I was there at the church."

"Okay...what happened?" he asks skeptically.

"First of all, it was an accident."

"Now you have me worried. What happened?"

"Well, your mom made me try on her wedding veil because she wanted to see me walk down the aisle wearing it. I was wearing those shoes you got me that are a touch too big, and long story short, I slipped out of them when walking, tumbled into a lit candle, and it rolled off the holder and right onto the veil. It caught on fire, and the only reason I still have hair at this point is because Breaker doused me in holy water."

Brian doesn't initially react.

He just stands there, a confused look on his face. After a few moments, he says, "Are you being serious?"

"Yes, I wouldn't lie about this. Trust me."

"So you set my mom's veil on fire?"

"Not on purpose," I say quickly. "It was all an accident. And that, uh, that wasn't the only thing that happened."

"What do you mean that's not the only thing that happened?"

"Well, you see, after the church, I went and changed because the holy water soaked me, but we had another appointment to pick out invitations, and well, I got a paper cut while flipping through the paper, didn't realize it, and ended up flicking my blood on your mom's face and all over the paper."

"What?" he asks, his eyes wider than ever now. "You flicked your blood at my mom?"

I tug on the lapels of his jacket. "Once again, not on purpose. All a mistake, but I thought I should tell you because I'm sure she called you to beg you to end things with me."

Brian's expression lightens as he pulls me into a hug. "Lia, she wouldn't do that."

"I don't know. She was pretty upset."

"She was probably upset, but she does like you. I'm sure an apology is all that's needed."

Yeah, that's what I thought too.

"Either way," he continues. "I'm sure it's fine. Are you okay, though? Almost setting your hair on fire and bleeding heavily doesn't sound like a fun day in wedding planning."

"Yeah, pretty traumatic, but that wasn't the real reason I came over here."

"It wasn't?" he asks. "Jesus, if that's not the reason, then I think I should mentally prepare myself."

I slip one hand under his jacket as I say, "Uh, probably." I'm not a confrontational person, but I know this needs to be addressed. "So when we were at the church, before the fire, your mom said something to me that didn't really settle well."

"Whatever it was, I'm sure she didn't mean it," he says, jumping to her defense right away. Needless to say, it bugs me that he never jumps to my defense, especially not in front of my future mother-in-law. "She's stressed with all the planning. I'm positive she'll say a lot in the next coming weeks that won't settle well. Don't take offense to it."

Lovely.

Can't wait for that.

"No, this was something you said...about me."

His brow furrows, and he tilts his head to the side. "What did she say?"

I drop my hands from his and say, "Well, she said that you don't like my glasses and that they're childish, that I would be better without them."

I wait for his backtracking.

For his denial.

For any sort of indication he didn't say that.

But he doesn't.

"Did you...did you say that to her?" I ask.

He glances away and then nods. "I did. She was talking about the wedding pictures and how your glasses might mess them up, and I said that maybe you'd consider contacts since the purple glasses were kind of childish."

"Oh," I reply, feeling really stupid. It's not every day your fiancé tells you you're childish. It's not something you want to hear either.

"Lia, I don't want you to take offense to that."

My head snaps up. "How could I not take offense to that, Brian? I've had these glasses forever. They're the ones my mom helped me pick out. They're special to me. They mean something."

"Oh, I'm sorry. I didn't know that," he says. "I just thought it was one of your...quirks. You know, like how you ironically wear shirts with characters from Harry Potter."

"I don't wear those ironically. I wear them because I like them."

"Well, either way, I didn't realize there was any meaning behind the glasses. I'm sorry, Lia."

I don't know what to say.

Thank you for apologizing seems so sterile and robotic.

It's okay is not appropriate because it's not okay.

So instead of saying something, I just stay silent.

"Lia." He tugs on my hand. "I said I'm sorry. Please don't be mad."

"I'm not mad," I say, staring at our connected hands. "Just embarrassed, I guess."

"There's no need to be embarrassed. I should never have said anything. That was really shitty."

"Do you think they make me look ugly?"

"No, Lia," he says quickly. "Not at all."

"Do you think I would be more attractive to you without them? Because that's how it feels, how the comment feels, like...like I'm not pretty enough when I wear them."

"Lia, that's not what I meant. I think glasses look great on you. They're just, they're purple is all, and I would have thought that maybe someone your age would want something more sophisticated."

My shoulders droop as I mutter, "So I'm not sophisticated enough?"

"No," he groans while pulling on his neck. "Fuck, I'm not saying this right. Just...just forget I said anything at all."

Forget what he said? He insulted me, and that's not easy to forget.

I look up at him, insecurity racing through me, and ask, "Do you think I'm good enough for you?"

"What?" His eyes widen. "Of course, Lia. Why would you think that?"

Because I've thought that for a while.

Because I think that maybe we aren't on the same trajectory.

Because the things that are important to you, like money and status, are not *important to me.*

"Because there are moments where you try to change me. Like when we go to meals with your mother, you buy me clothes to wear."

"That's because she can be very particular, and I don't want her giving you a hard time."

"Or the glasses, or when we're in public, it's like you have this standard I have to meet for me to be attached to your arm."

"What are you talking about?"

"Just this past weekend, I said, *Let's go get ice cream*, and I was going to go out in my pajamas, but you told me to change."

"Lia, I could see your nipples through your white tank top. Do you really think I want people seeing that?" He grips my hips. "That's just for me."

I look off toward his office windows. "I don't know, it just feels like I'm not good enough for you."

"Lia, stop." He tips my chin toward him. "Of course you're good enough. Why else would I propose to you? Now I'm sorry about the glasses. I never should have said that, but please don't let that unravel you."

"I'm not unraveling, Brian. I'm just trying to make sure my boyfriend—"

"Fiancé," he says in a clipped tone.

"Yes, my fiancé. I'm just trying to make sure that he is marrying me for the right reasons."

"What are you talking about? Where is this coming from? We had a great weekend, and now, all of a sudden, you're doubting me? Does this"—he smooths his hand over his mouth—"does this have to do with anything Breaker said to you today?"

"Are you serious right now?" I ask, taking a step back from him. "Breaker was nothing but supportive, especially when your mother basically told me I was a bridge troll with glasses and that my opinion about my wedding didn't matter. Do not blame any of this on Breaker."

"Shit, you're right." He exhales and places both hands on the edge of his desk. "I'm sorry. I'm just wound up and apparently unable to stop myself from saying stupid things."

That much is obvious.

"Okay, well, I think…I think I just need to take a breath."

"No," he says, closing the space between us. "Don't leave."

"I need some fresh air, Brian."

"Then let's go on a walk. Let's go to the park across the street. Please, Lia. I feel like a dick, and I don't want you leaving mad."

I look at his pleading eyes and realize that maybe…maybe he is just as stressed as I am. Because if he was truly being mean about the glasses, then he wouldn't have any remorse, and there is clear remorse written all over his face.

"Okay," I say, nodding.

He holds his hand out to me, and I take it. Together, we walk out of his office, asking Beverly to take messages until he gets back. Once outside his building, we head to the quaint park across the street.

It's just a small three-acre lot, a place for people to sit and take a breather. A tiny circular walking path with towering cottonwoods offers a brilliant cover from the bristling sun.

Brian squeezes my hand as he says, "I'm sorry you had a rough day today, and I'm sorry this wedding stuff is so stressful. I know it's not easy on you."

"It's not," I say. "None of it has been easy. And if I were honest, I wasn't expecting a proposal."

"You weren't?" he asks, completely shocked.

"Not even a little. I mean, come on, Brian, we never even talked about the possibility of getting married, so I was caught off guard when you got down on one knee."

"But…we love each other. I mean, I love you."

"And I love you, Brian. That's not the issue. I just…I don't know. I thought we'd move in together, take that for a spin first before there was a ring involved."

"We sort of live together, at least half of the time. You have a key to my place, a dresser. I just assumed that wasn't something we had to tackle." He pauses. "Am I moving too fast for you?"

Yes.

This is all too fast.

Lightning speed.

And I don't know how I feel. Something is off. Something doesn't feel right, and I can't pinpoint it. All I can feel is this sickening churning in my stomach that won't stop. The church today, the way his mother treats me like a second-class citizen, the ability to insult me without a worry or care, and how none of this was even on my radar—it's too much.

But I can't say that to Brian. He's too sensitive. He'll take my worries and concerns wrong. He'll think something is wrong with him when, really, it's just time moving too fast.

I smile up at him and say, "No, just…just stunned is all and still trying to wrap my head around all of it."

He nods. "I'm sure my mother's plans aren't helping."

"Yeah, she's going a touch fast." I hold up my fingers, causing him to laugh.

"She's been wanting me to propose to you for a bit."

"Really?" I ask, surprised. "I would have guessed from our rather cold relationship that she wouldn't want you to propose to me."

"Mother might be cold and uninviting at times, maybe a touch harsh, but she also can see when I'm happy." Brian turns toward me. "And you make me happy, Lia. Very happy."

I smile at him. "You make me happy, too, Brian."

He pulls me in close, and as we continue to walk down the paved path, his embrace feels different. And maybe it's because Breaker held me a lot today, but this feels forced, almost like he's checking off a box.

Hold fiancée, *check.*

There doesn't seem to be any passion in the embrace.

Any need to be close.

And I hate to admit it, but the way he has his hand pressing into my arm, bringing me up to his shoulder, it almost feels suffocating.

"She's been wanting me to propose to you for a bit." Did Brian propose because his mother suggested it?

This hold, this moment, it doesn't feel right.

This, him, us...for the first time since I've met him, it doesn't feel right.

CHAPTER 7
BREAKER

Lia: You never told me where you're headed tonight. Care to share with a soon-to-be-married old hag?

Breaker: You know, with that ratty old robe you like to wear still, you do resemble the true definition of an old married hag.

Lia: I think that's the nicest thing you've ever said to me.

Breaker: You need to up your standards.

Lia: So where are you going?

Breaker: I don't want to tell you.

Lia: Why not…? Wait, is it embarrassing?

Breaker: No, but you're going to give me shit for it, and I don't want to hear it, so I'd rather pretend I didn't tell you and move on.

Lia: Breaker Pickle Cane, you tell me what you're doing with Birdy this very instant. I demand it.

Breaker: Oh, you demand it?

Lia: Yes, on the fake breasts of Mrs. Doubtfire, if you don't tell me, I'm going to do something to your apartment when you're gone, and you'll have no idea what it is because it will be so subtle that you wouldn't even notice.

Breaker: Firstly, we NEVER swear on Mrs. Doubtfire's breasts, that's…that's just criminal. Secondly, DON'T YOU DARE touch a thing.

Lia: Do you really think your capital letters will deter me?

Breaker: They should. There's venom behind them.

Lia: I'm unfazed.

Breaker: You're a tyrant. These demands are impossible to live with.

Lia: Just tell me. Pleeeeeeeeease.

Breaker: You're annoying.

Lia: I know, now stop avoiding the topic and just tell me what you're doing tonight.

Breaker: Fine. We're going to some cupcake class that her friend is teaching. Her friend wanted to fill the classroom to show her boss she's valuable, so Birdy recruited me.

Lia: A cupcake class? But…you hate baking.

Breaker: I'm well aware.

Lia: Like you hate baking so much, you refused to put icing on your toaster strudel. Your exact words were "I want nothing to do with the process. Just put it in my mouth."

Breaker: See, this is why I didn't want to tell you.

Lia: I'm just stunned is all. I didn't know Birdy mattered that much to you.

Breaker: She sounded desperate. She pleaded to the nice guy. What was I going to say? I don't bake?

Lia: That's what you would have told me.

Breaker: You're different.

Lia: If that's the case. Can we take a baking class to learn how to make a wedding cake?

Breaker: That would be a hard no.

Lia: You don't love me!

Breaker: Shut up. You know I love you more than anything.

Lia: More than your Star Wars stamp collection?

Breaker: Of course. I stuck that in storage. Clearly, it doesn't mean that much to me.

Lia: More than your Jack Skellington mug?

Breaker: Naturally. I love the mug, but I don't see it every day like I see you.

Lia: Okay…do you love me more than your signed Lord of the Rings poster?

Breaker: Oooo, now you're testing me. How about this, you come in a close second.

Lia: Oddly, I accept this.

Breaker: LOL. Okay, Birdy's here. Have to go.

Lia: Have fun! Send me pictures.

"I know this was kind of out of the blue, but thank you for agreeing to come with me," Birdy says as she ties on her apron.

Mine is already on, and I desperately want to strip it off me.

I hate aprons.

I hate flour and sugar.

I hate spatulas.

I hate oven mitts.

I hate everything on the table in front of me.

Nothing about baking is magical to me. Not a single thing. The only great thing about the act of baking is the result, but I would rather purchase the result than make it myself. There are too many risk factors making it terrible that I'm not willing to take a chance on.

Just buy…always buy.

"Not a problem," I say with a smile, even though I know the smile is fake.

"Baking is not really my thing," Birdy says as she adjusts the apron at her neck. "But Callie just got this job, and she really wants to impress her boss."

"I would be the same way." I offer a nice smile. I pick up the cat-themed spatula and say, "At least the theme is pretty cool."

Birdy tilts her head to the side. "Is that sarcasm?"

I shake my head as I take in the pink space. Walls covered in pink murals, aqua and seafoam-green utensils, as well as appliances with cats everywhere you look, Pussycat Cupcakes really went all out. "I like cats. I had one growing up named Jiggles. He was my best bud."

"Really?" she asks. "You're being serious?"

"Yeah." I chuckle. "I guess it would be hard to believe, but yeah, Jiggles and I were quite the pair. He would follow me around outside while I flew my model airplanes, and at night, he would cuddle on my pillow."

"Aw, that's so sweet. What happened to him?"

"Feline cancer. But he lived until he was eighteen, so he had a nice full life."

"Okay, so maybe I don't feel that bad about taking you to a cat-themed cupcake place then."

"Oh no, you should still feel bad." I wink at her just as her friend starts the class.

I'm surprised that the cupcakes are already made. For some reason, I thought we would be baking from scratch, but what I come to find is this is a decorating class, so we learn to make the frosting and how to pipe it onto the already cooled cupcakes.

After a tutorial on how to make the frosting, I dip my finger along the side of the mixing bowl and take a taste of the buttercream.

"Not bad."

Birdy does the same, and I watch as she slips her finger past her lips and lightly sucks on it.

Nothing about it is sexual, nothing at all, but for some odd reason—maybe because it's been some time for me, or because she is really fucking pretty—watching her suck the frosting off her finger makes the back of my neck sweat.

"Ooo, that's good." She wipes her finger on a towel. "What color should we do?"

Gathering myself, I say, "Well, we could go with the proposed color, pink. Or we can be rebels and pick something else."

"A pink pussy...cat seems too generic." Her pause makes me laugh. "But blue...that's clearly not an option."

"No one likes a blue pussy...cat," I say, causing her to laugh this time.

"Green makes me think *ill*. And a sick pussy is not something I want to eat."

"Or lick," I add.

"Exactly." She taps her chin, a smile playing on her lips. "What about red...uh, wait, I take that back." I laugh out loud, grabbing the attention of the other bakers. She rests her hand on my arm and says, "Shhh, you're gathering attention. If we're straying from the pink pussy, we need to be stealthy about it."

"Sorry, but definitely not red."

"That was a terrible suggestion. How about orange or yellow? Those feel right."

"How about both?" I ask.

"Now, I think you're onto something." She hands me a bowl and says, "I think if we split the icing in half, color one orange and one yellow, and then put them in the frosting tube at the same time, then we will get some sort of tie-dye effect."

I blink a few times at her and say, "Uh, I thought you weren't into baking."

"I'm not, but I do aimlessly scroll on TikTok. The algorithm has decided I like to watch baking videos. And secretly...I do."

"It probably decided that because you watch the video in its entirety instead of swiping up. This is on you."

She cutely raises her hand. "Guilty. But I don't watch for the education. I watch because I have a problem."

"I can see that. You know, this makes me think of you differently." I joke around as I stir in the yellow dye while she does the orange.

"I completely understand. If you want to leave, I won't stop you."

"You know, leaving would be the right thing to do in order to teach you a lesson, but I think I'll be the bigger man and stay."

She smirks. "Don't act like you're staying for me. You're just staying for the pussy cakes."

I laugh out loud again. This time, it disrupts the class enough for me to have to apologize and then turn back to Birdy, my cheeks flushed.

"Thank you for coming tonight; it meant a lot to Callie," Birdy says as we reach her white SUV.

"You know, I think I will say this once and only once because I don't want to give off the wrong impression about my likes and dislikes for baking, but I had fun."

She clutches her chest as she leans against her car. "Please, spare my feelings from the lies."

"I did," I say, moving in closer. "I had a lot of fun hanging out with you. Wasn't as awkward as the double date."

She reaches out and plays with the hem of my shirt. "Yeah, double dates are always a treat, especially when one half of it is a blind date."

I set the box of extra cupcakes on top of her car and move in closer so she has to tilt her head back to look up at me. "So are we still on for a hike and bird-watching? I didn't deter you with the way I took down three cupcakes in one sitting?"

Her lips tilt up. "No, watching you munch on those pussies actually made me want to hang out even more."

I chuckle. "You know, you could have shown this sense of humor on the double date."

"Oh my God, I would not be caught dead saying anything like that in front of Brian. He's so...stuck up, and my brother is just the same. Whenever I'm around Brian, I know I have to keep it together. Act posh."

"Why would you want to act like someone else, not be your true you?"

"Easier that way. I'd rather spend a few hours with my pinky up, acting fancy, than answering to my brother why I said *pussy* in front of Brian."

I push a strand of hair behind her ear. "Yeah, I can see not wanting to get into it with your brother. I often have that thought cross my mind. But even with a filter, my brothers and I seem to get into it somehow."

"Same." She sighs. "But to answer your question, yes, I still want to go hiking with you. And maybe, you know, if you have availability for dinner or something this week, I could be free." She winces and says, "That sounds so pathetic, like I don't have a life, but who am I kidding? I don't do much other than work out and go to work, so...if you are free, I'm pretty sure I would be too."

"Not pathetic," I say as I stare down at her lips, this overwhelming urge pulsing through me to kiss her. "Honest, and I like that." I lift my finger under her chin and hold my breath as I wait for her to signal that this is okay. That I can kiss her. She wets her lips and tugs on my shirt, indicating she wants this just as much as I do.

I lean down, bring my nose close to hers, and pause for a moment, giving her a second to be ready before I press my lips lightly against hers. It's a feather of a kiss, nothing too intense, nothing open-mouthed. Just sweet.

Just enough to curb that urge.

Just enough to get a taste of her.

When I pull away, she smiles up at me, her eyes glimmering under the city lamps.

"I'll call you," I say as I grab the cupcake box. I stick one hand in my pocket and watch as she opens her car door.

"I'm holding you to that." She steps into her car and then shuts the door. I take another step back, and while I watch her drive away, I let out a deep breath as I replay the kiss in my head.

It was good.

Sweet.

Yet, why didn't I feel anything?

———————————

Lia runs her fingers along a bouquet of hydrangeas while The Beave corners the florist about arrangement options. "So are you going to just ignore the fact that you went on a baking date and not tell me anything about it?"

I shrug as I pick up a pink hydrangea and put it up against Lia's perfectly freckled face. "Nothing to really say. It wasn't really baking; it was frosting cupcakes."

"And...?" Lia asks, trying to get me to talk, but...I don't know. I don't really want to talk about it.

"And I brought cupcakes home," I answer and put the flower back in its pot.

"Uh-huh, so you're telling me that's all that happened? Nothing else?"

"I mean, we talked and laughed, and she was pretty fucking funny. But yeah, that was it."

"Did you kiss her good night?" Lia asks, her voice dropping an octave.

I pause because this feels weird. I don't know why this feels weird. Things with Lia never feel weird, but talking about Birdy does.

"Um, from your pause, I'm going to assume that's a yes." She lightly pushes at my shoulder. "Breaker, why aren't you telling me what happened?"

"Because," I say, turning away from her.

"Because why?" she asks.

"Just because."

She moves around me so I'm forced to look in her eyes. "That's not an answer. You tell me everything, so why are you being weird about this?"

"I don't know," I say while exhaling and pushing my hand through my hair. "Probably because it feels weird. Okay? This whole dating thing feels weird. And I don't know how to handle it."

"Well, not talking to me doesn't help. We tell each other everything."

"I know." I dip my head back and look at the sky for a moment. "Fuck, Lia, I kissed her last night because I really wanted to." I look her in the eyes now. "All night, she made me laugh, and she's beautiful, and at one point, she sucked on her finger, and it made me fucking sweat." Lia smirks. "So when it came to saying good night, I wanted to kiss her, and I did." I tug on my hair. "And it was good. Sweet. Not too intense, just perfect. But I…I felt nothing."

"Nothing?" she asks.

I shake my head. "No, there was no spark, no desire to push her up against the SUV and further the kiss. It was just sweet." I shake my head again. "I think there's something wrong with me. This is why I don't date, because I never feel anything for anyone. Never. It's always just…average. And Birdy is not the type of girl I take home for the night and not see again. She's the dating type."

"Are you two done conversing over there?" The Beave calls out while snapping her fingers. "I have important things to discuss."

Lia turns toward me and says, "This conversation isn't over. You hear me?"

"Yeah, didn't think it would be," I say as we head on over to the florist.

"Ophelia, please don't drag your feet. It's unbecoming." Lia clamps her lips together, probably to keep her from snapping back. The Beave's mood has carried over from yesterday, and it has been fucking unpleasant. "Now, I just spoke with the florist and she said she can accommodate our order of red roses, but we need to act quickly."

"Red roses?" Lia sneers. "Those are so formal." *She hates red roses. Thinks they're so cliché.* Can't say I disagree.

"Exactly, this is a formal wedding, Ophelia. What do you expect to have at the wedding? Daisies?" The Beave snorts as if that's the most preposterous thing she's ever heard.

"As a matter of fact," Lia says, "I was thinking daisies would be perfect. They were my mom's favorite flower."

The Beave pauses and then clasps her hands together. "Ophelia, I appreciate your dedication to your mother's favorite flower. Very admirable, but this is a wedding, not a memorial. This is a celebration."

Oh fuck.

Lia gasps. It's under her breath—subtle—that you almost don't hear it, but it's just enough for me to notice.

Just enough for me to know what's going to happen next if I don't interject.

"Mrs. Beaver," I say, stepping in before Lia loses it. "I don't want to step on any toes here, but I believe it would be a kind and serving thing to honor Lia's late mother by including daisies. It would be a way to include her mother since she can't be here."

"But roses and daisies don't go well together."

"I can include daisies in the bride's bouquet," the florist says.

"I don't need a bouquet," Lia says, causing The Beave to snap her head in her direction.

"What do you mean you don't need a bouquet? What on earth would you possibly walk down the aisle with?"

"I made a bunch of knitted flowers with my mom and grandma. I've saved them so I could make a bouquet out of them one day."

The Beave is silent, and then slowly, she starts to chuckle.

The chuckle grows.

And grows.

It's probably the most offensive thing I've seen. This woman thinks she has class, but she actually has none.

"Knitted flowers? For a wedding? You can't be serious." The Beave waves her hand in front of her, dismissing the whole notion.

"I'm pretty sure she's serious, or else she wouldn't bring it up," I say, losing my cool.

Lia gently places her hand on my arm, letting me know she has this. "Mrs. Beaver, I appreciate your need to make this a beautiful wedding, but you need to remember that you're around to see your son get married, and my parents aren't, so incorporating them into the ceremony and reception is important to me."

"And it should be important to you as well," I say, backing her up.

Sensing the tone, The Beave straightens. Her expression morphs into one of understanding, and she quickly slips back into the prim and proper woman she attempts to portray herself as. She turns to the florist and says, "Well, if we could find a suitable way to incorporate daisies without looking tacky, we would appreciate it."

The florist glances between us, looking entirely too frightened. "I believe we can."

"What a nice compromise," I say as a bee buzzes near my head. I swat it away. "I think daisies and roses will go well together."

"Especially white roses," Lia says.

"Oh, come now, you can't be serious," The Beave says. "White roses? You might not be getting married in a church, but for heaven's sake, white roses? We're not lying to our guests." I watch a bee float around The Beave's head, but either she doesn't care or has no sense for nature because she doesn't move.

"Why would we be lying to the guests?" Lia asks.

The Beave folds her hands together and says, "Ophelia, I have turned a blind eye to your nighttime activities with my son, but not everyone is as forgiving. White roses symbolize purity, and I'm afraid you're anything but pure."

I watch as Lia's cheeks grow red with embarrassment. "I don't think that matters."

"Oh, it matters," The Beave says.

"Okay, then maybe pink," Lia suggests. "Doesn't that have to do with grace or something?"

"Grace and sweetness," the florist adds.

"That would be good then," Lia says just as the bee flies near her head, and I wince, knowing she's going to freak out. "Oh my God," she squeals as she shifts up against me, ducking.

"What on earth are you doing?" The Beave asks.

"It was a bee." It buzzes near her head again, and Lia squeals once again while jumping toward the left. "Don't sting me," she calls out.

"For heaven's sake, it's just a bee. If you can't handle that, how are you going to get married in the gardens at the club?"

"As long as they don't—booooother-her-her me," Lia says, hopping around again when the bee goes for her ear. "It's dive-bombing me. It knows I'm weak."

"Ophelia, you're making a fool of yourself."

"I'm sorry," she says as she straightens up, just in time for the bee to hit her in the ear. "Mother of God!" Lia screams as she flails her arm out to the side, unfortunately striking The Beave right in the boob.

Plop.

And together, we all watch in horror as the fragile woman flails her arms up in the air, a croak falling off the tip of her tongue as she teeters backward.

There's no stopping the inevitable.

We all see it happening.

She's headed right for the stacks of hydrangeas.

And with a crash, a groan, and a tumble, the nursery falls silent as The Beave sinks into the table of flowers.

Buckets of water fall everywhere.

Hydrangea branches snap.

And a wince felt around the world appears on all of our faces.

"Get me out of here at once," The Beave says. I rush to her side and help her out, only to quickly go to Lia's side for protection because the inner depths of hell are about to part, and I'm pretty sure if I don't hold on tight enough, Lia is going to be sucked in.

"Oh my God, I'm so sorry," Lia starts, but The Beave holds her hand up to stop her.

Straightening her jacket and wiping the water from her face, she looks up at Lia and says in a voice I think was only intended for nightmares, "There will be red roses at the wedding with very minimal daisies. End of discussion." And then she takes off, her assistant at her side.

We stand there, a touch stunned as the florist leaves as well. After a few seconds, Lia says, "That, uh...that wasn't ideal."

I can't help it. I let out a low chuckle and say, "Who knew you would get to second base with your mother-in-law today? What did it feel like? In my head, they're just sacs of dust."

She coughs a few times. "Is that what I'm tasting? Boob dust?"

I let out a wallop of a laugh as I drape my arm over her and guide her toward the exit. "Just be glad your arm didn't fly low, or else you would have a mouthful of vagina dust."

"Vagina dust...isn't that just Old Bay seasoning?" she asks, causing me to snort.

"Oh fuck...I love you."

———

"You know, I've never seen someone's blood boil in real life. You always hear the idiom, but you never actually see it." Lia takes a bite of her burrito as we sit outside Alberto's, one of our favorite places to go when we're downtown. "But wow, we witnessed The Beave's blood rippling through her ghastly veins today. It was something else."

"If looks could kill, we'd both be dead."

"Dead on the spot. Did you catch the look the florist gave us? I'm pretty sure she wanted to shrivel up and disappear."

"I think that's how everyone feels when The Beave is around."

Lia takes a sip from the large lemonade we decided to share. "Thanks for sticking up for me. I appreciate it."

"You don't need to say thank you. That's what a Pickle of Honor does."

Lia chuckles but then grows quiet. "Do you think it's stupid to do the knitted flower thing?"

I shake my head. "Makes me like you that much more." Her eyes lift to mine. "I think it's really sweet, and if I were in your shoes, I would want to do the same thing. This is an important day in a person's life, and it's only right to honor those who can't be there. I think your mom would love it if you walked down the aisle with something you made together."

"Agreed." She sets her burrito down. "I keep thinking about the walk down the aisle and how my dad would have held me tightly, told me how much he loves me, how proud he is, and how he always dreamed of that day. The day he could give me away. And now…now I won't have that. I'll have to make the walk alone, and that's daunting."

"I'll walk you down the aisle," I say. "You won't be alone. You'll have me."

"The Beave would never go for that, as you're supposed to go ahead of me since you're the Pickle of Honor."

"By the way, if Pickle of Honor isn't on the programs, I'm going to rage." She smirks. "But I don't care what The Beave wants. I want you to be happy, to feel like you're surrounded by the people who love you, and if that means I'm doubling down on responsibilities, then who fucking cares?"

"Thank you. Ugh, I hate that this has all been so morose. I feel like when you get married, it should be this big celebration. So far, it's felt like a version of hell. The only reason I've made it through these past two days is because of you. I'm pretty sure I would have folded after the guest list number."

"It will get better. Once all this planning is out of the way, it will be smooth sailing."

"I hope so." She lifts her burrito and takes another bite. "So you going to finish that conversation about Birdy?"

"What else is there to say?" I ask with a shrug. "I think I'm going to give it another chance, just because she's cool and I had a good time with her. Maybe it was all the sugar I ate, but I told her I would take her hiking, so I'm going to do that, and we'll see where it goes from there."

"Why are you pushing it? If you don't like her, you don't like her."

"It's not that I don't like her," I say. "I actually do. I just didn't feel anything when I kissed her, and I expected more, you know? Maybe I was nervous. She was tugging at my shirt, and that was hot, so maybe I got in my head."

"She was tugging on your shirt?" Lia asks, her burrito halfway to her mouth. "Like to take it off?"

"No, like to keep me in place. I liked it. And her lips were super soft. I wonder if I open-mouth kissed her if that would have been better?"

"You didn't open-mouth kiss her?" Lia asks. "So it was just tight-lipped?"

"Yeah, like a peck."

"Well, that's probably why you didn't feel anything. A peck doesn't give you much room to interpret attraction."

"Huh." I scratch the side of my jaw and grab our lemonade. "You know, you might be right."

"I know I am."

"Don't be humble or anything."

"When have we ever been humble around each other?"

"Never," I answer. I lean back in my chair. "What are you doing tonight?"

"Headed over to Brian's. Things have been a little sticky lately between us, and he's feeling it, so he asked me over. He's making dinner."

"Did you talk to him about the glasses?"

She wipes her mouth with a napkin and nods. "Yeah, he admitted to saying that to his mom." Fury boils in my stomach. The man is still such a douche, and I can't ever see myself liking him. "But apologized.

I don't know. I feel like this is when all the rotten things come out in a relationship. It's best it comes out now, right? So you know you can work through all of it."

"Yeah, probably." Just then, my phone beeps with a text. I glance down and see that it's from Huxley. "One second." I hold up my finger and then read the text.

Huxley: Can you come over to my place tomorrow? We have some updates I would like to go over.

I text him back quickly.

Breaker: Sure. What time?
Huxley: Nine. See you then.

I glance up at Lia. "Looks like Huxley has some updates."

"Ooo, Shoemacher is going down."

CHAPTER 8
BREAKER

I'M FUCKING BORED.

Staring at my computer and the Tetris blocks blotting down the screen, I realize that my life is pathetic.

Yup.

This is what I'm doing, playing Tetris on my computer like some seventy-year-old man, all because my best friend is hanging out with her soon-to-be husband, and my brothers are off having copious amounts of sex with their wives. See, this is exactly what I was talking about. I need a life outside of my norm.

I need people to hang out with.

I need activities.

I need something other than sitting at home by myself, wearing a Batman Band-Aid over my nipple because I thought it was funny.

Standing from my desk, I stretch my arms over my head, and I go to text JP to see what he's doing, then pause. I know what he's doing, his wife.

Huxley too.

And it's not even like I can text Banner—our new business partner and friend—because he hooked up with someone at JP and Kelsey's wedding. Everyone is coupled. EVERYONE!

Stupid, I should be coupled too, not sitting around my house, drinking freaking orange juice and attempting to beat my own personal best on Tetris at seven o'clock at night.

I pick up my phone, click on the thread with Birdy, and shoot her a text.

> **Breaker:** What are you up to? I'm pathetically playing Tetris alone at the moment.

I walk to my bedroom, where I strip out of my shorts and put on a pair of black joggers just as she texts back.

> **Birdy:** I'm watching Sex and the City while feasting on one of our pussy cakes.
> **Breaker:** LOL. Want some company?
> **Birdy:** Always. I'll ping you my address. By the way, dress comfy. I'm in loungewear.
> **Breaker:** Slipping on a plain T-shirt as we speak.
> **Birdy:** Oh, did I mention no shirt is necessary?
> **Breaker:** I think you skipped that detail. See you soon.

Birdy lives in a really nice apartment.

Gated community, lavish pool, and expertly landscaped. Not sure how much she pays for rent, but it's probably more than I do, which I find funny given the vast difference in our bank accounts.

I pull into a parking spot outside of her building, grab the box of cupcakes from our class off my seat—never show up empty-handed—and jog up the steps toward apartment 3C.

I knock on the door three times, and I'm tempted to kick the footboard but remind myself that's something I do with Lia and hold back. The locks are undone, and the door opens for me to find Birdy on the other side wearing a pair of silk shorts and a simple black tank top.

"You brought cupcakes? I thought you wouldn't have any left after how you took them down in the class."

"I went on a one-day detox." I hand them to her just as she steps up to me, places her hand on my chest, and greets me with a kiss on the corner of my mouth. That was unexpected, but I didn't mind it.

"I'm glad you're here." She then takes my hand and pulls me into her apartment.

I slip my shoes off, lock the door behind me, and then follow her into the living room, where she takes a seat on the couch and pulls me down with her.

Her apartment is what I would have expected from her. Pristine white furniture with beige and tan tones spread throughout the space. It's clean, sharp, modern, and serene. Not one action figure decoration and not one poster. Very grown-up.

A far cry from my place.

And Lia's for that matter.

Sitting on her knees, she turns toward me and says, "I need to talk to you about something."

"Uh, okay," I answer as I turn toward her as well.

"Well, more like apologize."

"You apologized enough about the baking class," I say. "And I had fun, oddly."

"It's not about the baking class. It's about…" She winces and then adds, "The kiss."

"Oh, uh, what about the kiss?" I ask her.

"I know it was awkward."

"What are you talking about?" I ask, knowing damn well it felt a touch awkward.

"I was nervous and clammed up when I kissed you. I'm honestly surprised you're even here after that kiss. When I got your text, I gasped. I was waiting on a late-night Friday phone call telling me you can't meet up to hike."

"Birdy—"

"I'm a better kisser than that," she says in a panic. "Much better. I'm just, God, I'm so nervous around you."

"Why?" I ask. "I don't think I'm very intimidating."

"You're not. That's the problem. If you were some alpha asshole, then yeah, I probably wouldn't feel so jittery around you, but you're a nice guy, a sweet one, and you're the kind of guy who's hard to find, especially in Los Angeles. I keep telling myself I'm going to blow it, and I truly thought I did with that kiss."

"You need to stop overthinking things," I say, even though she's completely right. I thought the same thing about the kiss. Guess I wasn't alone on this. That's comforting. Maybe it was the tight-lipped thing after all.

"I'm sorry. I'm just so caught up in my previous relationship that it's difficult to shake those thoughts in my head. But I'll do better."

"Take your time," I say as I drape my arm over the back of her couch. "I don't plan on going anywhere, and as it stands, we're still going on that hike on Saturday."

"Good, because I went shopping today and got the perfect outfit for it."

"Oh yeah?" I ask with a laugh. "Wasn't sure there was a perfect hike slash bird-watching outfit out there."

"If you look hard enough, you can find it."

"Tell me more about this outfit."

"Oh no, no sneak peeks. It will be a surprise."

"Well, if it's not a shirt with a bird on it, I will be incredibly disappointed."

All she does is smile, and it's really cute. She's really cute. And funny. And sweet. Pretty much everything I would probably look for in a match. It's why I need to try harder to make this work.

"So did you go wedding planning with Lia today?"

"Yup, checked out some flowers."

She draws closer. I can tell she wants to be more intimate, so I shift my body to face her more, and then I draw a circle with my finger over her bare shoulder. There seems to be relief in her eyes, so I continue.

"What did you end up choosing?"

"Now, Birdy," I admonish. "What kind of Pickle of Honor would I be if I gave out the secrets of the wedding?"

"Pickle of Honor? This needs some explanation."

"Lia and I are huge Scrabble nerds. We were in a club together in college, and one night, it was just me and her playing, which is usually how the club gathering ended anyway. I was exhausted but needed to beat her at one more game. I had the workings to spell *pickle* and accidentally spelled it wrong. And of course, I was a cocky son of a bitch back then, especially when Scrabble was involved, so I called out my points like a master, and she pointed at the board, saying I spelled it wrong. It was humiliating, and the name stuck. I'm her pickle."

She chuckles. "You know, *pickle* could be thought of as something else."

I pause and then shake my head. "Trust me, this pickle has never gone there."

She laughs some more. "Well, I love your friendship. I think it's sweet. Do you have a lot of close friends? Or just Lia?"

"Well, I used to hang out with my brothers until they got married. That's put a real damper on our basketball games. I still see them, but it's more of a group thing, which grants their wives access to my personal business. They can be very needy when it comes to knowing all about my single life and how they can make me...un-single. And then there's my friend Banner, who just started working with us. He's pretty cool, but he's seeing this girl Kenzie, well, sort of seeing her. I don't know where they stand. So he's occupied with that." I nod my head slowly. "Looks like I'm at that time in my life where everyone pairs up."

"I know what you mean," Birdy says. "When I was with my ex, it was as if everyone was getting married or having kids. We did couple things together, and when we broke up, it was as if no one had time for me."

"That's shitty, but I know the feeling."

"Can't blame them, though," she says. "They're in love after all."

"I guess so. I think that's what has put a fire in me to meet someone. I'm not desperate or anything, but I also don't want to be lonely."

"I totally get that. I'm the same way. I don't need someone to be happy, but it's fun to do things with someone...you know, like hiking." She reaches out and plays with the fabric of my shirt.

"And icing pussies."

Her smirk is really sexy when she looks up at me. "Exactly. Like icing pussies."

Taking a risk, I tug on her hand and say, "Come here." To my luck, she listens and straddles my lap. I lean against the couch cushion so I'm looking up at her. "How was work today?"

"That's what you're going to ask me while I'm sitting on your lap?"

"Yeah," I answer as my hands fall to her thighs. "I have all of my everyday conversations like this. You should see the fistfights I get into with my brothers over who gets to be the bottom and who gets to be the top."

She lets out a sultry laugh while she draws circles on my chest this time. "Oh, what an image that has formed in my head."

"We find if we sit on each other's laps, we can focus on the conversation and block out distractions. I've had hour-long conversations on JP's lap where we've brainstormed over our next business venture. If it wasn't for the obvious HR violation, we would have everyone sit on each other's laps."

"You know, maybe you're onto something. My marketing brain is thinking that you could form some sort of device that prevents pelvis-to-pelvis contact but allows the same position. Oh, and you can add some horse blinders to really keep out the distraction."

"Wow, Birdy. Wow. That's positively genius."

She brushes off her shoulder. "Thank you, but the idea goes to you. I'm just the dream maker."

"Is that what you call yourself at work?"

"When I strike it big with a huge idea, of course. I quietly print out a certificate of completion with the name *dream maker* on it. I have a whole folder of them. In my desk drawer."

"A whole folder would imply that you're very good at being a dream maker."

"I am."

We spend the next hour or so talking about anything and everything, her sitting on my lap, me holding her thighs and not making a move at all. Not one single move.

She tells me about how she loves to go surfing—something I've never done in my life—how she is a huge fan of all types of cereal—the more sugar, the better—and how she once had a dog with three legs and said he was the best dog she ever had.

I shared with her my desire to own every *Star Wars* bobblehead ever made, how I believe the original bromance of our time is C3PO and R2D2—and she proceeded to tell me she's only watched the most recent episodes and how she doesn't get the whole Kylo and Rey fetish. I nearly balked with disappointment.

"Are you thirsty or anything?" Birdy asks.

"Nah, I'm good. I should probably get going, though, because I'm sure you need to wake up early tomorrow." I rub my hands over her thighs.

"I do happen to have a five thirty wake-up call."

"Yeah, I have a meeting with Hux tomorrow at his place."

"Okay, well…" Her fingers dance along my shirt. "I guess I should walk you to the door." She gets off my lap and then holds out her hand. I take it, and we walk over to her front door together. I slip on my shoes, and when I'm done, I stand tall and find her leaning against the wall right next to the door, her hands behind her back. "Thank you for coming over."

"Yeah, I had a nice time, even though you're not a fan of the Kylo Ren and Rey love affair."

"I just can't get on board," she says, holding steady. "Sorry. Doesn't work for me."

"Such a disappointment," I teasingly reply and then take a step forward. I hook my finger under her chin, close the space between us one more time, and hover right above her lips, waiting for her.

She closes the rest of the distance between us and smooths her hand up my chest while her mouth opens, encouraging mine as well. I drop my free hand to the wall next to her head, propping myself up, and deepen the kiss, letting my tongue explore now.

Her hands float up to my cheeks, where she cups them. Her tongue matches my strokes, and for the first time in a few months, I make out right there in the entryway of a girl's apartment.

I revel in the feel of her soft lips.

I sink into the grasp she has on my cheeks.

And when she gasps for a touch of air, I commit it to memory.

I've forgotten what it feels like to be intimate with a woman, and this feels good.

When I pull away, her lashes lift as her eyes connect with mine. I smile down at her and say, "Better?"

"Much." She runs her tongue along her lips. "So much better."

"Good." I lean down and press one more kiss to her lips before pulling away. "I'll see you Saturday for that hike."

"Yes, Saturday," she replies as I open the door to her apartment and head out. "Night, Breaker."

"Night, Birdy," I say just before I take off down the hall.

———

"Morning, Breaker," Lottie says as she answers the door to her house. "How are you?"

"Good," I say. "What about yourself?" She isn't dressed for the day yet, still in a robe with her hair up in a bun.

"Doing okay."

Huxley appears just then and loops his arm around her waist. He presses a kiss to the side of her head and says, "Can I get you anything?"

She shakes her head and pats his hand. "I'm good." And then she walks toward the kitchen, Huxley's eyes watching her every step.

"What does it feel like?" I ask him.

When he turns toward me, he asks, "What does what feel like?"

"To be that in love. You're so protective, possessive, infatuated. I don't think I've ever been like that with someone."

"Of course you have," he says. "You're that way with Lia."

"Lia and I aren't romantically involved."

"You might not be, but you know how you get when Brian's mom picks on her, that instinctual feeling like you will do fucking anything to make sure no one hurts your girl? That's the feeling. That deep-seated feeling that never goes away."

I slowly nod my head. "I get that feeling with Lia, but not on a romantic level, on a best friend level."

"Well, when you finally fall in love with someone, that feeling you have with Lia will transfer over. Why do you ask?" He heads toward his office, and I follow him.

"I've sort of gone out with this girl the last few days, and she's pretty awesome. Beautiful and smart. Great sense of humor. We don't have much in common, but she's sweet, quick-witted, and interesting. I went to her place last night, and we talked a lot, she even sat on my lap for a while, but I didn't have this overwhelming need to touch her. I kept my hands on her legs because I felt like that was the right thing to do, and when I kissed her good night, I really fucking liked it, but I don't know, I don't think I felt anything with her."

"Was she a bad kisser?" Huxley asks as he takes a seat at his desk. I take a seat at the one across from him.

"No, a really good kisser actually." I heave a heavy sigh and lean forward, hands clasped. "I don't know, man. I think I'm going through some shit, and I don't know how to process it. I think this lawsuit and the wedding are fucking with my head."

"Do you want to like this girl?" Huxley asks.

"I don't want to be left behind. Alone. Everyone I know is either married, getting married, or in a relationship. I'm just over in my lonely apartment playing fucking Tetris on my computer."

"That never bothered you before. You love Tetris."

"I still do," I say softly. "Fucking love it, but I don't know, it just feels like I'm at a point in my life when maybe I should have a serious girlfriend. I've never really had one before, and that's sort of weird, right?"

"You never needed one before. You've leaned on Lia for female companionship, and when you've wanted sex, you've had your fun. You've had the perfect setup for quite some time."

"Wait, do you really think that's it? That's why I haven't had a true girlfriend? Because I've leaned on Lia all these years?"

"Yes," Huxley says, exhausted. "It's frightening that you haven't taken note of that before. It's so fucking obvious."

"Not to me," I say as I lean back on my chair and press my hands into my thighs. "Do you think that's why I haven't found someone? Because I've been content with Lia?"

Huxley rubs his temple, his short patience showing. "Yes," he answers. "That's exactly why, because why do you need a girlfriend when Lia is all you've ever needed?"

"Jesus. I never thought of it that way." If that's the case, then it conversely means that Lia *wasn't* content with just me. I have never been what she needed because she started dating Brian. So even though she's worried about things changing between us, they already have. She now *needs* Brian, which means she doesn't need me as much. Man, have I been blind.

"Glad I can enlighten you. Now, can we get back to why you're really here?"

"I guess so," I say as my mind whirls. "But just one second. Do you think I should...I don't know, stop hanging out with Lia so much?"

Huxley pinches his brow now. "Why would you do that? You're just going to hurt her feelings."

"Yeah, but she has Brian, so shouldn't there be like...a transition of power?"

"You're not the goddamn president of the United States."

"I know that," I say, exasperated. "But with Brian and Lia getting married soon, shouldn't I back away a bit? Brian already has issues with how much time Lia and I spend together. Like, I should hand him the torch, right?"

"I don't know. If you think you should, then go for it. Now can we talk about the lawsuit, please?"

"Sure, sorry," I say and then pause. "It's just that I saw Birdy last night and the kiss was good, but I didn't feel a spark, and I wasn't sure if I should be feeling a spark or if it's too soon to feel a spark? I don't know, did you feel a spark with Lottie?"

Huxley tosses his pen onto the desk and leans back in his chair. "You tell me, do you think I felt a spark with my wife?"

"From what I've observed, I would say yes."

"Immediately," he says. "I might have thought she was annoying, frustrating, and downright irritating most of the time, but there was no doubt in my mind that she was the prettiest fucking thing I'd ever seen, and I wanted her in my bed."

"Ah," I say, nodding. "Same, you think, with JP?"

"Dude, seriously? Come on, you saw JP when he met Kelsey for the first time. The man had heart eyes coming out of every orifice of his body."

"Yeah, I know." I glance to the side. "It's not like that with Birdy. But I also wonder if I have a mental block now, and I'm not allowing myself to feel for her the way I should because of the leaning-on-Lia thing. Do you think that could be an issue?"

"I think there's going to be a huge fucking issue soon if we don't stop talking about this and get down to business."

"Yeah, okay...sorry." I chew on my thumbnail. "Real quick though, what are your thoughts on Kylo and Rey? Is it weird I'm considering dating someone who doesn't believe in the love affair as I do?"

"Jesus fucking Christ."

CHAPTER 9
LIA

Lia: Password is on tonight. Am I coming to your place, or are you coming to my place? I need to run to the grocery store if you're coming over here. I don't have any Sour Patch Kids or Sprite.

Breaker: Oh, I need to take a rain check.

I stare down at my phone, confused.

A rain check?

I'm pretty sure Breaker has never used that term with me...ever.

Lia: A rain check? Is this my Pickle? Just want to make sure he wasn't abducted or anything.

Breaker: Not abducted, just have plans.

Oh.

Plans? With whom?

Birdy?

I mean, I shouldn't care, but it's *Password*, and we always watch *Password* together.

We pause the game, and one of us finds out the password and makes the other guess; then we let it play out on screen. During the whole process, we drown ourselves in handheld calzones from our favorite pizzeria, suck on Sour Patch Kids until our tongues are raw, and wash it all down with Sprite, which always causes us to burp through the remainder of the night.

It's tradition!

So why would he just…book other plans?

I lift from my desk, where I've been working on a detailed Excel sheet, and then walk over to my bed and flop down on it. I should just tell him to have fun and see him on Friday when we meet with The Beave, but for the life of me, I can't let this go, so I text him back.

Lia: Plans, huh? With Birdy?

I send the text and wince, hating that I'm so curious.

Breaker: JP and Lottie actually. We're going to some bar JP's been talking about. Thought about asking Birdy to go, but not sure yet. That would be four times in one week that I see her. Don't want to look desperate.

Lia: Four times? That's more than you've seen me.

The disparity weighs heavily on my already churning stomach. Four times? That's…that's so much.

Breaker: Well, there was the double date, then the baking thing, and I went over to her place last night, so if I invited her out tonight, that would be a bit much, don't you think?

I think three times is a bit much.

Also…he could invite me to go out to the bar with everyone. Clearly, I'm not doing anything tonight.

Lia: You went there last night? Did you go for a reason?

Breaker: Just to hang. We talked a lot. She's not a fan of Kylo and Rey, which was a tough pill to swallow, but hey, you can't win them all. She did think one of the fan accounts I showed her was pretty hot.

Lia: She doesn't like Kylo and Rey together? I'm pretty sure that is terms for never talking to her again.

Breaker: It was easy to forgive, especially since I'm taking her on a hike on Saturday and a bird-watching tour.

Lia: Oh, cool. The same tour we go on?

Breaker: Yeah, it's the best one. She seems pretty excited about it. Said she got an outfit and everything.

Lia: Does it have a bird on it?

Breaker: She said it was a surprise.

Bet it's a sports bra and shorts. She seems nice and all but also...a bit thirsty.

Lia: Well, what am I supposed to do about Password tonight?

Breaker: Have Brian come over. He should start playing with you anyway.

Lia: What do you mean, "anyway"? This is our game.

Breaker: Yes, but you'll be married soon. I can't keep coming over on our set nights. This is a good change, Lia.

Lia: Wait...did you make plans on purpose? To guide me into some sort of transition?

Breaker: I forgot how smart you are.

Lia: Uh, I don't need you transitioning me. I'm a big girl, Breaker.

Breaker: Okay, so then go be with your fiancé. Talk about your wedding, make sure he knows what's happening with it.

Lia: Why does it feel like you're distancing yourself?

Breaker: I'm not, Lia. I'm just trying to prepare you. Once you get married, everything changes.

Lia: You say that as if it's a punishment.

Breaker: It's not, but the fact of the matter is, I can't be there for you like I am now. I can't be your companion, and you can't be mine, simple as that.

Lia: Companion? Where is all of this coming from?

Breaker: Nowhere, it's just facts. That's what's happening with our lives—we're evolving, changing, and this is just the next step. Now I have to go. See you on Friday.

I stare at my phone, reading over our texts repeatedly, trying to figure out what's happening. Sure, I'm getting married and will soon be living with my husband, but that doesn't mean I need to cut ties with Breaker or stop interacting with him. Hell, he's seen Birdy, someone he barely knows, more times this week than me.

And that makes me sad. All of this makes me sad. And the one person I would talk to about it just said he would see me on Friday.

Tears well in my eyes just as a knock sounds on my door.

I sit up from my bed, hopeful that it's Breaker and that his texts are all just a ruse. I quickly wipe under my eyes, run to the entryway, and throw open the door, where I find Brian on the other side, holding a bouquet of roses and wearing a large smile.

"Hello, sweetheart," he says, and I swear light sparkles off his freshly whitened teeth. "Thought I'd surprise you with some flowers and"—he picks up an overnight bag—"a sleepover."

"Oh, wow," I say, trying to make my voice sound excited, not disappointed. "I was, uh…I was not expecting that."

"Yeah, neither was I." He hands me the flowers. *Red* roses, which I despise due to how cliché and unoriginal they are. Something I thought Brian knew. "It was actually Breaker's idea." *Ah…what?* "He also told me to pick up Sour Patch Kids and Sprite, so that's in the bag as well. Not sure why, but he said it's what you guys need while playing *Password*."

"Breaker told you to do all this?"

"Well, the flowers were my idea, but game night was his. Said since he won't be around as much, I should learn the things you love." Brian leans in and gives me a kiss on the cheek. He pushes past me into my apartment as I stand there stunned.

Breaker set this up?

He wants Brian to learn all the things I *love*?

Why is he doing this? Why is he trying to extract me from his life?

I'm sure he's probably doing this to be nice, but it's hurtful.

And no way am I going to be able to enjoy this night unless I get to the bottom of it.

So taking a chance, I say, "Uh, Brian, I need to make an important business call. I'm going to run over to Breaker's so I don't bother you."

"Oh, I can be quiet if you want."

I shake my head. "Trust me, these walls are paper-thin. You could hear everything. Just make yourself comfortable, and I'll be back shortly."

"Okay. Love you."

I smile at him. "Love you."

Phone in hand, I slip out of my apartment and go straight to Breaker's. There is a very slim chance that he's there, but at least I can try, and if he's not, I can call him from his apartment.

I knock on the door gently and then give it a few moments before checking the door; it's unlocked. I push through just as Breaker approaches the entryway.

"Lia, everything okay?"

I shut the door behind me and fold my arms at my chest. "No, everything is not okay."

"Okay..." he drags out. "Well, I was just headed out—"

"Really? You're not going to ask me what's wrong?"

"I have a feeling I know," he says as he moves back toward his guest room, and I follow him. It's the room farthest away from my apartment. We've fought in here before while Brian was in my apartment, and there's no doubt that's what he's thinking now. He takes a seat on the guest bed and says, "What's going on?"

"What's going on?" I say in a hushed but forceful tone. "How about you tell me what's going on, because last I checked, you're pawning our traditions off onto Brian."

"I'm not pawning them off. I'm including him."

"I don't need you to include him. I do my own things with Brian. What I need you to do is stop pushing me away."

"I literally saw you yesterday. How is that pushing you away?"

"You saw me for wedding things. You're pushing me away from our normal stuff."

He glances away, yet I can see he wants to say something. Something is on the tip of his tongue, but he's holding back.

"Just say it," I push.

He bows his head and shakes it.

"So is this how it's going to be, Breaker? I'm engaged to be married, and now you won't even tell me what you're thinking?"

"I can't tell you what I'm thinking."

"Why not?" I ask.

"Because it's about you," he whisper-shouts.

I take a step back, trying to understand why he seems so jittery, so irritated.

"Well, if it's about me, then just tell me. Clearly, it's something you need to get off your chest."

"Fine," he says, and then his eyes meet mine. "You want to talk? We can talk. We've relied on each other too much, and I realized today that I'm not in a relationship because of you."

"Excuse me?" I ask. "Uh, care to explain how that's my fault?"

"Because you became my safety net. Why do I need a companion when I have you to fall back on?"

"So basically, because I was being a good friend, you're mad at me and trying to extract me from your life?"

"No." He tugs on his hair in frustration. "That's not what I'm saying."

"Then what exactly are you saying, Breaker? Because it seems to me like you're having some sort of relationship crisis because I'm getting married, and now you're desperate to find someone, and the one person you have been seeing isn't exactly what you were looking for. Therefore, you're blaming me for all of it."

"Wow." He stands up now, his height towering over me. "That's not what I was fucking saying. Way to twist my words."

I throw my hands up in defeat. "Then what are you saying?"

"We're just…we're too close."

"Too close?" I nod sarcastically. "Okay, so the friendship we've built over the last decade is too good. That's the problem?" I step away. "Okay, good to know. I'm sorry for caring about you so much and being a part of your life to the point that I've actually hurt you."

"Lia, don't," he says, reaching for me.

"No, you don't," I say as I turn around on him. "That's really shitty, Breaker, for you to push me away because you think I've prevented you from finding someone to be with. I've done nothing of the sort. Your dating life is your problem, not mine. Maybe instead of looking at the people who love you and support you to blame, try looking inward. I'm not the reason you're not with someone. The reason you're single is because you don't ever think anyone is good enough. Your standards are so impossibly high that no one will ever match them. That's the problem. Not me."

I turn on my heel, but he catches up and tugs on my arm.

"Lia, wait."

I snatch my arm away and say, "And what's the big deal anyway? Why now? Why do you have to find someone now? Just because I'm getting married, you think you need to get married too?"

"No," he says, a furrow in his brow.

"Then why is this a thing right now? Why are you making this an issue? I've dated other guys. Yes, not many, but I've had boyfriends. Why is this so different?"

"I don't know," he says, looking distraught.

Maybe an hour ago, I would have sat him down and talked through his feelings with him, but not now, not this time. My *fiancé*, who wants to spend time with me and do something *I love*, is in my apartment waiting for me. Breaker is being ridiculous and thoughtless. He can stew in his own vomit for a while.

"Maybe that's something you need to figure out." I head toward his front door.

"Lia, I'm sorry, okay?"

"No, not okay." I turn around again. "This is not how we treat each other. I don't know what's going through your head right now, what could possess you to have these thoughts and drastic ideas of pushing me toward Brian when I don't need pushing, but I will tell you one thing. It's going to drive a wedge between us. If that's what you want, then job well done." I reach the front door and say, "And don't worry about Friday. It's just looking for a dress, so I won't need your help with that." And then I leave his apartment, pause in the hallway, in the space between my door and his, and I sink down to the ground where I quietly cry. *What the hell is happening to us?*

"Uh, I don't know...dishwasher?" Brian asks as I flop back on the couch.

"How could you possibly get *dishwasher* from the clue *shark*?"

"I don't know," Brian says, frustrated. "This game makes no sense."

"How does it not make sense? You offer a clue to your partner, and then they try to guess, simple as that."

"But your clues aren't helping."

"I gave you three clues. Mouth, dentist, and shark."

"Yeah, great clues. How the hell do those even go together?" he asks.

"*Teeth!*" I shout. "My God, Brian, the password is *teeth*! You should have gotten it with *dentist.*"

"Well, this is my first time playing. I'm sorry I'm not as good as Breaker. Maybe if you weren't shoving all this godforsaken sugar down my throat, I would have been able to guess."

"I wasn't comparing you to Breaker," I say through clenched teeth.

"You didn't have to. I could see it written all over your face."

"Great assumption," I say as I offer him a thumbs-up and then stand from the couch. "Because apparently, you know exactly what's going on in my head, besides what I'm really thinking about, and what I'm really thinking about is freaking TEETH! God," I shout, utterly frustrated. "I'm going to bed. Feel free to go home if you'd like."

I leave the living room and head straight for my bedroom and bathroom, where I close the door. Since I'm already in my pajamas, I go to the sink and splash water on my face. I dry my face and then stare into the mirror as tears fill my eyes.

I don't have a moment to blot them away before Brian opens the bathroom door and leans against the counter.

"I'm sorry, Lia."

I can't look at him. I'll cry.

But I can't move either.

I feel paralyzed.

Nothing seems to be going right.

Breaker is trying to remove me from his life.

Brian is an idiot and doesn't understand a simple clue like *dentist.*

I've lit a veil on fire, flicked blood on my future mother-in-law, and punched her in the boob.

The wedding planning is going at lightning speed despite the accidents.

I'm embarrassing myself left and right.

I got in a huge fight with my best friend, something I don't do very often.

And the worst part of it all is that I have no one to turn to.

No one.

I grip the counter even tighter as my body sways, the pressure I've been carrying mounting on my shoulders as my breathing picks up.

"Hey, are you okay?" Brian asks as he steps up closer.

"N-no," I mutter right before my legs give out on me.

Brian quickly scoops me up, my name a frightened plea as he carries me to the bed.

"Jesus, what's going on?" he asks as he brushes his hand over my forehead. "You're pale. Lia, what's happening? Do you want me to call for help?"

I shake my head as my lip trembles, and tears fall down the side of my head. "No. Just…just let me get some sleep."

"You think I'm going to leave you like this? You almost hit your head on the counter. There's no way I'm leaving." He sits right next to me and places his hand on my stomach. "Talk to me, Lia. What's going on?"

"I just…" My lips tremble some more. "I'm just freaking out," I say, not wanting to tell him the truth. Things are already weird between Brian and Breaker—that much is evident after the display in the living room—I don't need to make Brian mad at Breaker for putting me in this mental state.

"Freaking out about the wedding?"

"About…us," I say, which is partially true.

"What about us?" he asks.

"We can't play *Password*. We're getting married, Brian. We should be able to play *Password*. And…and the wedding planning is a nightmare. I've set things on fire and bloodied people and swatted your mother's breast, and we can't seem to agree on much. And you don't care about the plans, which is fine. I know you're busy, but…it doesn't seem like we're on the same wavelength."

"We are," he says. "That's just a stupid game, which proves nothing. What we do in our everyday life, our thoughts, and our morals, that's what matters. And we are on the same wavelength there. Right?"

"Yes," I say quietly, even if he doesn't get it. Maybe it's from watching my parents as I grew up, but I just feel there needs to be a deeper connection. I want him to be able to guess what I'm going to say next. I want him to be able to understand me without even having to talk, and I don't think we have that. "But…do you know everything about me?" I ask.

"Of course I do," he says. "And what I don't know, I'll spend the rest of our lives finding out. Getting married to someone doesn't mean you know a list of facts about your partner like some reality trivia game. I'm marrying you because you make me happy, because I can't imagine a day when I don't think about you in my life, and because I love you, Lia. I'm not marrying you because I happen to know what you like to order from the sandwich shop around the corner or because you can telepathically answer a stupid *Password* question. Those are all menial things when it comes to getting married. It doesn't matter." He moves his hand to my heart. "This matters. Our love matters."

I hear the words he's saying.

I'm nodding as I listen.

And when he curls into me, spooning me from behind so we both can get some sleep, I go along with it because I can't do anything else to stop the sensation of feeling empty inside.

———

"Lia, hey," I hear a voice say just as I enter Morning Perk for a quick coffee before heading to the dress shop.

I turn to the right just in time to catch Birdy approaching.

Great, just what I need.

Ever since my fight with Breaker, I haven't felt like myself. I've been going through the motions of work, talking with Brian, even answering some emails from The Beave, and just saying yes to whatever asinine plan she presents. At this point, I don't care.

I haven't heard from Breaker since the fight, which in our world feels like decades.

I'm sad.

Depressed.

I miss my parents. God, I wish my mom was here. I wish I could ask her if Brian is right. If it took years for Dad to understand all her idiosyncrasies. If what Breaker and I have took years and is *only* good because we've had a decade together, and if I need to be confident that things will eventually click with Brian. *Those are all menial things when it comes to getting married. It doesn't matter... Our love matters.* Is he right? I. Don't. Know. *My mom would know.*

I really wish I could crawl into a hole and not deal with any of this. I just feel so...fragile, and that's never a word I've associated with myself.

But right now? Birdy.

"Hey, Birdy," I say, trying to tack on a smile.

"Oh wow, your hair looks so shiny," she says while touching the ends. "It's beautiful."

"Oh, thanks. I went to the salon around the corner and got it blown out. I'm trying on dresses today, and my soon-to-be mother-in-law told me to make sure my hair resembled what I wanted on my wedding day."

"Beautiful," Birdy says, and I can't tell if she's genuine or not. "Is your color natural?"

"Yes," I say. "My dad descended from a long line of redheads."

"I'm jealous." She smiles brightly, and God, she really is just perfect, isn't she? Great smile, bright blue eyes, and a perfect body. No wonder Breaker has been hanging out with her a lot. "So you headed over to the dress shop now?"

"Yes, I'm just going to grab some coffee first because I'll need some caffeine to get through this shopping trip."

Confused, Birdy asks, "Shouldn't shopping for a wedding dress be fun?"

It should be when you're not fighting with your best friend.

"My future mother-in-law can be difficult." I leave it at that.

"Well, she shouldn't have a say in it, but that's just my opinion. Anyway, I won't keep you from your appointment. I just wanted to say hi and thank you and Brian for setting me up with Breaker." She clutches her hands at her chest. "He's amazing. I don't know how he's still single, but I lucked out, because he's everything I could ask for in a man." She leans forward and elbows me as if we're close comrades. News flash: we are not. "And quite the kisser. Oh my God."

Things I don't need to hear right now.

"Well, I'm glad to hear it," I say with a big smile that is as fake as fake can be.

"Okay, have fun. I'm going to meet up with Breaker right now." She twiddles her fingers at me as my heart sinks down to the floor.

"Yeah, bye," I say as I turn toward the line, my breath picking up. He's meeting up with her right now?

I know I told him not to bother showing up for the dress shopping, but he really isn't going to be there?

No one is going to be there besides The Beave.

Is that what my life has come to? I don't have any other friends?

I don't have any other support?

All I have is Brian and his mother?

Once again, tears well in my eyes, but I don't let them fall, not here, not in the coffee shop. I make quick work of ordering myself a coffee, and thankfully, they're quick to deliver. With coffee in hand, I decide to walk to the bridal shop, which is a few blocks down. No need to drive.

As I head down the street, I clutch my coffee close to my chest and let out a deep breath.

Mom was supposed to be here today, and she's not.

I've isolated myself so much since their deaths that I've slowly lost any other friendships I had besides Breaker because he was the one who held me when I cried. He distracted me when I was feeling sad. He kept me moving forward.

And now that we're not talking and in a weird place, I've never felt more alone in my entire life.

When I reach the bridal shop, I hold my breath, waiting to see any sign of Breaker, but as I draw closer, all I can see through the windows is The Beave, pulling dresses for me to try on.

For a moment, the thought of running away crosses my mind. Taking off and just…leaving. Fleeing, getting away from all of this, but as the thought comes, it quickly washes away because that will do nothing to solve the problem. It will only trigger it more.

So with a cup of coffee in hand, a fake smile on my face, I walk through the doors of the bridal shop.

"Ah, there she is," The Beave says when she spots me. "My dear, look at your hair." Here come the insults. "It's so lovely." She walks up to me and strokes the long strands. "I would prefer you have an updo for the wedding, but this is quite appealing."

Color me shocked. Was not expecting that, and even though it is nice to avoid any snark, scowl, or insult from my future mother-in-law, it does nothing to curb my morose mood.

"Thank you," I say and then glance around the empty bridal shop. "Are we the only ones here?"

"Oh, I blocked off the shop for us so we won't be disturbed by any other people searching for a dress. I thought having the shop to ourselves could ensure we stay focused on what we're looking for."

We…funny how she uses that term about *my* dress.

"We do have at least three to find," she adds.

Oh, I forgot about that.

"Yes, a lot of shopping to do," I say as I look around one more time, just in case Breaker is here and I missed him.

"Now, where is Breaker so we can get started?" she asks.

Well, that confirms it. He's not here. Another dose of anxiety and depression rips through me.

"Oh, uh, something came up," I say. "He won't be able to make it."

The lie feels so lifeless coming out of me, I barely believe it myself, but it seems to appease The Beave because she snaps her stupid fingers and says, "Well then, let's get started. We'll be trying on ceremony dresses first. I had them pull classic silhouettes as well as elegant off-the-shoulder pieces."

"Great," I say, going through the motions.

"Right this way, Miss Fairweather-Fern," one of the shop assistants says.

"Please just call me Lia. If you need to add a *Miss* in there, *Miss Lia* is just fine. Using my whole name is a mouthful."

The assistant smiles at me and then leads me back to a very large dressing room where a few dresses have been hung, waiting to be tried on. Three very grotesque ballgown-shaped dresses, three slender-silhouette dresses—which look more like nightgowns than anything—and two mermaid-style dresses that look like they have absolutely no give.

"Here is a robe for you," the assistant says. "Why don't you get changed out of your clothes and dressed in the robe, and an attendant will come in and assist you?"

"Great. Thank you." When the door closes, I set my coffee and purse down on the provided table and then slip out of my shirt and pants. I'm not one to be naked in front of strangers, so I wore a pair of boy-short underwear that covers up a lot—I'm sure The Beave would be horrified—and my least revealing strapless bra.

I slip on the light pink silk robe, cinch it at the waist, and then I sit down in the chair and stare at the dresses.

I hate them.

All of them.

Too many embellishments.

Too slinky.

Too poofy.

Not enough space in the dress to walk.

They're nothing I would pick for myself.

I always thought I'd wear something simple with maybe a touch of lace, not these full, fabric-filled dresses that need a crane operator to get it on.

What is supposed to be a fun once-in-a-lifetime moment has quickly turned into a sad, bleak day that I'm sure will live forever in my mind as a dark memory, right along with the moment I found out my parents passed away.

I rest my head against the wall behind me and bring my coffee to my lips. I just want this to be over. I want it all to be over.

The planning.

The wedding.

The pain.

I want to be transported back to a time when everything was okay with Breaker, and I wasn't not so alone, but surrounded by loved ones. I want him at my side, telling jokes, making me laugh, and letting me know that no matter what, he'll always be there for me.

But he's not.

Not today.

Tears well in my eyes, and I quickly blink them back.

No, don't cry.

Please don't cry. Not here, not now.

Not in front of Brian's mom.

Knock. Knock.

Fuck. I blink the tears back some more and quickly dab at them. Maybe I can pass the watery eyes off as excitement for the dresses. With a heavy heart, I call out, "I'm ready."

The door opens, and I expect the assistant to walk through, but instead, Breaker steps in, absolutely stealing every ounce of oxygen from my lungs. His eyes connect with mine as he gently shuts the door behind him.

My heart races at the sight of him.

My emotions get the best of me.

And before I can stop myself, I let out a sob and then clutch my hand over my eyes as I cry.

"Shhhh," he says as he kneels in front of me and presses his hand to my cheek.

I slink down to the floor with him, and I wrap my hands around his waist, sinking into his chest and his comforting embrace.

"I thought…" I say through tears. "I thought you…you weren't coming."

He strokes my hair and holds me tightly. "I would never miss this, Lia."

"But…we haven't…talked." I pull away to look him in the eyes. He swipes at my tears with his thumbs.

"I thought we needed a second to gather ourselves." He strokes my cheek. "I didn't handle things right with you, and I thought that if I gave us a second, I could express what I've been feeling rather than blaming you for my problems."

"I don't want to talk about it," I say. "I just want to hold you."

He cups the back of my head as I go in for another hug, clinging to him desperately.

"I can't lose you, Breaker."

"You're not losing me, Lia. Never. I would never let that fucking happen."

"Promise?" I ask, insecurity so heavy in my voice that I can taste it.

"I promise you," he says with sincerity.

I sniff and say, "I ran into Birdy at the coffeehouse, and she said she was meeting up with you. I thought…I thought you ditched me for her."

"Never," he says softly while stroking my hair. "I had to give her some binoculars to practice with for our hike tomorrow."

"Really?" I ask as I lift to look him in the eyes.

"Yes, really. This is an important day, Lia; of course, I would be here for it."

"Thank you," I say softly as another wave of tears hits me.

He stands from the floor and grabs a box of tissues, only to sit back down with me. This time, he leans against my chair and pulls me to his side.

I wipe at my nose, and we just sit there in silence.

He's here. With me.

The thought rocks me, and once again, I tear up.

"What's going on in that head of yours?" he asks.

"Just grateful you're here. More grateful than you probably know."

"No matter what happens between us, Lia, I will always be there for you. Always. Okay?" I nod, and he presses a kiss to the top of my head before saying, "As much as I just want to sit here with you, I have to get back out there. The Beave is already pissed at me because I showed up late, and I don't want to make her madder."

"Don't leave," I say in a panic. "Help me into these dresses."

"Uh, don't you want an attendant to do that?"

I shake my head. "I'm so freaking raw right now, Breaker. I can barely breathe. I need you in here, with me, by my side. Please stay…"

CHAPTER 10
BREAKER

THOSE PLEADING GREEN EYES.

The tears falling over her cheeks.

The desperation in her expression. I feel useless.

I don't think I've ever seen Lia like this. Ever. Which could only mean one thing—she's not in a good headspace at all, and no way am I going to leave her to herself.

"Of course, I can stay," I say as I stand and pull her up with me.

Knock. Knock.

"Miss Lia," the attendant says. "Are you ready to try on some dresses?"

Lia looks up at me with a terrified expression, so I go to the door and part it open. "Actually, I'm going to help her into her dresses, if you don't mind. Can you pull a few simple gowns with some of that lace detail on them? Especially the one that is up front on the mannequin."

"Yes, of course, Mr. Cane."

I shut the door and turn back to Lia. "If I'm going to wiggle you in and out of these things, then we're going to put you in dresses that are actually your style. None of this poofy, embellished bullshit. I'm no expert, but these are atrocious." That makes her smile, but it's not the full kind of smile I'm used to. It's a blip. A blip will have to do.

"They're not great," she says, walking up to them. She picks up one of the silky ones and says, "This is the same fabric as the robe I'm wearing. People would be able to see every lump and bump on my body."

"Well, for one, you don't have lumps and bumps besides the two on your chest, and secondly, I'm not sure those are the kind of dresses you wear undergarments with."

She cringes. "I need undergarments. I'm not one to show nipple to a crowd of people."

"Only a select few?" I joke around.

"Obviously," she says before leaning against the wall of the dressing room.

"What are you doing?" we hear The Beave ask the attendant. "Why are you taking in more dresses? We haven't even seen her try on the first ones."

Lia's eyes plead with me, so I excuse myself from the dressing room and walk up to The Beave, who's sitting in a chair with an untouched glass of champagne in her hand.

"Mrs. Beaver, could I possibly have a word with you?" I ask, keeping my tone neutral.

"Well, of course," she says as she stands, and together, we walk off to the side, out of earshot. If anything, this woman likes to uphold appearances. She doesn't want anyone to hear a conversation they shouldn't. "What on earth is happening in that dressing room?"

"The dresses that were chosen are beautiful, but they're not quite Lia's style." I lower my voice some more and say, "She's very upset right now, and I don't want to cause a scene, so I thought we could try on some dresses that suit her more."

"Upset? For what reason? This should be fun."

"I agree. That's why we shouldn't dictate what she wears and be happy for what she thinks looks beautiful on her."

The Beave's eyes narrow. "Are you saying that I'm trying to be too controlling?"

Whatever gave you that idea?

Insert giant eye roll.

"Not at all," I reply with a smile. "I know you're trying to be helpful, but I say let's give Lia a moment to pick, and then if she can't find anything she likes, we offer suggestions. Does that work?"

"I suppose."

"Great." I hold my arm out to her, and she slips her hand against my forearm so I can escort her back to her seat. "I apologize for being late, by the way. I had a meeting that held me up."

"You are a busy man. How is the lawsuit?"

"Still confidential but should be brushed away soon. Huxley has it all under control."

"I would assume he does."

I help her take a seat and then ask, "Do you need me to get you anything, or are you good right now?"

"Quite well, thank you."

"Okay, then I'm going to go help Lia. We'll be right out."

I go back to the dressing room, knock, and then enter, only to find Lia standing in the middle of the room, wearing an off-the-shoulder cream lace dress that accentuates her waist and gently flows to the ground.

Holy.

Fucking.

Shit.

My mouth goes dry as my eyes slowly work their way up her torso, to her neckline, and then to her face and…something hits me. Something so strong, so foreign that I don't know how to categorize it. Like this overwhelming sense of…breathlessness. For a moment, my heart actually stopped beating, and the world stopped spinning, and everything was on pause as she came into view.

"What do you think?" she asks as the attendant exits the dressing room, leaving me alone with Lia.

What feels like a million butterflies take flight in my stomach as I attempt to put words to what's going on in my head.

"Is it bad?" she asks as she turns toward the mirror to look at herself, revealing a low cut, showing off her slender back. My eyes drag down to where the fabric hits just above the curve of her ass. "I think it's kind of whimsical, but do you think it's too much? It was the one that called out to me the most." She turns back around again, and her stunning eyes plead with me to say something. "You hate it."

I shake my head.

Holy fuck do I NOT hate it.

There's nothing to hate about it.

It's... Jesus Christ...she's...she's fucking gorgeous.

Swallowing hard, I say, "No, I don't hate it. You look...fuck, you look stunning, Ophelia." My words sound ragged, untamed, and unpolished, like something is stuck in my throat, and I can't quite get it out.

The prettiest fucking smile I've ever seen crosses her lips as she says, "Really?"

I grip the back of my neck as I give her another once-over. "Yeah, you look—" I swallow hard. Just...fuck. She looks so good, so fucking gorgeous that my mouth keeps watering, my heart is beating a mile a minute, and I want to just...reach out and touch her. "Wow," I answer. "Just... really fucking beautiful."

"You're blushing," she says.

I can feel the heat in my cheeks.

"Yeah, I just, uh, wasn't expecting to walk in here and see you in a dress."

Or to lose my breath.

Or to feel this urge to...fuck me, to kiss her.

That's what it is. That's what this heavy, foggy feeling is in my chest.

The butterflies.

The unintelligible thoughts in my head.

The desire pulsing up my legs.

The thought of kissing her consumes me, and I've *never* had that thought before, not since the first night I met her. It's like those ten years have rushed back in a fury, like a snapshot of time unfolding in a blink of an eye, taking me all the way back to the moment I ran into her in the hallway. Where I first saw those perfectly placed freckles of hers and the confusion in her expression.

Where her eyes fixated on me for the first time through her purple-rimmed glasses.

When the uneasy yet confident side of her personality shone bright.

I thought she was so fucking beautiful.

So funny.

So charming.

So real.

And then I found out how smart she was, how she had all the same likes and interests as I did. Throughout that night as we played Scrabble, I kept thinking I was going to ask her out when all was said and done, but then…she asked to be friends. She *needed* to find a friend. Instead of acting on my initial reaction, I pushed it away, only for it to perform a full-frontal attack on me when I was least expecting it.

Right now.

In this fucking moment.

She turns back toward the mirror, and I catch her gaze finding mine in the reflection. "Should I show her?" she asks, her voice laced with insecurity. "I don't want her to hate it."

"I don't care what she says. We're getting that dress," I say, my voice coming out more breathless than I want it to.

"But it's the first one. Isn't that a bad sign? Shouldn't I try on more?"

I shake my head. "No, sometimes, you just know." I wet my lips. "And this dress, Lia, this one is for you."

She shyly smiles and then turns around again and walks up to me. I watch her every step, my body stiffening with every inch she nears. And as she presses her hand to my chest, my stomach bottoms out, and my legs tremble beneath me. "Thank you for being here, Breaker. I don't think you will ever know how much this means to me."

"No, uh, problem," I say, swallowing again.

She stands on her toes and presses the lightest of kisses to my cheek. Even though it means nothing other than friendship to Lia, to me, it feels like she just branded me and marked me as hers for eternity.

And then, without another word, she opens the door and shows The Beave her dress, leaving me in a state of upheaval.

What the fuck just happened?

Breaker: Hey, do you think you could meet me for a cup of coffee in like ten minutes or sooner or whenever? I just need to talk, and I don't want to talk to my brothers because they're going to give me shit. I need someone neutral.

Banner: Color me intrigued. Want to come over to my place? Just in case you need privacy?

Breaker: That would be perfect. I'm driving over now.

Hands on the steering wheel, I keep my eyes on the road as I work my way across town to Banner's apartment, which is just ten minutes away from where I live.

I met Banner through Ryot Bisley, his brother. Ryot and Banner both came up with this great idea called The Jock Report—a social media conglomerate for everything sports where the athletes get to talk to their fans one-on-one. When Ryot told JP and Huxley about the idea, they immediately wanted to invest because they knew it was going to be huge. And it has been. Ryot and Banner, who were living in Chicago at the time— Ryot is a retired third baseman from the Chicago Bobbies—moved out here to California, where they opened an office and have quickly taken the sports world by storm.

I got to know Banner on a more personal level and realized we're pretty similar. Although he is a bit of a player, whereas I, apparently, haven't needed to play around. But we do both like computers and have built our own. We also determined that our brothers like to gang up on us whenever they get the chance, so we've formed a younger-brother alliance. Talking to him about what's on my mind will be perfect because he knows what the wrath of an older brother can do to you.

I turn right onto his street and then see an open parking spot right in front of his apartment building. Must be my lucky day—if that's what you want to call it.

Once parked, I hop out of my car, lock up, and head straight to his apartment. I hate showing up empty-handed, but when it's last minute, there's not much I can do about that.

When I reach his apartment, I give it a knock, and I hear him call out, "It's open."

Pushing through his front door, I spot him in the kitchen with two bottles of beer in hand. "Sounded like a beer kind of moment, am I right?"

"Really fucking right," I reply.

He nods toward his balcony. "Let's sit outside."

Banner has a really nice place. It consumes the entire top floor of his building with floor-to-ceiling windows, a massive open floor plan—more space than one person needs—and a large wraparound balcony. It's probably the type of apartment I'd live in if I wasn't living next to Lia.

I follow him out to the balcony, through his black-framed pocket sliding glass door, and then sit at his outdoor dining set under a black and white striped umbrella.

"I know I've only been here twice, but I don't think I'll ever get over your place," I say.

"Yeah, I feel pretty lucky. Although Ryot keeps trying to get me to move out to Malibu with him and Myla. Not ready for that yet. I love the beach, but out there, it almost feels like I'm settling down, and I'm not at that point in my life just yet."

I chuckle. "Forgive me if I'm wrong, but aren't you seeing someone?"

He drags his hand over his face in pain. "Don't get me started on that. This gathering is about you, not me."

"We can save some time at the end to dig deep into your nonrelationship."

"Ehh, that's okay. I think I'm good." He takes a sip of his beer and says, "So what's going on? Your text read *desperate need of help*, and if anything, I like a good story, so tell me."

I take a sip of my beer as well—actually more like a gulp—and say, "You know Lia is getting married, right?"

"Yeah, and you're the man of honor, right?"

"Right." I look out toward the skyline, unsure how to do this. "Hell, I don't think what I'm going to say will make a lot of sense. It will sound like a bunch of rambling, but I don't know how to talk about this without rambling."

"Good thing you came to me. I'm good at deciphering rambling. Lay it on me."

"Well, to begin with, I was shocked when Lia told me she was engaged. She and Brian, they, I don't know, have a different relationship. I feel like when you're dating someone, you're all in, right? Like, you want to spend as much time with them as possible."

Banner nods in agreement. "Yeah, I know that feeling."

"Well, they aren't like that. They can go a few nights without seeing each other, and I always thought that was weird, so when she said he proposed, and she said yes, I was truly shocked."

"Yeah, I would be too."

"And then she told me they're getting married in five weeks, well, more like four weeks now. And I don't know, this sense of panic consumed me. I couldn't quite place it other than I was afraid to lose her."

"That's natural since you guys are so close." Banner takes a sip of his beer.

"Right," I say, gesturing my hand toward him. "That's what I thought too. We are so close that I'm worried about losing that friendship. And I don't get along with her fiancé as much as I probably should, so I made an effort to reach out to him and solve that issue because I didn't want anything weird between us, anything that he could use against me so she doesn't hang out as much."

"Very smart."

"But then he ended up setting me up with this girl Birdy. On a double date."

Banner winces. "That smells like a whole bunch of awkward."

"It was. Very awkward, but Birdy turned out to be really cool and funny, and we've hung out a few times since."

"Okay, any chemistry there?"

"That's the problem." I lean back in my chair and take a sip of my beer. "I've kissed her twice now, and although the thought of being intimate with someone was appealing, each time I kissed her, it wasn't exactly what I was expecting. It just felt normal. Like every other woman I've ever kissed, and I don't know, I feel like there should be a feeling that's more than normal, right?"

"If you want to get down to it, yeah. When you kiss someone, someone you think you could date or be with, there should be a spark. Especially that first kiss. The first kiss tells you everything you need to know."

"There wasn't any spark. Not even a blip." I sigh heavily. "And then... today."

"Now we're getting to the good stuff," Banner jokes. I don't mind because he's keeping it really light, which I appreciate.

"Lia and I got in a fight two nights ago, and today was wedding dress shopping day. She told me not to come because of the fight, and there was no way I'd let her do that alone, so I showed up, and the relief on her face was something I wasn't expecting. And she clung to me like I was her lifesaver."

"Uh-huh…" Banner drags out.

I press my lips together and finally say, "Well, when I saw her in her dress…" I shake my head. "Dude, I swear to God it was an out-of-body experience. I don't think I've ever felt anything like it. My mouth went dry, I started to sweat, but I was cold at the same time. I couldn't breathe, but my heart was beating so hard that I thought my chest would explode. And then…" I look away. "When she made eye contact with me, it was like a million butterflies took flight in my stomach, and I swear to you, at that moment, I had this overwhelming need to kiss her. Like, it was pulling me to the point that I almost did it. I've never felt that way, ever, besides the first day I ever met her, and now, well, I'm totally fucked in the head, and I don't know what's going on."

Banner slowly nods his head, taking it all in. He sips his beer and then sets the glass bottle on the table. "I'll tell you what's going on." He looks me in the eyes. "You're in love with your best friend, and you just finally realized it."

"Come on, dude," I say, groaning. "That's what my brothers would have said."

"Because they're right, and I know you don't want to hear it, but why do you feel like you don't have a spark when you kiss other women? It's because deep down, you know they're not Lia. These weird out-of-body feelings you're having are because the woman you love is getting married in four weeks, and you're panicking about it."

"But…"

"No *buts*, man. Face the facts: you love her, and the sooner you admit that to yourself, the better."

I drag my hand over my forehead, his words stabbing me in the stomach, in the chest, racking up my anxiety.

Is he right?

Do I love her, and I'm just realizing it now?

My mind conjures up the image of her in her dress and how I felt, how I wanted to be the man who kissed her in it, how I couldn't take my eyes off her, how I felt absolutely sick knowing that dress wasn't meant for me but for Brian instead.

"Jesus fucking Christ," I say as I look up at Banner. "Fuck, I think I like her."

Banner shakes his head. "Nah, man. You love her. End of discussion."

I pace my living room, Banner's words on replay in my head.

I try to tell myself he's not right.

That it's conjecture that seems like it could be spot on, but really isn't.

That maybe I'm just reading all these feelings wrong.

But every time I hear her move around in her apartment, my skin breaks out into a clammy sweat, because I'm pretty sure…Banner is right.

After I left his place, I came back to mine, where I opened another beer, and I've walked circles around my apartment. Never stopping, just pacing, trying to get a grip on these feelings, trying to convince myself that Banner is wrong, that I'm wrong, that all of this is fucking wrong.

Panic.

Nausea.

Worry.

It's swirling around, making me feel crazy. Making me uncomfortable. Making me think things I shouldn't be thinking like…

What if I had kissed her in the dressing room? What would she have done?

What if I marched over to her apartment right now and told her how I'm feeling?

What if I pathetically asked her to reconsider the wedding?

Knock. Knock.

Oh fuck.

That has to be her. No one else visits me.

Unsure of what to do, I clench my sweaty palms and say, "Uh, yeah?"

"Breaker? It's me. Open up."

"Oh, uh…Lia, is that you?" I even roll my eyes at myself.

"Yes, Breaker. What are you doing? Open up."

"Ha, sorry," I call out, even though I don't move. "Um, just give me a second." I spin around in a circle, trying to figure out what to do as if something can be done.

Nothing, you dipshit, nothing can be done. It's not like you can take a washcloth and soap to your feelings and scrub them away quickly. Doesn't work like that.

Face the facts. This is going to be awkward for you.

Reluctantly and with heavy steps, I head over to the door, open it, and then lean on the edge, attempting to look like the epitome of a casual man NOT in love with his best friend. "Hey there, uh, how are you? Doing good? Wow, the heat today, am I right?"

Her brow curls up in question. "Why are you being weird?"

"I'm not being weird, I'm just…uh, striking up a conversation. Am I not allowed to talk about the weather with my best friend? Anyway, is there anything I can help you with?"

With a skeptical look on her face, she says, "Can I stay here tonight?"

"Uhhhh, what now?" I ask, blinking a few times.

"Brian left for San Jose tonight for an emergency meeting with one of his clients, and he won't be home until Sunday. I'm just, I'm not feeling super great, and I don't want to be alone."

"Ah, I see." I nod slowly.

"So can I stay the night?"

Ha. Spend the night here with me? That seems like an absolute disaster waiting to happen. I'm barely hanging on by a thread, and the cure to all of that is a temptation I can't consume.

What could I possibly say that would communicate *I'm pretty sure I love you and therefore you can't be here*?

There's nothing.

Absolutely nothing.

So…

"Of course," I squeak out. "Yeah, you know, because you've done that before. You've stayed the night, so that shouldn't be weird."

Her brows narrow even more. "Why are you all fidgety and sweating on your upper lip?"

"Sweating?" I wipe my mouth. "That's not sweat. Probably just left-over residue from my drink."

She eyes me suspiciously. "You're acting weird, Breaker."

"You know, I had a beer." I pat my stomach. "Might have been an off-brand beer, probably isn't settling well. Maybe I should just let you get to sleep. The guest room is made up." I move to the side so she can enter the apartment. "Go ahead, make yourself at home."

"I don't want to go to bed yet. It's only eight."

Feels like freaking eleven at night after the day I've had.

"Huh, well, guess that might be a touch early." I let out a long whistle. "I guess we could hang out."

"Yeah, I was hoping we could." She clutches her arms around her waist, and I realize she's sad. And if I'm sure of anything, it's that I care about Lia more than anything, more than anyone, so my instincts kick in.

"Everything okay?" I ask, putting aside that I have feelings for my best friend, and now I don't know how to act around her.

"No." Her eyes brim with tears. "I'm not okay at all."

Shit.

Time to set aside my feelings and focus on her.

I pull her into my apartment and shut the door behind her before bringing her over to the couch and taking a seat.

"What's going on?"

"I'm sad." She swipes at her nose. "Today was surreal, a moment I thought I would share with my mom one day, and the fact that she wasn't there, it's just killing me, Breaker. I keep wondering, would she have liked the dress I picked out? Would she have cried? Would she have taken a picture with me celebrating the moment?"

"Yes," I say flatly. "Yes, to all of those things."

"I love that dress," she says. "But a part of me just feels empty about everything, and I wish I could be happy about getting married, but I have my doubts, I have my worries."

"About Brian?" I ask.

"I don't know," she answers quietly. "I love him, but I feel like my entire life has been strained ever since he proposed. I don't feel right, not like myself. I feel trapped in this little box of what's expected of me, and now, I think I'm starting to lose my mind over it." Her eyes meet mine, and she says, "When we were fighting, I had no one to turn to. Not a parent, not a friend, and I didn't want to tell Brian because he probably would have used it as fodder as to why I shouldn't hang out with you, despite him saying he's okay with our relationship." She glances down at her hands. "I'm starting to realize how much I lost when my parents died." Her eyes well up again, and she leans back on the couch, crying.

I don't know what to say, because I agree with her—she lost so much when she lost her parents. I think she settled with Brian because he was there at the right time, but how the hell am I supposed to say that to her?

She's already going through a rough time, and clearly, my motives have been skewed ever since my realization this morning, so instead of saying something, I say nothing and just listen to her cry while I hold her hand.

After what feels like an hour, she turns toward me and says, "I just want to go to bed."

"Okay." I stand and pull her up with me. "Let me get you situated in the guest room."

She shakes her head. "No, I don't want to be alone. Can I sleep with you?"

That would be a hard no.

Very hard no.

No way can I let the woman I love sleep in my bed while she belongs to another man. Nope, that's asking for trouble.

"Uh, don't you think that might be a little inappropriate?" I ask gently, trying not to rock the boat on the emotions.

"We've done it before. Why would it be any different now?" she asks.

Very valid point.

Because we have done it before, so…what's changed?

Well, you love her, that's changed, and you're still trying to sort through those untimely feelings.

She's engaged, that's what is different. That's a sound excuse. And will save me from utter embarrassment and the possible agony of sleeping in the same bed with her.

Yup, let's go with the engaged thing.

"Well, you're engaged now." The moment the words slip out of my mouth, I watch her shoulders droop and her lashes flutter down in disappointment.

It's like a fucking knife to the heart, twisting and gutting me as I watch her slowly turtle in on herself. *Yup, you did that, you ass.*

"But," I find myself saying like a dipshit, "if that doesn't bother you, then sure."

Her eyes float up to mine. "It doesn't."

I plaster on the fakest smile I can muster. "Okay, well, great. Let me just lock up and get ready. You know where your toothbrush is."

Yup, we've done this enough that she has a toothbrush here.

It started back in college when she'd sleep on the futon in my dorm, and I'd sleep on my bed. We'd spend countless hours talking until one of us passed out.

When we graduated and our beds got bigger, we'd just share a bed and fall asleep facing each other. The next morning, we'd order donuts, drink coffee, and play dominoes.

But this feels different.

My body feels itchy with her around.

My mind feels like mush, like I can't conjure up the right thing to say.

So this should be fun. *thumbs up*

I pour out the rest of my beer and lock up my apartment. Then I wait a few seconds in the living room, mentally preparing myself. Sure, it's the same bed, but it's not like we'll be touching.

It's not like I'll be sharing a pillow with her.

There will be at least two feet of neutral zone between us, and if I'm good at anything, it's respecting the neutral zone. I'm a gentleman, after all.

With a touch more confidence, I make my way to the bedroom, where I find Lia sitting on the edge of the bed, wearing one of my T-shirts.

Fucking…great.

The sleeves swallow up her shoulders while the shirt extends to her midthigh, covering enough, but making me sweat from the mere thought that her naked body is under that fabric. My fabric.

"I borrowed a shirt. I hope that's okay."

"Yup," I squeak and then clear my throat. "Sorry, don't know why that came out like that." I awkwardly chuckle, and then in a deep voice, I say, "Yup, all good." When she just lightly smiles, I point my thumb toward the bathroom. "Just going to get ready, and then we can do all the sleeping because I love sleep. It is truly the natural medicine we all need in life."

"Are you okay?" she asks with an inquisitive look.

"Great. Real great." I fist-pump the air. "Sleepover. Huzzah."

Huzzah?

Jesus Christ, Breaker.

Why don't you just go stick your head in a microwave after that?

I slap my hands together. "So yeah. Brushing teeth now."

I turn on my heel, head into the bathroom, and shut the door.

I grip the counter, glance up into the mirror to see how truly pathetic I am, and that's when I spot her pink lace bra hanging on one of the hooks behind me.

Oh hell.

My muscles contract, creating a tangled, claustrophobic sensation that squeezes me so hard that all air escapes my lungs.

Panic. It pierces through me because, yeah, that's her fucking bra.

Her bra that's probably warm from wearing it all day.

Her bra that cups and props her tits up.

Her bra that makes me wonder just how fucking good she probably looks in it.

Clearing my throat, I say, "Uh, Lia, you left your bra hanging in here."

"I know. I didn't want to fold it," she calls out.

"Okay, but why isn't it on?" I ask stupidly. I know why it's not on. Who wants to wear a fucking bra to bed? Not me.

I hear her step up to the door and then open it. She pokes her head in and says, "I never wear a bra to bed. Breaker, I've hung my bra there before."

Ehhh, has she, though? I think I would have noticed, especially with the cup size banging a hole in my brain, that she has big tits. She has big tits.

"Are you sure you're okay?" she asks, her hand falling to my chest.

"Whoa, hey there, watch out, heh, heh." I let out a breathy laugh. "Hands to ourselves, let's remember that."

"What?" she asks, her face drenched in confusion.

"Um." I swallow hard. "You just startled me because your hand was cold."

"You're wearing a shirt."

I glance down at my chest. "Oh yeah, well, the fabric must be thin.

Brrr, maybe go warm up those frigid paws of yours; don't want to catch a cold."

"It's the middle of summer." She takes a step back. "If you don't want me to stay over because you have something else going on, then just tell me, Breaker."

"No, I have nothing else going on."

What are you doing, you moron? That was your out!

"Okay, well, then I'll just let you get ready for bed."

She moves back toward the bedroom, and I shut the bathroom door behind her.

Jesus Christ.

Get it together, man. You're better than this. You're smoother than this. You're Breaker fucking Cane. Stop acting like a total nitwit, strap on a goddamn pair, and be the best friend this woman needs.

And for fuck's sake, stop embarrassing yourself.

I take the next few minutes to go to the bathroom, brush my teeth, and create a mental wall that is completely impenetrable. Mark my words, when I slip into that bed, there will be no—and I mean NO—romantic thoughts of my best friend. Platonic. That's what we're going for. All the platonic-ness one can muster.

Is that even a word?

Doesn't matter. That's what's happening.

Because if anything, I'm a Cane, and Canes are born with the crafty ability to hold strong, to not buckle, and to rely on their mental fortitude to get them through any situation.

There. Pep talk complete.

I exit the bathroom, turn off the light, and head over to the bed where Lia is already resting under the covers, her beautiful silky hair fanned out against the dark of my pillowcase like a fucking...NO!

No thoughts of any fanning hair and how it's a beautiful contrast against the navy pillowcase.

No goddamn poetic sonnets based around how the moonlight looks on her Irish alabaster skin.

Nothing.

Focus, Cane.

I move toward my side of the bed and ask, "Uh, you comfortable?"

"Always. I love your bed," she says as she snuggles in even closer.

"Good," I answer as I slip under the covers and turn off the light, letting the moon illuminate the space through the sheer gray curtains hanging over the window.

I turn toward her in bed, where she scoots closer, her knee knocking with mine.

Watch it, lady. Distance, maintain distance.

"You're really jittery tonight," she says. "Is it something I said or did?"

Yes, you just exist. That's the problem.

"No," I answer as I stare into her beautiful eyes. "Maybe I'm just restless, you know, with not having a job at the moment."

"Are you sure? Because you've been weird ever since we left the dress shop."

Because I couldn't stop thinking how goddamn beautiful you are.

Wait, is that putting up a wall? No, it's not. Then again, when she stares at me with those large mossy eyes, I can't seem to switch my brain back to protective mode.

"Stubbed my toe in there," I say out of the blue.

"What?" she asks.

"Uh, yeah. Stubbed my toe and haven't felt right ever since."

"You're being stupid," she says while playfully pushing at my chest. "Is this your way of trying to make me feel better?"

"Yes," I say, almost out of desperation. "Yup, you know me, always joking around."

"Well, I appreciate the attempt, but I think I just need to get some sleep and rest my mind."

"Yeah, might be best." I smile. "Well, good night."

"Night, Breaker."

She turns away from me, and I mentally let out a large sigh. Well, thank God for that. Not sure what I would have done if she wanted to continue to talk. Now, I can just rest here in peace and not worry about staring into her eyes, getting lost in her late-night voice, or even thinking about—

She scoots backward.

Uh, what is she doing?

Then some more.

Excuse me, you're getting kind of close.

Her ass bumps into my leg.

Warning! Warning! She's way too close.

"Whatcha got going on there?" I ask her, my body stiff as a board.

"Can you hold me, Breaker?"

Absolutely. Not.

Has she lost her goddamn mind?

Hold her?

In the same bed?

Like…she wants us to *gulp* spoon or something. What the hell has gotten into her, and why now? Why, on the day that I realize I love this girl? Is this some sick joke that I'm unaware of? Some prank that I'm caught up in? If so, it's not fucking funny.

No way on God's green earth am I about to spoon Lia.

"Please, Breaker. I could really use the comfort."

Well…fuck…me.

"Um, do you think Brian would like to know that I held you at night?"

"I don't know."

"Yes, you do," I say. "He would hate it."

"It's not like it matters. I'm not cheating on him. You're my best friend, my family, the only person who can truly make me feel at peace. If you were a girl, I'd ask you to do the same."

"You would?" I ask.

"Of course. I used to spoon with my mom all the time."

Ah, so she sees me as a motherly figure. I can't hear that enough.

"It's okay if you don't want to," she says in such a defeated tone that I can actually feel my heart twist in my chest.

"No, I can," I reply quickly. "Just, you know, checking all of my bases is all." I lift my arm and hover it over her for a few seconds. Do I just... cuddle her? Or should I just lightly drape my burly man arm over the curve of her waist to make it seem like we're spooning, but in reality, I'm just using her as a human armrest?

The human armrest thing feels very rewarding, so I gently place my forearm on her waist, my hand extended straight out and lifting the blankets.

Eh, that doesn't work, so I lift my arm again and hover. I adjust, touch down on her waist, and notice the same thing.

Nope, back to hover.

I don't know where to drape. Not over her boobs; those, as we found out from her hanging bra, are loose and wild at the moment.

There's her stomach, but is that too intimate?

Which leaves her pelvic area, and well, not so sure that's a great idea either. Hand-to-pelvis doesn't scream platonic, more like one stroke away from legs spread and loud moans.

Luckily, I don't have to debate it too long because she lowers my arm around her stomach and scoots in closer so her body is plastered against mine.

Right up against me.

Back to chest.

Butt to...*gulp* crotch.

Sweet Jesus, man...do not get a goddamn boner.

Penis, do you hear me? This is not a moment to defy me. Be a good fucking listener.

*Think of flaccid things. FLACCID. Flaccid, floppy, dangly, pendulous...
limp. There you go.*

OH, I could think of things that are so repulsive that I'd rather hurl my
head into my trash can than think about.

Ahhh, I know.

I squeeze my eyes shut and conjure up images of JP and his dirty
pigeon friend. *What's its name?*

Cocoon?

Carl?

"Clementine?" I accidentally say out loud.

"What?" Lia whispers.

"Uh, Clementine," I repeat, for God knows what reason.

"Like the fruit?"

"Sure," I answer.

"Why are you saying that?"

"Can't think of JP's pigeon friend."

"Kazoo?"

"Ohhhhh, right." I smile to myself. "Kazoo."

"Why are you thinking about JP and Kazoo?"

So I don't get a boner.

*Because your ass is pressed right up against my pelvis, and if I even move
a little, I know the friction will be enough to give me a semi.*

"He was talking about him earlier today, and I couldn't think of his name."

"Oh...well, it's Kazoo."

"Yup, logged that away."

She places her hand on top of mine and says, "I think I need to change,
Breaker."

Change her clothes? Into what?

She's barely wearing anything as it is.

My mind floats to her in lingerie, walking toward me, sexy as shit with
her tits...NO!

Kazoo, think of Kazoo and the way JP blows kisses at the damn thing. Revolting.

Satisfied, I say, "Do you need pants or something?"

"No, not that kind of change. I mean, like my life needs to change."

That snaps me out of my *I'm in love with my best friend* fog. "Change? What do you mean *change*? You're perfect as you are, Lia."

"I feel like I'm in a rut, that I've been going through the motions and not truly allowing myself to experience the things I need to experience."

"What do you mean?"

She twists so she's on her back, and my hand rests directly on her stomach. Her head tilts to the side just enough so our eyes connect in the dim light of the room.

"Ever since my parents passed away, I don't think I've given myself a chance to live. I mean, I'm about to get married in four weeks, and it feels almost like a death sentence rather than a thrilling event. And I'm not sure if that's because I'm mourning my parents or The Beave is ruining the process, but I'm not having fun. I want to have fun. I want to do things I've never done before. I want to live a life my parents wanted me to live, and I don't think I've been doing that."

My thumb smooths over her stomach, the touch intended to comfort her. "What are some things you want to do?"

"I don't know," she says quietly. "But I think there needs to be a change."

"If you feel that way, I will one hundred percent support you," I say, and she shifts so she's facing me now, her face only inches from mine. Her shirt bunches up around my hand at her waist.

"You will?"

"Of course, Lia, but I need you to know, right now, as you are, you're perfect, okay?" The way she's looking at me, her proximity, and the feelings pumping through me rapidly give me my voice. "There's absolutely nothing I would change. Not your heart and the way you care for the people around you. Not your mind and how you can shift from sassy to intelligent in seconds. Not your soul and the way you carry your scars with pride." I grip her shirt and repeat, "You are perfect."

Her mouth parts, her plump lips glistening.

Her eyes widen with each breath she takes.

And it might be my imagination, but I can feel her draw even closer, leaving no space between us.

In the root of my stomach, this deep, twisting, agonizing feeling spreads through me to the tips of my limbs, this urge to touch her, to slip my hand under her shirt and feel her skin, to bring my mouth closer to hers where I'd see if she's tempted just as much as I am.

"Th-thank you," she says finally, her voice soft and sweet.

I wet my lips as I attempt to control my breathing, my hand twisting in the fabric of her shirt just enough that I can feel her warm skin on my wrist. "You don't need to thank me, Lia. It's just facts."

"Still, I needed to hear that. So thank you."

"Anything for you," I say as I glance down at her lips and then back up at her eyes.

What I wouldn't do for those lips right now.

Just one kiss. Just one taste.

From the corner of my eye, I catch her chest rising and falling harder as she moves in an inch.

Fuck me.

I loosen my grip on her shirt and, instead, rest my warm palm against her exposed hip. I find the seam of her underwear and gently press my index finger against it as my blood burns for more. *You're so close, just... just slip your finger under the seam, see what she does. Gauge her reaction.*

My pulse thunders as I glide my finger along the seam, my mind telling me to stop, my heart screaming at me for more.

I want her so fucking bad that it's painful. When I gaze into her eyes, I don't see anything other than admiration. It's a fucking look from her

I will always cherish, I will live for, because it shows me just how much she trusts me.

Even as I'm bordering on crossing a line, she trusts me.

So I slip my finger softly under the seam of her underwear, right on her hip.

She smiles.

My cock springs forward and all the blood rushes down my body as she reaches her hand between us and cups my cheek. Her thumb slides across my scruff, and I freeze in place as she moves in closer.

Fuck. She wants this. Right?

She wants this just as much as me.

I remove my hand and slide it to her back, where her shirt has lifted so I can feel her warm skin at the tip of my pinky. I'm so fucking tempted to slide my fingers down her back, under her underwear, and grip her ass.

But I want to see where she goes with this. I want to see what she wants from me. So I brace myself, waiting, not stopping the way she's closing in on me, but welcoming it because, fuck, I want this.

I should care that she's engaged.

I should care that we're best friends and this could ruin everything.

But I don't because I want her lips. I want to taste them. I want to see if the thought of how she tastes and feels in my arms is just as good as I think it is.

Her mouth grows closer and closer.

My veins feel electric.

My muscles tighten.

My breath seizes in my chest.

And then she presses her lips…to my cheek before saying, "Good night, Breaker." Then she turns back around, snuggles into her pillow, and that's that.

Nothing else.

I squeeze my eyes shut for being such a goddamn fool, for even wanting more.

She's fucking engaged, you moron. Best you remember that.

CHAPTER 11
LIA

THE APARTMENT IS QUIET. BREAKER is still in bed sleeping while I sit on his couch, coffee in hand, staring out the window at the view, the same view I have from my apartment. Yet, I feel more comfortable here.

More at home.

It's why I wanted to come over last night. I felt so out of control, and I needed that comfort.

And that's exactly what I got.

Despite our fight this week and things being awkward between us—that whole *I stubbed my toe* thing was really weird—I can still rely on him. He held me last night, told me how much he appreciated me, and didn't let me feel lonely for even a second.

I take a sip of my coffee and then glance down at my list. With my mind racing, I woke up early, came out here, and started writing down the things I wanted to do before I got married.

I wanted to be thoughtful in my checklist, not just write things down to write them down. So I've narrowed it down to five items.

Do something that makes me feel pretty.

Create a circle of trust.

Spend a day saying yes.

Stand up for myself.

Follow my heart.

I stare down at the list, a large smile on my face as I realize this is exactly what I need to get out of this rut, this dark pit I feel like I've been sinking into. And I already have some ideas on how to check these off.

"What do you think, Mom and Dad?" I whisper. "Think this is a way to jump-start my life again?"

A warm sense of comfort rushes through me. It might all be in my head, but I almost feel like I can sense their approval.

"Good morning," Breaker says as he steps into the living room, scratching his chest and looking like he needs at least two more hours of sleep. "How long have you been up?"

"About an hour. There's coffee warming if you want some. The raspberry kind of course."

"As if you need to say anything, I could smell it from the bedroom." He stumbles over to the kitchen, his feet scraping against the tile as he makes it to the coffeepot and pulls down the Jack Skellington mug I got him one year for Christmas. It was one of his favorite movies growing up. Since buying presents for a billionaire is incredibly hard, I decided to go the sentimental route. He uses it often. Once he pours his coffee, he turns toward me and nods at my paper and pen. "What are you writing?"

"The next greatest novel. It's about a dragon who slays…on the dance floor and out on the battlefield."

He sips his coffee and then says, "Does the dragon dress in drag?"

"Obviously."

"I'd read the hell out of that, especially if it's as riveting as *Lovers, Not Brothers.*" He walks over to where I'm sitting on the couch and takes a seat as well. "Does your dragon have a name?"

"Anita Sparkle Claw," I answer.

"She sounds feisty."

"With one touch of her talon, you're transported into ye old ages full of glitter battles and fleshy sword fights."

He chuckles. "Fleshy sword fights, huh? I like the sound of that. Very intriguing."

"I'll be sure to send you the rough draft."

With a smile over the lip of his coffee mug, he nudges my leg and says, "Seriously, what are you writing?"

"A list."

He circles his hand. "Care to elaborate?"

"Well, I've been thinking about how I haven't been feeling right, and to get myself out of this rut, I came up with a list of things to do before I get married."

"Like a bucket list?"

"Yes, but this could be called the knot list."

"Knot list?" he asks, his eyebrow lifting in that cute way of his.

"You know, instead of kicking the bucket, I'm tying the knot."

"Aah, I'm following you. Okay, so what's on your list?" I hand it over to him, and I watch as he reads it over, slowly nodding. "Well, for one, you're already pretty, so no need to worry about that."

I roll my eyes and steal the list from him. "I want to do something that makes me *feel* pretty. Something different, and I have an idea. Want to go with me?"

"Go with you where?"

"To check off the first item on my list. I want to go today. Get this ball rolling."

"Oh," he says and then winces. "I, uh, I have that date with Birdy today."

"I forgot about that." I glance to the side, disappointment heavy in my shoulders. "That's okay. I can do this by myself." I flash my eyes up to him. "But some of these I'm going to need a cohort in. I won't do it alone."

"Any other day, I'm free," he says. "I'm there for you."

"Thank you." I smile and bring my knees into my chest.

"Care to tell me what the thing is that you're doing today?"

I shake my head. "No, I want it to be a surprise."

"Okay." He takes another sip of his coffee. "And what about this circle of trust? Am I in it?"

"You're the core of it."

That makes him smile. "Good. Just checking." He glances around and asks, "So did you get breakfast, or am I supposed to house you *and* feed you?"

"I think you know the answer to that."

He sighs and stands from the couch. "What's it going to be? Waffles? Pancakes? Omelets?"

"The pickle special, please."

He glances over his shoulder. "If it's going to be the pickle special, then you better get your little behind in here and help."

"But I'm emotionally spent," I playfully whine.

"Not an excuse. Get in here, now."

"Fine," I answer, exasperated.

"So are you nervous?" I ask Breaker as I sit on his bed, cross-legged, drinking my third cup of coffee this morning.

"Nervous about what?" he asks as he sifts through his dresser for clothes. Fresh from the shower with a towel wrapped around his waist, he still has droplets of water cascading over his skin from places he missed while drying.

I watch his finely tuned back muscles flex, the corded sinew on either side of his spine when he moves to the right and when he moves to the left. When he stands with a T-shirt and shorts in hand, I catch the way his towel conforms to his butt, giving me the smallest glimpse of his glutes and the hard work he puts in at the gym. And when he turns around, I avert my eyes because there's something about his chest, the thickness of his pecs, and the carved divots of his abdomen that make me blush.

Staring down at my coffee cup, I say, "Nervous about your date with Birdy."

"No," he says confidently.

"Not even a little?"

He shakes his head. "Not even a little."

"Well, she did make it quite clear that you two were having a good time. She said you were a really good kisser."

"That's because I am," he says, then smirks at me.

I roll my eyes. "Humble much?"

"Never."

He disappears into his bathroom, and I call out, "Are you doing anything tonight? I was hoping we could play Plunder or Codenames. But I can find something else to do if you plan on carrying your date later into the night."

He pops out of the bathroom wearing a pair of black athletic shorts and a black T-shirt. Funny that he took so long searching through his dresser for that outfit. It's as plain as plain can get.

"I'll let you know," he says as he takes a seat on the edge of the bed with a pair of black socks.

"Are your panties black too?"

"Don't call them *panties*." I laugh as he continues. "And you know they're black. How could you forget after that one night you were so wasted, you wore them over your head and passed out?"

"Can we not talk about that?"

"You brought up underwear. Therefore, I wanted to bring up one of my favorite memories of you."

"That's one of your favorites? Wow, you really need to reconsider your memories."

He turns toward me, and I get a whiff of his cologne—fresh and bright—which makes me want to sink my nose into his chest. "If we're talking favorite memories, I think yesterday a core one hit me hard in the chest. Wasn't expecting it."

His voice grows serious, so I know what he's about to say is not a joke. "What was it?" I ask.

His eyes lift, and he says, "Seeing you in that wedding dress. You seriously took my breath away, Lia."

My cheeks heat as I bring my coffee cup to my lips. "Thank you." And then, because the moment is so serious, I say, "Do you know what my favorite memory of you is?"

"The time I misspelled *pickle* while playing Scrabble so you could forever have a nickname for me?"

I chuckle. "No, but that's up there." I push a strand of hair out of my face. "The day you graduated. I can still see the exuberant hug you gave your brothers while you were in your cap and gown. It was so beautiful to see brothers that connected to each other, that supportive. It made me love you that much more."

He smiles. "I've been very lucky in the brother department, even though they can be pains and they ditch me for their wives now."

"Can you blame them? Have you seen their wives?"

He laughs. "Yeah, I have, and the fact that they got married so close together doesn't really help me because they're both still honeymooning."

"I'm pretty sure they'll be honeymooning for a while."

He drags his hand over his scruffy jaw. "I'm pretty sure you're going to be doing the honeymooning pretty quickly as well."

I shrug. "Probably not as long. Brian is not that obsessed with me. I'm guessing he'll be the guy who brings work on his honeymoon." The words come out of my mouth before I can stop them. When I glance at Breaker, his brow is furrowed, and I can tell he wants to say something. "Who knows, though?" I continue. "He can be very attentive at times."

Breaker stands from the bed and stretches his arms over his head, revealing a patch of skin right above the waistband of his shorts. "If it were me, I'd spend a great deal of time honeymooning." His eyes connect with mine. "No way would I let you out of my sight." My cheeks flame, and he quickly realizes what he said so he adjusts. "I mean *my girl*. No way would I let my girl out of my sight."

And I believe that to the fullest.

There was only one time I ever heard Breaker have sex, and he must have forgotten I was home, but I can still remember like it was yesterday. The girl wasn't obnoxious at all. She actually sounded sweet—if that isn't weird to say—but it was Breaker's dirty mouth that I can still hear, deep and sultry, telling her how he was going to fuck her and for how long. It was the sexiest thing I've ever heard, completely unexpected, and it took me a day or two to be able to look at him normally again.

If he was honeymooning, I have no doubt that he would be rabid about it, even though he gives off friendly vibes. He gets along with just about everyone. He is possessive, protective, charming, just like his brothers. No word of a lie. I have envied Lottie and Kelsey a few times. Brian always seems happy to see me, but he's never particularly. . .ravenous. There have been times I've felt more *appreciated*, like a fine wine, rather than defiled. And I *know* Lottie and Kelsey have been defiled many, many times by their Cane husbands. *And Breaker would be no exception.*

"Well, your girl would be very lucky," I say, trying to break the tension that immediately filled the room. "I just don't think Brian is that kind of guy. We barely have sex now as it is."

That makes Breaker pause and then slowly turn to me. "What?" he asks.

Oh crap.

"Uh, I don't know why I said that," I say awkwardly.

"Is it true?"

I can't look him in the eyes when I answer, "Brian just has a lot going on, and I have to respect that."

"Fuck that," Breaker says, growing angry. "He should be fucking you every chance he gets. He should appreciate the fact that he gets to be with you. That he gets to pleasure you. It shouldn't even be a question about whether or not you're fucking at night. He should want you every goddamn second of every goddamn hour. And if he's not pleasuring you the way he should, then that's something you need to discuss."

"He's been tired, Breaker."

"That's no goddamn excuse." He pushes away from the bed and grips his hair. "Fuck, if you were my fiancée, my wife, I'd never let you leave the bedroom. Your voice would be hoarse from every fucking orgasm I gave you."

Once again, my cheeks flame and my stomach twists with uncertainty, heat, and this weird, bubbly, airless feeling as I stare up at him. And when his eyes meet mine, I wait for him to change his wording again, but he doesn't.

"Anyway…" He blows out a heavy breath. "I should get going. Feel free to stay as long as you want."

"Okay," I answer awkwardly. "Have fun on your hike."

"Thanks." He makes it to his bedroom door and then glances over his shoulder. "Can't wait to see what you do today. Love you, Lia."

"L-love you," I say, stuttering over the words, not because I've never said them to him before, but because of the way his eyes penetrate me when he says it, like he's trying to convey something. Like he's trying to tell me something else, something deeper, but before I can decipher exactly what it is, he's heading toward the living room and then out his door. To his date. With Birdy.

I set my coffee mug on the nightstand and flop back on the bed.

What the hell was that all about?

CHAPTER 12
BREAKER

"ARE YOU BOTH THERE?" I say into the phone once I conference Huxley in.

"Yes," they say at the same time, and then Huxley adds, "This better be fucking good. Lottie is waiting for me."

"Kelsey is cooking pancakes naked, so yeah, hurry the fuck up," JP says.

God, their lives are so annoying…annoying because I'm jealous. So fucking jealous.

"I need to talk to you guys because I'm going to do something stupid. I can feel it. I need to come back to work. I need to distract myself with something, anything; please, just let me come back to work."

"Uhh…the desperation is thick. What's going on?" JP asks.

"I almost fucked up," I say. "Or maybe I did, I don't know, but fuck, it's not good. It's really not good, so please just let me come back to work. I'll wear a wig, a fake mustache, I'll even do another job. Just anything to get me away from…from this hell."

"A mustache, huh?" JP asks.

"Tell us what the hell is going on," Huxley says in that father-figure voice of his.

I take a deep breath while I squeeze the steering wheel of my car at a red light. I *should* be stressed by the goddamn lawsuit being hurled toward me. I should be worried that the Cane name is being disparaged. But no.

I'm stressed about the woman I love *who I just told I'd fuck hard enough to make her hoarse from orgasms*. The fuck? But first... "I, uh...came to the conclusion that I have feelings for Lia."

There's silence.

And then, "I fucking told you he was going to figure it out in a week," JP says. "Spending that much time with a girl you're harboring feelings for while she attempts to plan a wedding with another man, yeah, that will give you a swift kick to the scrotum."

"Can we not play the *I told you so* game?" I ask.

"But we did," Huxley says. "We told you this would happen."

"Okay, great, wonderful, you two are modern-day matchmakers. Congratulations. Now, can we please move on?"

"Glad you can be big enough to acknowledge that," JP says.

"How does this pertain to work and fucking up?" Huxley asks.

"I can't be around her anymore. I need reasons I can't help with the planning of her wedding."

"So you're just going to crush her like that?" JP asks. "Dude, that's not cool."

"What the hell am I supposed to do?" I ask. "I just told her if she was mine, I'd never let her go. I would fuck her every chance I had."

"Whoa, what?" Huxley says.

"Uh, dude, that's a bit extreme for not even admitting your feelings. How? Did you just announce that you'd fuck her out of the blue?"

"No." I drag my hand over my face. "We were talking about the honeymoon phase, and I mentioned how I wouldn't let her out of my sight but quickly changed it to *my girl*. But then, after that, she tells me that she and Brian barely have sex *because he's tired*, and I just fucking lost it. All I could think about was how this lucky son of a bitch was taking advantage of her and how he didn't deserve her, and I told her that if she was mine, we'd be fucking all the time, so yeah...there you have it. I need to not be around her anymore, and if I could return to work, that would be great. Thank you."

"You can't come back to work yet," Huxley says. "Not until Taylor says it's clear."

"So what am I supposed to do? Keep being her man of honor when clearly all I want is her?"

"You could do some next-level shit and jeopardize her wedding so she doesn't get married at all," JP says.

"Don't listen to him," Huxley cuts in. "That's a terrible fucking idea. Why don't you just tell her how you feel?"

"Please," I scoff. "We all know how that goes. I tell her how I feel; she doesn't feel the same way. She ends up patting me on the shoulder, and then we don't talk anymore."

"Where are you getting your evidence from? Movies and TV shows?"

"Of course, where else?" I ask as I pull into the parking lot of the trailhead.

"Probably not your best source of reality," JP says. "I think Huxley is right. You tell her, and if she doesn't feel the same way, at least you know, and you can move on."

"What about that Birdy girl? Can't you move on with her?" Huxley asks.

"I'm about to tell her I can't see her anymore because I like someone else, and I don't want to lead her on. Also, I've kissed her twice now and felt nothing, and I think it's because I want Lia and only Lia."

"That much is obvious," JP says.

I press my fingers into my brow and say, "So what should I do?"

"We already told you what to do," Huxley says. "Tell Lia how you feel. If you don't, you're going to regret it."

"But she's on this mission now to do things before she gets married. What am I supposed to do about that?"

"Well, if you think she might not feel the same way about you, then help her understand how you're a better match for her than Brian," JP says.

"Yeah, I agree," Huxley chimes in.

"How do I go about doing that?"

"Be everything Brian is not," JP says. "Without crossing the line, obviously, you can't go fuck her and be like, *See, I fuck you, and Brian doesn't.*"

That actually makes me chuckle. "I would never do that, but I get what you're saying." I lean my head against the headrest and ask, "Do you really think it could work?"

"Never know until you try," Huxley says.

"And I just want to state for the record one more time about how right we were about this."

"Shut the fuck up," I say, causing them both to laugh. "I hate you."

"No, you don't," Huxley says. "You just hate that we're always right."

"Yeah, that too. Okay, Birdy is here for our hike. Got to go."

"Be gentle with her," JP says.

"No, I thought I would kick dirt at her and tell her to get lost."

"Not recommended," Huxley adds right before I say bye and end the call.

I look out the window to where Birdy steps out of her white SUV wearing a matching set of maroon biking shorts and sports bra. And from where I'm sitting, I can see a small bird pattern on them.

Fuck.

I squeeze my eyes shut again.

I don't want to make her feel bad.

But I'm going to. There's no way around it. She definitely thinks we're about to have a fun bird-watching hike. *How do I tell her otherwise?*

Grumbling to myself, I get out of my car just as Birdy steps up.

"Hey, you," she says in a cheery voice just as her hand lands on my chest, and she stands on her toes to press a kiss to my jaw. "How are you?"

Fucking awful.

"Good." I tack on a smile. "Uh, I like your outfit, very themed for bird-watching."

"I told you it was good." She beams up at me, and I realize I must tell her now. I can't go on this hike and pretend everything is fine and then tell her after. That would be brutal. She must sense my uneasiness because she asks, "Is everything okay?"

I pull on my hair and shake my head. "No."

"Oh, what's going on?"

"Come talk with me," I say as I take her hand in mine and lead her around to the back of my SUV and open the trunk. I take a seat, and she does the same. "I've been a fucking idiot, Birdy, and I dragged you into my idiocy."

"What do you mean?" she asks.

I look up at her and say, "I like someone else, and I thought that maybe if I just ignored it, I wouldn't think about it. But it's become more and more clear that I like this person, and I don't want to lead you on."

"Oh," she says, looking down at her hands and making me feel like the absolute shithead that I am. "I'm guessing it's Lia, isn't it?"

I could deny it, but what's the point in lying?

"Yeah," I say softly. "Like I said, it's really fucked up, and I can't pretend the feelings aren't there while I try to date you at the same time. It wouldn't be fair."

"I appreciate that," she says softly and then asks, "Does she know?"

"No," I say quickly. "Not even a clue."

"Are you going to go for it?" When her eyes connect with mine, I realize at that moment who I'm talking to, who set me up with her. Brian. Fuck.

"Uh...no," I answer, but the lie even sounds stupid to my ears.

"I won't say anything," she says. "I don't care for Brian all that much. I think he's a tool, and honestly, I think Lia could do better. I don't know what she sees in him."

"Me either," I say softly.

"You should go for it," Birdy says. "You two have such a strong connection."

"That's nice of you, but you don't have to talk about this. I know it's got to be weird."

"Sure, it's weird, and am I disappointed? Of course. I think you're amazing, Breaker, and if you asked me out on a date, I would one hundred percent go, but I also know when a guy isn't interested or is hung up on someone else. I had a feeling that might be the case. I could just tell by the way you two interacted and the way you spoke about her. Something is there, and I really think you should try to figure it out."

"But she's getting married in four weeks. Doesn't that make me look like a giant ass? Like I couldn't have figured this out sooner? Now I'm going to come swooping in and tell her how I feel? It doesn't seem appropriate."

"Not sure there is a standard for an appropriate time to tell someone you love them. But the last thing you want to do is not tell her and regret it forever."

"That's what my brothers said."

"Did they also say, *I told you so*? Seems like something they would pick up on."

"Yeah, pretty sure everyone picked up on it besides Lia and me." I sigh heavily. "Jesus, Birdy, I'm just so sorry."

"Don't be." She takes my hand in hers. "I'd rather you tell me the truth. Frankly, this might be the most real conversation I've ever had, and I appreciate it."

"Well, thanks for being so cool about it."

"Do you still want to go on a hike? Maybe we can talk about Lia, and I can help you."

"You don't want to do that."

"I do," she says convincingly. "I'm all about true love, and I think you and Lia have that. She just needs to see it too. Plus, I can't waste this outfit."

"True," I say as I hop off the back of the trunk. I hold my hand out to her and help her down. "Can I give you a hug?"

"Of course," she says as she pulls me in.

"Thank you for understanding."

"Thank you for being honest." When we push away, she says, "Now, if you happen to have a single friend who is kind, sweet, doesn't hurt to have some looks, and can be as honest as you, then I would love to meet him."

"You know...I just might have someone in mind for you."

Her eyes light up. "Really?"

I shut the trunk of my car and nod. "Yeah, he's a former baseball player. What do you think about that?"

"Um, I say yes, please!"

I chuckle, and we head up toward the hiking trail.

"Goldfinch, right?" Birdy asks.

"That's right," I say, feeling like a proud teacher. "Look at you getting it after the twelfth time."

She chuckles. "Well, don't say you can't teach me anything. Clearly, I'm a master at bird-watching."

"Clearly." We make our way up the hill, almost to the crest. "I'm irritated that we haven't seen more variety."

"Well, you know, the crow and goldfinch have sealed the deal for me on this bird-watching thing. I think I'm an avid fan forever."

"Your sarcasm is easily detectable." I let my binoculars rest on my chest. "If this was a real date, I'd be thoroughly embarrassed by the showing. Here, I'm taking you on some exotic bird tour, and we find a gaggle of crows and a dozen goldfinches."

"Could have been worse, could have been just the crows."

"Very true." When we reach the crest of the hill, we pause and take a second to check out the view of the city.

"Not too bad," Birdy says as she finds a boulder and takes a seat on it. "Care to join me?"

I take a seat as well. "I'm glad we still went on the hike. I think it's helping clear my head."

"Good, which means you might be ready and open to talk about all things Lia."

"Ehhh, not sure that's the case."

She bumps her shoulder with mine. "Come on, I have some insight. I'm a girl, and I know Brian. I could give you some pointers."

"Yeah?" I ask. "I guess that wouldn't be too bad to maybe...see what you have to say."

"Glad you're open to it." She chuckles. "First of all, you need to know Brian's weaknesses, and I will tell you right now that communication is one of them. He's also a workaholic, he's not very thoughtful, and even though he proposed to Lia, it certainly wasn't his idea. It was his mom's because *she* wasn't happy with him not being married yet. Do I think he loves Lia? Of course, but do I think he could marry anyone? Also, yes. I don't think the ability to deeply love and be in love with someone is in his bones. I've seen it with his girlfriends growing up. They were more like accessories than anything."

"Yeah, I got that feeling from him. He and Lia started dating not long after she lost both of her parents, and I believe there was comfort in having him around for that type of affection I couldn't give her." I wince and say, "Please don't say that to anyone. I don't want Lia to find out I'm breaking her trust."

"Don't worry, Breaker. I'm on your side. I won't say anything...especially since you're dangling a baseball player in front of me."

I chuckle. "A good one at that."

"I'm counting on it, but seriously, I think one of the best things you can do is be there for her more than you already are. Knowing Brian's relational deficits, why not emphasize your strengths in those areas? She knows *you*. But is she aware of the man you'd be in a romantic relationship?"

"That's what my brothers said."

"Your brothers are smart. And do everything with her, maybe even flirt just a touch."

"I don't want to cross the line."

"Then don't, but you should subtly let her know that you're attracted to her. Start hinting at how you feel so that when you do tell her, this isn't a total shock, and she doesn't have some assumption that you're trying to ruin her wedding. Not that I think Lia would process information that way, but just in case."

"Yeah, that's actually really smart." I kick some dirt away. "Fuck, this feels terrifying."

"Well, feel free to call me anytime and ask for advice. I think you have a leg up on Brian. The only thing that could hold you back is her fear of facing the truth. And the truth is, I don't think she truly loves Brian. I've seen how she interacts with you and how she interacts with him. There's warmth when you two are together, a connection. I don't see the same thing with Brian."

"I don't either." I drape my arm over Birdy's shoulder and say, "We're going to have to stay in touch, you know. I really appreciate your honesty and help right now." *And hope I'm not putting my trust in the wrong person.*

"Just promise me, when you two get married, because I know it's going to happen, invite me and offer me a plus-one." *That's something I can do.*

"I very well might dedicate a toast to you if this all works out. You gave me a bout of confidence I wasn't feeling this morning."

"If you ever need someone to pump you up for overtaking Brian, I'm your girl. He might have introduced you to me, but he still is an idiot."

"Yup, can't disagree with you there."

We both laugh and then stand from the boulder. I was right all along. Brian is a douche.

"Shall we head back? The birds are letting us down today," I say.

"Yes, and we can go over all the ways you can be flirtatious without crossing the line. It's time for the Win Your Girl Bootcamp. You in?"

"Teach me all the things, wise one."

Breaker: Stopped by Masala Palace and grabbed some chicken tikka, reshmi kabab, paneer korma, and garlic naan. You in?

Lia: Are you kidding me? I think I just drooled reading that text message. I'm home, want me to prepare the game board and table?

Breaker: Obviously.

Lia: On it. Please choose your Plunder ship color.

Breaker: Why are you asking? You know I'm always green.

Lia: You've lost the last three times, so I didn't know if you wanted to change it up. Maybe switch your luck.

Breaker: Green for life.

Lia: Okay, prepare to be annihilated. Also, I have a surprise to show you when you get here.

Breaker: Yeah, does this surprise happen to be one of the things you're checking off your list?

Lia: Yes.

Breaker: Well, I can't wait. See you soon.

Food in hand, I step off the elevator of our apartment building and head right to my front door. After Birdy and I made it down the hill, I gave her a hug goodbye and then traveled back up the hill myself, this time thinking about everything. Letting my mind wander, my mind process, ruminating on my true thoughts and feelings.

First and foremost, I love her. I let that sink in. I let myself sit in my feelings and understand them. Lia is the most precious person in my life. She's my ride or die. She means everything to me.

She's my girl.

After I let myself accept that, I went on to accept that everyone is right. I need to tell her about my feelings, but I need to ease her into it. It might scare her if I jump out at her with these feelings.

Also, I need to give her time to check her goals off her list. I don't want to get in the way of that. I want her at her best when I approach her with my feelings, which will give her time to adjust to the new way I'll approach our friendship.

After some time up on the hill and just living in the moment, I made my way back down again and ordered food, knowing Lia wouldn't be able to say no to Indian food. It's one of her absolute favorites.

With excitement in my chest, I reach my door, turn the knob, and enter, half expecting Lia to be standing there, waiting for me. When she's not, I call out, "Hey, I'm here."

"In the bedroom," she says. "Come here."

Confused but also excited, I drop the food off at the table and make my way to my bedroom, where the door is cracked open. Whatever she wants to show me, she sure is making a big deal about it—which I love.

I push the door open and glance in. That's where I find Lia standing in the middle of the bedroom, her hands clasped together in front of her. She's wearing a pair of leggings and a crop top—not her normal type of shirt since it shows off a touch of her stomach, but it looks great on her. Really good on her, but that's not what's gathering my attention. Nope. It's that her long red hair has been cut and dyed. Thin blonde streaks are woven through her hair that now sits just above her shoulders, with long flowy bangs and messy curls that fit her personality so well.

"Holy...shit."

She is wearing a large smile as she says, "Do you like it?"

"Ophelia," I whisper while I take a step forward. "Jesus Christ, you look hot."

Her smile glows even brighter. "Really?"

I close the space between us and reach out to touch her short locks. "Yeah," I say breathlessly.

"It's a little spunky, but I feel like a new woman with all that hair lifted off me, and I thought the highlights would be fun, but I kept them minimal because I still like my red hair."

I take her all in as my heart beats wildly in my chest. Jesus fuck, she was gorgeous before, but now, I don't know if I'll be able to keep my hands to myself.

And before I can stop myself, I tell her exactly what's on my mind.

"You look fucking sexy. Not that you didn't before, but Jesus fuck, Lia. You look so fucking incredible. I love it."

"Thank you," she says, a light blush staining her cheeks. "I sent a picture to Brian; still waiting to hear back from him. I hope he likes it as much as you do." *I bet the fuck he does. But I don't fucking care.*

"He will," I say, still touching her hair as this wave of lust pours through me.

I want to sift my hand through her hair. I want to pull her close. I want to slip my hand under her crop top. I want to show her just how much this transformation turns me on. And it's not just how she looks. It's her confidence, her smile, and how proud she is of herself. I want to pin her to my bed and run my mouth up and down her neck.

"And the outfit, it's not too much, is it? I thought I'd try something new."

I look down at her crop top and the hint of her lace bra strap lining her shoulder as I shake my head. "No, not at all. You look really fucking amazing, Ophelia."

"Ooo, two Ophelias. You must really approve."

I swallow as I squeak out, "Yeah, I do."

I approve so much that I'm struggling to remind myself that she's engaged, and that I need to take this slow. That I can't touch her the way I want to.

Pulling it slightly together, I ask, "But more importantly, how do you feel?"

"Well, after your reaction, I feel really sexy."

"You should."

"I'm just excited to see what Brian has to say." Ah, yes, we're all waiting on bated breath for Brian's reaction. Did you hear the sarcasm in that? From the kitchen, her phone rings, and she glances up at me. "Speak of the devil. I bet that's him. I'll answer, and you can divvy out the food. Don't hoard the garlic naan."

"Wouldn't dream of it," I say as she moves past me, and my eyes follow, falling straight to her rear end.

Fuck, would you look at that?

Bubbly, pert, all shown off in her skintight pants.

I swear the universe is testing me and will decide my fate on how I can control myself in this situation. My best friend, who I've always thought was incredible, turned into a smokeshow in a few short hours.

I reluctantly remove my eyes from her ass and fall in step behind her. While she reaches for her phone, I open up the bag of Indian food as my eyes casually drift in her direction, taking another opportunity to check her out.

Even her tits look incredible in that shirt.

Yup, the universe is testing me for sure.

"Hey, Brian," she says cheerfully. "How are you?"

I try to block out her conversation because I don't want to hear him tell her how much he loves her new hair, so I focus on dividing up our food.

That's until I hear her say, "What? You don't like it?"

That snaps me to attention. I forget all about the food and focus on her instead.

The confidence—which was propping her chest up only a few moments earlier—vanishes.

Her beautiful smile that had stretched from ear to ear falters.

And I can feel the pained disappointment in her voice as she lowers her voice to reply.

"I wanted a change," she says. "Because I wasn't feeling myself. Yes, I feel like myself now." She pauses and then turns away from me. "Brian, can we talk about this later?" Another pause and then, "For how long? A week? I mean, it's not like I can stop you, right? Business is business." I crumple the paper bag in my hand as I continue to listen, my hatred for the man growing stronger. "Yes, but we're supposed to get married shortly. It would be nice if you were here." It would be great if he wasn't. "Okay, fine. Yeah, talk to you later." She hangs up and drops the phone to the side of her.

I wait a few moments, and when I notice she's not going to move, I decide to move to her. I sit down next to her on the couch, lift her chin so she's looking at me, and that's when I notice the tears.

I'm going to fucking kill him.

"I'm sure you got the gist of that conversation," she says. "But he didn't like my hair. Said it was a mistake."

Yup, murder is in his future.

"He's wrong," I say as I cup her cheek and swipe the tears away. "He's so fucking wrong because the moment I saw you, my heart skipped a beat, Lia. You look gorgeous. So fucking stunning that I had to remind myself that you're my best friend."

"You're just saying that." She shakes her head.

"I'm not," I say as my eyes fall to her lips and then back to her eyes. "I'd never just say something to appease you. Brian is an idiot because the fact that he can't see how you shine with this new hair, can't see your confidence, is his loss."

"He thinks his mom is going to be really mad." *Who the fuck cares? Is he still attached by his umbilical cord, or what?*

"Good," I say. "I hope she is mad. Gives us more fodder to fuck around with her."

She lightly chuckles. "He's also going to be gone for a week, maybe more. I guess what he's dealing with in San Jose requires more attention than he initially thought, so that's great. Not like we're getting married or anything." She sighs. "God, why did he have to be such an ass? Maybe he's stressed."

"Being stressed does not give anyone an excuse to be a dick. And he was a dick. Flat out. I need you to realize that. What he did was an inexcusable dick move. Do you hear me?"

She blinks and then nods. "Yes."

"Good. Now, we're going to forget that just happened because we have a fun night planned, and I'm not going to allow him to ruin that. Understood?"

"Yes," she says again, and then she falls into my chest. I wrap my arms around her and let her cry it out for a few more minutes. All the while, I think about what I would have done if Brian dismissed her boldness in person.

"You've barely touched your naan," I say. "That's unacceptable."

"I'm sorry," she says, pushing it to the side. "I'm just…not in the mood."

"Is that why we haven't started playing Plunder?"

"Maybe I should go back to my place."

"Yeah, okay, as if I would let you do that," I say. "With that frown you can't seem to shake, no way would I allow you to just sulk away. Nah, sorry, you're here with me for the rest of the night."

Her eyes well up again, her lips tremble, and I tug on her hand to sit on my lap right as she bursts into tears again.

"I'm sorry about all of this," she says quietly as we sit on my couch, watching old reruns of *Family Feud*.

After she ate a few more bites of her food, we packed everything up in containers and stuck it in the fridge. Since she wasn't in the mood for a board game, we both took a seat on the couch, where we've been mindlessly watching reruns ever since. I've wanted to pull her in close several times, to stretch her legs across mine, to massage her feet, to do anything to touch her, and to make her feel better.

"Don't apologize," I say.

"I know, but I didn't even ask you how your date with Birdy was. I just kind of bogarted the night with my issues."

"You didn't bogart anything. You have the right to be upset. Brian let you down, and you need to work through those feelings. There's nothing to apologize for."

"Still…" She turns toward me now. "How was bird-watching with Birdy?"

I shrug casually, keeping my eyes on the TV as I say, "We decided just to be friends."

"What?" she asks. "Why?"

I shrug again. "Just don't think I was into it like she was."

"And she was okay with that? She said she was so excited about meeting you."

"She was," I answer. "We had a real honest conversation about it, actually. She could tell I wasn't feeling it and said it was okay. She'd rather know now than have me drag things on. We still went on a hike together. Did some talking, and I told her I would hook her up with one of my friends who I think would be perfect for her."

"Who?" she asks as her lips lightly turn up.

"Penn."

Momentarily forgetting her woes, Lia leans over and grips my forearm. "Oh my God, Breaker, they would make the cutest couple."

"I think so, plus Penn is really honest and is the kind of guy she's looking for."

"Is he dating?"

"I think so, just hasn't found anyone he wants to be serious about. I think that could be Birdy."

"Well, look at you being a matchmaker. I'm sorry it didn't work out, though; I thought you were looking for that kind of relationship," she says.

"I was, but she wasn't what I wanted."

"What do you want?" she asks.

You.

Everything about you.

Your soul.

Your mind.

Your heart.

Your body.

I want all of you, every last fucking inch of you.

"Still processing that. I'll let you know when I'm ready."

"Oh, you have an idea?"

"Yes, I have an exact idea, but it's going to take some finagling, so let's put this conversation on pause."

"Okay, that's not evasive at all."

"Not at all." I wink, which causes her to push me with her foot.

"That's annoying."

"At least we've moved past Brian being a dumbass."

She leans against the back of the couch. "He really was being a dumbass, wasn't he?"

"He was because from where I sit, he's completely missed the fact that you're a total smokeshow with that hair."

"Smokeshow, huh? What was I before?"

"A smokeshow," I answer. "But without confidence. This new haircut just makes you shine brighter."

"I was feeling really confident."

"He's a certified troll for saying anything negative. Bet you he thinks you're too hot now, like you're out of his league, and he's worried you might wander off."

"Well, if he keeps acting like an ass, I very well might."

That's the spirit. Wander off, straight into my arms.

Not wanting to push the subject, I turn back to the TV and say, "Are we going to apply to be on *Family Feud* again this year? We have Kelsey and Lottie, who we can add to the team, as well as JP, so I think the odds are in our favor. Kelsey would have precise answers, JP would have the funny covered, and Lottie will cover the wildcard topic."

"We'll never get picked."

"That's not the kind of attitude I like to hear. We must manifest this shit. Come on, we were born to be on *Family Feud*. You and me during Fast Money? We'd annihilate. Steve Harvey wouldn't know what to do with himself because we'd destroy it. And who knows, I'm not opposed to paying people off to get on the show."

"I told you, we'll get on the show on our own merit, not what number you can write down in your checkbook."

"Yeah, but the checkbook would be a surefire way to make it happen."

"Where are your morals, Breaker Cane?"

"Iffy at best when it comes to *Family Feud*."

"I can see that." Growing more serious, she says, "Thanks for hanging out with me tonight, and being my own personal hype man about my hair and my outfit. It truly did make me feel special."

"Well, you should feel special. Because you are. I'll hype you all day, every day."

"And that is why you are my best friend," she says.

Yeah, if only I was so much more.

CHAPTER 13
LIA

Lia: What are you doing?

Breaker: Staring at my ceiling, dreading having to go to my brother's house.

Lia: Sunday brunch?

Breaker: Yes, but all they're going to do is fawn all over their wives while I sit there with a mediocre Bloody Mary in hand, watching them.

Lia: Oh, funny thing…I like mediocre Bloody Marys.

Breaker: Is this your way of inviting yourself?

Lia: I need more friends! I need girl friends, to be precise. Lottie and Kelsey seem cool, and if they're going to be on our Family Feud team, then I need to get to know them.

Breaker: So you are inviting yourself?

Lia: Please…Pickle.

Breaker: Ugh, fine, but I swear to God, Lia, if you start spouting off embarrassing shit about me like you did at the last brunch before the wives were around, I'm going to kick you right in the crotch.

Lia: Oh no, not a kick to the crotch. *shivers*

Breaker: Yeah, a giant old foot right to the camel toe.

Lia: I had a camel toe ONCE! Do not use that against me.

Breaker: I can still see it like it was yesterday…

Lia: And you were saying you don't WANT me to say anything embarrassing about you to your brothers...

Breaker: Oh, would you look at that? The camel-toe image vanished.

Lia: Funny how that works. When do I need to be ready?

Breaker: I leave in twenty. Dress slutty.

Lia: Slutty? Why?

Breaker: Might be fun to send Brian another picture.

Lia: Too soon, Breaker, too soon.

Breaker: LOL, noted. See you in twenty.

"I need to buy some of your cologne," I say as we pull up to Huxley's place, a large white coastal-style house with black-framed windows and accents. It's beautiful with its manicured lawns and fresh flower boxes under the windows. Picturesque. The type of house I'd want one day.

"Why do you need to buy some of my cologne?" Breaker asks as he parks in the circular driveway.

"It smells sublime. I think I want it for myself."

"You can't wear my cologne," he says, giving me a strange look.

"Why the hell not?"

"Because we can't smell like each other. Besides, I like the smell of your perfume. Viktor and Rolf really suits you."

"It's scary how you remember my perfume. I'm not sure Brian could even describe the scent to me if I asked him."

"A subtle combination of rose, jasmine, and orchid," he says, his eyes landing on me.

And then we stare at each other for a few seconds, in the car, with the world whipping around us. How does he know that? I wouldn't be that precise with the way it smells; yet Breaker knows everything.

Every last thing about me.

He knows that when I get my period, I get horrible migraines, and he's always there with ibuprofen, caffeine, and Sour Patch Kids.

He knows that I'm not that big on working out, but that sometimes I get in moods of wanting to work out, so he always has a variety of classes I can join when I come to him. He keeps them in a note in his phone.

He knows that without even having to ask, he should buy Comic Con VIP tickets for us and think up our costume ideas because I love going. Still, I can't handle the stress of it all, and I'd rather be told what to wear and when than to figure it out myself.

And apparently, he knows exactly what I smell like. Notes and all.

Not sure I could say the same about Brian. Then again, like Brian said, we have our entire lives to figure it all out.

So why does that sentiment feel sour on my tongue now?

"Come on," he says while opening his car door. "I'm starving, and they're serving make-your-own breakfast tacos."

Shaking my head from any thoughts of Brian, I open my door as well, just as Breaker moves around his car and grabs the door for me.

"What are you doing?" I ask, looking up at him as my hand slides into his.

"Helping you out."

"Why would I need help?"

"Uh, I don't know...you don't wear dresses often, so I wasn't sure if you knew how to walk in one."

I press my palm to his face, which causes him to laugh and pull away.

"Can't a guy be a gentleman without being chastised about it?"

"Can't a girl wear a dress without being teased about it?"

His teasing falls flat right before he says, "You can, and if I didn't say it before, you look beautiful, Lia." Those bright blue eyes stare back at me, sincerity so heavy that it almost feels...real. Like him holding my hand is real, and his words are spoken from a different place, a place that isn't just friendship.

"Thank you," I say, waiting for him to guide us to the door, but he doesn't.

He stays put, standing in front of me, his eyes scanning the navy-blue maxi dress I paired with a few gold necklaces. I styled my hair with some soft waves like the hairdresser did yesterday and added a heavy dose of mascara to make my eyes pop.

His hand reaches up to my hair, where he twists a few strands between his finger and thumb.

And for some reason, my breath catches when his eyes meet mine again.

"You don't need a dress to look beautiful. You're beautiful in just your flannel shorts and T-shirt, but you also look great in this."

I swallow hard, my nerves feeling frayed because, what's going on? It's like a switch has been turned on in him...or turned off, and he's more... affectionate. His compliments seem more intimate. And the way he looks at me has some hunger to it.

Before I can process anything, he slips his hand back into mine and tugs me toward the front door.

"Have you ever seen a breakfast taco bar?" he asks as if he didn't just stare into my soul with his commanding eyes.

"Uh...no."

"It's fucking mouthwatering. Huxley gets it catered. There are mimosas, Bloody Marys—mediocre ones, of course—a giant fruit display, plus a variety of croissants that I'm pretty sure will rock your world. They've rocked mine a few times." He pats his stomach.

"Yes, that six-pack of yours really tells me how the croissants have rocked you," I say.

A charming smirk passes over his lips right before he drops my hand and rings the doorbell. "Notice my six-pack, huh?"

"The astronauts on the ISS noticed your six-pack."

He presses his hand to his chest. "Don't flatter me. My ego won't be able to fit through the door."

I nudge him with my shoulder just as the door opens, Huxley appearing on the other side.

There's something to be said about the genetics the Cane brothers possess because every one of them is extraordinarily handsome. All with dark hair, square jaws, sculpted bodies, and personalities that would make any leading lady fall for them.

Huxley has that tall, dark, and brooding thing going on, but can switch right out of it when he needs to, like right now, as he smiles at me.

"Lia, it's great to see you. Been a while since my brother brought you around. Congrats on the engagement."

"Thank you," I say. "And congrats on your wedding as well. Breaker showed me pictures."

"He should have brought you," Huxley says, eyeing his brother.

"Charise was a fine date," Breaker says while shifting to the side.

"Lia would have been better." Huxley steps to the side as well and gestures with his hand to walk in. "Everything is on the back patio. Enjoy."

"Thank you," I say as I step into his beautiful house, where the entryway has a large picture of him and Lottie on their wedding day. The sun is setting in the background. He's holding her possessively by the jaw as he kisses her. It's raw, beautiful...erotic, a picture Brian and I would never take.

A position Brian would never hold me in.

A kiss I don't think we'd ever share.

He doesn't have that in him, that craving, grasping-for-air nature. He doesn't see me as his and only his. He doesn't look at me and think...
mine.

That's never bothered me, but for some reason, looking at this picture of Lottie and Huxley, and the words Brian said to me last night, it's...it's bothering me now.

"You okay?" Breaker asks, coming up next to me.

"Yes," I answer. "Beautiful photo of them."

"It was a beautiful wedding," he replies and then smooths his hand to my lower back, right above the curve of my ass. "Ready to get some tacos?" he whispers in my ear right before he guides me toward the back of the house, his palm nearly searing my skin through the fabric of my dress.

"Yes," I answer as my voice gets caught in my throat.

He must not notice because he leads me out back where JP and Kelsey are filling their plates while Lottie fills up a champagne flute.

"Hey," Breaker says with a wave of his hands, causing all three sets of eyes to land on us. "Brought Lia with me because, frankly, she invited herself."

I pinch his side, causing him to laugh. I whisper, "Because of that, game on." I address everyone and say, "Breaker said the Bloody Marys are mediocre."

"Oh, you bitch," he whispers, causing me to laugh.

"What?" JP asks. "My Bloody Marys are not mediocre."

"You have no idea what you just did," Breaker mutters.

"I have an inkling," I answer as JP sets his plate down, grabs Breaker, and takes him over to the drinks, where he runs through every step of making the perfect Bloody Mary.

"Hey, Lia." Kelsey waves and grabs a plate. "Help yourself."

"Thank you," I say as I take the plate from her and then look over the buffet.

What looks to be fresh tortillas are stacked under a warmer. There are scrambled eggs, a variety of cheeses, salsas, refried beans, bacon, sausage, avocado, and cilantro. Breaker was right. This looks amazing. To the right is a colossal bowl of fruit salad made up of strawberries, blueberries, raspberries, blackberries, and cherries. And to the right of that…the croissants with a bowl of jelly.

"This looks amazing," I say.

"Take your time," Kelsey says. "We'll be here for the next few hours, slowly picking away at the buffet. It's an event. I would start with two tacos and a drink."

Lottie slides in next to me and says, "Then go for the bowl of fruit as a palate cleanser."

"Then a croissant, only one to start," Kelsey adds.

"Then some water," Lottie says. "Then another taco, then croissant, then fruit…then croissant."

"Keep it slow and steady on the booze drinks." Kelsey hands me a mimosa.

"I'm not going to remember that, so I might need you two to guide me."

"We got you," Lottie says and then points at a table on the other side of the pool. "Meet us over there unless you want to listen to JP drone on for half an hour about how he makes the best Bloody Marys."

"He better get it all out now," Kelsey says. "I don't want to hear about it when we get home."

Chuckling, I fill my plate with two tacos made up of scrambled eggs, refried beans, cheese, bacon, and avocado, and then head over to the other side of the pool, in the shade with the girls. Just what I wanted.

"I'm so glad Breaker brought you," Kelsey says. "We're always telling him to bring you, but he says you spend a lot of weekends with your fiancé."

I nod. "Yeah, he's out of town this weekend, so I was free."

"Well, thank goodness for that," Lottie says. "By the way, the knitted pot holders you gave us are my favorite thing ever."

"Mine too," Kelsey says. "I need to know how you made them. I've wanted to pick up a hobby for a while, but I don't know where to start."

Lottie grips the table and says, "Oh my God, we should start a knitting club."

"Don't tease me," I say. "I've always wanted to be part of a knitting club."

"Oh, we're not teasing." Lottie looks over her shoulder and calls, "Myla, over here."

I glance over my shoulder and spot Ryot Bisley—former third baseman for the Chicago Bobbies—I know this because Breaker told me—and his wife, Myla. They recently joined forces with the Cane brothers, so seeing them here is no surprise.

Ryot tugs on Myla's hand, whispers something in her ear. I watch as their eyes connect. An unspoken affection for each other passes by right before he pinches her chin and kisses her lips gently.

The sight of them makes my stomach hollow out as the thought, *I want that*, passes through my mind.

But don't I have that?

Don't I have that with Brian?

I want to believe that I do. I want to be able to sit here and think, if I brought Brian to this brunch, that he wouldn't send me on my way and focus on the powerful man who he has at his fingertips but rather speak quietly in my ear, hold my hand, want to let everyone know that I'm his.

Myla makes her way over here, her curvy body something to behold. No wonder Ryot is watching her walk away. Hell, I can't take my eyes off her either.

"Hey, girls." When she spots me, she says, "We haven't met. I'm Myla." She holds her hand out, and I take it.

"I'm Lia, Breaker's best friend."

"Oh, I've heard so much about you. Congrats on your engagement."

"Thank you," I say, even though it's starting to feel like congrats aren't in order.

"Are you not eating?" Lottie asks right before she takes a large bite of her taco.

"Please." Myla takes a seat. "As if I would skip out on taco bar. Ryot said he'll get me a plate and bring it over."

"That's so sweet," I say.

Myla smiles while her eyes find Ryot. "That's Ryot, always thinking of me first before himself." Myla waggles her brows. "Even in bed." She then leans forward and says, "Girls, last night, I'm not kidding, I'm pretty sure I had an out-of-body experience."

"Please, do share with us," Lottie says as my cheeks heat. "And then we need to solidify this knitting club thing, because I'm serious about it."

"Ooo, I'd love to knit," Myla says.

"Then I think it's official," Kelsey adds while sipping her mimosa. "We're going to become knitters, and Lia is going to teach us everything."

"Wait…" Myla pauses. "Did you make those knitted potholders?"

"That was me."

"Okay, you need to teach me because I love those things." God, she's so beautiful and friendly.

"See," Lottie says. "They're a crowd-pleaser and a much better wedding gift than the crystal orb we got from one of Huxley's clients. What the hell are we supposed to do with that? Huxley wants to pawn it and then donate the money to someone random, like slip it in a card, hand them the card, and leave. I argued that what if that business associate ever came to our house and wanted to see the orb? We had to keep it. So it's stuffed away in a closet. Anyway." Lottie turns toward Myla. "Tell us about the sex."

"Ryot really loves going down on me. I truly think it's one of his favorite things." I pick up my drink and start to sip it because I've never had such open conversations like this before. Not even with Breaker. Actually, never with Breaker. "Well, last night, he was sucking on my clit, while he had a vibrator inside me, and I nearly flew off the bed."

I suck in my drink wrong and start coughing.

"You okay?" Kelsey asks while rubbing my back.

"Yes, sorry." I cough a few more times. "Just drank that wrong."

"You sure?"

I nod, my cheeks flushed from embarrassment.

A vibrator while he's going down on her? Who knew that was even a combination?

"Huxley did that to me the other night, easily the best orgasm ever. Sure, I love it when he's inside me, of course, but something about his tongue makes me lose my mind."

"Same with JP," Kelsey says. "But he likes using his fingers over a vibrator, and I do too because he is able to hit me in just the right spot."

"What about you, Lia?" Myla asks, and then all eyes fall on me.

"Uh…" I look around. "Well, Brian, he uh…"

He doesn't have sex with me a lot.

He doesn't like going down on me.

He doesn't like it when I give him a blow job because he says I don't do it right…

"He's not much of an oral guy," I say, silencing the table.

The air immediately shifts from pleasant and fun to awkward and uncomfortable.

"But we're working on that," I say out of desperation, not to look like a total loser. "He's busy a lot, so it's hard to find time, especially since we don't live together."

"Oh, yes, when you live together, that will change," Lottie says, but I can tell she's just saying that to be nice.

"Totally," Myla pops in.

"Living together changes everything." Kelsey smiles.

"And you won't have Breaker on the other side of the wall anymore, which I'm sure will be better," Lottie says. "I can't imagine what that must be like."

"Especially after we ran into that girl who went to your wedding," Kelsey says, trying to remember what she said. "What was her name?"

"Charise," I say.

"That's right." Lottie snaps her finger at me. "Oh my God, she told us she had never in her life had orgasms like the ones she had with Breaker."

Ones?

Plural?

"She went on forever about it in the grocery store—kind of awkward. She said she really wanted to see him again and asked us to say something. We didn't," Kelsey says. "He's not a relationship kind of guy."

"Makes you think, though," Lottie says as she stares off at the men. "We might have underestimated the youngest Cane brother. He comes off all sweet and charming, but I bet you he's the sexiest in bed out of all of them."

"I could see that," Myla chimes in.

"I don't think it's even a question," Kelsey says. "I'm pretty sure that's the case. Just look at him. No man can have those eyes and not fuck someone to their deathbed."

Oh.

My.

God.

I don't think I'll ever be able to look at Breaker the same.

"Also"—Kelsey leans in—"and you guys have to swear I never told you this, but JP told me a story once about Breaker."

Lottie wipes her mouth with a napkin and says, "Tell us. Breaker has always been a mystery to me. I need to know more."

Kelsey glances at me and says, "I'm sure you know this already, but JP told me he was on a business trip with Breaker once, and he picked up a girl at a bar. He took her back to the penthouse that he was sharing with JP. He said he had never heard a girl come that many times in his life. And it wasn't just in their bedroom. Apparently, Breaker didn't care about doing her in the kitchen, or on the dining room table, or out on the balcony."

I swallow hard as a light sweat pricks out over my skin. Why can I see it in my head? Why can I clearly visualize his strong, masculine body pulsing into a woman on a balcony?

"With his brother in the other room?" Lottie asks and shakes her head. "God, that's ballsy but really hot. I'm sort of into that whole *people are watching me* thing, but of course Huxley would never."

"Neither would Ryot," Myla says. "The number of times the man has whispered *mine* into my ear."

"Same," Kelsey says. "JP would rather cut off his own penis than allow anyone to see me naked."

I think about Brian and what he'd do. My initial thought is, he would… if the people paid us. And how shitty a thought is that?

"Anyway," Lottie says. "Back to this knitting club. What do we need to get started?"

And just like that, we're back to knitting.

Not sure I will recover from this conversation because, holy shit, I learned far too much about my best friend, things I never knew. *Plural orgasms.* I didn't know that was a thing. And then Breaker's words come back to me from yesterday.

"Fuck, if you were my fiancée, my wife, I'd never let you leave the bedroom. Your voice would be hoarse from every fucking orgasm I gave you." Hoarse. From every fucking orgasm.

I clear my throat and try to act normal as the thought of Breaker fucking someone flashes through my mind. "Um, well, we will need yarn."

"Hold on." Lottie pulls out her phone and types away. "I'm taking notes. We're going to make this happen."

———

All the ladies have a croissant in hand, and together we "cheers" them in the middle of the table, and each takes a bite.

Ooey, gooey, buttery, and flaky with a hint of jam. Good God, it is the most magnificent thing I think I've ever tasted.

"Oh my God, this is good," I say with a mouthful.

"If I wasn't so concerned about my waistline expanding, I'd have these every day," Lottie says. "Reign is our personal chef, and he spends all afternoon prepping these. He makes sure they're piping hot in the morning. And his homemade jam is heaven."

"JP is trying to steal Reign, and he asked me to help him," Kelsey says. "I told him there was no way I was getting in the middle of that fight."

"Smart move, sis," Lottie says, playfully staring down Kelsey.

"You know"—Myla examines her croissant—"I might have to ask Ryot to get in the mix of stealing Reign. I have no problem with some friendly competition."

Lottie glares at Myla. "Need I remind you that I'm feisty, and I don't mind using my nails as claws."

Myla leans close and says, "Need I remind you that I grew up in a military household where I learned to hold my own. I will destroy you."

"I have secret rage," Lottie fires back, making us all chuckle.

"That means nothing to me," Myla counters with an evil glare.

"You know," Kelsey cuts in. "Maybe I'll just do you all a favor and steal him for JP, and that way, we don't have to see anyone's rage."

"Or I can just take him," I say, raising my hand.

All the girls turn toward me, and Lottie is the first to smile. "I think you'll fit in just nicely."

"I agree," Kelsey says.

"I think so too."

I sip my mimosa and smile because I could not agree more. This is exactly what I was looking for: a group of girls I could talk to, bond with, and just laugh with when it feels like the world is falling apart around me.

Of course I have Breaker, but for that moment when we weren't talking, it felt like I had no one, and that made me so sick to my stomach. Talking with these girls, making friends, fulfills one of the items on my checklist—build and create a circle of trust. I know it's early, but this could be the beginning of that.

"You haven't told us anything about the wedding," Kelsey says.

"True," Lottie chimes in. "The only thing I've heard is how breathtaking you are in your dress."

"You heard that?" I ask.

"Yeah. Breaker was telling Huxley all about it. I think his exact sentence was, She *stole my breath.*"

"Wow, if Breaker said that, I can only imagine what your fiancé will say," Myla adds.

Yeah, I wonder what Brian would say. I know what his mother thinks—she was not a fan.

She wasn't a fan of any of the three dresses she forced me to get.

"I'm sure he'll love it," I say, even though I can't be entirely sure, especially after his response last night about my hair and outfit.

"Where is the wedding?" Kelsey asks.

"The Pier 1905 Club," I answer. "Brian's family are members. The wedding will take place in the gardens."

"Oh, that should be pretty," Kelsey says.

"Yeah," I say on a sigh and realize that maybe this would be a good way to bond with the girls. Bond on a deeper level. "It's not my ideal location, but I'm sort of stuck with it since my soon-to-be mother-in-law is a distant relative of Lucifer himself."

"Really?" Lottie asks, setting her drink down and turning toward me. "Is she one of those moms who wants to have control over everything?"

"Yeah. *Mother* has her quintessential wedding in mind, and none of my ideas are even on Mother's radar."

"How is she getting away with this?" Kelsey asks. "Does Brian know?"

"Oh yeah, he knows, and he's completely impervious. He keeps telling me to let his mother make all the decisions because the wedding isn't a union of love for his family. It's more of a horse and pony show. Clearly, I don't have the same opinion."

"Uh, and why isn't Brian backing you up?" Lottie asks.

Great question.

"He's a mama's boy, and I'm pretty sure he still believes he must do anything to please Mother. Also known as The Beave. He constantly seeks his parents' approval, and this is just another instance of that."

"Well, that's ridiculous," Kelsey says, outraged. "I like the nickname, though. Your wedding should be one of the most special days of your life, not a day filled with someone else's version of love."

"I agree. Breaker has been pretty good at helping me keep things from getting too scary. The mother-in-law wanted us to get married in a church, but Breaker helped move it to the garden. The dresses she wanted me to wear were atrocious, and Breaker put his foot down on that too. Honestly, I'd be lost without him."

Kelsey and Lottie exchange some sort of knowing look before they turn back to me. "It's because Breaker always thinks of you first," Kelsey says softly. "He truly cherishes you. I'm sure he doesn't say all the things to you that he says to us, but you are his number one. There's no question about it."

I look over my shoulder where I find Breaker laughing with his brothers and Ryot, all holding Bloody Marys in hand, looking like a pack of men's world fitness models getting ready for their next shoot. Breaker glances at me just at the same time, and with a simple wink in my direction, my stomach tumbles out of my body.

"Yup, always puts you first," Lottie seconds as we all take a sip of our drinks.

———

"Did you try the croissants?" Breaker asks as he sits on my lounger and places his hand on my shin.

"I did," I say as I can feel the warmth of his palm once again.

"And…"

I attempt to look anywhere but into his eyes, but it's useless. They're the brightest blue, which means they're pulling me into his gaze—his comforting, warm gaze. "They were fantastic," I manage to say.

"Told you." He gives my shin a squeeze. "Seemed like you were having fun with the girls. What's this I hear about a knitting club? And how can I get an invite? I bet Lottie and Kelsey have no idea the skills I have."

His charm soothes the tension I was just feeling. "Your ability to knit barely registers as a skill. You can knit a line, and that's pretty much it."

"Lies!" he says. "I knitted a scarf."

"Your 'scarf' was three lines knitted together, and you said it was for a mouse."

"Yeah, so, mice need to stay warm, too. And maybe if I was invited to the knitting club, I'd grow my skills into something more, like a knitted hat."

"Last time I tried to teach you, you pierced the wall with your knitting needle because you were frustrated."

"The yarn was aggravating me. I'm better now, less temperamental."

"Uh-huh, sure."

He nods at me. "Scoot over." I move to the side of the large lounge chair just as Breaker sits next to me and loops his arm around my shoulder. Together, we lie there, staring up at the cloudy sky as everyone around us chats and enjoys some bottomless mimosas and JP's apparently not-so-mediocre Bloody Marys. "What else did you guys talk about?"

How you're probably a stallion in bed.

How you made a woman come so many times in one night that JP was actually impressed.

"Uh…things," I say.

"Things? That's so descriptive. Wow, I never would have thought." I poke his stomach, causing him to laugh. "Seriously, what did you talk about?"

"The wedding and how you seem to care about me."

"I do care about you." He pulls me in closer so I can rest my head on his chest. "You're important to me. Did you tell them how I've been your knight in shining armor when it comes to The Beave?"

"In so many words but not quite that eccentric."

"I think it's important to know that I've been the hero of this journey down the aisle. It's vastly important."

"To whom?"

"The world."

"You're so ridiculous."

"Maybe, but you were the one who made me the Pickle of Honor."

"How could I possibly forget?" I ask as his hand strokes my shoulder. It feels nice to have human contact. Not just groping hands and pecks on the cheek. *Does Brian miss me when he's gone? Miss holding me? Touching me?*

"I'd hope that you wouldn't. Did you talk about anything else?"

"A few things," I answer. "But nothing I want to talk about in the back-yard of your brother's house."

"Okay, shall we leave, then?"

"We don't have to. I mean, it's nothing important."

"Yeah, but if we stay any longer, JP will make me drink another Bloody Mary, and I don't think I can stomach it. I nursed the one he gave me two hours ago and then dumped it in a bush when they weren't looking."

"No, you didn't."

He points at a shapely bush off to the right near the fence gate. "That one, right there, if it starts to die, we will know why."

"Aah, just another secret I'll have to hang over your head."

"Okay." Breaker flops onto his couch and puts his hands behind his head. "Give me all the dirt. What did you talk about?"

When we returned to our apartment building, I went to my place and changed because there was no way I was lounging around Breaker's apartment in a dress. I switched over to a pair of flannel shorts and a regular T-shirt. I also washed off my makeup because it made my eyes feel weird. Breaker changed into his athletic shorts and a shirt that features the art of the inner workings of a computer. He thinks it's cool, and I tell him it's one of the nerdiest things he owns.

"It's really not that big a deal," I say as I sit cross-legged on his couch and clutch a throw pillow.

"It has to be a big deal if you didn't want to talk about it in Huxley's backyard. So spill, Lia, what is it?"

"God, you're annoying. Fine, but you can't tease me or make fun of me about it, okay? I'm sort of sensitive about the topic."

"Okay," he says as he sits up and turns toward me. "What is it?"

"Well, Myla started the conversation off with how, uh...her and Ryot were...enjoying themselves."

"Having sex?" Breaker asks.

"Yes, having sex. And before you say that's not a big deal, it is a big deal because I normally don't talk about those things, so I feel weird, okay?"

"Okay," he says soothingly, and I'm glad he's sensed my tone and is not going to make fun of me.

"So she was talking about how Ryot is really good at giving...oral, and then Kelsey and Lottie chimed in. I just felt weird because Brian really doesn't do that, and when I try to give him...that, he pushes me away and says that...well, that I'm not that great at it."

"He said that to you?" Breaker asks, his brows narrowing in anger.

"Not precisely with those words, but yeah. And I don't know, listening to them talk about their sex lives, it made me think that maybe I need to step it up, you know? Maybe I need to try harder."

"Doubtful," he says while looking away.

"You don't know that. Maybe I suck in bed."

"Ophelia," he says, his voice terse. "You wouldn't suck in bed."

"You don't know that. For all we know, I could be a real dead fish. I mean, I thought I knew what I was doing when it came to a blow job, but maybe I don't." My eyes connect with his. "Like...what do you enjoy when a woman is down there?"

He pulls on the back of his neck. "Every guy is different."

"But it's a mouth on your penis. I'm pretty sure any guy enjoys a mouth on their penis, so…what do you like?"

He clears his throat. He's uncomfortable. Of course he is. God, I bet he's never had to complain about one of his hookups being bad in bed. They've probably all had more experience than I have, especially given he's the prodigious man stud in bed. No wonder he's uncomfortable. He's the sexiest Cane brother with wicked talents.

"You know what, never mind. This was stupid. I shouldn't have brought it up. It's just that I don't think my sex life is good, and shouldn't it be good right before I get married? Shouldn't we be having sex all the time? Phone sex even? We just…aren't. He goes to bed and doesn't even spoon me. I keep telling myself it's because he's exhausted from work, but…Huxley and JP and Ryot are tired, but they still—"

"I like when the girl plays with the tip slowly at first," he says, his voice deep, almost tortured. He lifts his gaze toward me, and I register what he said. His stare is so intense that I'm immediately captured. *Drawn.* "I like to be teased, taunted, unsure if I'll be granted permission to enter her mouth. I like it when she drags her tongue around the head, then flicks the underside over and over until I'm so hard, I'm aching for more." My cheeks heat. I'm transfixed. "I love cupping her cheek to show her that if she wants to take me, I want her to. And when she does suck me into her warm, wet mouth, I love watching her eyes, seeing them water, seeing how she can take me all the way back to her throat. And as she's pumping me in and out, I fucking beg for the lightest drag of her teeth over my length, just enough to tantalize me."

"Oh," I say as I shift, my body heated. This is…this is the first time I've ever heard him talk like this, and it's making me feel all kinds of tingly. "And, uh…that will make you orgasm?"

"Hard," he answers. "And I prefer my girl to swallow, as I like watching her throat work while I stiffen in her mouth."

My mouth has gone dry.

And a dull throb is pulsing between my legs because oh my God, I never would have expected this from him. I mean, sure, I knew there was a dirty side to him—I've heard it—but teeth dragging…this is what the girls were talking about, this very thing.

"I see." I nod slowly. "Well, that was informative."

"What do you like when it comes to a guy going down on you?" he asks.

"Umm, well…I'm not quite sure because Brian doesn't really do that."

"I would," he says quickly while wetting his lips. Speaking directly to me, his eyes so intense, he says, "I'd go down on my girl. Because I'm desperate to taste her, please her, and drive her wild, I'd slowly spread her legs and work my way up her inner thighs, teasing her. I'd drop kisses over every inch until I could see her dripping for me. Ready for my tongue to devour her. Her clit would be so hard I'd be able to flick it with my tongue. She'd be panting, nearly breathless. My fingers would widen her lips so I could drag my tongue over her clit in one long stroke."

Oh fuck, why can I *feel* that?

"That's, uh"—I squeeze my legs together—"that would be nice."

"That would be only the beginning. I love to hear my girl scream, to pull on my hair, to dig her heels so far into my back that I feel it the next day. I love to suck on her clit, taste her, pulse my fingers into her, and make my face sloppy with her arousal. And then, I like to do it all over again. I take. I fucking take every last ounce of pleasure from her, and then that's when I let myself come, when I know that she has nothing left to give me."

My skin breaks out in a sweat as a dull throb starts to pulse through my veins.

I smack my lips together. "Well, that, uh, that is not the way Brian does it." Not even close. "So this was educational. Maybe I should try the whole tongue-flicking thing."

"Do you want to try it?" he asks.

"What do you mean?"

"Do you want to go down on Brian?"

"I mean, isn't that what I'm supposed to do?"

"You're not supposed to do anything. But when a woman goes down on me, it's because she wants to, because she finds my cock so enticing that she can't function without tasting me. I want my girl to be desperate, needy, and begging for me, so when she does take me in her mouth, she worships it. Just like I would worship her aching pussy."

Jesus…hell. *Because she finds my cock so enticing that she can't function without tasting me… Just like I would worship her aching pussy.*

Hearing him say *pussy* is next level. How it rolls off his tongue with ease as if he says it all the time. And he probably does. This conversation has shown me exactly the type of man he is when he's intimate with a woman. Dirty talking, desirous, dominating. A stark contrast from the sweet, funny best friend I know so dearly.

"Well, I want to pleasure him," I say. "I think everyone wants to be able to pleasure their partner." *Do I find Brian's cock so enticing that I can't function without tasting him?* Obviously not.

"What do you do with him?" he asks as he scoots closer to me, placing just a few inches between us now so our knees knock together and his arm is draped right behind me.

Can he tell how…turned on I am from this conversation? Can he feel the heat coming off me? Can he see my rosy cheeks or see the light sheen of sweat that has broken out over my skin?

God, I hope not.

"Uh, what do I do with Brian? Well." I clear my throat, feeling uncomfortable. I'm the one who started this conversation, so I might as well go all in. "We obviously kiss."

"That's a given," he says, his eyes falling to my lips.

I have to look away because it almost seems like there's hunger in his pupils, but that could just be the heightened awareness from what he just said. "And you know, touch each other. He fondles my breasts and, uh"—I swallow—"I touch his balls and penis. But, we kind of just get into it, you know? He really likes to fuck me from behind."

Oh my God, I can't believe I just said that. My cheeks are burning with embarrassment.

Breaker tugs on a strand of my hair and twists it around his finger. "Does he spank you while he's fucking you?"

"What?" My eyes widen before I shake my head. "No. He's never spanked me."

"Shame. Bet you would get wet from it." Dear Jesus. "Do you strip for him?" he asks, his voice so deep that I'm barely comprehending what he's asking.

I rub my thighs gently, trying to keep my mind on his question and not his responses. "I did a few times."

"Lap dance?"

"Uh, not really. But I have purchased some lingerie that I know he liked. It was black see-through lace."

Breaker wets his lips again and nods. "That's hot, Lia."

"Yeah?" I ask, my cheeks now flaming.

"Very hot. I love when my girl wears lingerie. I love when she wants to dress up for me, show me her body, grind on me. It's all about the teasing, so even if you're not comfortable with giving a lap dance, trust me, if you were in lingerie and just lightly grinding on my dick, I'd be fucking ecstatic."

"But…what do I do, just sit there?"

"And move your hips. It's his job to further the moment by running his hands up your thighs like this," he says as he drags his fingers over my leg, shooting a punch of lust straight between my thighs.

Fuck, that feels good.

"Oh," I say breathlessly.

"And he's supposed to smooth his hand over your stomach, especially if you're facing the other direction, your back to his chest. He's supposed to attempt to touch your breasts but not really touch them. He's supposed to get close, to run his finger along the underside but pull away. He's supposed to turn you on so much that when he moves his hand back down your stomach and plays with the waistband of your underwear that your legs part even wider. You should be wet, throbbing, so turned on that you're ready to come when he slips his fingers right against your clit."

I can't breathe.

I can't speak.

I can barely hear him over the roar of my pulse in my ears.

Turned on…yeah, I'm there.

I know that I'm wet, I know that I'm throbbing, and that Breaker knows exactly how to entice a woman.

"Does he finger you?"

"Umm…sometimes," I say.

"Does he suck on his fingers after he fingers you?"

"Uh, no, that's not Brian."

"That's the best fucking part," Breaker says as he wets his lips. "I love tasting a woman. I love having the flavor of her on my tongue as I drive into her."

"Oh, yeah, Brian has not done that," I say stupidly as I try to look away from his magnetic eyes.

"How does he fuck you? Does he tie you down? Does he let you ride him? Does he use toys?"

I swallow and wish at this moment that I had a drink, anything to quench my thirst from this conversation.

"Just regular, you know, nothing too fancy. Like, we do, uh, different positions, but nothing outside of that realm." I cover my face and say, "This is so embarrassing."

"Why?" he asks, lowering my hands from my face.

"Because clearly you're more voracious in bed, and I look like a basic vanilla-bean girl compared to you."

"Don't compare yourself. That's the first way to make yourself feel bad."

"It's hard not to compare when discussing toys and tying up. And then the girls earlier with all their talk about how their men like going down on them. Maybe…maybe something is wrong with me."

Breaker forcefully grips my chin, and when our eyes lock, he says, "Nothing is wrong with you. Fucking nothing. It's all about chemistry and maybe…maybe you just don't have that with Brian." Why do I have a feeling he might be right? "Tying you up, using toys, is that the kind of stuff you want?"

"I don't know what I want; I just…I think I want more than what I have now."

"You deserve more," he says, his voice choppy now. "Your pussy deserves to be tongued, consumed, and fucked so hard that you can't walk the next day." My breath grows heavy, the air becoming harder and harder to suck in. "You're so fucking sexy, Lia, and if it were me—"

Knock. Knock.

If it were you, what? I want to scream as he turns to look at the door.

I catch the narrowing of his brows and wonder if he knows who is here, because whoever it is, he doesn't seem too happy about it.

"Who is that?" I ask, as if Breaker can see through the door.

"No idea." And for the first time since I've known him, I watch him walk toward the door, my mind focusing on his backside, the tightness of his ass accompanied by what he just said to me. *You're so fucking sexy, Lia.*

I play that on repeat, over and over, until I hear him answer the door. "Oh, hey. Uh, what are you doing here?"

"Is Lia here?"

Brian? He's here?

I move over to the entryway, where I see Brian with a single duffel bag in hand.

"Brian, I thought you were on your business trip."

He glances at Breaker and then back at me. "I was, but I didn't like our last conversation, so I returned for the night. I have to leave first thing tomorrow morning."

"Oh." I twist my hands in front of me, my body temperature immediately cooling down.

"Can we go to your place, please?" His eyes plead.

"Yeah, can you just give me one second? I'll meet you over there," I answer as I stand there awkwardly.

"Sure." Brian glances at Breaker. "Good to see you, man."

"Yeah, you too," Breaker says as Brian takes off. Breaker shuts the door and sifts his hand through his hair. I watch the bottom of his shirt lift to show off the waistband of his briefs. "So Brian's home."

"He is," I answer. "That was unexpected."

"Very." Breaker leans against his hallway wall, looking almost defeated. I can't imagine why, though. "So you should probably go talk to him."

I take a step forward. This need to touch him is so overwhelming, but I hold back because I'm not sure what would happen if I did. If I gave in to this mystifying sensation that's pulsing through my blood, I might not be able to stop myself. "Yeah, I probably should." I toe the ground, needing to say something else, so I ask, "Should I talk to him about sex?"

His sharp eyes focus on me as he says, "I mean, if you want to. If you think it's a good time."

"I think it needs to be said, don't you? We're getting married in four weeks."

"That you are," he huffs and then pushes off the wall. "Yes, Lia, go tell him what you desire, and don't be afraid to tell him everything." Breaker takes a step forward, closing the space between us. He pushes a stray hair behind my ear and speaks softly. "Tell him you want his tongue between your legs. Tell him you want him to tease you, to taunt you, to make you feel so goddamn wet that you could just come from him rolling your nipples between his fingers."

My breath becomes shallow again, and my eyes fall to his lips as he continues, "Tell him you want him to fuck you. To fuck you so mercilessly that you can't take the constant hammering of his dick inside you until you come so hard that you can't think of sex any other way but carnal."

My lungs seize.

My toes tingle.

And my body is tempted to crumple right here on the floor from the erotic energy running through me.

I want that.

I want that carnal feeling he speaks of.

I want to feel a man so deep inside me that it makes my eyes well with tears.

I want to be stretched, licked, and fucked to the point that I can't remember anything besides this undeniable feeling of him and only him.

"What if he doesn't want to fuck me?" I whisper, my insecurity rearing up.

Breaker pauses and loops his index finger under my chin. He lifts my gaze to meet his. Very carefully, he says, "Then he's not the man for you because, Lia…you deserve to be fucked. Just like you deserve to be worshipped. *Hard.*"

And before I can say another thing, he walks away.

CHAPTER 14
BREAKER

"DUDE, DIDN'T YOU JUST LEAVE us?" JP asks when he opens his door.

I push past him and head straight to his kitchen.

"Uh, come in. Not like I'm doing anything important."

"Where are your disgusting Bloody Marys?" I ask as I move around his kitchen.

"Uh, if you recall, the brunch was over at Huxley's. He has everything," JP says when he follows me into the kitchen.

"Then where's your alcohol? I know you have some. Where is it?"

"Okay, I need you to slow down for a second." He rests his hand on the counter. "Why are you all jittery?"

"Just give me fucking alcohol, okay?" I take a seat on one of his kitchen island seats and push my hands through my hair.

"What's going on?" Kelsey asks, walking in with a concerned look.

"Breaker apparently needs alcohol but has yet to say why."

"Because I'm in love with my best friend who's getting married in four weeks. Do I need any other explanation?"

"No, I think that will do it," JP says like a dick, and then he moves to a cabinet on the right of the fridge and pulls out a bottle of Scotch. "Will this do?"

"Yes, whatever, I don't care. Just give me something, anything."

Kelsey sits beside me and places her hand on my back soothingly. "What's going on?"

"I feel like I'm going to lose it." My body shakes with adrenaline as my emotions rip through me.

JP slides a glass of Scotch toward me, and I immediately down it and slide the glass back to him. "More."

"Oh-kay," he says.

"Breaker, talk to us," Kelsey says.

I swallow the next glass and set it down, gripping the cylinder with both hands. "Do you remember when you two were in San Francisco, and you weren't an item yet?"

"Yes," they both say at the same time.

"And the night Kelsey was going out with that other guy and, JP, you didn't know how to handle it because you really liked Kelsey? You got trashed that night and sent that stupid email."

"Yes, unfortunately."

"Well, that pain you were feeling, that's what I'm feeling right now." I tug on my hair. "Fuck."

"Where is Lia now?" Kelsey asks.

"At home...with Brian." I slap my hand on the counter and say, "And the worst thing about it all is because thanks to your little girl chat at brunch, she was asking me all about sex because apparently Brian is a real fucking dud in the bedroom and doesn't go down on her."

"What?" JP asks in disgust. "That's like the best fucking part, making your girl come on your tongue."

"That's what I said, and she was asking for advice on how to give a good blow job." I hold out my glass, and JP quickly pours some Scotch in it. "And I fucking told her how to give a good one. Right there, I told her everything, so now she's over at her place, probably kneeling in front of Brian, the fucking douche, sucking his dick, because I'm the goddamn asshole who told her how to do it. Fuck!" I lean back in my chair and down the Scotch before setting the glass back down again.

"Wow, there's a lot to unpack there," JP says. "You really taught her how to give a good blow job? Why?"

"I don't know, because I lost my mind. Because I can't look her in the eyes and see the sadness Brian puts there. Because I couldn't let her feel bad about herself when she's clearly trying, and he's not. So yeah, I told her how to please him, and now that they're in her apartment, I couldn't stay there. I couldn't listen to her pleasure him. There was no fucking way, when all I want is for her to be with me. I mean, Jesus Christ, I was doing fine," I yell, thrusting my arm out. "I was doing perfectly fine, and then I saw her in that wedding dress, and it's like…my world snapped, and I can't stop spiraling. Why couldn't I have figured this out a year ago? A month ago, anytime where there wasn't a countdown to doomsday when she attached herself to another man who does not fucking deserve her? Not even close."

"To be fair, Huxley and I have been telling you for years you like Lia," JP says.

I glare at him while Kelsey says, "JP, that's not helpful."

"Wasn't trying to be helpful, was trying to make a point, like I've been trying to make for years now."

"You're an asshole," I say to him.

"How do you want me to respond?" JP asks, thrusting his arms out. "Do you want me to hold your hand and tell you everything will be okay? That we'll always know you as the better man? News flash, man, she's getting married. And if you don't do something about it, then she's going to go off with the douche, and you're going to be left to die alone in your apartment."

"Seriously, JP," Kelsey groans. "You're being rude."

"I'm being real. If he wants her, then he needs to tell her."

"No, he can't," Kelsey says, surprising me. "Trust me, if he just knocks on her door and tells her he loves her, she won't take it well. He needs to continue to show her how he's better."

"That's not working out for him. Lia is giving the other guy a blow job because my idiot brother taught her the tricks of the trade." He turns to me. "Were you trying to turn her on? Were you trying to be all sexy-like?"

"Don't fucking say *sexy-like*," I say. "And it was a hot moment, okay? I saw her cheeks blush. I was showing her that I'm the kind of man who'd make her orgasm several times in one night, not stupid Brian."

"And how did that work out for you?"

"Not fucking well," I answer and press my fingers into my forehead. "I think Kelsey is right, though; I don't think I can just tell her. I feel her questioning him, questioning herself. But fuck...she's also the person who doesn't like to give up. So she'll do anything to make it work, and I bet that's what she's doing tonight. Maybe...maybe I can fake getting hurt or something." I perk up. "Yeah, like, I can break a leg or something, and then you guys can call her and tell her I'm in the hospital, and that will drag her away from Brian tonight, and she won't give him a blow job."

"Are you hearing yourself right now?"

"I am." I stand from my chair now to pace the kitchen. "This is a great idea because it will garner me sympathy, and she'll want to take care of me of course because that's who she is, and when she's taking care of me, I can move in more, steal her from Brian. This is genius."

"This is stupid because if you break your leg, how the hell are you supposed to run away when Brian finds out what you did? The guy might be a douche, but that man has simmering rage, and I think he could be a good fight," JP says.

"Uh, besides all of that, breaking a leg is not the way to get the girl," Kelsey says. "God, you guys are such idiots."

"Breaking my leg is the best idea so far. What else should I do? Oh!" I snap my fingers. "I can tell her I got food poisoning from the Bloody Mary."

"The fuck you will," JP says. "Don't fucking taint me for your own benefit."

"That's the only thing I had that she didn't, and food poisoning will drag her away from Brian."

"Uh-huh, and how do you suppose you throw up in front of her?" JP asks.

I glance around the kitchen. "Have any raw chicken?"

"For God's sake," Kelsey says, rising from her chair. She takes me by the arm and sits me down. Her hands rest on my shoulders as she stares me in the eyes. "You're not going to do anything tonight—"

"But—"

"If she happens to give him a blow job, then so be it. That's the price you pay for trying to show her how you enjoy one. But what you need to remember is that she heard everything you said. She listened intently, and if I know Lia like I think I do, that will stick in her mind. Every time she looks at you, she's going to think about how you like to be sucked, how you like to be between a female's legs, and how *easily* you can please a woman. She will remember that, and that's the new foundation you work off."

"Babe, seriously, keep talking like that and we're going upstairs."

Kelsey glances up at JP and says, "Unless you start being helpful to your brother, who clearly is in agony, then I won't be going upstairs anytime soon. He loves her, JP, and he deserves to be with her." She turns her attention back to me and continues, "This is go time, Breaker. Forget about what happens between Brian and Lia. Act like he never came home and charge forward. Trust me, we spoke about you in our little girls' gathering, and there's intrigue there, and it's not best friend intrigue. I think you have a chance, but you need to do this right. Brian will falter. He already has, so be patient."

"I have four weeks," I say in desperation.

"She will break before that, trust me. Between you and Brian, you have the history, the sex appeal, and the ability to make her happy. She'll see that quickly. Brian is a blip. You are forever."

"Babe." JP clutches his chest. "Damn, that was sweet."

"That was sweet," I say.

"You're making my heart all aflutter," JP adds. "And naturally, my dick hard."

Jesus.

Ignoring my brother, I ask, "You really think Lia and I are forever?"

"If anything, Breaker, I love *love*, and I would never mess with that. I truly believe you and Lia are soulmates. I'm just glad you're seeing it now."

"Okay." I nod. "So what do I do now?"

"Well, when I was spiraling, I decided to donate money to make myself feel better," JP says. "I know of a great pigeon rescue that could use another donor."

I look him dead in the eyes and say, "I'm not feeding into your pigeon obsession. You can fuck off with that."

LIA

"So how was your flight back?" I ask, unsure of what to say to him. His presence is completely unexpected. I'm having a hard time processing that he's even here, let alone digesting the conversation I just had with Breaker.

"It was fine. Got some work done, thankfully," Brian says as he loosens his tie.

Yes, thank God for that. Can't imagine what would happen if he didn't get work done.

"Well, uh, are you hungry? I can order food."

"I just really want to talk to you." His eyes go to my hair as he approaches me. Does he still hate it? He hasn't said he loves it, that's for sure. He takes my hands in his and asks, "Is everything okay?"

"What do you mean?"

"Here, let's sit," he says as he brings me over to my couch. Once we're seated, a few inches between us, he continues. "I know the wedding planning has been stressful on you, and I'm worried that maybe you're not handling it all well, hence the haircut and color."

Excuse me?

"What do you mean? I cut my hair and highlighted it because I wanted to, not because of the stress of the wedding."

"Lia," he says in his condescending tone. "I've known you for over a year now, and you've never made such a drastic change like this before. I'm just worried the stress is overwhelming, your parents aren't around, you're trying to find some semblance of control, and your appearance is the one thing you feel you can control. So you cut your hair. I'm worried this pattern will continue, and who knows what you will do next."

I rear back, absolutely offended by his assumption. Firstly, where does he come off, even thinking he has a say in my appearance? Secondly, does he truly not see how happy I was in that picture I sent him?

"Brian, it's a haircut. It's not like I went off and tattooed a penis on my face. And my decision to do this has nothing to do with you and everything to do with me. I wanted to feel pretty."

"You were just fine before. There's no need to change anything."

"Just fine?" I ask, rising from the couch. "I was just fine before? Couldn't think of a better adjective than that?"

He presses his hand to his forehead. "*Pretty*, I meant *pretty*." He lets out a huff. "It's been a long day. I've been worried about you, and getting this flight was hard, so excuse me if my words are not what they're supposed to be right now."

"I need your words to not be condescending, and I don't think that's too much to ask."

"Where is this all coming from?" he asks. "I feel like you're angry with me."

What clued you in? Good God.

"I am angry with you," I shout. "Jesus, Brian. This whole wedding and dealing with your mom and your reaction to my hair, it's been a nightmare. And you...you never want to have sex with me. Why is that?"

He looks at me, confused. "Yes, I do," he says.

"No, you don't. We haven't had sex in two weeks. Don't you think that's weird? Don't you think we should be at each other's bodies every chance we get, peeling off our clothes and finding pleasure in each other?"

"It's been a rough couple of weeks, Lia."

"We didn't even have sex the night you proposed. I fell asleep while you were on a business call."

"With clients from Japan. What choice do I have?" he asks, his voice growing angrier.

"You have a choice, and it's called me, but you don't choose me. Am I just some sort of...accessory to your life checklist?"

"No, Lia," he says as he stands and moves toward me. "I love you. You're going to be my wife."

"Then why don't you want to have sex with me?"

"I do," he says, his hands going to my shoulders. "It's just...it's been hard lately, okay?"

"Are you...are you cheating on me? Are you getting sex somewhere else, and that's why you don't want to do it with me?"

"Lia," he says sternly. "Don't even fucking say that. You know that's not the kind of man I am." And I believe him because he might work long nights and sometimes say the wrong thing, but I know for certain that Brian would never do that. His dad cheated on his mom many times, and he saw how that hurt her. He always said he would never do that to his wife.

"I know. I'm sorry," I say, feeling shameful for bringing it up. "Do you think we're in some sort of rut? I mean, you don't even like it when I give you a blow job."

"I've never liked them, Lia. It's not just you. I feel bad when a girl has to just sit there and suck on my dick, okay?"

"But what if I wanted to?" I ask, trailing my fingers up his shirt.

He stops my touch and links our hands together. "I still feel like it's demeaning. You deserve better than to have to pleasure me like that."

"It's not demeaning," I say. "It's a way to show your partner how you love them."

He shakes his head. "It's demeaning to me."

"Okay, then what about like...spanking or toys? We've never tried that."

"Because we don't need that kind of fanfare. I don't need a vibrator to get you off. I can do that myself." *Not every time, though...*

"It's not about you not being able to get me off. It's about having fun, doing new things."

"Let's just stop talking about it, okay? That's not a concern at the moment."

"It is for me," I say, my voice rising. "I don't want to marry someone who doesn't want to have sex with me, Brian."

"Excuse me?" he asks. "You don't want to marry me?"

"No, I do. I'm just saying we're having some issues, and I think they need to be sorted before we get married. I think it's important."

"The only issue I have is that you seem to be getting these ideas in your head about me, and I have no clue where they're coming from. We were fine before all of this, so why now? Why are you second-guessing our relationship?"

"I'm not second-guessing, I'm just trying to iron out some kinks, and I don't think I should be chastised for that. I mean, when I've asked you for your support with your mom about the wedding stuff, you take her side. Don't you think you should be taking your future wife's side?"

"Why does there have to be a side? Why isn't there a compromise?"

"Because your mom doesn't understand the word *compromise*."

"Pretty sure she's cut down the guest list, we're now getting married in a garden rather than a church, and there are daisies in the wedding to represent your mom. None of those were on my mother's list to begin with."

"Your *mother* shouldn't even have a list. Your mother shouldn't be this involved."

"She's representing me, Lia. Since I'm busy, she's taking on the responsibility of standing up for what I want."

"Oh really?" I ask. "So you believe it's imperative to have roses at your wedding?"

"Yes, I think they're elegant."

"Please, Brian. You couldn't care less what's happening at the wedding. You're just going to show up."

"That's not true. I want what's going to look nice, what's going to represent the family, and a day we can remember forever."

"It's not always about image," I say as I move past him.

"Why do you keep arguing about this? You're getting your way with things. Why are you making a big deal about it?"

"Because if this was what I wanted, we wouldn't be having it at the club, we wouldn't be inviting people I don't know, and I wouldn't be changing into three dresses."

"But it's not all about you, Lia. You might be the bride, but I'm the groom, and there has to be pieces of me in the wedding planning as well. My mother knows what that is."

"Well, maybe if you talked to me about what you wanted, I could help pick those things out."

He blows out a heavy breath. "You're creating a fight over nothing. Like I said, something has gotten in your head, and you're trying to find any excuse not to...not to go through with this. And if that's the case, Lia, just tell me now. I don't want to get to our wedding day and have you run out on me because you finally found the courage to do so."

"Brian, I'm not trying to get out of this," I say, feeling defeated. "I'm just trying to get you to understand where I'm coming from. I want us to be okay. I want you to be on my side. To want me. To not think I'm going through some sort of crisis because I changed my hair. I mean…are you going to judge me when I walk down the aisle? Are you going to think my dress is ugly? Is that something I should worry about?"

"No, my mother sent me a picture. It's a pretty dress."

I pause and tilt my head to the side. "Your mother…sent you a picture of my dress?"

"Yes, she wanted to make sure I approved."

"That's not…that's not something you need to approve. That's my decision."

"Do you hear yourself?" he asks. "You're being so selfish. This wedding isn't just about you, Lia."

"I didn't say it was," I yell. "God, you're so infuriating. I'm so glad you freaking came here to fix things. Good job." I move toward the kitchen and grab myself a sparkling water.

"Does any of this have to do with Breaker?"

I pause, the hairs on the back of my neck spring to attention, and I feel my inner rage spike to DEFCON 1 levels.

"I swear to God, Brian," I say as I spin on my heel. "Bring him up one more time, and I will end this engagement, this wedding, and this relationship. This has nothing to do with him and everything to do with us and our disconnect."

"I don't feel a disconnect."

"Because you're not here," I shout. "You're so blind, so clueless. I mean, hell, I'm offering to put your dick in my mouth, and you can't even fathom the idea. You should want your dick in my mouth."

"You want to suck me off?" he yells. He sits down on the couch and leans back. "Fine, Lia. Suck me off."

"You're such an asshole," I say as I walk back to the bedroom.

BREAKER

"I don't feel very good," I say as JP and Huxley walk me to my apartment.

"Because you had three shots of Scotch in ten minutes, realized your mistake, tried to counteract with buttery croissants and water, and now your stomach has no idea what to do with itself," JP says.

"If you puke on my shoes, I'll murder you," Huxley says.

"Why did I have to come home? I don't want to hear her having sex." I rest my head on Huxley's shoulder. "I bet she's a sweet moaner."

"Can you not speak so closely to my face?"

"I bet she has the best-tasting pussy ever, like…a fresh field of flowers."

"When was the last time you ate pussy?" JP asks as we reach my door. Huxley unlocks it and lets us in.

"I can't remember, but I bet you hers is fantastic."

"Just dump him on his couch," Huxley says.

"No, my bedroom. I want to smell the pillow she used the other night. It smells like her. I want to clutch it."

"I don't think I've ever seen a more embarrassing display of a man," JP says. "If only Kelsey didn't take my phone away so I couldn't record anything."

"Kelsey is an angel sent from the heavens above," I say while clutching JP. "And Lottie, well, she's funny, and I like that she busts your balls all the time, Huxley. I've never seen a woman put you in your place like her. God, the way you grovel around her, talk about embarrassing. But that's what I'd do with Lia, I would worship the ground she walks on."

"That's great," Huxley says as he pushes me back on my bed. I tumble onto it with a plop.

I hold my feet up and say, "Shoes. Please take off my shoes."

Huxley points at me, then JP, and says, "Go ahead, remove the shoes."

"Why don't you remove the shoes?"

"Because I'm the older brother, which automatically puts me in the managerial role."

"Are you saying you'll manage how I take off his shoes?"

"Yeah, now take them off."

"How about you both take one off?" I say, wiggling my feet. "I could also use some more water. And maybe a bucket. I don't want to puke on the floor, and I have a good feeling that might happen."

JP turns to Huxley and says, "Shoes or puke pail and water?"

He groans and walks off toward the kitchen.

"He's such a grumble gus, isn't he?" I ask.

"I hate you right now, you know that? You interrupted my entire Sunday. Kelsey was supposed to spend the day naked in the house, and now I've had to drag your sorry carcass around and take off your god-damn shoes."

"And socks."

He slips off my shoes, followed by my socks, just as Huxley comes into the bedroom with water and a puke pail.

"Wow, you two are true heroes. The best brothers a guy could ask for." I spread my arms wide on my bed. "Come give me a hug."

"And risk you puking all over us? No, thank you," says JP.

Huxley pulls on the back of his neck, observing me. "Do you think we need to stay with him?"

"He's not that drunk, just stupid drunk. He'll sleep it off and be fine."

"I can tell there's a headache in my future." I pause and then sit up. "Wait…did I donate to the pigeons?"

JP shakes his head. "I tried to get you to, but Kelsey stopped me."

"Thank fuck for that angel of yours." I let out a large sigh, then grab the pillow Lia used, pulling it into my chest, where I give it a large squeeze. "Fuck, she smells so good. Like a field of flowers."

"I thought that's what her pussy tasted like," JP says. "You need to work on your descriptors."

"She's just flowers everywhere. One giant flower." I moan out her name. "Oh, Ophelia."

"Okay, shit's getting weird," JP says, taking a step back. "I think we have the right to vacate the premises."

"Yeah, I think you're right." Huxley pats my foot. "Call us if you need anything."

"I need you to break up the wedding. Thank you, and have a good day."

"Yeah, we'll get right on that," JP says as they both walk away.

"Angels, all of you are angels." And then I pass out into my pillow.

LIA

The front door shuts, and I bring my legs to my chest, holding them closely.

After another two hours of fighting, Brian and I both thought that maybe it was best to take a moment to cool off. He's going to his place for the rest of the night while I'm staying here. He asked if I was going to go talk to Breaker, and I told him I had no intention of going over to Breaker's place. I'm not even sure he's home, as I heard him leave earlier, so I have no idea what he's doing.

And I'm not in the mood to see anyone.

Am I wrong in this situation? Am I being selfish? I don't think I am. I'm not asking for much from him. I'm just asking him to talk to me, to want me, to be the fiancé I deserve. And if he can't give me the attention I deserve right now, who's to say he'd be able to give it to me when we're married? *And The Beave sent a fucking photo of the dress I chose to see if he approved? What am I? A preschooler?*

I don't think I've ever been more confused in my life.

I rest my head against the couch just as my phone lights up with a text message.

Breaker: How was the blow job?

If only he knew.

Lia: Nonexistent.

The dots pop up, indicating he's texting back, so I lie on my side on the couch and pull a blanket over me while I wait for him to respond.

Breaker: Shame. I gave you some good tips. Really good. Like… so good.
Lia: I'm sure you did.
Breaker: I really like the sucking of the tip, it feels so fucking good, Lia.

Uhh…okay. Not sure what's going on, but maybe it's a continuation of the conversation from earlier.

Lia: Yes, you stated that earlier.
Breaker: What about you, do you like…the tip?
Lia: Uh, wouldn't know, you know, since I haven't done it.
Breaker: You would like it. I know you would. I can see it in your eyes. Fuck, I bet you give the best head.

My cheeks flush again, and I'm so unsure of what's happening that I consider walking over to his apartment to see if he's okay. Instead, I just text him back.

Lia: So far, reviews aren't in my favor.
Breaker: Because you're sucking the wrong dick.
Lia: Apparently.
Breaker: What did he do? Did he get to taste you?
Lia: No.

My breath picks up, becoming more labored as I wait for him to text me back.

Breaker: Good.

Good? I sit up now as I stare down at my phone.

Breaker: He doesn't deserve to taste you.

I glance over at the wall we share as if I can see through it. What's he doing? Is he home?

Lia: Is everything okay, Breaker?
Breaker: You tell me.
Lia: What is that supposed to mean?
Breaker: Why are you texting me and not fucking Brian right now?

My palms sweat, my fingers slide along my phone, nothing making sense, but also, the sound of his sultry voice from earlier repeats in my head.

Lia: We got in a fight, and we're taking a second to cool down.
Breaker: Did he say some bullshit about you again? I swear to
    God, I will end him if he did. You're so fucking beautiful, Lia.
    Don't let him make you think otherwise.

I drop my phone onto the couch and stand, my heart racing.

What is actually happening?

This is Breaker. We always stand up for each other, but this feels different. It *sounds* different.

My phone buzzes again, and I see that it's from Breaker. My mind tells me not to look, but my heart is begging me to.

The heart wins out.

Breaker: What did he say to you?

I pace the length of my living room as I text him back.

Lia: Just asked me if I'm having some sort of crisis because of my haircut and my questions about sex.

Breaker: Bro is a goddamn fool. He should be fucking you every chance he gets, especially with your new hairstyle. So sexy, Ophelia, fuck...

I let out a low groan, my eyes swimming with uncertain tears. Because how can Breaker, my best friend, talk like this? How can he say everything I want Brian to say? Brian can hardly even look at me, kiss me, or acknowledge that I'm a slight distraction from his ever-consuming work.

Another text comes in.

Breaker: Why isn't he fucking you?

Giving up on trying to figure out what is going on, I move to my bedroom, where I flop on the bed, my headboard hitting the wall.

Lia: I don't know, Breaker.

Breaker: Did you just lie down in your bed?

Lia: Yes, are you home?

Breaker: Yes, in my bed, thinking about you.

I squeeze my eyes shut and count to five before I answer, before I say something stupid—because I'm extremely emotional.

Lia: Why are you thinking about me?

Breaker: I'm always thinking about you.

Lia: You can't always be thinking about me.

Breaker: I am. When I wake up, I wonder how I can possibly interact with you, how I can catch a glimpse of your smile. Throughout the day, I know that if I need a pick-me-up, some comfort, or fun, you're the person I want to see. And at night, when I go to sleep, you're the last thing I think of before I shut my eyes.

My teeth roll over my bottom lip as I text him back.

Lia: You say that as if it means more.

Breaker: Maybe it does.

Lia: What are you trying to do?

Breaker: Nothing.

Lia: We don't say things like that to each other.

Breaker: Yeah, well…maybe we should.

Lia: What are you talking about?

Breaker: Never mind. You won't get it. You have Brian.

Lia: Breaker, what the hell are you trying to say?

Breaker: Nothing. Not a damn thing. I need to sleep this shit off. I'll talk to you tomorrow.

Lia: No, talk to me now.

When he doesn't reply, I text again.

Lia: Breaker, do I need to come over there?

Lia: Breaker…

I stare at my phone, waiting for a response as my heart races. What is he talking about? It almost seems like…like he has feelings or something, but that can't be right. This is Breaker. He doesn't do *feelings*, right?

When he doesn't text back, I almost walk over to his apartment until I hear one solid heavy knock against the wall.

Then four.

Then three.

And then there's silence.

One knock. Four. Three.

My mind quickly translates it: *I love you.*

He's never knocked like that before. Never three words, never by himself. So what does that mean? What does this all freaking mean? Tears of frustration rise to my eyes as my phone dings with a text message.

Hoping Breaker is texting to explain it all, I quickly check the screen, but I'm quickly disappointed.

Brian: I'm sorry about our fight. I love you very much, remember that. You'll be my wife in four weeks, and we have the rest of our lives to figure out the details.

Groaning, I toss my phone to the side and cover my eyes with my hands.

I need to escape from all of this.

CHAPTER 15
BREAKER

JP: How're you feeling, Big Boy?

Clutching a cup of coffee, I text JP and Huxley back in our group thread.

Breaker: Don't call me that. And not fucking great. I texted some really stupid shit to Lia last night.

JP: I'm going to need a copy of that text thread for my own enjoyment.

Huxley: I normally don't participate in JP's shenanigans, but I'm interested in what you said as well.

Breaker: Love how supportive you two are.

JP: If anything, we're here for you, bro.

Breaker: Yeah, I can tell.

Huxley: What did you say?

Breaker: Oh, pretty much everything besides I love you, and I wish you were mine. Just skirted around all of that. Her responses showed clear confusion, for obvious reasons, and now I have to get myself together to go taste cake with her and her soon-to-be mother-in-law because the fight she got into with Brian last night clearly wasn't bad enough for her to warrant calling off the wedding.

JP: Sounds like the seventh circle of hell.

Breaker: Pretty much.

Huxley: Are you going to mention the texts?

Breaker: Should I? Or should I just act normal, as if nothing happened?

JP: I would go with the nothing happened. Don't bring attention to your stupidity. She has enough stupid to deal with when it comes to Brian.

Huxley: I don't tend to agree with JP very often, but I would have to say he's probably right on this one. Just act like everything is normal.

Breaker: And what happens when I see her, and all I want to do is reach out and kiss her?

JP: Uh, remember consent is a real thing.

Huxley: You can't just kiss women without them saying yes, so there you go. Avoid the lawsuit. We already have one we're dealing with.

Breaker: Thanks for the reminder. Okay, I have to get going. Not going to mention the texts, not going to kiss her, and I'm going to act like everything is normal.

JP: Best plan of action.

Huxley: Still going to wait on the texts from last night.

Breaker: Hux, you're starting to sound like JP.

JP: Can't say that's a bad thing.

I stand, take one last sip of my coffee, and then go back to my bathroom where I brush my teeth and then rinse with mouthwash as well. I check myself in the mirror one last time and then head toward my front door just as there's a knock on it.

Right on time.

I muster up a smile, open the door, and say, "Morning, Lia," in the cheeriest, nonawkward *nothing happened at all* tones.

Dressed in a purple pair of shorts and a white lace top, she has styled her hair half-up and half-down, pulling the front strands away from her face, which emphasizes her gorgeous green eyes.

Fuck, she's so beautiful.

"Hey," she says shyly. I need to drive our conversation right past last night's awkward texts and straight into denial, acting like it never happened.

"Are you ready to go?" I ask while I pat my stomach. "It might be early, but I held off breakfast so I can take down some cake."

Actually, eating cake is the last freaking thing on my list at the moment since I still have a touch of booze belly, but we make sacrifices for the ones we love, right?

"Uh, yeah. I didn't eat breakfast either."

"Two peas in a pod, aren't we?" I loop my arm around her, shut my door behind me, and walk her toward the elevator. From the confused look on her face, I might need to tone down the chipper attitude a bit. I hit the *down* button and stick my hand in my pocket. "Get a good sleep?" I ask, not sure what else to say.

"Not really," she says.

"No? Were you thinking too much about what flavor The Beave will force you to get? My guess, something boring like vanilla on vanilla."

She glances up at me while the elevator doors open. I can sense her confusion and her desire to talk about last night, but like I said, we're plowing ahead. No need to dwell on the past and things I might have said under the influence.

Denial.

Denial.

Denial.

"So what do you think the flavor will be?"

We ride the elevator down as she says, "Uh, well...you're probably right. Vanilla on vanilla."

"But we're going to fuck up that idea, aren't we?" I wink at her.

"Yeah, I guess we are."

"That's the spirit." We step off the elevator and walk toward my car. "Now, there's one thing we need to talk about before we arrive at the bakery." I open the passenger car door for her and say, "Where do we stand on red velvet? We're both huge fans, but is it crazy enough to drive her nuts?"

The smallest of smirks pulls at her lips. "I don't think so. We might have to ask for the cotton candy flavor."

She steps up to the car, and I grab her hand to help her into her seat. For the briefest of moments, her eyes fall to our connected hands before they fall back on mine.

"That's my girl," I say. "Cotton candy, all day, every day."

"Ah, Breaker. I wasn't sure you needed to be here with us during the cake tasting as well," The Beave says, her nose surprisingly stuck up in the air much more today.

"Oh yeah, I'll be here for everything. Plus, it's cake. Can't miss a chance for some free samples."

On the drive over, Lia and I denied everything from last night beautifully and instead spoke about many, many, and I mean many cake flavors that could throw The Beave into an absolute fit. It was as if we found a topic that we could exploit and ran with it.

"Very well." The Beave pulls her lightweight jacket that matches her skirt together. "Shall we head in?"

"We shall," I say, which causes Lia to chuckle.

I hold the door open for them and then slide in behind Lia, where I poke her in the side and then whisper in her ear, "Don't laugh at me, or The Beave will know we're in cahoots."

"Pretty sure it's too late for that," she says just as the baker greets us.

"Mrs. Beaver, thank you so much for joining us today."

"Of course." She gestures to Lia and says, "This is Ophelia, the bride, and this is her friend Breaker Cane."

"Hello, it's very nice to meet you."

The door opens behind us, and I turn around just in time to see Brian walk into the bakery. From the mere sight of his punchable face, my irritation rises. What the fuck is he doing here?

"Ah, there you are, sweetheart," The Beave says.

"Brian," Lia says, startled. "What, uh, what are you doing here?"

"I was able to move a few meetings around. Couldn't miss the cake tasting." He leans in, grabs her by the back of her neck, and kisses her on the lips. When he releases Lia, he turns toward me, pats me on the shoulder, and says, "Hey, man. I got it from here. You can take off."

Uhhh…

I glance at Lia, hoping she doesn't agree with this decision, and to my luck, she says, "No, Breaker can stay. I'd love to have his opinion still."

Thank fuck for that.

"Okay, sure. The more, the merrier," Brian says with a smile that reads fake.

That's right, you motherfucker. As if he can just fucking waltz on in here and act like he's the doting fiancé.

Sure, it's a cake tasting for his wedding, but he's acting like he's been at every meeting, and he hasn't. The more, the merrier…he can fuck off with that.

"Well, then, why don't you four take a seat, and I'll get the samples ready for presentation? I'll be out shortly. In the meantime, can I have my assistant grab anyone champagne?"

"Please," The Beave says. "One for everyone."

More like one for each hand, thanks.

I reach to pull out Lia's chair for her, but Brian gives me the stink eye of all stink eyes, so I back off. Instead, I pull out my own chair and mentally thank myself for being so gentlemanly. The Beave sits next to me, Brian sits next to The Beave, and Lia sits between the Beave and me like a happy little family.

Not uncomfortable at all.

"Now, I've informed the baker of our preference of flavors," The Beave starts out with.

"What would those be?" I ask. "Because I don't think you asked Lia."

"I told her what Lia likes," Brian says.

"Oh, and what did you say?" I question.

Brian straightens and says, "Vanilla bean with vanilla frosting."

Ha, we fucking knew it.

"That's not what she prefers," I say as the hairs on the back of my neck rise, a dogfight about to break out. "If she has to suffer through something as drab as vanilla, then she prefers to pair it with a raspberry lemon curd. She also enjoys red velvet with cream cheese frosting, but the cake must have chocolate chips in it. If there are no chocolate chips, she wants nothing to do with red velvet. But her favorite flavor is lemon blueberry, which I'm sure is not an option you considered."

Brian's eyes narrow, and he turns to Lia. "You have been just fine with vanilla before."

Lia looks back and forth between us. "Well, it's not my first pick."

"But a pick at that," The Beave chimes in. "And since we will have over three thousand attendees, going with the most common flavor will obviously be the most beneficial choice."

"Three thousand?" Lia asks, looking at The Beave, then Brian. "I thought we cut that list down."

"We were going to," Brian says, "but I spoke with Mother last night, and we think it's best not to insult anyone." *Except your damn fiancée.*

"Not insult anyone?" I step in. "How do you even know three thousand people? That seems absurd to me."

"Well, good thing it's not your wedding," Brian shoots back. "Maybe when you're finally able to get someone to fall in love with you and walk down the aisle instead of creeping on other men's girls, you can choose how many people attend the wedding."

"Hey," Lia says. "Brian, he's not creeping on anyone."

"Now, now," The Beave says, trying to talk us down, but my hands are clenching into fists under the table.

Where the fuck does this guy get off?

He doesn't even know her favorite cake flavor, and he thinks he can mouth off to me?

Before I can respond, The Beave cuts in, "Brian and I had a long conversation about the wedding planning that I frankly thought was getting out of hand, and we agreed on some things last night."

"How the hell could you have a conversation without Lia?" I ask, my anger rolling back my politeness.

"Pardon me?" The Beave asks. "Mr. Cane, it would do you a service not to swear at me."

Yeah, I'm not taking this bullshit today.

"Mrs. Beaver, it would do you a service to treat Lia with some respect. In case you've forgotten, my brothers and I own this city, this state, this country, so unless you want your reputation to completely and utterly tank, you will tell Lia exactly why the plans *you've* already made are not satisfactory."

From the corner of my eye, I spot Lia's silent gape as she turns toward me.

I'm not fucking around today. Not after what Lia told me about Brian. Not after what I said to her last night.

Enough is enough. They aren't going to push around my girl, not for one more goddamn second.

"Where do you get off threatening my mother like that?" Brian asks, his hands gripping the edge of the table as if he's about to flip it.

The Beave pats his arm. "Relax, darling, I can handle this."

Poised and calm, The Beave presses her hands together and says, "As you are aware, this union was not my first choice for Brian—"

"What do you mean?" Lia asks, her eyes falling on Brian.

"Mother, that's not true. You like Lia."

"I do. I think you are a lovely girl, but if I had my way, Brian would marry someone with status, and unfortunately, that's not the case here. And therefore, I am paying for a wedding that reflects *our* status, even though he's marrying you. That is why we switched back to the church, took out the daisies, and invited the people we originally wanted to invite."

Wow.

She can't be fucking serious.

How can someone with an ounce of a conscience go behind a bride's back and change everything about her wedding that she agreed upon?

I glance at Brian, waiting for him to say something, to stand up for Lia, but instead, he just sits there like the pitiful, pathetic man he is.

Looks like I'm going to have to stand up for her, prove to her that I'm the man she can rely on. I'm the man who deserves her hand. I'm the fucking man who can and WILL make her happy.

I go to open my mouth with a retaliation when Lia turns to Brian and says, "You allowed her to do that? It's one thing to just sit there and allow her to insult me to my face about how I'm not the pedigree of woman *she* would prefer for you to marry, but to have a conversation with her last night, after we fought, and let her change everything about our wedding? Did you do that out of spite?"

"Okay, here are the samples," the baker says, setting a tray in front of us, clearly not sensing the strained tension at the table as her assistant passes around the champagne. "We have as requested, the vanilla bean cake with vanilla frosting, the vanilla bean cake with chocolate frosting. The chocolate fudge cake with vanilla frosting, and the chocolate cake with chocolate frosting." She sets some forks down and says, "Enjoy," before she takes off again.

When the baker is out of earshot, Brian says, "I didn't do anything out of spite. My mother was consoling me after our fight, and we discussed how the wedding was stressing you and that we should just let Mother do the planning."

Lia sits a little taller, her confidence growing. "The only reason the wedding planning is stressful is because we're being forced to get married in four weeks, your mother is trying to take over, and no one seems to be listening to me besides Breaker."

"Because Breaker wants nothing more than for our relationship to fail," Brian says. Oh wow, look at that. We finally have something we can agree upon.

"He's been nothing but supportive. He even gave me tips on how to give you a blow job...one you didn't want."

"Jesus, Mary," The Beave says, clasping her hand over her chest as Brian stares me down. I just shrug my shoulders because, honestly, what else can I do at this point? I lean back and take a sip of the bubbly while I enjoy the theatrics. "Can we show an ounce of decorum?"

"Why the hell are you talking to Breaker about our sex life?" Brian asks.

"What sex life?" Lia announces, and it takes everything in me not to laugh. "You barely even look at me when I'm naked."

Babe, I would look at you naked every fucking chance I got. Then proceed to fuck you until you can't take anymore.

"Ophelia, lower your voice," The Beave chastises.

"Why? So people don't hear that your son would rather spend his nights working on his computer than fucking me in bed?"

I'm pretty sure the gasp that escapes The Beave's mouth can be heard three blocks away.

And the clutching of her pearls is the perfect addition to her outrage.

Oh, this is good.

This is really fucking good. I can't hold back my smile or stop from wishing there to be more.

Keep it coming, Lia.

"Lia, enough," Brian says. "That is a completely inappropriate way to talk to my mother."

"But she can act like I'm a second-class citizen, and you have no problem with that? Don't you see the issue here, Brian?"

I do. *mentally raises hand* I see it bright as day.

Speaking quietly and in an even tone, The Beave says, "Let's all take a deep breath and focus on the cake."

Lia completely ignores her and turns toward Brian. "You will always take her side, no matter what. She can say to my face how I don't meet her standards, but because she's so desperate to see you married, she'll *settle* for me as a daughter-in-law. Do you understand how fucked up that is, Brian? Why would I want to enter a family who treats me like that? Why would I want to be with a man who allows his family to treat me like that?"

Brian's eyes flit to his mom and then back to Lia. "Mother is right. I think we all need to take a deep breath."

"I don't need a deep breath," Lia says. "I have never in my life seen anything more clearly." She stands from the table and pulls her engagement ring off her ring finger and places it on the table.

Another expertly placed gasp by The Beave echoes through the bakery.

I want to slow clap, encourage this valiant behavior because, God Almighty, seeing Lia fired up like this makes my goddamn nipples hard.

"I'm done, Brian. I should have been done a while ago, but maybe I just needed the coldhearted evidence about *why* I should be done."

"What are you talking about?" Brian asks, panic setting in his eyes. I can't tell if it's panic from what his mother might say, from the image being portrayed of him, or if he truly is concerned about Lia. Sad that there are so many options to choose from.

"You treat me like I come third in your life, directly behind work and your mother, and I don't want to be with someone who doesn't consider

me their number one. You insult me when you say things like I'm having a mental crisis, I never should have changed my hair, and you hate my glasses. You hurt me when you don't want to touch me at night, when you don't want to even try something new. I think the only reason I've been hanging on for so long is because when I met you, you helped me through the grief of losing my parents. But now, I just wonder if that was out of the kindness of your heart, or if that was you trying to use the loss of them to get closer to me."

"Lia, that is not true."

She pushes the ring toward him. "I'm done. I'm done with everything. I'm done feeling like shit when you're around. I'm done worrying if you'll actually kiss me or not when you see me. I'm done asking myself if I'm good enough for you, good enough for your family. And I'm done dealing with your psychopath mother. I need more. I want more. And I sure as hell deserve more. Come on, Breaker."

I stand from my chair, ready to be at her beck and call. But because I have manners, I first address the table before I leave. "Always a pleasure."

I'm about to guide Lia out the door when she turns back around and says, "Also, the club is probably one of the ugliest places I've ever seen, and nothing about it is elitist other than trying to look elite." She then reaches toward the table, palms the chocolate cake with chocolate frosting, and scoops it into her hand. "I'm taking this with me because it's the only decent flavor on the platter."

And then she turns and walks out the door, me trailing her with the biggest fucking smile on my face.

———

"Holy shit," I say as we reach my car. "Lia, I can't fucking believe you did that."

She's shaking and pacing as she holds the cake in her palm. "Oh my God, oh my God...did I just say all of those things?"

I grip her shoulders, stopping her from moving, and bend at the waist to look her in the eyes. "You fucking did and, Jesus Christ, I'm so proud of you."

"You are?" Her lip trembles, and I can see that the adrenaline is starting to wear off.

"Yes, Lia. That was so fucking amazing and well deserved. Jesus, my nipples got hard in there listening to you."

That makes her smile. "Hard nipples, really?" I thrust my chest out at her, and with her non-cake-filled hand, she runs her fingers over the hardened nub. "It *is* hard."

"See. Hell, I'm so proud of you. How do you feel?"

She nods, her head bobbing lightly. "I feel…I feel good." Her eyes connect with mine. "Free."

And that makes me smile. I pick her up and twirl her around as I press my head close to hers while she holds the cake out.

"We need to celebrate."

I set her down, and she holds the cake between us. "I have cake."

"I think we need more than just cake, but yes, let's eat."

She lifts her hand to her mouth and takes a large bite before offering it to me. I second the bite, and together, while standing in front of my car, we eat her stolen cake out of the palm of her hand.

After a few moments, she says, "I think I know what I want to do."

"Let's hear it."

"Grab some pizza for lunch, lots and lots of hard cider, go back to your place, and play Plunder."

"That's how you want to celebrate?"

"I couldn't have asked for a better idea," she says, meeting me once again with that beautiful smile.

"Then let's eat some pizza and play Plunder." I open the door for her and grab a few napkins from my glove compartment for her cake hand, and while I help her clean up, I ask, "Just want to make sure, are you happy? You just called off a wedding and broke up with Brian."

Her eyes meet mine as she says, "I am. It was the right move, thanks for checking."

"As long as you're good, then let's celebrate."

"I'm good. Promise."

———————

Holy fuck. Holy fuck.

Holy.

Fuck!

I pace my bedroom as Lia gets changed at her apartment. After we left the bakery, we went to our favorite pizza place, ordered two large pizzas—one sausage with onions, the other pineapple and pepperoni—ran by the store for two twelve-packs of Angry Orchard, and then came straight home. She said she was going to take a quick rinse in the shower, because she felt gross after being in the bakery, and change.

Which leaves me here, staring at my phone, waiting for my brothers to text me back.

Finally, my phone dings, and I swipe at it to read the message.

JP: Wait, she broke up with him right there in the bakery, ring and all? Holy shit.

I type back in a fury just as my phone dings with another message, this one from Huxley.

Huxley: Wow. I have nothing to say other than wow.

Breaker: Yeah, tell me about it. I was in awe, and my nipples got hard.

JP: I appreciate a hard nipple on a man. Shows me that he registers with his emotions.

Huxley: You need help.

JP: Just telling it like it is.

Breaker: Can we not go on a tangent? I have minutes before she comes over, and I need to know what to do.

Huxley: What do you mean you need to know what to do? She just broke up with her fiancé and called her wedding off. You do nothing. You be a friend.

JP: Uh yeah, dude. Were you thinking about making a move? That's fucking tacky as shit. Give her a second to mourn before you go sniffing around, letting her know you want to bone.

Breaker: First of all, I just don't want to bone. Second of all, I'm already keeping my self-control on a short leash. I don't know how much longer I can hold out.

Huxley: Don't fucking do anything. Jesus, that would be terrible timing.

JP: Yeah. Real bad, man. What do you want to be, the rebound guy? Fuck, no. Give her a moment to figure it all out.

Breaker: Yeah…fuck, I think you're right.

Huxley: Of course we are.

JP: Seriously, nothing else. You don't want to ruin anything. Tread carefully, and when the time is right, strike!

Breaker: Okay…just a little bit longer, that's all I have to keep telling myself. Oh shit, she just came over. Talk to you later.

I set my phone on my nightstand and then head out to the living room, where Lia hovers over the pizza boxes wearing a pair of black and green buffalo-plaid flannel shorts and a white tank top that shows off an inch of her midriff. And her black lace bra is as visible as they come, making my mouth water.

She's worn this outfit around me several times, but now, it feels like it's my undoing.

I want to do so much to that outfit, to the woman wearing it.

I want to slip my hands under the crop top. I want to run my fingers along the lace. I want to drag those shorts down, revealing whatever she's wearing underneath.

But the boys are right. I would be stupid if I attempted anything at this point. I need to keep things neutral. Friendly.

Platonic.

"I'm going to start with a slice of each. What about you?" she asks, holding one of my plates in her hand.

"Yeah, I think I'll do the same. I'll grab drinks."

"I'll meet you on the couch." We purchased one pack of hard cider that was already chilled and put the other in the fridge. I grab two that are cold, some napkins, and walk over to the couch where I have already set up Plunder. Think if the games Risk and Battleship had a baby, it would be Plunder.

"Oh my God, can we just talk about that cake for a second and how dry it was? The Beave actually thought that was the best in town. No offense to the baker...but woof."

I let out a low chuckle. "Are you going to require a dessert to make up for that? Because I can get something delivered. Anything for your heroism today. Taking down The Beave requires all the good things to come your way."

"Hmm." I hand her a drink, and she hands me my pizza. I rest the napkins between us. "You know, I've always believed donuts can be eaten at any time. Let's get a dozen glazed jelly from Arnold's."

"Let me grab my phone. I'll order." I move back to the bedroom, grab my phone, and then pause when I see a text from Brian.

My stomach drops, and I wonder why the hell he's trying to communicate with me. What would he have to say to me?

I should just delete it. Not even read it.

If only my head worked that way. Unfortunately, it doesn't because curiosity gets the better of me.

> Brian: I know you're with Lia. She's not answering my messages.
> I know we haven't been on the best of terms, but can you
> please have her call me?

"Ha!" I laugh out loud. "Okay, sure, Brian." I delete his text message and move back toward the living room.

In his fucking dreams.

———————

"Arrrrrrrrr, ye land lubber, hand over ye resources," Lia says while holding out her hand and twiddling her fingers.

"But if you take the last of my rum, I won't have anything. Do you really want to end the game like that?" I ask on a hiccup. "Taking a man's rum?"

"I said, 'Hand it over.'" She jabs my side with the fake hook she brought over from her apartment.

I hold my hands up in defeat. "Fine. Take my rum, but I hope you burn in hell."

She holds up the rum in absolute victory and hops up on the couch, parading around.

I lean back and watch. "Victory is mine once again," she coos right before flopping back down on the couch and tossing her hook to the side. "I think I need another drink. Want one?"

I glance at the already eight empty cans between us and say, "Maybe some water. If we keep this up, we will be passing out at eight."

"Is that a problem? Copious amounts of sleep are good for the body, you know?"

"Very true. Fine, grab me another. I'll clean up the board."

"Clearing the evidence of my victory already? You're such a poor sport."

"Lia, I just lost three times. It is five at night, and I have nothing to show for myself today other than cheering you on as you told The Beave off, demolishing cake from your hand, and eating six slices of pizza."

"Seems like you accomplished a lot to me."

"Not as much as you."

She playfully fluffs her hair and says, "Well, no one can accomplish as much as I did. I palmed a cake and stormed out of a bakery."

I chuckle. "I don't think I'll ever get that image out of my head."

She grabs us both a drink, and I abandon cleaning up the game when she hands me a cider. We crack them open together and take long swigs.

"You know, I was thinking about your list of things you wanted to accomplish before you got married."

"What about it?" she asks.

"I think you should keep doing it. Clearly, it's given you this beautiful confidence to take charge of your life, and it would be a shame if you stopped. Plus, you checked off another one of the things on your list."

"You remember what's on my list?"

"Lia, I remember everything about you," I say right before I list her items off. "Do something that makes you feel pretty. Well, you did that with your hair and shopping. Not that you needed it, but I can see that you love it, and I love it too." Her cheeks blush. "The second was create a circle of trust. Well, you have me, and I think you bonded with Kelsey, Lottie, and Myla the other day, as well as started a knitting club. That's a great start."

"It is. I really like them. They're fun."

"The third one was to spend a day saying yes. You just name the time and place, and I'll be right there by your side the whole time."

"Let me catch up on the work I've put off, and then we'll make a day of it." She takes a sip of her drink and pulls her legs into her chest.

"The fourth was to stand up for yourself. Well, you can check that one off because damn, Lia, you took the world by storm today, and it was so fucking amazing to watch. I was in awe."

"Thank you. It felt good." She looks off to the side and says, "I can't believe he'd just sit there and let her say those things about me. It just shows that maybe he wasn't really in love with me, and I don't think I was in love with him. At least not recently. It's hard to be in love with someone when they don't treat you like they love you. They can say the words, like he did, but he didn't prove it. He didn't act on his love. It's about the little things, you know? The things you don't even notice until they're done. Like…like stocking my favorite coffee because you know I can't drink anything else. Brian never did that."

"I'm not that douche. And I wouldn't want you drinking anything else." I wink.

She smiles softly. "I think my choice today also coincides with my fifth task: following my heart. It's scary to break off an engagement because you don't want to disappoint people, or hurt feelings, but I just felt it, you know? After speaking with the girls, things felt off, not right. And then when Brian didn't even defend me, I knew it was over."

"I'm glad you listened to yourself."

She rests her head against the couch and asks, "Did you hate him?"

I finish the rest of my drink, chugging that one pretty hard. "Brian? Yes. I did. With the fury of a thousand men."

"Wait, you hated him that much?" she asks.

"Uh…yeah, Lia. The only reason I tried to get along with him was for you. Not because I thought we could be friends or that I thought he was a good guy. It was all for you."

Her eyes connect with mine, and she wets her lips. I wish I knew what she was thinking, if I could read what was going on in her mind, because it would make this so much easier. I wouldn't be as scared of making a move…when the time is right of course.

"You should have told me."

I shake my head. "I didn't want to influence you. My feelings on the matter should never have been taken into consideration."

"But, Breaker, if I had married Brian, wouldn't that have been like one of your brothers marrying someone you hated?" Not even close. But I do get her drift.

"Yes and no." This is where I could go for it and explain what loving her means to me, but it's too soon. I know that. I could give her a taste, perhaps. "Lia, if I have learned anything through your brief and torrid engagement with Brian, it's this. I love you too much to be happy to love you less."

"What does that mean?" She looks so confused and forlorn.

"It means that the only way I'll be happy if you marry someone else is if you are one hundred percent committed to him and him alone. If you were marrying me, no fucking way could I share you with another man, best friend or not. And I wouldn't expect your husband to love you any less than that." Because if you married me, I would be both. Best friend and husband. Period.

She glances away, and I can only hope that something clicks inside that beautiful brain of hers. I know now that I could never give her up. That's what love is.

CHAPTER 16
LIA

I CAN'T HANDLE IT WHEN he says things like that.

His captivating eyes tell me that I should always be put first, and it's what I always wanted to hear from Brian. It's the one thing I asked from him, yet Breaker offers it up so easily.

If you were marrying me, no fucking way could I share you with another man, best friend or not. And I wouldn't expect your husband to love you any less than that.

I drop my feet to the ground and down the rest of my cider. "Do you want another?" I ask him as I walk to the kitchen.

"Sure," he answers, but I can hear the trepidation in his voice.

I don't bother to ask him what's wrong because I already know. He's worried I'm drowning my sorrows in booze, but I'm not. I'm trying to drown the red-hot emotions pulsing through me every time he looks my way. I'm aware I'm the one who asked him to be my friend—*and only my friend*—all those years ago. I'm also aware that his sisters-in-law don't believe he's a relationship kind of guy. So I need to stop imagining things.

However...I can't get the thoughts out of my head of how he goes down on a woman.

How he prefers his dick to be sucked.

How he'd treat his woman like she's precious.

Nor can I stop thinking about what his bedroom eyes look like. Are they darker? Clearer?

Not to mention, the way he so shamelessly tells me how beautiful I am...it's starting to beguile me because I shouldn't be looking at my friend like that. I shouldn't be having these thoughts, so if I have to use alcohol to help me subdue them, then I will.

I crack a can open for each of us and hand him one.

"Let's watch a show," I say. "Or watch a movie. We can watch *The Thin Man*."

"Are you sure you don't want to annihilate me in another board game?"

"I'm trying to save your pride."

"Aren't you considerate?" He grabs the remote, and I suck down my drink. My head is starting to feel fuzzy, which is just what I want. I welcome all of the fuzziness.

"Oh, I recorded some reruns of *Password* in case you wanted to play." He wiggles his eyebrows at me. "You game?"

"You know I always am."

"Good." He winks and then takes a large gulp of his drink as well.

———

"Stop." I laugh so hard I nearly pee my pants. "Stop...how am I supposed to guess *spoon* from *dairy*?"

He is buckled over, laughing on the floor in our empty cider cans.

"Because you slurp dairy up with a spoon," he says as he lies on the floor, arms spread, staring up at the ceiling. His shirt has pulled up a few inches, and I catch sight of his brilliant abs.

"You could have said *spork*. You've lost your touch."

"I'm drunk," he says as he kicks a few cans away. "And I just ate a donut, so my mind isn't working well."

I fall to the floor and crawl over to him, my hair falling over my cheeks as I stare at his smiling face. I reach out and pat his cheeks a few times. "You used to be so smart. What happened to you?"

"You and your drinks," he says right before he wraps his arm around my waist and rolls me to the floor right next to him.

"We didn't drink that much."

"We drank ten cans each," he says.

"Over like...ten hours."

"Lia Fairweather-Fern, it has not been ten hours. And we've gulped down three in the past hour, so...we are drunk."

"You might be drunk, but I'm not drunk."

"Oh yeah?" he asks. "Stand and walk in a straight line."

"Easy," I proclaim as I roll to the side and then slowly push myself up to standing. He props himself up against the couch to watch me. I take a deep breath and say, "Watch this excellence."

I put one foot in front of the other and start walking, my legs wobbling while I lose balance and nearly crash into the island chairs, causing Breaker to roar with laughter.

"Okay, sure, you're not drunk."

"That's not my fault," I say as I take another deep breath.

"It's not? Then who's operating your legs?"

"Me, but...it's my bra's fault," I say. "It's constricting the blood from reaching my toes, and that's what makes it hard to walk."

"Wow, that's quite the scientific reasoning."

"Well, you try walking with a bra," I say right before I reach in front of me, snap open the front clasp of my bra, and then pull the whole thing off. I toss the bra at Breaker and say, "You try."

He glances up at me as he holds my bra in his hand, and then his eyes travel down my neck, past my collarbone, and right to my breasts, where my nipples press hard against the white of my shirt fabric.

"That was hot, Lia." He wets his lips and then examines my bra. "Really hot."

His eyes fall to my breasts again, and I can feel all inhibitions fall away as I stick my chest out and say, "Trying to get a good look?"

"Yeah," he answers with a shameless smirk.

"Well, cut it out." I kick my foot toward him. "This is serious business." I take a deep breath and hold my arms out to the side. "Watch me walk with beauty and grace."

"Let's see it." Although, when I sneak another look at him, he's still looking at my braless breasts.

I place one foot in front of the other and glide, not missing a step and proving that in fact I'm not drunk.

"Ha," I say when I finish. "Told you it was the bra."

"Puh-lease," he says while he stands. "That was all luck. Bet you I can walk straight with this bra on."

"Oh, you think so?"

"I know so." He sets the bra down on the arm of the couch, pulls his shirt over his head, and tosses it to the side.

Hello, pecs.

"Uh, what are you doing?"

"Putting the bra on," he says as he reaches for it and attempts to fit his arms through the loops. "Fuck, why is this so tight?"

"Uh, maybe because you are much larger than me."

He has one arm strung through a strap but is turning in circles, trying to grab the other strap. After a few turns, he props one hand on his hip and turns toward me. "Can you fucking help me instead of just watching me run in circles like a dog trying to catch his tail?"

"I'm actually good just watching."

He grumbles, takes the bra off, and then fits it on backward so the back of the bra runs across his nipples. Since I'm so much smaller than his broad shoulders, his arms turn in, being pulled by the straps of the bra.

He glances down at himself and then back up at me. "You know, I don't really think this is a good look for me."

I let out a roar of a laugh while I shake my head. "I've seen better."

"Then let's just get this over before I lose all sense of myself and start matching your lipstick with my nipple color."

"What?" I chuckle. "Why would you match it with your nipple color?"

"I saw this girl talk about it on TikTok. How the perfect shade of lip would match your nipple. That not true?"

"Why are you watching makeup tutorials on Tik Tok?"

"I don't search them out. They just pop up. The girl had a Boston accent. I think her name was Mikayla. Really fucking entertaining that I watched a few of her TikToks. No shame. She's actually really inspirational. Lives her life the way she wants. And hey, now you know to match your lipstick to your nipples. You're welcome." He then holds his arms out and walks in a straight line, holding steady the whole time.

"You know this doesn't count, right?" I ask. "You're not wearing the bra correctly."

"Uh, because it's not big enough."

I shrug. "Not my problem."

"Then what the hell is this? What am I doing?"

"You tell me, you're the one who whipped the bra on."

"Ridiculous," he says as he takes it off and then slingshots it right at my face.

The fabric slaps me across the cheek, and I gasp in shock. "Oh my God, you could have taken my eye out."

"Dramatic much?"

"I bet I have a red mark." I grip my cheek and play it up.

"Death by bra, that's a first."

"Uh, excuse me, sir. I have no doubt in my mind that many a woman have met their creator because of a poorly manufactured brassiere, most likely designed by a man who has zero concept of the kind of damage a destructive underwire can have on an unsuspecting soul."

"You do realize a bra is a choice, right?" His smirk tells me he's only teasing, but that doesn't stop me.

"Oh sure, right, a bra is a choice, so if I started walking around with my tits out, you think I won't have complaints about erect nipples or showing too much?"

He sticks his hands in the pockets of his athletic shorts and says, "No complaints here."

"Ugh, pervert." I walk over to the kitchen and grab another cider for us both.

"You can't be serious. This might make me puke."

"Or sleepy. I prefer the sleepy." I crack both open and hand him one. We cheers and then take a seat on the couch, our shoulders pressed together as we stare at the TV in front of us.

After a sip, I say, "You know, there's no one else I would want to spend my time with after I called off a wedding and broke up with my fiancé other than you." I rest my head against his shoulder.

"Same, Lia."

We both take a drink.

"When you first saw me in the hallway of your dorm, did you ever think this is where we would end up? Neighbors, best friends, attached at the hip?"

"Uh…not at that moment, but after that night, I had a good inkling."

"How so?"

"We just matched. Like when everyone left Scrabble that night, and we were alone, I felt like my missing puzzle piece was put into place."

"I felt the same way." We both lift our drinks to our mouth and take long pulls. "I would be lost without you, Breaker."

"I would be lost without you, too."

"Doesn't seem like it," I say, my mind turning morose. "You have so much going for you. Your business, you have a strong family bond and sisters-in-law who are so much fun. You have promise, a community surrounding you, and so much opportunity."

"And you don't have any of that?" he asks, his tone suggesting he's wondering where I'm going with this.

"I have you. I'm building a circle. And I have a job that I love, but I don't know, I just feel like you have so much more."

"What I have, you have. You know Huxley and JP treat you like a sister. And you've built your business from the ground up; not many people can say that. Are these feelings stemming from not having your parents around?"

"I think so," I sigh. "God, do you think I will ever get over it?"

"No, I don't think losing your parents is something you get over; I think it's just a tender hurt you learn to live with. It will take time, but it will get easier with each day."

"I can still feel them sometimes," I say softly before taking another large sip of my drink. "At night, when I feel alone in my apartment, I can sometimes feel that they're there, watching over me."

"They are," Breaker says. "They're always watching over you. And you know, when you're feeling alone, you can always come over. That's what I'm here for."

"You are." He slips his arm behind me and pulls me in close. "You are so important to me, Breaker."

"You're important to me too, Lia."

I sit up and look him in the eyes. "Like...what would I do without you?"

"I try not to think about what a day without you in it would look like," he says.

I stare at him, his eyes flitting back and forth between mine, my eyes traveling over his face as a smile tugs at my lips.

"Why are you smiling?" he asks before finishing off his drink and setting his can down.

I join him and set my empty can on the coffee table. "You're a far cry from the guy I met back in college. Remember that caterpillar you grew on your upper lip? Atrocious."

"Hey, there were a few girls who liked it."

"Amanda Fulton? Yeah, because she liked every guy with two nipples and a penis, she pretty much looked past the nose fur."

"Were nipples really a requirement for her?"

I palm his face and push him away, causing him to laugh. "I'm tired." I let out a large yawn.

"Because we drank too much," he says.

"Well, I want to go beddy bye."

"Then go to bed." He leans against the couch and puts both of his hands behind his head.

"I will," I say as I stand on wobbly legs. "Just need to go to the bathroom first."

I move toward his bedroom, and he says, "Where do you think you're going? Your apartment is down the hall."

"But the comfortable bed is right over here. Thanks." I offer him a wave and then head toward his master bathroom, where I take care of business and brush my teeth.

I don't bother with my hair because it's already a mess. I move toward his bed and climb into the cool sheets. Yes...this is perfection.

For Christmas one year, Breaker bought me the same sheets as his because I said I love them so much, but for some reason, they don't feel the same on my bed. I think it's the mattress. That, and his bed smells like his cologne, which could make anyone want to sink in deeper.

"Just make yourself at home," I hear him say as he moves around the bathroom.

"Don't mind if I do." I scoot toward the middle of the bed and lie on both pillows, leaving him with limited options. He always claims I'm a bed hog so might as well live up to it.

I hear him flush the toilet, followed by the sound of him brushing his teeth. When he turns off the bathroom light, he moves into the bedroom and lowers the motorized shades—something I don't have in my apartment—and puts the room into complete darkness.

The bed dips from his weight, and then he slides up against me.

"You have my pillow." He tugs at it.

"Hey, I'm using that."

"You can't use both," he complains.

"I can do whatever I want. I got here first."

"Yes, but this is my bed." He tugs again, but I hold on tight.

"Fine. If you're going to be like that, then I have no choice than to do this." He slips his arm around my waist and pulls his body flush against mine so he can share the pillow.

"Are you saying this is a punishment? Because it doesn't feel like one." Really enjoying his warmth at the moment.

"It will be when I roll away in the middle of the night, and you fall off the bed," he replies.

"And they say chivalry is dead."

He chuckles. "If you were my girlfriend, then yeah, I'd let you do whatever you want. But that's not the case here. You're just the trolling best friend."

"Trolling, wow," I tease. "Care to explain to me how this hold is different? Because it seems like you're spooning me like a girlfriend."

"Nah." He blows out. "This is friendly. If you were my girlfriend, my hand would be in an entirely different place."

"Ugh, men, always wanting their hand between a woman's legs."

"That's not where I was thinking."

"Oh sorry, boobs." I roll my eyes, even though he can't see them.

"Not what I was thinking either," he whispers.

"Oh…uh…butt crack? Not my first choice, seems stifling to a hand, but to each their own."

He lightly chuckles, and I can feel him shake his head behind me. "Wrong again."

"Well, call me confused because I can't think of any other place to stick your hand. I mean, down my mouth, but that feels like a choking hazard."

"I wouldn't stick my hand in any of those places," he says as he slowly splays his hand across my stomach, causing it to hollow out from his touch. "You see, it's not about the obvious touch. It's about the subtle one." He glides his hand down to the patch of skin on my stomach that's exposed and very lightly runs his finger across it. "This is how I would touch her. Just light enough to let her know I'm here, but not too much to make her think I want more."

"Oh," I say, slightly breathless because, Jesus, that feels good. "Brian, uh…he never touched me like that. He wasn't much of a cuddler."

"His loss," Breaker says as he continues to run his fingers along my skin.

"He never did much with me. It makes me wonder if he just didn't find me attractive."

"Impossible." His fingers toy with the hem of my shirt, slipping just lightly under it. "You are desirable, Lia." His voice dips, his lips close to my ear while his hand slides another inch under my shirt, causing my body to heat.

I lie there, stunned, and unable to move through the fog of alcohol consuming my brain. I keep thinking, *What is he doing? Is he really touching me intimately?* But in the back of my mind, I want him to move faster.

"I've never felt desirable," I say as his warm palm connects with my stomach now, his hand fully under my shirt.

"Because you haven't been with the right man," he says, shifting his body closer so I feel the heat of his bare chest on my back. "If you were with the right man, then he'd always know how to treat you so you *know* you're desirable."

His hand inches up my stomach just enough that his thumb lightly drags across the skin under my breasts.

Fuck.

Heat consumes me, and my cheeks are on fire as my stomach dips and bows while he slowly inches his hand back down my stomach until he reaches the spot just above the waistband of my shorts. A tingling sensation shoots through my veins as his pinky runs along the elastic of my shorts. I bite the side of my cheek, my pulse pounding so hard I can hear it in my ears.

"Everything about you is desirable, Lia," he says as he pulls me in even closer so my butt lines up against his pelvis. And then, surprising me to my core, he dips his pinky finger past the waistband of my shorts. I gasp, my chest filling with unexpected hope that he'll dip farther, but before I can even consider the ramifications, he drags his fingers back up.

His touch is so light, barely even there, but with the feel of his chest against mine and the briefest physical contact, my entire body's reacting, causing a cool sweat.

"You're…you're making me feel…"

"What?" he asks as he plants his hand just below my breasts.

His thumb moves up and down, up and down, barely missing where I want him to caress me, creating this inferno so deep in my bones that I start to ache.

Ache for his touch.

For his hand.

For him to move it farther south.

An action I never thought I'd desire from my best friend, but here I am, mentally wishing and begging for him to spread me and make me feel anything but empty.

"Breaker," I say, my voice breathless.

"Hmm?" he asks, moving his hand back down so the tips of his fingers slip past the waistband of my shorts.

Yes, God, yes.

Go farther.

Touch me, please.

My eyes squeeze shut as my pelvis voluntarily tilts up. I shouldn't want this. I shouldn't need this. I shouldn't want to get lost at this moment.

This is the alcohol, right? This is the loss of a fiancé...right? I'm feeling lonely.

I'm confused.

That's all.

I don't...I don't want Breaker. He's my best friend.

But then his fingers drag along the skin right above my pubic bone, and my body shifts, twisting an inch to my back. It's subtle, but it forces his fingers to fall even closer.

Throbbing.

Burning.

Hoping.

I want more. And right when I think he's going to guide his hand between my legs, he glides his hand back to the middle of my stomach. I groan in frustration.

"Were you going to say something?" he whispers, his lips so close to my ear that I might combust.

"I...don't remember," I answer.

"I think you do remember. You just don't want to say it." His fingers dance up my stomach to my rib cage. "You were saying I'm making you feel..."

I wet my lips as I strain for his touch, but he doesn't move. He keeps the hold on where his hand goes, always maintaining control.

"Just tell me, Lia," he says, his lips dragging over my ear, causing chills to break over my skin.

"Turned on," I say on a heavy breath. "You're making me feel... turned on."

"It's because you're so goddamn sexy," he says just as the tip of his thumb slides against my breast.

"Oh...fffff-uck."

"Jesus, you're so hot," he whispers just as his pelvis presses against me, and my eyes pop open in pleasure from the feel of his erection against my backside.

Oh my God.

He's just as turned on as me.

His fingers slip along my stomach, and this time, without hesitation, slide under my shorts, where his pinky glides back and forth, right above my mound. He's not touching me where I want him to touch me, but at this moment, I'm more turned on than Brian has ever made me.

I want it. Badly.

I want this.

I want release.

And I'm so worried that if I say something or move, this burning desire will dissipate. And I don't want it to because I'm feeling something, like... like I'm starting to come alive from a deep, dark sleep, one that I've been in for over a year.

Needing to give him more access, I twist so I'm almost all the way on my back.

The new angle causes his grip to grow tighter, and as he moves back up my stomach, my chest grows heavy, my nipples harden, and I wait.

I pray.

I hope that he'll touch me more.

That he'll fully touch me this time.

Eyes shut, I hold my breath, my legs trembling as he inches closer and closer to my breast.

Almost there.

Just touch me, please.

He must be able to read my mind because his hand slides right under my breast, and his thumb drags across my nipple.

"God," I moan, my back arching as I fall all the way to my back now, showing him I want more. I want so much more.

"Jesus Christ, you have the softest tits," he says, his erection against my leg now, his lips right against my ear. "What I want to do to these."

"Wh-what?" I ask.

"Strip you out of this shirt and plant my head between your tits. I want to test their weight in my hand, pinch your hard, pebbled nipples, suck on them until you scream, and then mark them with my teeth. I want you to wake up the next day and see that you were owned the night before."

My legs involuntarily spread as the dull throb between them becomes a pounding need. Breaker's deep, raspy—*sexy*—voice, the one I heard through the wall once before, is breaking every ounce of restraint I have. He's using it on me. *Me.*

I expect him to move his hand back down, but instead, he drags his thumb over my nipple again, and again…and again, causing a hiss to escape my lips.

I thrust my chest into his hand, wanting him to make good on what he said, but he retreats, and I groan in frustration.

"Breaker," I say breathlessly.

"You need me, don't you?" he asks, a sense of cockiness in his voice. Even that's more of a turn-on than anything.

"Yes," I whisper, wanting to shed my clothes.

Thankfully, he moves past my shorts and then right between my legs. I spread them in delicious anticipation, and to my delight, he slips two fingers along my slit. He doesn't press inside, doesn't even try to get me off, he just glides them over the sensitive skin. So I spread even wider, causing them to slip inside where he feels just how turned on I am.

"Fuck," he says in such a tortured voice that I feel the rumble of it all the way down to my bones.

He removes his fingers, dragging my wetness up my stomach, and when I think he's going back to my breast, he removes his hand from my stomach, and I watch in fascination as he slips his fingers into his mouth, sucking on them both.

My breath catches in my throat as he slides them past his lips and says, "I knew your pussy would be the sweetest thing I ever fucking tasted."

"Breaker," I say, my mind nearly exploding. "What...what are you doing?"

"Attempting to control myself," he says.

"We're...we're drunk," I say for some reason, maybe to make myself feel better for crossing a line with my best friend.

"We might be, but I've thought about tasting you for so goddamn long now."

"What?" I ask, stunned. "N-no, you haven't. This was... You were just showing me how I can be desirable."

"Yeah, Lia," he says, his eyes connecting with mine. "You're so fucking desirable." And then he slips his hand back toward my breast, bringing his index finger up to my aching nipple, and pinches it.

"Oh God," I groan, my hand falling between us, right against his hardened cock.

This is not what we do.

We don't cross this line.

But feeling him so hard right now while he plays with my nipple makes me do something I don't think I was ever prepared for. I dip my hand past his shorts and run my fingers down his boxer briefs, along his...

"Oh my...God," I say breathlessly as he continues to twist my nipple. "Breaker, you're...you're huge."

And he is.

Long.

Thick.

Easily the biggest I've ever felt.

My fingers work along the ridge of his veins through the fabric of his briefs and then back up to the head.

His breathing picks up, but he doesn't stop turning me on, playing with my nipple.

I want more, so much more, so I turn all the way onto my side, facing him. I can barely see his face in the darkness of the night, but can see the outline of his carved jaw.

"I'm turned on," I say as if he didn't know that.

"So am I."

"I want a release."

"Me too," he says.

"We shouldn't be doing this. This is crossing a line."

He doesn't say anything to that. He just smooths his hand to my back and down my shorts, gripping my ass tightly.

"Breaker, I need you to say something. Tell me this is crossing a line."

"I'm not going to say anything to stop this. Not a goddamn thing."

"Why not?" I ask, my heart hammering.

"I think you know."

I shake my head. "I don't, Breaker. I don't know."

Once again, he remains silent, and just when I think he's not going to do anything, he rolls onto his back. He pushes down the blankets, and then he grabs me. In one smooth motion, he lifts me on top of his lap, right over his erection.

"Oh God," I breathe out heavily.

He reaches between us and adjusts himself so I'm resting along his ridge.

"You want a release, Lia? Take it," he says with confidence. "Use my cock."

The demand is so naughty, so erotic, something I never would have expected him to say, yet it switches something inside me. Instead of shying away, I feel myself listen to him.

"L-like this?" I ask as I move my pelvis, my clit sliding along his erection.

He nods. "Just like that."

"With our clothes on?"

"Yes. Have you never dry humped before?"

"N-no."

"Then I'll help you." He sits up on the bed effortlessly, as if I'm not on top of him, and lines his back against his headboard. I'm still pressing against his erection, but this position makes me feel the pressure of his girth on my clit.

His hand falls under my shirt and moves up to my breast, where he cups it and gives it a gratifying squeeze. My head falls back and my pelvis juts forward, creating such a delicious friction that I repeat the movement.

"Just like that," he says, his thumb playing with my nipple now. "Ride my dick, Lia. I want you to focus on your pleasure. I'll get off when you get off."

He'll get off when I get off? The selflessness, it thrills me even more.

I rest my hands on his shoulders, and as he plays with my nipple, I pick up my pace, moving my clit over his cock, loving the way it feels and the intense pressure pulsing through me, just as he pulls my chest forward and sucks my breast into his mouth through the fabric of my shirt.

A gasp pops out of me as he moves his mouth across to the other breast, sucking and nibbling as well. There's just enough protection from my shirt to frustrate me, so I drag the neckline down, exposing the top of my breasts. He doesn't skip a beat as he sucks on my cleavage, moving from one side to the other, using his teeth the whole time.

"Yes," I call out, feeling shy but also crazy at the same time, like I can't keep in the pleasure. I don't want to. I want to let it out. I want to release it all.

I've been so frustrated, so bottled up, that it feels like Breaker just popped the cork, and I'm finally letting myself live for a moment.

I rock harder against him as the pressure between my legs builds, and my bottom half starts to go numb. I can tell my impending release is just a few moments away.

"God, yes," I whisper as he bites down on the side of my breast, the pain of it turning quickly into pleasure, and I guide his head to the other side. "More," I say as he drags my neckline lower, a rip sounding through the silent room. His mouth finds my nipple, and he pulls it in with one large suck. *Holy fuck, that feels incredible.*

I groan and ride his length, pulsing harder and harder.

He moans, and a wave of goose bumps erupts over my skin.

He bites down on my other nipple, ripping my shirt completely open, and I grind harder against him.

His mouth is so delicious, his hands so attentive, his mind in it to please me, not himself. It's so sexy, so incredibly gratifying that I grip the back of his neck, toss my head back, and I let the pleasure of his delicious cock against my clit take me over the edge.

"Fuck, Breaker," I call out as I ride him faster, my orgasm piercing through me at such a fast pace that I do everything in my control to keep it going, to make the feeling last as long as I can. Just as it starts to wane, he groans against my breast, he pulses up against me, and then he's groaning into my shoulder as he comes as well.

I'm so startled, so intoxicated by the sound of him coming that I just sit there, stunned, holding him, not caring that my shirt is ripped open or that he was just sucking on my breasts. Or that I just crossed the biggest line with my best friend ever.

"Jesus, fuck," he whispers as he catches his breath. He lifts his head and then leans against the headboard. In the dark of the night, I can catch the rise and fall of his chest, but that's about it.

Oh my God, we just made each other come.

I...I can't believe it.

Now that it's over, I feel so shocked.

Unsure of what to say, I move off him and then whisper, "Can I borrow a shirt?"

"Of course," he says. "I can get it for you."

"No, it's okay. I can grab it." I get out of bed, feeling so awkward that I close my ripped shirt together and move over to his dresser, where I grab a shirt and then go to the bathroom. I shut the door behind me, lean against the counter.

What the hell did I just do?

I...I just humped my best friend to the point that both of us orgasmed.

I'm freaking out.

Big time.

We crossed a line, a big one, and I'm pretty sure I just ruined everything.

There's a knock on the door, followed by, "Lia, you okay?"

No.

I'm not at all.

"Yeah," I call out. "Just, uh, changing and going to the bathroom. Be out in a second."

"Lia, do you want to talk about this?" His voice is sincere and comforting. Not the same as the man who told me to use his cock for pleasure. This is the Breaker I know. The Breaker I love.

"What?" I squeak out. "No, of course not. Nothing to talk about." I change out of my shorts and my shirt and slip his shirt on, leaving me in nothing but his clothes...that smell just like him of course.

With turmoil twisting in my stomach, I go to the bathroom, clean up, and then don't bother to look in the mirror before I leave because what's the point? I know what I'll see—someone incredibly scared about what just happened.

I exit the bathroom to find Breaker on the other side of the door, holding a new pair of shorts.

"Hey," he says as he lifts my chin so I'm forced to look him in the eyes. "You good?"

I tack on a smile because if I've learned anything from Brian in the past year and a half that I was with him, it's to know how to fake a smile. "Of course. Just really exhausted now." I pat his bare chest. "Took it out of me. Do you, uh, want me to go back to my place?"

"No." His brow furrows. "No, I want you to stay here with me."

"Okay, just wanted to make sure." I smile and then start to move past him when he presses his hand to my stomach, stopping me.

"You sure you're okay?"

"Positive."

I know he's not convinced, but he lets go of me. He moves toward the bathroom while I make my way to the bed and slip under the covers. This time, I just use my pillow, staying on my side while my mind races. I probably just messed up my friendship. It was amazing when his mouth was on me. I got so lost, so quick, and in the moment, I didn't care about anything other than the friction and heat we were creating.

Was it really all worth it?

Was it worth ruining this friendship?

Fresh from the bathroom, Breaker walks up to the bed, where he slips in. I half expect him to stay on his side, but he pulls me close to his chest by the stomach and buries his head in my hair.

I'm breathless, unsure of what to do.

He's snuggling again.

He's spooning me.

His entire body is in control of mine.

"You sure you're good?" he asks, his breath caressing the back of my neck.

"Yes," I whisper, my heart racing a mile a minute.

"Okay. Night, Lia."

I swallow hard and whisper, "Night, Breaker."

He snuggles in closer while I lie there, wide awake.

Instead of falling asleep, I remain restless, captured in his strong arm, battling between reveling in the way he holds me so close and freaking out that I just ruined everything.

When he drifts off and his grip loosens, I take that moment to slip out of bed, out of his bedroom, and over to my apartment, where I lie awake the rest of the night.

You fucked up, Lia.

You fucked up big time.

CHAPTER 17
BREAKER

SMILING TO MYSELF, REMEMBERING LAST night as if it was just a minute ago, I stretch my arm out to the side to bring Lia in close to me, but when my arm hits the empty mattress, I crack my eyes open to find nothing but an empty bed.

"Fuck," I mutter as I press the heel of my palm to my eye.

She ran.

I should have fucking known.

In the moment—*God, it was amazing*—she was right there with me.

But after, even though she didn't want to admit it, I felt her running as fast as she could. Mentally, she was checking out of the possibility of an us and freaking out over the fact that there could possibly be an us.

I sit up in my bed and look around the room for any trace of her. Maybe, if I'm lucky, she's in the kitchen or the living room with her favorite cup of coffee, but then again, I don't smell it.

I quickly go to the bathroom as a dull throb starts pounding at the base of my skull, reminding me of the many drinks I had last night.

I'd like to say mistakes were made all around, but to me, last night wasn't a mistake. The only thing I regret is not talking this out and not following my gut instinct that she wasn't okay afterwards.

But I don't regret teasing her.

I don't regret biting my way across her supple chest.

I don't regret the way her warm center felt sliding over my length.

And I don't fucking regret hearing her moan as she brought herself to orgasm.

I wash my hands and move toward the living room and kitchen, which is completely empty.

Just what I suspected. So without another thought, I walk out of my apartment, down the hall, and knock on her door.

I wait a few moments, and when she doesn't open, I knock again.

A few more seconds and nothing.

Panic starts to set in.

"Lia, you in there?" I knock.

Dead silent.

Fuck.

I go back to my apartment, and I find my phone. I consider calling her, but for some reason, I have a feeling that will go straight to voicemail, so I text her instead, trying to keep it light and not clingy or pathetic at all, even though that's how I'm feeling.

Breaker: Morning, here I thought I was going to have to make you breakfast. Looks like I lucked out.

I set my phone down and go to the kitchen, where I make a pot of coffee, grab the ibuprofen from my cabinet, and toss a frozen breakfast burrito in the microwave. While everything is cooking and brewing, I grip the kitchen counter and stare down at my phone, willing it to ding with a text.

When my coffee finishes brewing and the breakfast burrito is done, and I don't have a response, sheer panic sets in.

"Fuck," I whisper as I push my hand through my hair.

What did I do?

Huxley and JP were right. I should have just been the friend she needed last night. I should have kept my hands to myself. I should never have ripped her shirt and sucked on her tits.

That was so fucking—

Ding.

"Oh, thank fuck!" I shout as I lift my phone and see it's a text from her.

Lia: What would you have made?

Relief washes over me at her lighthearted response.

On a sigh, I sit down with my burrito, ibuprofen, and coffee and text her back.

Breaker: Currently eating a breakfast burrito from the freezer, so maybe that.

Lia: Really, you would have heated up a breakfast burrito? Wow.

Breaker: What would you have wanted?

Lia: A Danish at least.

Breaker: Well, if you'd have asked, I would have retrieved.

Lia: Shame. Now we'll never know.

Breaker: Why did you leave? Was I not letting you hog the bed?

Lia: Early morning meeting.

Ehh, why don't I believe that?

Probably because I know her schedule, and she never, and I mean never, has an early morning meeting. That's just not how she operates. If she has a meeting with clients, it's always midmorning or afternoon. Early morning isn't in her vocabulary.

Breaker: You lying to me?

Lia: Do you really think I'd lie to you?

Yes.

I do.

And she is.

So I can either sit back and go with her lie, or be the person I've always been with her and be honest. The easier way out is to go with the lie. But the best things in life are never easy, so I decide to call her out.

Breaker: After what happened last night, you'd lie.

It takes her a few moments to text back, but she does, thankfully.

Lia: Can we not talk about last night?
Breaker: Why, do you regret it?

Please say no. Please say no.

Lia: I…I don't know, Breaker. It was…weird.
Breaker: Wow, can't hear that enough.
Lia: Not like that. I mean…the during part was, well, it was amaz-
ing, but you're *you* and that makes this weird.
Breaker: I get that, but that doesn't mean you need to pull away.
Lia: I'm not, I'm just taking a second to digest what happened. I
mean a lot happened. We learned a lot about each other in
a few short minutes.
Breaker: I didn't learn anything, just confirmed a lot of things in
my head. Fucking amazing tits that taste like heaven.

I know I shouldn't say it, but I don't want her thinking that I believe any of that was a mistake because it wasn't. It was…it was the start of something new, and I don't want to shy away from it.

Lia: Breaker, I'm being serious.
Breaker: Yeah, so am I. I always knew you had amazing tits, but

sucking on them last night? Fuck, it was one of the hottest things I've ever done, and I can still taste you on my tongue.

Lia: I…I don't know what to say.

Breaker: You don't need to say anything. Just know that there's nothing to regret, at all. And it doesn't change anything. I'm still your best friend. Always will be.

I wait for another text, but it doesn't come in.

After I finish my breakfast and take ibuprofen to combat my raging headache, I take a shower and then check my phone again.

Nothing.

So I decide to sleep off the headache. When I wake up an hour later, still nothing.

I think I might have fucked up.

———

"Thanks to all the evidence you provided us and the due diligence of the team, we put together a strong case to counteract the lawsuit and force Gemma to extend an apology through the media," Taylor, our lawyer, says.

Huxley clasps me on my suit-clad shoulder, clearly happy about the news.

Me, on the other hand, I can barely muster a *yippee*.

After I woke from my nap, I received a text from Huxley—I thought it was Lia, and I swore up a storm—asking me to come into the office at two. Since he was asking me to step foot into Cane Enterprises, I knew it had to be the end of the lawsuit.

And it is, but given the last twenty-four hours with Lia, I honestly couldn't care less about whatever is going on with the crazy Shoemacher lady.

"That's fantastic," JP says. "Does she have a written statement she'll read?"

"She's working on it with her lawyer now, and we'll approve it before she goes live with the apology," Taylor answers.

"Please send it directly to me when it comes in," Huxley says before holding his hand out to Taylor. "Your hard work on this case will not go unnoticed. Thank you, Taylor."

"It was my pleasure, Mr. Cane," Taylor says as he snaps his briefcase closed. He offers JP and me a handshake before he heads out of the conference room, his two assistants at his side.

When the door shuts, Huxley turns toward me while gripping the conference table. "Are you happy?"

"Yeah," I say as I lean back in my chair, clearly not showing the kind of excitement they were expecting.

"Are you?" JP asks. "Because it looks like someone ran over your dick, and you're mourning the loss."

"I assumed you'd be thrilled to come back to work," Huxley says. "Which we should have a company-wide conference about. We need to set the record straight. Those who can't attend in person will be required to attend online."

"Probably best we do that," JP says. "But I want to know what's going on in Breaker's head right now. I want to know why he's not pumping his fist in the air and saying *huzzah* like he normally would be."

Both my brothers stare me down, their reluctant gaze not faltering as I let the room sit in silence. After a few seconds, Huxley says, "Did you fuck things up yesterday with Lia?"

"What?" I ask, playing dumb. "What would make you think that?"

"Great observation," JP says, patting Huxley on the back. "Handsome, smart, and observant. That's why he's at the helm."

"I didn't fuck things up with Lia," I groan in annoyance. Even though, yeah, I did, big-time. I've been checking my phone through this entire meeting, and not one single text message from her.

"You didn't?" JP asks, now pacing around me. "So tell me, what did you do yesterday with Lia?"

"Just hung out," I say. "Ate some pizza. Played some games. Had a few ciders."

"A few? HA!" JP rips. "Look at those bags under his eyes, Hux. Does it look like he had a few ciders?" JP points at me with a pen he picked up off the conference table.

Huxley leans forward and examines me. "They look sunken."

"Precisely," JP says with a dramatic flair. "Which means he had a lot to drink last night. So tell us, Breaker, how many ciders exactly?"

I roll my eyes. "I don't know, like ten."

"Ten?" Huxley asks. "That's a lot for you."

JP leans in and says, "Hence the dark circles under his eyes. And check out his hair. It's all disheveled, even though there seems to be product in it." JP walks behind me and threads his pen through my hair. "Unkempt, which is a result of…"

Huxley scratches the side of his jaw and says, "Running his hand through it."

"Aha," JP replies, making me want to punch him right in the stomach for how annoying he's being. "And why would he have sunken eyes and be running his hand through his hair?"

Huxley sits across from me. Looking smug, he says, "Because he fucked things up with Lia."

"You guys are so fucking wrong," I say as I lean into my chair. "This was fun, though."

"Are we?" JP continues to pace behind me. "Then why are you wearing two different-colored socks?"

"What?" I glance down at my legs and then back up at JP. "I'm not wearing socks."

"Exactly!"

"What?" I ask, so confused.

JP pauses, turns to Huxley, and says, "I might have lost track of what I'm doing."

With a giant eye roll, Huxley looks at me. "Give me your phone."

"Why?" I ask, sweat starting to form on the back of my neck.

"I want to see it."

"Look at your own phone," I reply.

"No, I want to look at yours because if I'm not correct about you fucking up with Lia, then there's nothing to hide, right?" He wiggles his fingers. "Hand over your phone."

"Yeah, good one," JP says, now taking a seat next to Huxley. "Hand him your phone."

"No, that's stupid." I fold my arms, knowing they're closing in on me.

"What's stupid is your denial," Huxley says. "So hand us the fucking phone or admit you fucked things up."

"I didn't fuck things up," I shout, and then quietly add, "Just perhaps, made things a touch complicated." I break because there's no point. They're going to figure it out, so I might as well get their abuse over and done with so I can figure out what to do with Lia.

"Complicated." JP slaps the conference room table. "We knew it."

Jesus, did he have a lot of coffee before he came in? He's extra fucking annoying.

"What the hell did you do?" Huxley asks, looking annoyed. Why is he annoyed? This is my life, not his.

I pull my hand through my hair, and JP quickly points at me. "See, anguish. He's tousling his hair with anguish. We were right all along. Huzzah!"

"Don't fucking say *huzzah*. It's bad enough when Breaker does it," Huxley says. He then turns to me and continues. "I don't have time to fuck around with you growing a pair to tell us what you did wrong. I'm taking Lottie out tonight, and I don't need you two messing it up. So just fucking tell us so we can tell you how you're an idiot and then help you find a solution."

"Fine," I groan. "We got drunk last night; she went to my bed to sleep; I cuddled with her and somehow ended up with my hand up her shirt and touched her tits. She moaned and grabbed my dick. We dry humped, and then afterward, she freaked out and left in the middle of the night. We spoke for a brief second this morning through text, and she has yet to respond to me."

"You fucking idiot," Huxley says.

JP pinches his nose. "We told you not to do anything, and you deliberately disobeyed us. How do you think that makes us feel?"

"This isn't about you, JP," I say.

"You're right, you're right." JP looks me in the eyes. "You're an idiot."

"Well aware." I slouch in my chair and press my fingers to my forehead. "What the hell am I supposed to do now?"

"How about not dry hump your best friend?" Huxley says and leans back in his chair as well. "Let me ask you this. In the moment, did she love it?"

"Yes," I answer. "She was so into it, asking for more. But afterward, she freaked herself out."

"Probably because you're the only person she has in her life, and she's afraid she just messed that up," JP says with some helpful insight. I know, I'm shocked too.

"Fuck, you're so stupid," Huxley says. "We told you not to do anything other than be a friend."

"Yeah...well, easier said than done, okay?" I drag my hand over my face. "It was impossible not to touch her. Especially after she took off her bra, and she smelled so fucking good, and I just...fuck, I want her."

"Ever heard of patience?" JP asks. "Because if you exercised patience, you wouldn't be in this mess."

"Wow, thanks for pointing out the obvious."

"Hey." JP holds up his hands. "Don't get mad at me. I'm not the one who messed up. You are."

"Yeah, but you're not being helpful."

"Oh, I'm sorry. Did we miss the part when you asked us for help?"

I grind my teeth together and then say through clenched teeth. "Help."

JP turns to Huxley. "He wants our help."

"Yeah, I heard him. Not sure we can help him, though," Huxley says, grating on my nerves as well.

"Because we offered him help yesterday, and he didn't take it," JP continues. "And isn't that the worst, when someone specifically asks you for advice and then they don't take it, especially when it's solid advice?"

"It is." Huxley runs his finger over his chin. "Not sure he deserves more advice."

"Jesus Christ," I mutter before standing. I'm over this. I'm happy about being able to get back to work, but I'm not going to sit through this torture.

As I head toward the door to the conference room, Huxley calls out, "Fuck her."

"What?" I ask as I glance over my shoulder.

He turns his chair and looks me dead in the eyes. "Fuck her. Make it impossible for her to say no. You've already made the move, so live with that. You can't go back to being just friends, so show her exactly why she wouldn't want to be just friends. Fuck her. Fuck her hard. Fuck her good."

JP peeks his head over Huxley's shoulder and says, "Trust me, if he can get Lottie to fall for him, then listen to his advice." JP grips Huxley's shoulder. "He's right. You have the friendship down. Now show her why she can't resist you."

"She said it was weird because it was me."

"Then I suggest you introduce her to that side of you just like you introduced her to the sensitive, best friend side. You know how to fuck, so prove it."

I pull on the back of my neck as I say, "You think that will work?"

"Only one way to find out," JP says. "But for the love of God, use protection."

"Wow, thanks for that," I say as I open the door to the conference room and head to the elevator to leave.

I hate to admit it, but they might be right. Lia is comfortable being my friend because that's how she knows me. But boyfriend? Being intimate? She's not comfortable with that side of me just yet, so I might as well introduce her and make her comfortable.

Breaker: Are you home?

Breaker: You can either answer, or I can walk in on you doing whatever the hell it is you're doing in your apartment. Either way, I'm seeing you tonight.

Lia: I'm taking a walk. Be home in ten.

Breaker: I'll be waiting for you.

I lean back on her couch, wearing nothing but a pair of athletic shorts—got to show her the goods even if she didn't ask for them—and I listen as she unlocks her door. Not sure she's expecting to see me on her couch, but either way, I'm not fucking moving.

I gave Huxley's advice some thought, and I agree with him completely, but I don't want to fuck her right away. That would be far too aggressive. I need to ease her into it, which is exactly what I plan on doing.

Her front door opens and she walks in, headphones on her head, a light sheen of sweat coating her skin from the ninety-degree weather outside. She's wearing a pair of pink athletic shorts and a Smurfs T-shirt that I'm pretty sure is from her youth. When she glances up, she stutters back from the shock of seeing me and presses her hand to her chest.

"Jesus, Breaker." She removes her headphones and sets her phone down on the kitchen counter. "You could have told me you were in here."

"I said I'd be waiting for you."

"Well, I didn't think in my place."

I walk over to her. "How was the walk?"

Her eyes fall to my chest but quickly rise to my face. "It was fine."

I cross my arms and lean against the wall. "What did you think about?"

Her eyes scan me again before she moves toward her bathroom. "Nothing in particular."

"Oh, I see." I follow. "So you didn't think about the way I sucked on your tits last night?"

She stumbles into the bathroom door before looking over her shoulder. "Oh my God, Breaker."

"What?" I smile. "It happened, might as well talk about it."

"I don't want to talk about it."

She steps into the bathroom and goes to shut the door when I stop her. "Why not? Was it so good that reminiscing will only make you hot again?"

Her eyes grow angry, and it takes everything in me not to burst out in laughter. "No. I don't want to talk about it because it was awkward. I don't know how to be around you now, so bringing that up only makes it worse."

"Interesting. I thought bringing it up makes it better."

"It doesn't." She shuts the door and turns on the shower.

After a few seconds, I knock on the door and say, "Need help in there?"

"Go away, Breaker."

I chuckle and move over to her bedroom, where I sprawl across her bed and place my hands behind my head. I wait there for a few minutes, and when I hear the shower turn off, I prepare myself. It might be awkward for her, but I'm going to make it way less awkward.

The bathroom door opens, and she walks into the bedroom wearing nothing but a towel around her torso. Her hair isn't wet, but little droplets careen down her chest.

"Oh my God," she shouts as she stumbles back into the bedroom door. "I thought you left."

"Lia, you know me better than that." I let my eyes travel down her body and back up. "New outfit? I like it."

She rolls her eyes and goes to her dresser, where she pulls out a pair of shorts and a shirt. I hop off the bed and walk up behind her just as she's shutting her second drawer. She stills when she feels me.

"What are you doing?" she asks as I drag my finger over the slope of her neck.

"You had some water right here," I say, my voice growing deeper than usual from a simple touch of her soft skin.

She turns around so her back is against the dresser, and she's facing me. "That's what towels are for," she says. Her chest is rising and falling at a more rapid rate.

"Seems like you missed it," I say and then move my finger along her collarbone. "And here, you missed some water here."

"I was quick with drying off," she says as she leans back against the dresser.

"Yeah, why was that?"

"I don't know," she answers as she wets her lips.

"Well, you did a shit job, because you have some water here too," I say as I move my finger along the swell of her breast.

Her teeth roll over her bottom lip as her chest rises against my finger. I take that as a good sign and continue to push forward. I move my hand to where the towel is tucked under her arm and toy with it, seeing what her reaction would be. When she doesn't say anything, I give it a soft tug, loosening the terrycloth.

"What are you doing?" she asks.

"Helping you dry off," I say. "Unless you don't want me to help. I'd be more than happy to just watch."

"Why, uh, why would you want to watch?" she asks. She slips into the mood, just like that. Easier than I thought, but I still want to move at a snail's pace with her because I don't want to fuck this up. I have one chance to make her mine, one fucking chance, and I'm not going to forget patience this time.

"Because," I answer as I tug on the towel again, loosening it all the way.

The reason it's still on her is because I'm holding it up, yet she makes no move to stop me. "I didn't get a good look at those tits last night."

And then, I release the towel, letting it fall to the ground between us. My eyes immediately fall to her breasts, and I grow hard instantly as I take all of her in.

Firm yet supple breasts with light pink nipples beaded to a point entice my mouth. Her body curves in at her waist and flares at her hips. Petite, but just enough to grab on to. Her pussy is bare, which makes my mouth water even more, and as I drag my gaze back up to her face, I see the hunger she has in her mossy-green eyes.

"I need a better look," I say as I take her hand in mine.

"Better look at what?" she asks as I walk her to the window of her bedroom and flip open the curtains. "Breaker," she says as she recoils against my chest.

"They're tinted. No one can see," I whisper against her ear. That seems to relax her enough for me to gather both of her hands in mine and then lift them above her head and pin them against the floor-length window.

A gasp falls past her lips before she says, "Wh-what are you doing?"

"Drying you off," I answer and then press her hands against the window. I speak directly into her ear as I say, "Don't move these. Got it?"

"Breaker—"

"Got it?" I repeat, this time sterner.

She nods her head as she shakily says, "Yes."

Satisfied she won't move, I pick up her towel from near the dresser and walk back toward the window where she's waiting.

I don't rush. I take my time as I consume every inch of her with my eyes. This woman has absolutely captivated me from day one, and the fact she's letting me see her like this and touch her is enough to make me go fucking crazy with desire.

I place the towel over my hand and step up behind her. "I'm just going to dry you off, okay?"

She nods so I bring my towel-covered hand to her front as I press my bare chest to her back. I slowly move it over her stomach and then up to her breasts. When I connect with them, her head rolls to the side as a light moan fills the silence of the room. I move to the other breast and make sure to twist her nipple to cause her to gasp. I drag the towel up to her neck, where I grip her tightly, not choking her but enough to show her I'm in command.

I place my lips close to her ear as I say, "Spread your legs."

"Breaker…" she whispers right before I feel her swallow.

"Spread them, Ophelia," I repeat, and this time, she listens. "Good girl." I drag the towel down, between her breasts, past her stomach, and straight between her legs. Her head falls back against my chest as she groans.

I can't help the smile that spreads across my face as I move the towel back up her stomach only to lower my body so her ass is right in front of my face. I bring the towel to the two round globes and act like I'm drying them off, but in reality, I'm giving them a gentle squeeze.

Her ass is so perfect, and I'll be a happy man the day I get to spank it. But not today.

I drag the towel down her left leg and then all the way back up, where I briefly pass over her pussy, and then drag the towel down her other leg. Meanwhile, she holds still, her hands propped against the window.

"There," I say as I toss the towel to the side. "Let's see how I did." I place both hands at her ankles and then slowly drag them up the sides of her legs, using my fingertips rather than my palm. Goose bumps break out over her skin as I continue to work my way up until I'm standing and my hands are at her waist. "Dry so far," I say as I walk my hands up her stomach, and then with my chest against her back, I cup each breast and pass my thumbs over her nipples.

"Fuck," she whispers as her head once again falls back.

"You like your tits being played with, don't you?" When she doesn't answer, I squeeze her nipple and say, "Don't you?"

"Yes," she breathes out heavily.

"I thought so." I keep hold of one breast, lightly massaging it, while I drag my other hand up to her throat and grip it firmly. "You also like it when I hold you like this, don't you?"

She nods against my chest, and her confirmation turns me on more.

"Good answer. Seems like you're dry, but I just have one more place to check." I keep my hand at her throat, my thumb pressed into her jaw, as my other hand floats down her stomach, past her belly button, and straight to the spot between her legs. I slip one finger over her slit and revel with just how fucking turned on she is. "Ophelia, I thought I dried you off." I drag my finger over her clit, causing her to moan. "But you're incredibly wet. How could that be?"

I remove my finger and bring it up to my mouth, where I let her hear me suck on it, while still holding her by the neck. "Fuck, you taste so good." I place my hand on her hip as I speak softly to her. "Now, you have two choices. I can either lick you clean or bring the towel between your legs again. You tell me what you want."

She gasps for air, and I let up on my hold only a touch.

"What's it going to be?"

"I...I don't know," she responds, too shy to ask for it. Well, that's not what I want to hear, so I'm going to have to force her to beg for it. I know she wants me, and I know she wants this. It's getting her out of her comfort zone that I need to work on.

"Okay, then I will decide for you. I'll use the towel."

I release her neck and reach for the towel just as she says, "No."

I pause and ask, "No, what?"

"I...I don't want the towel."

I smirk and then bring my hands up to her breasts where I gently play with them, letting my fingers pinch and tug on her nipples. "Then what do you want?"

She takes a few shallow breaths before she says, "Your...your tongue."

I moan into her ear, letting her know I'm pleased, as I say, "Good choice."

And then without warning, I spin her around so her ass is against the window now, and I pin her hands up again. "Keep these there and spread your legs wider."

She does as she's told, and when I think she's ready, I press a kiss to the swell of her breast, and then drag my tongue to her nipple where I lap at it a few times. She writhes against my mouth, wanting more, but I take my time. I go at my own pace, and when I'm ready, I move down her stomach, kissing the entire way until I'm kneeling in front of her.

Her breaths are short and jagged now, her stomach completely hollowed out, her pelvis leaning toward me as I kiss her pubic bone and then her hip flexor and then her inner thigh. She groans in anticipation, so I move to the other side, driving her wild with desire, and when she's had enough, I spread her with two fingers and then bring my tongue to her clit, lapping her up in one long stroke.

"Oh my God," she nearly screams as her legs tremble in front of me.

"So fucking good," I say as I dive my tongue against her clit, loving every goddamn second of this. She tastes so good. She feels so good.

So right.

As if this is where I'm supposed to be.

This is what I'm supposed to be doing.

I spread her even wider and use my tongue to flick against her clit.

"Oh…oh, Breaker," she cries as one of her hands falls to my head. Normally, I'd tell her to put her hand back where I put it, but I allow her to touch me because I feel like she needs that connection.

Her fingers sift through my hair and tug on the short strands as I continue to lap at her clit over and over again, loving the way her grip on my hair grows tighter as I bring her closer and closer to the edge.

"Feels…feels so good," she says as her body slides against the window. She must need a better position, so I lift, grip her around the waist, and then slowly lower her to the floor. I press my hands against her inner thighs and spread her even wider, giving me much better access.

I slide my tongue along her slit in a long, slow motion, and she tries to clench her legs together, but I don't allow it.

"Oh my God," she whispers as her hand finds my hair again.

With my nose pressed against her mound, I flatten my tongue against her arousal and slide it up and down, watching as her breathing picks up, her mouth falls open, and she tugs on my hair.

"Fuck, Breaker. Jesus, I'm...I'm..."

I pick up my pace once again, flicking fast at her clit repeatedly, watching her excitement grow. Her pelvis arches, both of her hands fall to my head where they keep me in place, and she voluntarily spreads her legs as her chest rises and lets out a deep moan.

"Oh God!" she screams as she comes, her pussy drenched. I lap it all up, licking her until she has nothing left to give.

Her hands loosen in my hair, and they fall to her sides as she attempts to catch her breath.

Satisfied, I lift from the floor, and as I stare down at her, my erection painfully in need of some attention, I say, "Get dressed and meet me at my place in ten. I'll order food, and we can play a game."

And with that, I head back to my apartment to jack off in the shower.

Holy fuck.

Holy fucking fuck.

Now it makes sense why I've held out.

It's *her* taste.

Her body.

Her everything that I've wanted...probably for longer than I think.

CHAPTER 18
LIA

I STAND IN FRONT OF Breaker's apartment door, my clit still throbbing after what he did to me, unsure if I should knock or simply walk in.

Normally, I'd just walk in, but after the past twenty-four hours, I'm not sure what I should be doing now.

Breaker went down on me.

He not only went down on me, but he made it seem like I was his Thanksgiving feast and he was starving. Never in my life have I felt such euphoric pleasure, and that was with his tongue. And he asked for nothing in return. Just took what he wanted and left.

I have no idea how to process it all.

And even though I want to hide away in my apartment because I don't know how to act, there's no way he'd allow that. Also, I want answers. I want to know what's going on.

So I grip the door handle and walk into his apartment to find him sitting on his couch. His hair is wet now, and he's wearing a different pair of shorts, but that's it, just shorts.

I've seen him with his shirt off plenty of times, but he normally has a shirt on whenever we hang out. Not sure what changed today, but I'm not going to complain. He's so handsome...sexy, with his carved pecs and his strong, muscular arms. Not to mention the stack of abs he has for a stomach and the deep V that's sculpted into his hips. He's so good-looking that I've told myself through all these years never to look because he was my friend, but now...now I'm allowing it.

"There you are," he says in a jovial tone, as if he didn't just have his head between my legs. "I ordered Thai. Should be here in twenty. How do you feel about playing Codenames? We haven't played that in a bit."

I stand there, stunned.

Because the man who I'm staring at right now is very different from the man who was just gripping my throat, telling me I was a good girl for listening to him. The man in front of me is my best friend. The guy I've grown comfortable with, the man I've relied on for so long. But the man from ten minutes ago, he's...he's on another level, and I don't know how to handle it.

"You okay?" he asks.

"Uh...not really," I say as I cross my arms. "I'm just a touch confused."

He pats the couch. "Come talk to me."

I hold up my hand. "I think I'll stand here, thank you."

"Okay." When he smiles, I can see in his eyes that he knows exactly what he's doing. "You can talk there. What's up, Lia?"

Lia...

Lia?

Just so casual. Totally neglecting the fact that he dominated me in my own bedroom while using my full name and commanding my body to do things I've never done.

"What's up?" I ask, my voice rising. "How about the fact that you're my best friend but just made me come so hard that I'm not sure if my clit is still attached?"

He chuckles and says, "Trust me, it is. But if you want me to check, I don't mind going down there again. This time, though, I'd prefer you sit on my face."

"Breaker," I shriek before covering my eyes.

"What?" He laughs.

"We don't say those things to each other or do those things..."

"You might not, but I do now." He lifts from the couch. "Want something to drink?"

I watch him casually move around his apartment, grabbing a cup, filling it with ice, and then pouring a Gatorade into it.

When I don't answer him, he grabs another cup, fills it with ice, and tops it off with the rest of the Gatorade. Eyes on me, he brings the drink over and offers it to me.

For some reason, my body registers just how close he is, how much taller he is than me, how much more muscular...

My internal body temperature spikes all over again.

"Here," he says softly.

"I didn't say I wanted a drink."

"After all the panting you just did in your bedroom, you're going to want the electrolytes." He smirks, and I needle him in the stomach, causing him to laugh.

I take the drink from him and follow him into the living room, where I sit on the opposite side of the couch.

"Trying to keep your hands to yourself?" he asks. "I get it."

"No, I'm trying to keep you away."

"If that were the case, you wouldn't have come over here."

"As if you would have allowed me to stay at my apartment," I scoff before taking a drink of the lime Gatorade. Ugh, that's refreshing. I really did pant a lot. My mouth feels dry.

"I would have if that's what you needed, but clearly, by you being here, you needed...me." He smirks again and sips from his glass.

"Umm, arrogant much?"

"Nah, just telling it like it is."

"Then tell me this, what the hell are you doing?"

He glances down at himself, taking in his person, and then back at me. "Looks like I'm enjoying a cool drink with my friend. What are you doing?"

"Stop playing around," I say. "Tell me what's going on? Are we...are we friends with benefits or something? Because that never works out. Trust me."

"Do you think we're friends with benefits?" he asks, staying as elusive as ever.

"No. I think we're friends, and one of us has lost our mind."

"It's okay," he says, winking. "I'm sure you'll get your head on straight again soon."

I grind my teeth together. "I was talking about you. You're the one who's lost his mind."

He scratches the side of his head as he says, "Huh, odd. I don't feel like I have. I feel pretty normal actually."

"Oh my God, Breaker," I shout. "You're starting to make me mad."

"I can sense that. How can I make you less mad?"

"By telling me what the hell is going on. I mean…do you like me or something?" The question sounds so childish coming off my lips that I hate myself for asking.

"I've always liked you, Lia," he answers.

"I mean…romantically."

"Well." He rubs his jaw with his hand. "Let's see. I think you're incredibly hot. You taste like fucking candy. Your tits will forever live in my dreams, and I can't wait to have your legs wrapped around my head, so take that as you will." He smiles and then leans toward the coffee table to organize the game.

And I let that sink in.

Not sure I'd ever have thought Breaker would say something like that to me.

Never thought he'd ever touch me the way he has.

But the way he answered me, not actually saying he likes me romantically, more what he likes about me, puts me on edge.

"I'm not just someone you can fuck around with," I say before I can stop myself.

He pauses and turns so our eyes meet. "You think I'd do that to you?" he asks, his voice growing darker.

"I don't know, Breaker. It feels like I'm just a toy at the moment."

He pushes back, then turns his body toward me. "That's insulting, Lia. Do you really think I'd treat our friendship so cheaply?"

No.

I think he takes our friendship very seriously.

"Then what is it?"

"How about you stop trying to label things and just enjoy? I know what I'm doing."

"Would be great to let me know what that is."

He turns back toward the coffee table and shuffles some cards before saying, "Let me worry about it. You just sit back and relax."

He cuts the conversation off with that.

The rest of the night, we eat Thai food, play Codenames, joke around, and don't speak about what we've done. When it's time for bed, he walks me back to my apartment, and when I think he's going to kiss me, he pulls me into a hug and kisses the top of my head.

When we're in bed, he knocks on the wall four times, and with an uneasy feeling in my chest, I knock back three.

———

"Look at this multicolored yarn," Lottie says. "And it has glitter in it."

"Oh wow, that's nice," I say while the girls show me all the supplies they bought for our first knitting club gathering.

After the whole *towel and going down on me* situation, I texted the girls and asked them if they wanted to meet up, and luckily, they were free the next day. They think they're going to learn how to knit, when in fact, I have ulterior motives. I need to figure out what's going on with Breaker so I know how to approach it. *Him.*

"I got just plain red," Myla says, looking defeated. "I didn't know we were allowed to get a glitter yarn."

"You live and you learn," Lottie says with a smirk while Kelsey sits in our circle after stepping out to answer a call.

"Okay, sorry about that. JP thought we were going out to dinner tonight, and I had to remind him that's tomorrow."

"Where are you two going?" Myla asks.

"To this new sushi place that he's been wanting to go to for a while."

"Is it Nori?" Lottie asks.

"Yes. Did Huxley take you?"

"Last week," Lottie answers. "It's so good." She then turns to me and says, "Are you a big sushi fan?"

"I love it. Breaker and I used to get it all the time in college. There was a place downtown that wasn't too pricey, but it was amazing."

"Speaking of Breaker," Lottie says with a smile. "I heard through the grapevine that he's been making a move."

The grapevine being her husband.

"What?" Kelsey says. "JP didn't say anything to me."

"That's shocking," Lottie says as she leans over and picks up one of the cookies I made for tonight. "He's a bigger gossip than Hux."

"I even heard a whispering of something," Myla said. "But my husband and his brother can't keep anything to themselves, and Breaker hangs out with Banner enough for there to be a leak between them." Myla looks up at me. "So, is it true?"

With all eyes on me, I know this is what I wanted, but it doesn't make it easier, just makes the conversation flow better.

"Uh, yeah, he did."

The girls all clap and cheer, but it all feels so weird.

"That boy has had it really bad for you," Lottie says. "God, I'm so glad he finally did something about it. How was it?"

I pause and tilt my head to the side. "He's had it bad for me?" I ask, confused.

Lottie glances at Kelsey and then back at me. "I mean...what?" She blinks a few times.

"You said he has it bad for me. What do you mean?"

"Uh, I don't think I said that, right, Kelsey? I didn't say that."

"Yeah, I don't think she said that."

"That's what I heard," Myla says with a smirk, and when the sisters look her way, she just shrugs. "Listen, we're here for a reason. These men of ours often have the upper hand, and any advantage we can have over them, the better, so we might as well be truthful with her. Yes, Breaker has had it bad for you."

"He didn't say that to you?" Lottie asks, looking guilty.

"No, he didn't. He wouldn't say anything really, other than he knows what he's doing."

"Of course he does," Kelsey says with an eye roll. "All the Cane brothers *know what they're doing* and we are mere pawns in their plans."

"Oh stop," Lottie says. "I don't see any of us complaining about the orgasms. Which by the way, you didn't answer me. Was it good?"

I press my lips together and nod. "Yeah, it was spectacular. Like… unlike anything I've ever experienced."

"It always is," Kelsey says while leaning back in her chair. "I swear these men have some sort of secret society where they learn how to precisely play with a woman so they're ruined for any other man."

"It's true," Myla says. "Ryot has always been able to control my body, rendering it useless."

"Huxley is the same. I hated him so much when we first met, but somehow, he kept me around by using just his fingers."

"Breaker used his tongue," I say, skipping over the dry humping because I just don't think that's something I can get into. "But he started it by 'helping me dry off from the shower.'" I use air quotes, causing the girls to laugh. "And before I knew what was happening, he had me pressed against my apartment window, completely naked, and was going down on me."

"God, that's so hot," Lottie says. "I love when Huxley fucks me against a window. It feels so naughty."

"So it was *magnificent* then," Kelsey says. When I nod, she adds, "Then why do I sense some hesitation?"

"Two reasons," I say. "For one, I literally just broke up with my fiancé and called off my wedding. I think it makes me look incredibly slutty."

"I don't think so," Myla says. "I think it's just you figuring out what you want, and that's important."

"I agree," Kelsey says.

"Me too. What's the second reason?" Lottie asks.

"It's Breaker. He's everything to me, and even though when we're in the moment, when he's touching me, making me feel things I've never felt before, I can't help but worry. What happens if this doesn't work out? What if something goes wrong? What if he gets bored of me and moves on? It's weird now when he's intimate; it's going to be so much weirder if I get attached and he decides to move on."

"Not going to happen." Lottie shakes her head. "Breaker would never."

"But he's never had a true relationship before," I say.

"Because he's had you," Kelsey says. "Because you've been everything he's ever needed, and now that he's figured that out, he's trying to take things to the next level."

"But…he hasn't kissed me. He's just given me orgasms."

Lottie and Kelsey pause as they exchange glances. Myla and I both look confused as Lottie shakes her head. "Oh no."

"Oh no, what?" I ask.

Kelsey winces. "We know exactly what he's doing."

"What?" I ask, growing anxious.

"He has a plan, a meticulous plan to make you fall for him," Lottie says.

"It's true." Kelsey nods. "The Cane brothers, well, they're something else. When they have their mind set on something, they make it happen their way. Meaning, he hasn't kissed you because he's waiting for the perfect moment."

Lottie nods. "Yup. The first kiss means something to him, so he's saving it."

"And going down on me means nothing?" I ask.

Kelsey and Lottie think on it just as Myla chimes in. "Have you guys ever been intimate before in your friendship?"

"Never," I answer.

She nods. "Then this is him probably showing you that it can be normal."

"Ah, yes," Kelsey seconds. "God, that would so be something one of them would do. Think about the amount of times JP teased me before we actually had sex. Or you and Huxley. It's their MO. It's what they do. They turn you into putty until you can't do anything other than follow them around, waiting for their next move."

"Facts," Lottie says. "The first time Huxley touched me was my last first—that's how powerful it was. Did it feel like that to you?"

I think back to my bedroom—not to when we were drunk—but to when he was pinning me against the window because we were both very much aware of what was happening.

"It felt…it felt like nothing I've ever felt before. It was as if I was just a mere instrument to him, and he knew exactly how to play me. I mean, I let him hold me by the throat. I let him put me into positions I never would have in the past, and I was convinced only by his touch, by his voice."

Kelsey and Lottie nod. "Yup, he's playing his cards with you," Lottie says.

"So what do I do?" I ask.

"Nothing," Kelsey answers. "There's absolutely nothing you can do. You can try to fight it, but I don't think it'll do much."

"I might be overstepping a bit," Myla says, "but it almost seems like you might have the same feelings about him. Am I right?"

"I've never truly thought about it," I say. "I always just considered him my friend. But this past week or so, it's been different. He's looked at me differently. He's told me how beautiful I am. He's said it before, but this was… It was as if he meant it from a different place. And then he started touching me lightly, here and there. Like this night when I felt really sad about losing my parents and asked him to hold me. We were in his bed, and nothing happened, but his hand did wander along my hip. I didn't think much of it then, but after the night we got drunk—"

"Whoa." Lottie holds up her hand. "What happened the night you got drunk?"

"I'm surprised your husbands didn't tell you." I set my yarn down, completely neglecting the knitting premise now. "It was the day I broke things off with Brian. Breaker and I went to celebrate, and we both got drunk and went to bed. We were playfully fighting over his pillow, and then he cuddled into me. I asked him if that was how he would hold his girlfriend, and he said no and then proceeded to show me *exactly* how he would touch his girlfriend."

"And how did he show you?" Myla asks, sitting on the edge of her seat.

My cheeks heat just thinking about that night. "With teasing touches. He'd slowly move his hand to just below my breasts and then slip his hand past the waistband of my shorts."

"Oh dear God." Kelsey fans herself. "Did the teasing lead to anything?"

I bite my bottom lip. "I, uh, I ended up dry humping him to completion."

"Both of you?" Lottie asks, and I nod. "Well…that's it then, you just opened it all up for him to take control."

"Yup," Kelsey says. "And then with the towel thing. He has his mind set, and you need to decide if you're going to let it happen or not."

"I…I really don't know. I don't want to lose him." He's told me he's loved me for years, and it's always been in friendship, but lately…lately it's felt like more. But how can I know the difference? And what if I'm not enough for him sexually and his interest in me dwindles like Brian's did? *What if I lose him too?* "If what you say is true, and he's trying to coax me into a relationship, what happens if he doesn't believe we work? As a couple? I don't think I could manage him not being in my life."

"Sometimes the best relationship comes from a strong friendship as the foundation," Kelsey says. "That's how it was with me and JP. We got really close, and I thought he was a great friend. Crossing that line felt natural to me."

"It doesn't feel natural to me," I answer.

Lottie taps her chin. "I think Breaker is going to help you see just how natural it can be."

Breaker: Just got off work. Headed to your place.

Lia: Are you really just going to invite yourself over?

Breaker: As if I needed an invite to begin with.

Lia: Maybe you need one now.

Breaker: Fine…Lia, can I come over and play?

Lia: What does "play" entail?

Breaker: Games. *eye roll*

Lia: Okay, as long as we're playing games. I can cook up some tortellini if you want. I got the fresh kind.

Breaker: Serve me a bowl. I'm making a quick stop.

Lia: What are you getting?

Breaker: Dessert.

Lia: Okay, see you soon.

"Hey," Breaker says, walking into my apartment. I glance over my shoulder just in time to see him remove his suit jacket, revealing his tight-fitting button-up shirt where the top few buttons are undone, hinting at his firm chest. "Smells good."

"Oh, thanks," I say as I turn around and face the stove, my face heating from the mere sight of him.

He walks into the kitchen, comes right up behind me, and places his hand on my hip while looking over my shoulder. I'm immediately aroused, and that annoys me. I shouldn't be this insane about the man. I should be able to control myself, but it seems like the girls are right. It's next to impossible to control yourself around the Cane men.

His hand slides under my shirt and grips my waist as he says, "Want me to grab drinks?"

"Uh, yeah." I gulp. "That would be helpful."

"Okay." He then lowers his face to my neck and places the lightest of kisses on my skin. "You smell amazing, by the way."

And then he pulls away, and I'm left stirring the sauce rather frantically as I try to control my pulse, which has skyrocketed.

It's the little things with him.

The attention.

The touches.

What he says.

All things I can now see that I wanted Brian to do—all things Breaker does without even asking. It's almost as if it's ingrained in him, and he doesn't need to think about it. It just happens.

"How was your day?" he asks as he grabs two Sprites from the fridge.

"It was fine," I say, still feeling stiff.

"Just fine?" he asks as he brings the drinks to the table.

"Yeah, nothing too exciting happened."

"Well, we'll have to change that," he says as he grabs plates, and I take the sauce off the stove. "I got this. You go sit down."

"You don't have to, Breaker."

He places his finger under my chin and holds me in place as he says, "I want to."

Okay, then.

I let him serve us, and when I take a seat, I watch as he rolls up his sleeves, which then plays in my head like some sort of porno from the way his muscly forearms flex. God, he really is so sexy. Why am I only letting myself notice it now? I mean, I've known he's hot, but the thought has never hit me like this before, like I want to do something about it.

With a plate in each hand, he walks over to the table and sets it down in front of me. He grips the back of my neck and says, "Need anything else?"

"Uh, I don't think so," I answer while his palm burns into my skin.

He gives me a light squeeze. "Let me know if you do."

Before he takes a seat, he scoots his chair closer to mine and then sits down, only to place his hand on my bare thigh.

I nearly choke on my tortellini.

"Problem?" he asks.

"Your, uh, your hand is on my thigh."

"And…"

"Is it supposed to be there?" I ask as I stare at his gorgeous smirk.

"As a matter of fact, it is." He stabs some tortellini with his fork and sticks it in his mouth.

Okay…I guess his hand is on my thigh then.

I turn back to my plate and try not to focus on the way his thumb caresses my skin back and forth slowly. It's like he's lulling me into some sort of sex-induced lullaby.

News flash, it's working.

"Aren't you going to ask me how my day was?" he asks.

I swallow and take a sip of my Sprite. "How was your day?"

"Pretty good. We had a company-wide meeting to go over the Shoemacher case, and then we fielded questions. It took up a great deal of the day. We split up the questions by department so we didn't keep people waiting. I was glad to be back in the office."

"That's good. You happy?"

He glances over at me and smiles. "Very."

And for some reason, I don't think he answered about work.

———

"I can do those," Breaker says as he comes up behind me while I'm at the sink, washing the pots. His hands once again slip under my shirt and past the waistband of my shorts to land on my hips. With his chest right against my back, the position feels more intimate than anything I ever did with Brian.

"I can handle it."

"You sure?" he asks, his fingers sliding inward, causing a dull throb to ache between my legs.

"Yes," I answer as I rest my head against his chest. Just for a moment.

He chuckles, and I can feel the rumble throughout my whole body. He brings one hand even closer in, resting just above where I want him. "I have no problem cleaning up. You did cook, after all." His lips tug on my ear, and I drop the sponge in the sink and fully relax into him.

"I...I can do it."

"Okay." He nibbles on my ear again. "I'll get dessert ready." He removes his hands, and I almost let out an unsatisfied moan to call him back.

Throughout dinner, he kept his hand on my thigh as we talked about the old theater in Culver City opening up again and the old movies they'd play. He was attentive, he laughed with me, he listened, and he asked questions.

Just like every other conversation we've ever had.

Yet this felt different.

Everything feels different.

And it's scary.

What's especially scary is the way I feel empty when he walks away. That should be the most concerning thing out of all of this. I *never* felt anything like that with Brian. I shouldn't be comparing things with Brian, but if what the girls said is true, and Breaker wants to move our friendship into a relationship, then Brian is the benchmark. And I'm coming to realize that it is a *very* low benchmark. He texted me again today, but that was it. I haven't read any of his messages because why bother? We're done.

End of story. No way would I feel this way if things ended with Breaker. *And that's what terrifies me.*

I finish washing the pot, clear out the sink, and then wipe down the counters. When I glance up and don't see Breaker at the dining room table, I call out, "Breaker?"

"In here," he says from my bedroom.

Oh dear God.

What kind of dessert could we possibly have in the bedroom?

I tug on the hem of my shirt as I head toward his voice. That's when I hear the bathtub filling with water. I poke my head around the corner to find Breaker turning off the faucet. The tub is full of water and topped off with bubbles, while candles provide the only light in the room.

"What's this?" I ask, unsure of what else to say.

Breaker turns toward me, and my eyes immediately fall to his unbuttoned shirt and exposed chest and stomach.

"Bath time," he says before walking up to me and taking the hem of my shirt in his hands. But he doesn't pull up. He waits for me to give him the go-ahead. A part of me wonders what would happen if I walked away, but the other part of me—the desperate part of me—wants to see what he has in store.

So I lift my arms, and he slowly drags my shirt over my head and then drops it to the floor.

"Turn around," he says.

And I do so.

He undoes my bra and lets it fall to the ground right before he drags my shorts and panties to the ground, leaving me completely naked.

His hands fall to my hips again as he presses his warm body against mine. His mouth caresses my cheek while his hands slide up my stomach to my breasts. Breaker seems to really like my breasts, which is definitely boosting my residual self-doubt from Brian's lack of interest. *Stop thinking about him. You have a hot-as-hell man touching your boobs.*

"You're so fucking addicting," he says as he pinches my nipples.

My head falls back, and his lips find my neck. He trails kisses up the column and then back down while he plays with my nipples.

"Fuck," I whisper as my body blazes.

"You like that, don't you?"

I nod, not holding anything back, because I do. I like when he touches my breasts, when he plays with them, when his fingers pinch and pull on my nipples.

"Good. Now listen closely, Lia. I'm going to need you to slip into the bathtub, rest your head on the end, and spread your legs. Got it?"

I nod again and follow his instructions. He helps me into the tub, and I sink into the luxurious warm water.

"How does that feel?"

"Amazing," I say as I get comfortable.

"Good." He then reaches into a brown paper bag that I didn't notice and pulls out a dildo. My eyes widen as he switches it on. The tubular part vibrates and rotates while a little part at the base flicks up and down.

Oh my God, is he going to use that on me?

My cheeks immediately flame as he sits on the edge of the tub.

"Have you ever used one of these before?"

"N-no," I say nervously.

"It's simple." He brings it to the tub and parts the bubbles from my breast before letting it vibrate against my nipple. "You just stick this inside your delicious pussy and let it do all the work."

"I-in the tub?"

"Yes." He flips it off and drags it down my stomach, causing it to hollow out right before he lowers his hand into the water and runs the dildo along my pussy.

"What are you going to do?" I ask.

"Watch," he answers simply. "Take my hand and help me guide it inside you."

"But it's so big."

He catches my eyes as he says, "If you think this is big, wait until I let you have my cock. Now guide it in."

Rocked by his words, I help him guide the dildo in, noting how it stretches me, but nothing painful. It just feels…incredible.

"How are you?"

"Fantastic."

"Good. Hold it in place." He switches it on, and I nearly fly out of the tub from the buzzing inside me and the clit stimulator on the outside.

"Oh my fuck," I say as water sloshes around me, my legs clamping tight.

"Relax," he says while pushing my chest down.

"But…oh my God, Breaker. It's too much."

"It's not. Just relax." He pinches my nipple, relaxing me immediately, which then intensifies the sensation between my legs.

"How?" I say as my head slowly moves from side to side.

"How what?" he asks as he releases my breasts and stands above me.

"How do you know what I need?"

I glance up to see his serious expression, hungry, greedy. "Because I know everything about you, Lia, even what will make you come."

"You do," I whisper as I sink into the water, letting the vibrator do the work. "It feels so good, like—" It turns off, and I look up at him to find him holding a remote. "What are you doing?" I ask.

"Controlling the situation." And then he turns the vibrator back on, shocking me and causing my legs to spasm.

"Oh my God," I moan.

The clit stimulator combined with the vibration is a sensation I've never experienced before, and I'm loving every second of it. Soaking it in, letting myself let go of all of my thoughts and concerns, focusing on how everything feels and the man in front of me, with his shirt open and his hungry eyes watching me.

"Play with your tits, Lia."

His voice feels like a drug, seeping into my veins and governing my every movement. Without question, my hands travel up my body to my breasts, and I push them together. To keep the vibrator in place, I clench my legs together. *Holy shit, that's intense.*

"Breaker," I whisper as I run my fingers over my hardened nipples.

"Shit, you're so hot," he says as I hear him unzip his pants.

My eyes immediately open and fall to his waist as he reaches into his briefs and pulls out his long thick cock.

Oh.

My.

Fuck.

Girthy.

Lengthy.

And so, so hard.

His gaze is on me as I take him all in.

My mouth waters, my legs quiver, and I know deep in my mind that I don't think he could fit in me. There is no way.

"Breaker, you're...you're so big."

"And fucking hard because of you." He turns up the vibration on the remote, and my eyes squeeze shut as my body is rocked with pleasure.

I hear him grunt and the telltale sign of his hand sliding up and down his length. It's so erotic. We're not touching each other, yet we're getting each other off.

"I'm going to be inside you soon," he says as I open my eyes to see him pulling on his cock, his chest muscles firing off, his abs contorting with every stroke. "And I'm going to fuck you, Lia. I'm going to make sure you feel nothing but my dick for the rest of your goddamn life."

The vibrator moves faster, and I can't do anything other than let him take over. So I bring one hand down to the vibrator, hold it in place, and then use my other hand to play with my nipple, running my finger around it in circles, flicking at it, and then pinching it the way Breaker does.

"Fuck, this feels so good," I say as my pelvis starts to move with the vibrations.

"Do you wish it was my cock inside you?" he asks.

"Your cock is too big," I say as my legs start to spasm with jolts of pleasure.

"My cock is perfect for your cunt," he says, his voice drawing me to look up at him. "You hear me?" he asks, determination in his expression. "My cock is fucking perfect for your deliciously tight cunt."

My chest fills with air as my head feels dizzy. I nod in agreement, only for him to press the button on the remote again, the dildo now vibrating at a frantic pace that causes my stomach to bottom out.

"Oh my God...oh fuck," I yell as my body seizes. The stimulator rubs my clit in just the right spot, causing my body to tingle all over.

An undeniable pressure builds and builds at the base of my stomach, letting my pleasure climb until it's sitting right there, ready to fall over.

"Breaker...oh my God," I groan.

"You need to come?" he asks.

"Yes," I grind out, and then in a flash, the vibrator is turned off. My eyes shoot open, and I breathlessly ask, "What are you doing?"

"Making you wait for me." He continues to pump his cock, but steps closer and closer to me until his pelvis is right at my face. "Suck me into your mouth."

"What?" I ask.

"You heard me, Lia. Suck my cock."

"But, I'm not—"

"Don't," he says. "Don't fucking tell me you're not good at it. Just from the look of your lips, I know you'll make me come in seconds. So suck my fucking cock into your mouth. Now."

So turned on but also unsure, I turn in the tub so I'm kneeling in front of him. With the vibrator still between my legs, I reach out and take his girth into my hand. His eyes squeeze shut just from the touch, which gives me confidence, and then I slowly bring him up to my mouth, where I lick along the rim.

"Jesus fucking Christ," he says as his palm lands on my head. He doesn't force me or encourage me. It's almost like he needs to have his hand there to keep steady.

I swirl my tongue around the head a few times, pull him into my mouth, and then release him, repeating the rhythm a few times. I watch in fascination as his chest rises and falls more rapidly. I love the way his fingers dig into my scalp, and the groans that fall past his lips are so erotic that it heightens my pleasure as well.

I swirl a few more times and then remember what he said about flicking the underside of his cock. I drag my tongue to the base and then lick all the way up to the point that I know he loves the most. And that's when I start flicking and pumping his cock with my hand at the same time.

"Motherfucker," he breathes out. "Fuck, Lia." His hand plays with my hair. "Your mouth. So goddamn good. So warm." I suck him in, and his legs buckle for a moment. I pull him all the way out, then push him farther in, and when I drag him out, I let my teeth slowly skim across his length. "Fuck!" he shouts as he stiffens, and then the vibrator turns back on in full force. I moan against his cock as rapture shoots through me.

"Breaker, I'm…I'm there."

"Then suck me hard," he says, and I do. I pull on his cock so hard that I feel like I'm going to hurt him. But I don't. I just spur him on even more, and my orgasm climbs closer and closer, my body going numb, my vision fading. All I can think about is how I want him to come. How I want to hear his moans.

I swirl my tongue, dip my mouth over his cock, pull back with my teeth, and when I can't hold on to my orgasm any longer, I moan loudly against the head of his length as my whole body spasms.

"So fucking…hot," he says as his entire body stiffens. "Swallow me," he says right before he pulses inside my mouth and comes.

I swallow every last drop, and when he's done, I fall into the bathtub, trying to catch my breath as I stare up at him. He drops to his knees and reaches out to me, where he grips the back of my neck, pulling me closer to the edge.

"Fucking Christ," he says, breathing heavily as his eyes are on mine. "Jesus, Lia."

"Did…did you like that?"

"Did I like that?" he asks, shocked. "I more than liked that. I just developed an addiction to your mouth." His thumb drags over my lips as he gently says, "My cock lives here now. This is my mouth. These are my teeth. This is my tongue." And when I think he's going to go in for a kiss as he pulls me closer, he kisses the top of my forehead and then pulls away. "Good night, Lia."

He pulls away, and with a surprise protest, I say, "Wait, you're leaving?"

"The plan was always to leave after dessert." He stands, and I watch him stuff his penis back into his pants, but he doesn't bother zipping up. "Get some good rest."

And then he's off without another word.

I don't know how long I stay in the tub, at least until the water goes cold. I drain the water, rinse off, and then I don't even bother with clothes as I brush my teeth and climb into bed naked, my mind flooding with thoughts of what we just did.

I reach to turn off my bedside light when my phone dings with a text message.

Breaker: Thank you for dinner, Lia.

I stare at the text for what feels like a minute. It's such a stark contrast to the way he left my apartment. How can he just turn it on and off like that? My mind is still whirling with every erotic thing that happened between us tonight. Doesn't he have the same thoughts? I decide to ask him because I need to understand this better.

Lia: How can you act like nothing just happened?

Breaker: I'm not acting like nothing happened. Trust me, I can still feel your mouth on my cock.

Lia: Then...then why are you acting so casual about all of this? I have no idea what's happening between us, and you're not helping.

Breaker: This feels normal to me, Lia. Like I should have been intimate with you for the last ten years, but I know it's taking you time to get there. I want you to see just how normal it is.

Lia: It doesn't feel normal. It feels weird.

Breaker: Did it feel weird when you were dragging your teeth along my dick?

Lia: Well, no. But that was in the moment.

Breaker: Exactly. Keep living in the moment and stop overthinking everything. Good night, Lia.

And then, then he knocks on the wall four times, and reluctantly, I knock on it three.

———————

I don't even bother getting my yarn out of my bag as I take a seat on Kelsey's couch. I called an emergency meeting after last night, and the girls were more than happy to accommodate. The men, not so much.

Lottie sets down a plate of mini quiches that Reign made, as well as a plate of his delicious croissants.

"Seemed like a croissant moment," she says.

Kelsey brings over a bowl of jelly, plates, and utensils while Myla files in with drinks.

"What's going on?" Kelsey asks.

Getting straight to the point, I say, "You guys were right. He has a plan, and he's executing it."

Lottie leans over and grabs a mini quiche. Before popping it in her mouth, she says, "The Cane men always have a plan...always."

"What happened?" Myla asks.

I go into detail about the night and how we shared a nice dinner, and he was all handsy, but conversation was normal. And then when it came to dessert...

"Wait, he had a dildo with a remote and then put you in the tub?" Lottie asks, blinking.

My cheeks are flaming as I nod. "Yes. And let me tell you, never in my life have I ever done anything like that. Not even by myself."

"I knew he was the kinkier one," Lottie whispers.

"That's not even the kinkiest part," I say.

Myla lifts her drink to her lips and says, "Please tell us."

"Uh, well, he told me to suck him off while the vibrator was still inside me."

The girls all sit there, partially stunned.

"And I did," I add.

Lottie swallows and asks, "How was his dick?"

"Like a freaking log."

The girls let out a boisterous laugh.

"Seriously, it was so big. I told him that wasn't fitting inside me, and he told me how his cock was perfect for my...cunt."

"He said that?" Kelsey asks. "Man, I don't know if I'm going to be able to look at Breaker the same way."

"I don't think any of us will," Myla says.

"Quick question," Lottie says, holding up her finger. "Did you suck him off?"

Starting to feel a touch more comfortable with these conversations, I nod. "I did and...I really liked it."

"Thatta girl," Lottie says while patting my leg.

"So what's the problem?" Myla asks.

"The problem is, everything still feels weird. Like when we're in the moment, nothing is weird about it. It's so natural. And sure, he stuns me with what he says and what he wants me to do, but after...after is what's killing me. And when I talked to him about it last night, he told me to stop overthinking everything."

"He's right," Kelsey says. "You need to just live in the moment."

"I agree," Myla says as she puts jelly on a croissant. "It sounds like he's trying to normalize it all, and if you're resistant, it's going to make it hard for him to do that."

"The big question is, do you want something more with him?" Kelsey asks.

I lean back on the couch and give it some thought.

Life without Breaker is a life I don't think I could handle, nor do I want it.

This new level of our friendship, it's different, but I also seem to enjoy it. That's a lie. I know I enjoy it.

Immensely.

"I think I do," I answer. "But that terrifies me."

"Understandable," Lottie says. "But you know Breaker won't do anything to hurt you, ever. He cherishes you."

"He really does," Kelsey adds. "Pretty much worships the ground you walk on."

"And he's intending to make something so much more of you two," Lottie adds.

"I guess so. But...the weirdness," I say.

"Then don't make it weird," Myla chimes in. "Take charge. Don't let him lead the way. Surprise him and initiate something yourself. Maybe that will take the weird out of it."

"Ooo, good idea," Lottie says.

"Oh, that makes me sweaty," I say. "I've initiated many times before, but Breaker is just so much more experienced than I am. I'd feel like an idiot if I tried to initiate."

"All you have to do is walk up to him and grab his penis, and he'll be good to go," Myla says, causing us to laugh.

"Yeah, I might need more than that."

"So you're open to initiation?" Kelsey asks.

"I think so. I mean, it makes sense. If I want something, I need to move forward on it as well, and maybe it will be less awkward if I take the first step."

"I think so." Myla taps her chin. "Oh, I know. You can send him a dirty text."

"Yes." Lottie slaps the armrest of the sofa. "A dirty text. That's perfect. You can hide behind the keyboard so you don't have to face the initial awkwardness, but you can also control the conversation."

"That is a great idea," Kelsey chimes in. "What should it say? Something that will really grab his attention. Like... *I like your penis.*"

Lottie rolls her eyes. "Excuse my sister. She's not that good at dirty talk."

Kelsey folds her arms. "Okay, what would you type?"

"Well, since you're putting me on the spot, I'm not going to be as eloquent as if I took some time to really think about it. But she could say something like... *I'm so horny just thinking about last night.*"

"Better," Myla says and shakes her head. "But not good enough. We need something that would match Breaker's style, something that would really grab his attention." She thinks about it for a second, and then a smile crosses her face. "Got it."

"Please share," Lottie says, crossing one leg over the other.

"Plain and simple...*I want to sit on your face.*"

"What?" I ask, my cheeks feeling like they just caught in flames.

"Yessss," Lottie drags out. "God, Huxley goes insane when I say stuff like that."

"JP loves that as well," Kelsey adds.

"You guys would text that to your men?" I ask in disbelief.

"Yup." Lottie pulls out her phone. "Watch. I'll text him right now and show you his response. We should all do it."

"I have no problem with that," Myla says and pulls out her phone, and Kelsey does the same. They all send a text.

"Seconds, just wait," Lottie says, and then her phone dings. With a smile, she clears her throat. "I said, *I want to sit on your face*, and he responded..." She wets her lips. "*Get home. Now!*"

Kelsey's phone dings with a text. "That would be my husband. And he said, *Babe, you know your pussy has a permanent reservation, party of one, on my face.*"

I smirk just as Myla's phone goes off.

She opens up her text and says, "Ryot texted a tongue and three drops of water. As well as, When *you get home, strip down. I'll be waiting in the bedroom.*"

Hmm, I wonder what Breaker would say.

Curiosity gets the best of me, so I take out my phone as well.

Lottie claps her hands as she says, "She's doing it."

They're right. I need to cross the bridge of awkwardness if I'm going to make this work, and I do. I don't want to lose him. I want more of him, but I'm just scared. The only way not to be scared is to jump in headfirst.

I pull up our text thread, and I shoot him a text.

Lia: Hey.

"What did you say?" Kelsey asks.

"I just said hey, figured I'd work him in first." My phone dings, and I read his text out loud. *"Hey, was just thinking about you."*

"Ooo, ask him what he was thinking about," Kelsey says.

I text back.

Lia: What were you thinking about?

My phone dings. *"About how I want to see you tonight. Come over to my place?"* I glance up at the girls. "Should I say it now?"

They all nod. On a shaky breath, I text him back.

Lia: I'll be there…I really want to sit on your face.

I squeeze my eyes shut and press *send*. "Oh my God, I can't believe I just said that to him. What if he thinks it's weird?"

"Guaranteed he won't," Lottie says. "He'll love it so much."

"He will," Myla adds. "Just wait."

I stare down at my phone, and when I see the blue dots indicating that he's typing, my stomach drops. And then a resounding ding sounds off through the living room.

Instead of reading it out loud at first, I read it to myself.

Breaker: Good. Your cunt is mine tonight. I'm famished.

My eyes widen when I look up at the girls.

"Ooo, his response has to be good," Lottie says.

I turn the phone around for all of them to read it together because I can't say what he texted out loud.

"Dear God," Kelsey says.

"Ummm, did Breaker just win?" Lottie asks.

Myla nods her head as she sits back. "Yeah, he beat out all the boys with his response." She then looks at me and says, "Have fun tonight. Looks like it's going to be one hell of a time."

CHAPTER 19
BREAKER

I OWE LOTTIE AND KELSEY a medal of honor because I know for a fact the reason Lia texted me earlier about wanting to sit on my face is because of them. I know they had a knitting club thing today because JP was bitching about how he wanted to go ravage his wife but couldn't.

Lia's participated in everything I've initiated so far, which has been out-of-this-world amazing. But then I read...*I really want to sit on your face.* Fuck, did that send an enormous smile to my lips. Does that mean she's starting to feel more comfortable with the idea of us? So soon? Fuck yes, I hope so. There is no doubt in my mind that the girls have convinced her to step outside of her comfort zone.

And I'm fucking grateful.

Lia is at her place now, changing, not sure into what, but she's changing, and I'm waiting impatiently for her to get here. I've thought about how I want to approach this because I want her to feel like she can take charge, but I also know that she's most likely going to be shy, so I'm going to have to read her.

I pace my living room, and when I hear the door next door shut, I hold my breath. I stare down my door, and after a few seconds, the knob twists open.

"Hey," she calls out.

I glance toward the entryway and catch her in a pair of green silk shorts and a white tank top. She's not wearing a bra. That's evident by how hard her nipples are.

"Hey," I say as I come into view.

Immediately, her eyes fall to my chest. I've noticed she's spent more time checking me out in the recent week than ever before, and I'm eating it up. It's why I keep going shirtless when I'm around her.

I walk right up to her, slip my hand around her waist and pull her into my chest, then kiss the top of her head.

Have I wanted to kiss her on the lips? Every goddamn second I'm around her, but I'm waiting. That first kiss, it's going to be a special moment, one I want to fucking remember forever, so I've held off even though it's pained me.

"How was knitting club?" I ask her calmly. Difficult, because my body is buzzing from her text.

"It was fun," she says as she pulls away. I can tell right away that she isn't displaying as much confidence as she was with her text, so I'll need to take charge.

Not a problem at all.

I take her hand in mine and move her to the couch, where I take a seat. I have her sit between my legs so her back is to my chest. We stretch our legs out along the couch, and because I already have music playing and the lights are dimmed, the mood is set.

Her head rests on my shoulder, and I circle her waist while one hand moves under her shirt so I'm touching her stomach.

"Did you see that the Blue Man Group is coming to LA?" I ask.

"They are?" she asks. "Please tell me we're going."

I chuckle. "You know, I could always take you to Vegas to see them. I'm rich after all. Hell, I can host our own private show here at the apartment."

"Flashing your money, are we?"

I like her lighthearted tone, so I go with it. "I feel like I need to impress."

"Do you know how you can impress?" she asks. "Recite all of the characters in Harry Potter in alphabetical order with corresponding house—if they have one."

"Hmm, something to work on." I smooth my hand over her stomach and then work my way up to her breast, barely skimming it with my fingers. "Do you know what JP told me today?"

"What?" she asks, her voice sounding breathless.

"Huxley apparently has a soft spot, and I'm not talking about Lottie."

"What do you mean?"

"Well," I say while dragging my fingers along her stomach, loving how it dips and expands with every breath she takes and every touch I make. "Huxley was in his office, and JP walked in on him and saw his eyes were teary."

"No, I don't believe it," she says while shaking her head. "Huxley doesn't cry."

"I know, that's what I said. And when JP asked him what was going on, Huxley shut down."

"Yeah, as if the man would share his feelings."

"Exactly," I say, loving how much Lia knows about my family. "But you know JP, he's relentless, and he irritated Huxley so much that he finally spilled and said he was watching a video Lottie sent him of a baby hearing for the first time after not being able to hear since birth. Huxley ended up showing JP the video, and they teared up together. Then of course JP donated half a million dollars to a foundation that helps families who can't afford the equipment needed to help their children hear."

"Oh my God, that's so sweet," Lia says. "I thought you were going to say something ridiculous like...JP's pigeon craze."

"That's where I thought it was going too," I say as I bring my hand back up to her breast. This time, I lightly cup it and drag my thumb over the bottom. "But I was surprised to hear that it was about a kid. It makes me think they're hiding something."

"What do you mean?" she asks.

"I don't know. I think Lottie might be pregnant."

"No." Lia shakes her head. "She had drinks with us the other night."

"Yeah, but JP also said he's seen some nonalcoholic knockoffs. Or she's skipped the booze portion of the drink."

Lia twists so she sits on my lap now, her back against the couch and her legs draping off the edge of the couch. "No, she can't be pregnant. I'm sure I would have been able to tell."

"Do you have uterus X-ray vision I don't know about?" I ask.

She presses her palm to my face, causing me to laugh. "You know what I mean."

"I really don't. I think she is. The signs are there. Huxley has been extra protective around her lately. More than usual. And he's canceled a few appointments. JP told me about it. He thinks they've been going to see the doctor."

I place my hand on her thigh as she stares off in wonderment. "I can't fathom it, Huxley being a father. Then again, I never, and I mean never, thought he would get married." She turns toward me now, straddling my lap. I accommodate the switch in position and slip my hands under her shorts, all the way up to the juncture of her hips. "But here he is, proving me wrong with every turn. Lottie really has domesticated him."

"Yeah, I'm glad they bumped into each other. I like Lottie a lot."

"Me too," Lia says. "And Kelsey, for that matter. Are she and JP trying to get pregnant?"

"I didn't ask, but from the look in JP's eyes when he was talking about Lottie possibly being pregnant, I could see the desire in his eyes. I think JP would make a great dad."

"I think so as well." She places her hands on my chest. "I like gossiping about your siblings. They present such an austere image that seeing behind the scenes of these powerful men is fun."

"What about me?"

"I know everything about you already," she says.

"Not everything," I answer.

She smooths her hands over my chest and asks, "What do I not know?"

"That the first night you came to my dorm, I told myself halfway through Scrabble that I was going to ask you out when all was said and done."

Her head tilts to the side. "No, you weren't."

I nod. "Yes, I was. I was gathering the courage to do so."

"Why didn't you?" she asks, confused.

"Because you said you wanted a friend, and I didn't want to ruin our connection, so I said, *Okay, I'll be your friend.*"

She wets her lips and asks, "So why now? Why have you changed that way of thinking?"

"Because," I answer as I grab the hem of her shirt and slowly drag it up and over her head, "I realized that seeing you marry another man was my absolute worst-case scenario because I have deep-rooted feelings for you, Lia." My hands go to her breasts, and she lifts her chest in a gasp as she moves her ass along my growing erection. "Do you think you could feel the same way?"

She glides her teeth over her bottom lip, and when her eyes connect with mine, she says, "I think so."

"Good," I answer before I pick her up and stand from the couch. Her arms wrap around my neck, and her breasts press against my bare chest. It's such a delicious feeling that I almost feel sad that I'm going to break the contact soon.

"This is all so...weird and new to me," she admits. "It's hard for me to wrap my head around it."

I carry her into my bedroom and lay her on the bed before I reach for her waist and take off her shorts, leaving her completely naked. Being able to see her naked whenever I want is like a goddamn dream. "I'm still trying to wrap my head around it as well," I say as I push my shorts down and grip my erection at the base. I squeeze it and let out a hiss as I take in her perfect body.

The swell of her hips.

The way her nipples are pebbled all the fucking time.

The slight part of her lips as she watches me stroke myself.

"Tell me this, Lia, how did you like having my cock in your mouth yesterday?"

She swallows deeply before saying, "I liked it…a lot."

"Good answer." I stroke my length, running my hand over the head while Lia's eyes remain transfixed on what I'm doing. "Did you play with the vibrator after?"

"No." She shakes her head.

"Why not?" I ask.

"Because." Her hand floats over her breasts, and I watch in jealousy as she plays with them. "I didn't think I was allowed to play…without you."

I swear my dick gets even harder from her response.

Wetting my lips, I then lower to the bed, where I hover over her with one hand on either side.

"That's an even better answer," I say as I lower my mouth to her chest, where I nip along her skin. "Feel free to play whenever you want without me, but"—I lift to look her in the eyes—"always think about me." And then I pepper her chest with kisses, going from one side to the other, sucking on her skin, nibbling, leaving my mark so when she wakes up tomorrow and looks in the mirror, she knows exactly who she belongs to.

Her hands drag up my back and to my neck, where she plays with the short strands of my hair. "Do you…do you really find me attractive?" she asks, surprising me.

She hasn't said very much during our last encounters, other than to tell me she was enjoying what I was doing, but today is different. She's bolder today, she's more open. More inquisitive.

To answer her question, I take her hand and place it on my hard-on. "You tell me," I answer.

She strokes lightly, and her touch feels like fire, stoking the flames with every move of her hand.

"And…and you really want me?" she asks.

I pull her nipple into my mouth and suck hard, causing her chest to lift off the bed. When I release the little nub, I say, "I think about you every second of every day, Lia. I want you more than I've ever wanted anything in my life."

I kiss down her stomach and hover there, loving how she's squirming for my touch. "Any other questions?"

She wets her lips and nods.

"Hurry up, because I'm fucking starving." I lower and dip my tongue against her pussy, causing her to moan.

Her eyes squeeze shut, and on a breathy moan, she asks, "Is this just fun for you…or is it something more?"

I bring my mouth to her pussy, and I spread her. I don't lick her just yet, I only hover, and when she glances down at me, I say, "This is so much fucking more." And then I dive my tongue against her clit.

"Oh my God," she says as her hands fall to my hair.

This is my fucking happy place, right here, between her legs, making her moan my name. And I'm so fucking mad at myself for taking this long to realize it. Sure, I was always attracted to her, but it took a goddamn second for me to figure out that I wanted her. And that makes me infuriated. *Because I nearly lost her.* I would have hated myself forever if I'd lost her.

I press my tongue along her clit, sliding it slowly, and when she lightly breathes out my name, I know it's time. I move away, and as she protests, I flip her to her stomach.

"Wh-what are you doing?" she asks.

I drag my hand down her spine and over the curve of her ass. After smoothing my hand over the round globe, without thinking, I smack her ass, leaving a red handprint.

"Fuck." She grips the comforter beneath her but doesn't protest. So I do it again. "Breaker," she breathes heavily.

"What?" I ask as I smooth my hand over the red spot.

"I...I don't know."

I spank her again, and this time, she lets out a hiss. "You like it, don't you?"

On a light moan, she says, "Yeah."

"But you weren't expecting to like it?"

She shakes her head.

Smiling, I spank her again...and again. The sound reverberates through my bedroom, and I know it's a sound I'm going to commit to memory because it's so sweet, hearing her softly moan with each slap.

I rub my hand along her ass, massaging it lightly, letting the sting of the spank be smoothed by my palm. And then after a few more seconds, I spank her again.

"Breaker," she cries out.

I smile and then prop her ass up into the air, where I slip my hand between her legs and feel just how wet she is.

"That's fucking right, Lia." I run my finger along her slit. "You're ready for me."

I release my hand, walk around the bed, and then lie down. I put my hands behind my head and say, "Okay, come here."

She peeks up from where her head is resting on the mattress and asks, "What do you mean?"

"You wanted to sit on my face. So come sit on it."

"Oh." Her cheeks redden to a dangerous shade of embarrassment. "I, well... We don't have to."

My eyes narrow. "You said you wanted to. Therefore, you will do it. Get over here. Now."

"Breaker, I just... I've never—"

I lift, grab her arm, and tug her toward me. Then I turn her around so her back is facing my front, and I position her to straddle my chest.

"What are you doing?" she asks.

I press my hand to her back and lower her down and then bring her ass right up to my face.

"Oh my God, Breaker," she says right before I slip two fingers inside her. "Fuck," she grinds out, and I can feel her breath on my erection.

Would I love for her to pull me into her mouth while I do this? Of course. But am I going to make her? Never.

I tilt her pelvis up more, and I bring her closer so my mouth is right against her drenched pussy. That's when I start swiping. Her legs clench around me, and she falls forward, her mouth right next to my cock.

As I lick her, her hands run up and down my inner thighs, so I spread them for her, and that's when she reaches under and cups my balls.

"Shit, Lia," I mumble as my head falls for a second.

"You like that?" she asks.

"Fuck yes," I answer and so she continues to cup them while her other hand grips my cock. "You don't have to," I say in a rush, even though I desperately want her mouth again.

"I want to," she answers before she sucks the tip into her wet, warm mouth.

Fucking heaven.

"So fucking good," I say as I continue to drive my tongue over her clit.

She gets comfortable, and while I play with her, she plays with me, and it's so sexy. I've never done this with anyone before, and I can honestly say I'm glad it's with Lia, because she's so damn perfect. Everything about this is.

She brings me in and out of her mouth while she plays with my balls. Immediately, my spine begins to tingle while my orgasm builds.

It's going to be quick. Really quick, so I focus on making her come. I harden my tongue and make short, quick flicks against her clit, causing her to moan against my cock.

"Jesus," I say. "Do that again, and I'm coming in your mouth."

She hums along my cock, and my toes curl while my balls draw tight. Shit, I need her to come.

I move my tongue faster, but it's no match for what she's doing to me, and my mind can only focus on one thing, and that's the orgasm that's teetering.

With one final squeeze of my balls and a pull with her teeth, my body stiffens. "Fuck, I'm coming," I say as I pump up into her mouth, and she swallows against the head of my cock. "Uhhhh, fuck," I yell as pleasure rips through me.

She laps at my cock once my hips stop moving, and that's when I realize that she hasn't come yet. So I flip her off me and onto her back. She looks up at me, a devilish grin in her expression. She's so satisfied with herself that I can't even be mad about how she took over.

"You're in trouble," I say as I spread her legs.

"Why?" she asks, her smile stretching from ear to ear.

"Because." I reach up and pinch her nipple, causing her to wince. "That was supposed to be for you. You weren't supposed to suck me into that beautiful mouth of yours."

"But I wanted to." Her satisfied eyes meet mine. "I wanted your cock, Breaker."

And Jesus fuck…I might just be hard again.

"Here," I say to Lia, offering her one of my shirts. "Wear this tonight."

She takes the shirt with a Rubik's Cube on the front and says, "You know, I could just walk back to my place and get clothes."

I help her put the shirt on over her naked body and say, "You could, but that would require you to walk around naked in a public place, and that's not approved by me. That would also mean you would have to leave, which is also not approved by me."

She chuckles and presses her hand to my chest. "No one told me you're the one in charge."

"Well, I am." I kiss the top of her head, so desperate to claim her mouth. "Which also means *Sorry, but you're sleeping here tonight.*"

"And why is that?" Her hands fall to my waist, and even though I just made her come a few minutes ago, I have this needy urge to do it all over again.

"Because I've let you sleep at your place the last two nights, and it's about time you spent the night here so I can wake up next to you first thing in the morning."

"I thought I was a pillow hog?" she asks as her hands smooth up my chest.

"You are, but it's something I can look past."

"Wow, you're a real hero." She chuckles and then pulls me into a hug. I smooth my hand over the back of her head.

"Everything okay?" I ask.

She nods against my chest but doesn't pull away.

"You sure? You just went really quiet on me."

"I'm sure. Just thinking."

"Tell me what you're thinking about," I say as I run my hand down her back and then back up.

"Just how crazy this is." She glances up at me. "I never would have expected to be in this position with you or in that position we were in a few moments ago. I suppose I'm still trying to grasp it all."

"You seem open to it, though."

"I am." She now pulls away enough so we're looking at each other. "I like you, Breaker, a lot. And I seem to have this full-blown attraction for you that I never knew I had. And when you're touching me, commanding me, it makes me feel safe, protected, like I'm...home. I just don't want anything to mess that up, you know?"

"I understand." I slip my finger under her chin and say, "I promise, I will do everything in my goddamn power to make sure nothing is messed up. Got it?"

She nods. "Yes."

"You trust me?"

"You're the person I trust the most," she answers.

"Good." I pull her into a hug again. "Then I need to ask you something."

"What?" she asks.

I lead her to the edge of my bed, and we both sit.

"You're making me nervous," she says as I take her hands in mine.

"Don't be nervous. I just have a question to ask you." With a smile, I say, "Will you go on a date with me tomorrow?"

"Stop… That is not your question."

"It is," I reply. "I'm serious, Lia. I want to date you, and now that I know you're open to it, I want to make it official."

"Really?"

I nod, and she glances away.

"What's wrong?" Something is clearly on her mind. "Is that not something you want? Did I read you all wrong?"

She shakes her head. "No, not at all. You didn't read me wrong. It's just that…this is all so sudden. I just broke things off with Brian and canceled the wedding. If I started dating you, don't you think that would, I don't know…look bad?"

"To whom?" I ask.

"I don't know…just people."

I slowly nod. "And who are these people you talk about?"

"Stop." She chuckles. "You know what I mean."

"I do, but I'm wondering when you started caring about what other people think. Because as long as I've known you, you really haven't cared at all."

"You're right. I haven't. I guess I just still have that fear."

"Well, if you're not ready, I'll wait. I can wait for as long as you want me to wait," I say. "I'm not going anywhere, Lia. If you want me to slow down, I'll slow down. If you want me to give you some space to think about things, I will do that too because I want you in this just as much as I am."

She bites her bottom lip and says, "I want this too, Breaker." She groans and then flops back on the bed while covering her eyes with her hands. "God, I'm so annoying."

I laugh and lie down next to her while settling my hand on her stomach. "Why do you say that?"

"Doesn't it seem obvious? That I should just be with you and not have any reservations holding me back? You're the clear choice, yet I'm so scared to take that step toward dating, because that would mean...that would mean our friendship is over."

"Uh...excuse me?" I ask. "What do you mean *our friendship is over*?"

"If we take that first step toward dating, Breaker, then this could end in two vastly different ways. We are together forever, which just seems crazy to even think about. Or we break up, and I doubt we can be friends after breaking up."

I scratch my cheek. "Why does being together forever seem crazy to you?"

"Well, do you even want to get married one day? Ever since I've known you, you haven't had a serious girlfriend, so is that something you want? Doesn't getting involved with me freak you out at all?"

"Not in the slightest," I answer. "And I think it's because in my mind, I've always been with you. You've always been mine."

"That's annoyingly sweet."

I chuckle and then cup her face. "You said you trust me, right?"

"Yes."

"Then let me lead the way, okay? Can you do that? I promise I won't push too hard."

She swallows and nods. "Okay, yeah, I can do that."

"Good girl." I smirk and then say, "Now, if you want to go back to your place and sleep, you are more than welcome to. Just borrow some pants of mine first. If you want to stay here, that's good too. But the choice is yours."

"I want to stay here," she says, her eyes on mine.

"Then let's get ready for bed because I'm exhausted." I lift from the bed and pull her up as well.

After taking turns going to the bathroom and brushing our teeth, I walk her to her side of the bed, pull down the covers, and help her in.

Once everything's locked up and my phone is charging, I slip in behind her, the cool sheets a stark contrast to her heated body. I slip my arm around her waist and pull her into my chest.

"You good?"

"Very," she says. "This is my favorite way to sleep. Ever."

I lay a kiss on her neck. "Mine too."

"Breaker?" she asks after a light pause.

"Hmm?"

"Tomorrow…is that date still an option?"

I smile against her silky hair. "It is."

"Okay. I think I want to go on it."

"You think, or you know?"

"I know, but can it not be some awkward date where you wear a suit and I get dressed up? That's not really us."

"Trust me, I know. I have something entirely different planned. Something I've been thinking about for a while."

"Really? What is it?"

"It's a surprise." I slip my hand under her shirt. "Now go to sleep."

"You're just going to leave me hanging like that?"

"Yup." I kiss the top of her head. "But block out your day tomorrow because you're mine."

"The whole day?" she asks.

"Yes. The whole day. I might not make you dress fancy, but I'm still going to make a lasting impression. Consider this your last first date ever."

"Awfully confident, don't you think?"

"It's not confidence, Ophelia," I whisper. "It's facts."

CHAPTER 20
LIA

"IS THE BLINDFOLD REALLY NECESSARY?" I ask as he stops at what feels like a stoplight.

"For the tenth time, yes."

"And dressing me yourself, was that necessary? Or did you just do that so you could play with my boobs?"

"Lia," he says in a stern voice. "I don't need to blindfold you and say I need to dress you to cop a feel. I can do that any time I want."

"Oh? And when exactly did my body become your body?"

"The moment you came on my tongue," he answers as his hand lands on my thigh.

"Okay, well, that's an answer."

He chuckles and says, "We're almost there, just a bit longer. And I have to say, you did an excellent job eating your donut this morning. You didn't get any crumbs on you."

"Not my first time eating a donut. And it was a different experience, eating it blindfolded."

"Ah, see, the day is already starting out to be a winning one." He stops the car and the window rolls down. "Good morning," I hear him say. "Surprising her, not kidnapping." That makes me laugh.

Whoever he's talking to says, "Enjoy, Mr. Cane."

And then Breaker pulls forward.

"Mr. Cane? Are you flashing your billionaire card today?"

"Perhaps," he answers with a smile in his voice. He squeezes my hand and pulls the car around until he parks.

"Are we here?"

"We are." He undoes his seat belt and says, "Stay here."

I hear him hop out of the car, and then within a few seconds, he's opening my car door as well.

"Am I going to have to walk blindfolded?"

"No," he answers as he reaches behind me and undoes the blindfold. It takes my eyes a few seconds to adjust, but when they do, I'm met with an underground parking lot.

"Where are we?" I ask and then that's when I see his shirt.

It's black and clings to every inch of his muscular chest, but it's the picture of Jack Skellington on it as well as the saying *Her Jack* that truly catches my attention. I glance down at my shirt, and it's of Sally with *His Sally* on it.

"Umm…are we at Disneyland?"

He tilts my chin up, and I come face-to-face with his beautiful smile. "We are."

My eyes well up, and I lean against the passenger seat as I say, "I can't believe you remembered."

He takes my hand in his. "Junior year in college, it was right after you went on that date with the squid eater. Perhaps one of your worst first dates ever. You came back to my dorm and bitched about how guys are such idiots, and they don't know how to conduct a real first date. I asked you what would be your perfect first date, and you said Disneyland. You would test the guy to see if he would wear matching shirts. If he did, it was a check in the plus column." He gestures to his shirt. "Pretty sure I'm doing pretty well so far." *Oh my God. Doing pretty well so far…* I'm simply stunned. I'm also feeling so emotional because how did he remember every detail of that conversation? *How?*

A tear falls down my cheek, and he leans in and wipes it away.

"Why are you crying?"

"Because," I say. "This is...this is thoughtful." I turn toward him. "You're the only person who has done something thoughtful like this for me. Ever."

"Because you're so special to me." His thumb caresses my cheek. "I'd move mountains for you, Lia." He wipes my tears again and then tugs on my hand. "Come on, no more crying. It's time to have fun."

I let him help me out of his car, and then as we walk and he holds my hand, I lean into his strong presence, into this man who has always treated me as if I'm his number one. The one who has remembered everything about me—from the type of coffee I love to my idea of the perfect first date.

I never imagined him like this, the doting man, yet it seems to fit him so perfectly. *He seems to fit me perfectly.*

I thought long and hard about why he's pursuing me. About his point last night—why he's never had a long-term girlfriend.

"I think it's because in my mind, I've always been with you. You've always been mine."

Those words, that declaration, floored me. From the moment something flicked on for Breaker, he has treated me as if I'm precious. Something I've never experienced. In fact, it's light-years away from how Brian treated me. Breaker's treated me the same way I've seen Huxley and JP treat Lottie and Kelsey. And *that* has given me more confidence to take this next step with Breaker. Because I believe him. I believe *in* him. He's not one to lie. *You've always been mine.* And if I've always been his, it's starting to become clearer that he's always been mine too.

Consider this your last first date ever.

When he said that last night, I wanted to believe it. As I cling to him, walking past row after row of cars, I believe it.

I can see it.

I can feel it.

"Breaker," I whisper as I hold his hand tightly. "You got us the VIP package?"

"More like the Breaker Cane package," he whispers into my ear.

The parking lot we parked in was some secret parking lot that lets you skip all the lines. We went straight to the VIP section where we were greeted with Mickey ears, *Nightmare Before Christmas*–themed, of course, and the cutest part of all of it is that Breaker is wearing his with no shame.

Reminds me of the guy I met back in college. Couldn't care less what anyone thinks about him, does what he likes, and doesn't think twice about it.

"Mr. Cane, welcome to Disneyland. I'm Jorge, your guide for today."

Breaker lends out his hand. "Jorge, it's a pleasure to meet you. Please call me Breaker."

"My pleasure," Jorge says and then puts out his hand. "This must be Miss Fairweather-Fern."

"Please, call me Lia," I say as I shake his hand.

"Miss Lia, it's a pleasure." Gripping an iPad to his side, he says, "I understand it's just your small party today. I received the planned schedule of events, and I have your reservations organized as well. It looks like we're going to have a great day."

"We are," Breaker says.

"Wonderful, and please, if you want to stop for any food or need me to pick up food for you while you're on a ride, I'd be more than happy to assist with that. I'm here to make your experience unforgettable."

"Thank you, Jorge," Breaker says.

"Well, if we're ready, I think the first thing on our schedule today is to ride the Matterhorn."

I glance up at Breaker, who is smiling because he knows—of course he knows—the Matterhorn is my favorite ride. I love how old and janky it is. Being tossed around makes me laugh more than the actual ride.

"Might as well start with a bang, right?" he asks.

"You're spoiling me today, aren't you?" I ask as Jorge leads the way through the park.

"I am, but not to impress you. I don't feel like I need to at this point." He brings our connected hands to his lips as he says, "I'm spoiling you because I want to, because I get to, and because you deserve nothing but the best, Lia." He presses a gentle kiss to my knuckles.

I don't know how this happened, how I became so lucky to be with this man, but somehow, the universe has made it happen—maybe it was with the help of my parents, who always loved Breaker, who always expected us to end up together. Maybe they had a little part in putting us together.

"You deserve so much too," I say to Breaker, who just shakes his head.

"I have all I need, Lia," he answers, looking me in the eyes.

———

"You ready for this?" Breaker whispers into my ear as the bar to our Peter Pan ship falls over our legs.

"Yes," I say as we take off into the darkness of the ride.

"Good, now pull down your shorts."

"What?" I ask on a laugh, and then I turn toward him.

"It's a two-minute ride, Lia. If I can't get you off in two minutes, then I don't know what I'm doing as a man."

"Stop." I push at his chest. "You're not getting me off on Peter Pan." Whispering, I add, "Children ride these rides."

"But it's the Peter Pan Challenge."

"Says who?" I ask.

"Says the behind-the-scenes sex enthusiasts."

"Yeah, well you can contact your sex enthusiasts and tell them they're freaks. Disney is sacred!"

"Sooo…is that going to be a no?"

I chuckle and shake my head. "That's a hard no. My God, Breaker."

He laughs and then loops his arm around me. "You know, I was only kidding."

"For some reason, I don't believe that."

Our ship flies through London and off to Neverland, the enchanting children's ride also one of my favorites. So far, we've made our way through all of Fantasyland, this being our last ride, and then we're heading to Star Wars: Galaxy Edge next. We haven't had to wait in line, and when we got off Snow White's Enchanted Wish, Jorge had waters and cream cheese—stuffed pretzels for us. We found a place to sit, and I devoured my pretzel. Of course we shared with Jorge, who was more than gracious about it. We stopped to take pictures in front of the castle as well as in front of the Matterhorn, and we even went into a gift shop where Breaker bought us matching Disneyland shirts with the year on them. Classic souvenir. Lucky for us, Jorge has been carrying our bag.

It's been so magical.

"Thank you," I say to him. "This has really been such a perfect day. The perfect first date."

"It's not over yet," he says. "We still have to hit up California Adventure after this."

"We're going to California Adventure?"

"Uh, yeah, it's going to be a whole day."

"Are we ending with fireworks?"

"What do you think?" he asks with a smirk.

"Wow, Breaker. You know…if you wanted a blow job that bad, you could have just asked for one. You didn't have to go through all of this."

He chuckles. "Oh, I know, Lia." His lips right next to my ear. "Trust me, I know how much you want my cock."

My cheeks heat, and I'm glad we're in a dark room, or else people would be able to read the expression and desire I have for this man all over my face.

———————

"I truly think I got a hard-on while riding Rise of the Resistance," Breaker says as we sit at our reserved seat in Docking Bay 7. "Like actual chills."

"Same," I say. "Although I can't speak on the erection that you're talking about, I did get chills. That has to be one of the most immersive experiences I've ever been a part of. And the way the cast members yell at you. I truly felt like I was a prisoner."

"Yeah, we're doing that again." Breaker leans back in the small circular booth we have to ourselves. "Makes me want to get out my Chewbacca costume and start running around the apartment."

"You still have that?" I ask.

"Yeah, and I still have your Leia costume, which…I think we need to upgrade, you know, since now I get to see you naked. I think I deserve you in the gold bikini."

"Oh my God, seriously? Are you going to be that cliché?"

"Yeah, you have a problem with that?" he asks.

I smirk and lean into him. "No, I actually think it would be really hot."

"Don't fucking tease me, Lia. You know I'll buy that bikini right now."

I'm about to tell him to do so when Jorge delivers our food. Breaker went with the smoked ribs, and I was drawn toward the shrimp noodles. He also drops off some Sprites and then says, "I'm going to take a break for a moment while you two eat. You have my number if you need anything."

"Thank you, Jorge," Breaker says right before he takes off.

"This looks delicious," I say as Breaker hands me a fork.

"It does." He slips his arm around my waist and pulls me in closer before resting his hand on my hip, keeping me right next to him.

As we dig into our lunch, I ask him, "Have you always been this possessive over the women you're seeing?"

"Nope," he answers before swallowing his first bite. "You're the only one."

"Can I ask why?"

"Why? Do you hate it?"

I shake my head. "No, I love it, but it's so different. I haven't ever met a guy who has held me like you do. Or wanted to touch me like you. And I guess I didn't know how much I liked it until you came along."

"Yeah, I didn't know how much I needed it either until I touched you." He smirks at me and then shoves a forkful of his food in his mouth, looking all goofy and ridiculously cute. When I shake my head at him, he nudges me and asks, "What?"

"You're just...God, you're annoying with how hot you are. You can just smirk, and it makes my stomach all twisted in knots."

"I consider that a good thing."

"Of course you do, because you think you have me wrapped around your pinky."

"Don't I?"

I fork a piece of shrimp and mutter, "Unfortunately."

He chuckles. "Don't be upset about it or anything."

"You're just charming and sweet and thoughtful, and ugh...it makes it hard to find fault in you."

"Are you looking for faults?" he asks as he sips from his Sprite cup.

"Aren't we always looking for faults?" I ask as I twirl noodles on my fork. "Without faults, we wouldn't be human."

"True," he answers. "So if you're looking for faults, I have something for you to chew on."

"Oh yeah, is it a real thing?"

"Very real. I think about this all the time and how I could have done better," he replies.

"Okay, let me hear it." I take a bite from my fork and listen intently.

"One of my greatest faults would be not asking you out on a date the first night I met you."

I roll my eyes. "Come on, Breaker."

"I'm serious," he says, and from the tone in his voice and the expression in his eyes, I can truly tell he is. "Ever since I got a taste of you, I keep thinking about how I'm such an idiot for not asking you out sooner, for not making a move earlier. I can't believe I waited this long to hold your hand, to have you in my bed. It makes me feel like a real fucking idiot. And all those years of not having a girlfriend, it's because of you. Because I had deep-rooted feelings for you that I wasn't allowing myself to feel. So yeah, there's my fault, being a legitimate idiot when it comes to how I feel about you."

"Wow, okay," I say, unsure of how to respond to that. "I don't know if we would have the same relationship that we do now. I probably wouldn't have been as open with you about certain things if I was looking for something romantic. When you're just friends, it's as if you can drop all the walls and be yourself, but when you're trying to be romantic with someone, you almost put on this façade to show that you're good enough to be with that person. I've sort of felt that way recently with you."

"Why?" he asks, turning toward me and abandoning his meal.

"It's nothing huge, just subtle things, but I've had some self-conscious moments, and I just think it comes with the territory when someone is more sexually experienced. I mean, this past week, Breaker." My cheeks redden. "I have never done half the things we've done. I didn't even know that kind of sexuality was in me."

"Do you still feel that way?" he asks.

"Sometimes. You're just… I don't know, it's stupid." I adjust my glasses on my head and turn back to my meal.

"I'm just what?" he asks, tugging on my hand.

Knowing he's not going to let this go, I say, "You're not the same nerdy guy from college. Sure, if I was able to look past the mustache back then and the floppy hair, I probably would have been intimidated, but I wasn't because you were goofy, and I loved that about you. Now that you're all grown up and…you know…muscular, there's an intimidating factor to your transformation. I don't feel like I'm in your league."

"Jesus, you can't be serious, Lia."

"I know, I said it was stupid, but it's hard not to feel that way when the guy who is…well, whatever this is between us, when he's gorgeous, rich, and extremely well endowed, with the kind of experience that would make any woman blush. I don't feel worthy."

He forces me to look at him by looping his finger under my chin. "I can't tell you how to feel, and those feelings are something I will help you work through, but I want you to know this right here and now. I'm the one who feels lucky, okay? I'm the one who feels like they're trying to dig their claws into you so you don't run away. That insecurity lives heavily in my heart as well. I fear you'll wake up one day and realize that you made a mistake, that you miss Brian, that you should never have called off the wedding. Or that maybe I'm the rebound guy, that I shouldn't have made a move on you so soon."

"Breaker, you know that's not the case."

"I want to believe that, but in my head, I know I didn't go about this the right way. I didn't pursue you appropriately, normally. I should have eased more into the sexual aspect."

"Why did you jump in headfirst?" I ask.

"Because I wanted to show you that there was chemistry between us. I didn't want to give you an inkling that there wasn't. And frankly, I wanted you. I want you. Badly, Lia. The moment you put on that wedding dress, everything changed."

I smile softly. If I think about his reaction when he saw me in the wedding dress, I'll get teary. I was so emotional that day, and Breaker's unconditional support was the only thing that held me together. I had never seen his face look so…adoring. Or perhaps wowed. *"You look… fuck, you look stunning, Ophelia."*

"I think everything changed in me at that moment too."

"I hate you," Breaker says. He's leaning against a low fence, taking deep breaths while I giggle next to him, Jorge taking in the scene as well and trying not to laugh.

"Why do you hate me?" I ask.

His eyes shoot to me as he says, "You know I despise that godforsaken ride. It's death waiting to happen."

"It's a kid's ride," I say about Goofy's Skycoaster.

"That is not a fucking kid's ride, that is...that is a nightmare." He takes a deep breath, and Jorge walks over to him. "Can I get you some water, Breaker?"

"Oh, he's fine," I say, but Breaker tells him differently.

"Water would be amazing. Thank you so much, Jorge."

"Not a problem. Be right back."

Once Jorge leaves, Breaker stands straight and grabs my wrist, pulling me in close to his chest. With a firm hold on me, he says, "You're going to pay for that later."

"Why? I didn't force you to go on the ride. That was your own choice."

"You taunted me and then pleaded. As if I can fucking deny you anything." He nods toward the ride behind me with the sharp C curves that make you feel like you're going to fall right off the track. "You knew I hated that ride."

"I would have been just fine riding that on my own."

"Bullshit." He chuckles, his chest rumbling against mine. "Jesus, you're such a liar. Face the facts, Lia, you're going to pay for that."

"What are you going to do? Spank me?" I ask.

His eyes darken as his hands fall to my lower back. "Yeah, I might just fucking spank you. I'll spank you so hard that your pussy is drenched, begging for my dick, and then...I'll leave you completely unsatisfied."

I swallow hard. "You...you wouldn't."

"And then, when you're lying there restless, your cunt throbbing for release, I'll make myself come all over your beautiful sloped back just to remind you who owns you."

Well, good God.

"Here you go, Breaker," Jorge says, coming up to us.

And as if someone turned off a light switch in him, Breaker goes from dominating alpha to cheery park guest. "Thank you so much, Jorge." He shakes his head. "That Goofy coaster gets me every time."

"Me too. My niece loves it, and whenever I bring her here, it's a requirement. I think she's testing my love every time she makes me go on it."

"I think Lia is doing the same...testing my love."

And with one wink, my stomach bottoms out. That wink, and his use of the word *love*, it just about makes me throw my arms around his neck and kiss him.

And...why hasn't he kissed me yet? For a moment, at lunch, I thought it was going to happen. Or earlier, when we were on the Ferris wheel, just enjoying the view while I sat on his lap, I thought that maybe it would happen then, but it didn't.

If he wasn't already intimately involved, I would have suspected that it would never happen.

Or even last night, that would have been the perfect moment, after we were done being all...carnal, when I rested in his arms, that would have been perfect. So I don't understand the wait.

"You ready for the next ride?" Breaker asks. "I think we're headed over to The Little Mermaid, right?"

I smile up at him. "Yup, I believe we are."

And then hand in hand, we move on.

"Right this way," Jorge says as he lifts a red velvet rope blocking a bench from the public.

After a few more rides, we were taken back to The Office, a secret restaurant in California Adventure with a beautiful view of the pier. It's where we were served some of the best lobster I've ever had. And the room was so cute. We had to walk through a vault to get into it, and then it was covered in cartoon pictures of animators.

Of course, Breaker had to sit right next to me in the booth, where he could always keep a hand on me and occasionally feed me food with his fork. I loved every second of it.

After that, we headed back to Disneyland, where we rode Indiana Jones one more time and then proceeded to pick up desserts from the Candy Palace. I got a Rice Krispie treat, and Breaker got caramel popcorn. We took the train around the park while we ate our desserts, and Breaker even got a cookie for Jorge. And then after one more ride of Space Mountain, where Breaker held my hand the whole time, laughing, Jorge took us to our roped-off bench that looked over the castle.

"Fireworks should be starting shortly. Can I get you anything else?" Jorge asks.

"No, thank you. I think we can take it from here."

Jorge nods. "And you have your pass to get back to your parking lot?"

Breaker nods. "Yup." He then reaches into his pocket and slips something into Jorge's hand. "Thank you so much for everything. You have been fantastic."

"Of course. Thank you, Breaker. Miss Lia, it was a joy meeting you. Before I leave, can I offer to take one more pic of you two?"

"Nah, I think we're good. Thank you, though."

And with another goodbye, Jorge takes off, leaving us alone.

"What did you slip into his hand?" I ask.

"One thousand dollars," Breaker answers casually.

"One thousand dollars? Oh my God, Breaker."

He chuckles. "What? He did a good job."

"You probably just made his day."

"Yeah, well, it's the least I can do after he made this day so special for us both." He drapes his arm over the back of the bench and snuggles me in close. "Did you have a good time?"

"I had the best time," I say as I lean into his hold. "This was the kind of day you always dream of, but it never really comes to life."

"Well, it's real. All of this is real," he says.

"Hard to believe."

People scavenge for spots in front of the castle, strollers bumping into sidewalks, crying children tired from the events of the day, and a lot of tired people vying for a spot to sit down. Weirdly, it adds to the magic.

I turn toward him and rest my hand on his thigh as I say, "Thank you for today."

"You're welcome, Lia. You know I'd do anything for you, right?"

"Yes, I know."

"So you just name it, and it's yours."

"I think…" I move my hand up to his chest. "I know I want something, but I'm nervous to say it."

He turns toward me more and asks, "What is it?"

Just then, the show begins, and the crowd hushes as music plays through the speakers placed throughout the park.

"It can wait," I say.

"Uh, no, it can't," he says. "Just ask me."

I move my hands to the hem of his shirt, and I twist it through my hands as I say, "It's going to sound really stupid, but I don't know. I guess I just want to make sure this is real."

"What is it?" Breaker asks.

When I glance up at him, the first firework shoots up to the sky, lighting up the dark night. "I want to make sure that we're, you know…actually dating. That we're exclusive, that…I don't know, that I'm your girlfriend or something."

The smile that crosses his face is the cutest thing I've ever seen. "You asking me to be your boyfriend, Lia?"

"I mean, if you want to put a label on it. I just don't want this to be a flash-in-the-pan kind of thing. You know? Like...just sex and fun. I don't want that."

His face grows serious, and he slips his hand behind my neck as he says, "You would never be a fling to me, Lia. Ever. What we have, it's serious, and I won't treat it any other way."

"Okay," I say as I glance away, gaining the courage to say what I want to say next. When my eyes fall back on his, I say, "Then if that's the case, kiss me."

His hand grows tight at the nape of my neck, pulling me toward him. I have never seen such a determined yet adoring look on his face before. I feel so...*loved*.

My breath catches in my chest. I wet my lips right before he brings me in the last few inches, and his mouth lands on mine.

I can feel my eyes roll in the back of my head as his soft lips capture mine.

Soft.

Demanding.

Absolute perfection.

It's the most intense, satisfying, and thrilling moment of my life—kissing Breaker, kissing my best friend, feeling the electricity bounce between us as our mouths collide. With fireworks exploding above us, his lips mold around mine, his other hand tilting my face ever so slightly, controlling the moment.

And I let him, because I can't do anything else other than fall into this man's grasp as his open mouth works over mine.

Pressing.

Taking.

Tense.

When his mouth parts, I part mine. When he turns to the right, I turn to the left. When his grip grows tighter, so does mine.

And when his tongue presses against mine, I moan and swipe my tongue against his.

He's so delicious.

I tangle my tongue with his, my hand growing tight around his shirt, needing him closer, needing more, and when I slip my hand under his shirt, he pulls away, stunning me.

I blink a few times just as huge fireworks burst above us.

Catching his breath, he stares at me for a few moments and then says, "I, uh…I don't want to give the kids a different show."

And I'm brought back to reality.

We're still in Disneyland.

Surrounded by children.

"Oh God." I press my hand to my chest. "I'm sorry, I just…I guess I got carried away."

"That's okay, so did I." A boyish grin spreads across his face. "You're a really good fucking kisser."

My cheeks heat as I say, "I was going to say the same about you."

He pulls on the small strands of his hair as he says, "Just another regret of mine. We could have started doing that a long time ago."

"Looks like we have some time to make up for."

"We do," he says as he grips my chin and places one more kiss on my lips. Even though it's a light, featherlike kiss, it packs a powerful punch because it was willing and a way to express his desire for me.

It makes my stomach flutter. It's confirmation that we are doing this… we are becoming an *us*. And I shiver as I hear my mom's sweet voice saying, *About time, sweet cheeks. About time.*

CHAPTER 21
BREAKER

HANDS GRIPPING THE BATHROOM COUNTER, I stare into the mirror and take a few deep breaths.

I love her.

I'm in love with her.

I want nothing but her.

That fucking kiss nearly knocked my socks off.

I've never experienced anything like it. Like the moment our lips met, an electrical charge shot through me, rebooting me to be a different man.

I feel the need to always have her at my side.

I feel the need to compulsively touch her.

I feel the need to strip her down and make love to her.

I want her to know that I'm hers, forever. That I don't want anyone else but her.

But I also need to take this one stride at a time.

I don't want to scare her away.

One goddamn step at a time, man.

I push off the counter and grab my toothbrush and line it with toothpaste.

After the fireworks, we walked back to the car hand in hand. On the drive home, I rested my hand on her thigh, and she placed her hand on top of mine. We talked about a new board game coming out that we wanted to play while reminiscing about the time we went to Disney when we were in college. It was a total disaster since we went during a peak time and were able to ride three rides total. Brutal.

When we got back home, I walked her to her apartment and lightly kissed her good night, reveling in the way her lips felt on mine and how I desperately wanted to invite her back to my place. But I said my good night and came back here to take a shower.

Hair still damp, with a towel wrapped around my waist, I brush my teeth just as I hear my front door shut.

"Lia?" I call out, my mouth foamy.

"Yeah, it's me," she says as I hear her approach.

I finish up brushing quickly, rinse my mouth, and head out to my bedroom where I find her standing in the middle of the room, wearing a silk robe, her hair damp as well.

"Everything okay?" I ask.

Her eyes fall to my chest and then to my towel before climbing back up to my eyes. She shakes her head just as she undoes her robe and lets it fall to the ground, revealing her purple lingerie set. A silky-looking tank top with matching lace underwear.

"I don't want to be alone, Breaker." She walks up to me and lightly brings her hands to my abs, where she travels them down to my towel. "I don't want to sleep alone, and I don't want our night to end with a good-night kiss at my door."

"No?" I ask as a light sweat breaks out over my skin.

She shakes her head and undoes my towel, causing it to fall to the floor. "You kissed me tonight, which means I want all of you. Nothing else holding us back. I want everything."

My cock grows between us as I reach up to her cheek and cup it. "You know I want the same thing, right? I just want to make sure you're ready."

She grips my hand and tugs me toward the bed. "I'm more than ready." When the backs of her legs hit the edge, I don't push her over. I drag her tank up and over her head, then drop it.

I slide my hands up her sides, cup her face, and then bring her lips to mine, where I kiss her all over again. This time, I'm not worried about our surroundings and allow myself to get lost in the moment. *In her.*

Her hands grip my wrists, holding her in place as our mouths part together and our tongues collide. It's the sweetest, most delicious feeling, having her cling to me like this, feeling how much she wants me, just like I want her.

Her kisses are intense, gratifying, and ethereal at times. Like I'm holding the most precious thing in the world between my hands.

And I believe that because she is.

She's so fucking precious, and I will never do anything to fuck this up. Never. I know how long it took to get here with her, and I will be damned if I fuck it up.

I tip her back on the bed and reach for her thong, dragging it down her legs and tossing it to the side. We both climb to the head of the bed, and when she spreads her legs, I settle on top of her, my body fitting perfectly between her thighs. I lightly stroke her wet hair as I stare down at her.

Our eyes connect, and for a moment, I feel the words at the tip of my tongue.

I love you, Ophelia.

I want to say them. I want to shout them. I want her to know exactly how happy she makes me, how I feel like my cup is always full when I'm with her. Nothing could ever hurt me because I have her in my arms.

But I swallow my feelings and bring my lips to hers where we make out, her hand driving through my hair, mine slowly working down to her chest where I lightly cup her breast.

Nothing is rough about my touch, nothing feral about it either. Because I don't feel the need to drive into her. I want to cherish this moment.

My mouth falls from her lips and trails along her jaw and down her neck. She clutches on to me as I reach her breast. I lick around her nipple, circling it a few times before lightly pulling it into my mouth.

"Yessss," she says as she plays with my hair, something I've grown fond of.

I move to her other breast and play with her nipple before I lick down her stomach and between her legs, where she spreads them for me. The act of her making room for me sends a bolt of lust through my chest because she trusts me.

And I want to keep that trust.

I press my tongue along her slit and drag it up, slowly.

"God, Breaker," she breathes out. "I love your mouth."

I swipe again.

And again, each time diving deeper and deeper until I'm pressing against her clit.

I want to bring her to the edge, to the point that she's going to come, and then pull away, so I continue to lap against her, loving the way her legs squeeze against my shoulders and how her nails dig into my hair and the way her chest rises and falls, twists, and turns with every stroke of my tongue. She's so responsive, very much a partner in our pleasure, and I love that about her. I don't have to guess what she likes because she lets me know.

Her legs tremble against my shoulders as they grow tighter and tighter.

"Yes...almost there," she says just as I pull away. "What?" she asks, the confused look on her face so cute that I want to kiss it right off.

"I want you to come on my cock." Her expression softens as she stretches her arms above her head. "Do you want that, Lia?"

She nods. "Yes, but hurry."

I smirk and reach over to my nightstand, where I pull out a condom and open the package. I glance over at her and catch her intense stare as I roll the condom over my aching cock and make sure it's rolled all the way down.

"Do you want me on top, or do you want to be on top?" I ask her.

"I…I don't know," she answers. "Maybe you on top."

I move back between her legs, and instead of slipping inside her right away, I lower my mouth to hers and kiss her again, parting her lips with my tongue.

She relaxes beneath me, so I spend time on working her mouth while I play with her breast, loving the way it feels in my palm, so soft, like velvet.

And when I think that she's truly relaxed, I line up my cock against her wet, ready entrance. From the mere feel of my dick near her, she tenses again.

"You need to relax, Lia."

"I know," she breathes. "I'm just nervous."

"Nothing to be nervous about." I kiss along her jaw, down her neck, and then back up. With my cock at her entrance, I carefully press into her, only an inch, and let her adjust.

"Oh God," she gasps. "Breaker, you're too big."

"I'm not, Lia. I'm perfect for you." I nibble at her ear and play with her nipple before moving my mouth back to hers. It takes her a second, but she kisses me back with the same passion. And I let her get lost in my mouth as I slowly move inside her again. She's so fucking tight that I break out in a sweat, my mind swirling with how incredible this is going to feel.

So fucking amazing.

"You okay?" I ask her while I kiss her jaw.

"Yes," she breathes, so I move another inch. "Jesus," she whispers.

"You sure you're good?"

"Yes. I just…I've never felt like this before."

"Do you want me to keep going?"

"God, yes," she says as she finds my mouth again and relaxes some more, making it easier for me to slip in. After a few more minutes, with her relaxing into my mouth, I'm able to almost insert myself fully.

Her chest rises against mine, and she tears her mouth away, taking a deep breath. I steal the moment to bring her breast up to my mouth, where I suck on her nipple.

"You're so good, Breaker."

Her words encourage me, so as I bite down on her nipple, I thrust my hips that very last inch, bottoming out as she clenches around me.

"Fucking…hell," I groan as I drop my head to her shoulder.

She holds me tightly, her breathing labored. "So full, Breaker."

I lift my head and find tears in her eyes. My hand quickly falls to her cheek as I ask, "Shit, are you okay?"

"Perfect," she says as she pulls on the back of my head and brings me close to her mouth.

This time, I kiss her deeply. I stretch my tongue farther into her mouth, and she matches the depth. Our colliding mouths send a rippling sensation up the backs of my legs that forces me to move my hips.

"I'm…I'm sorry," I say against her mouth. "I need release."

"Me too," she says as she shifts her pelvis.

"Fuck, Ophelia, don't move." I pin my hand against her hip. "You'll make me come."

She smirks and then moves her pelvis again.

My eyes fall to hers. "I'm fucking serious. You're so tight. I'm like seconds from coming."

"Then come," she says as her legs wrap around mine, bringing me even deeper.

"Shit," I mutter as I prop my hand against the mattress and start sliding in and out of her, making sure to drive down and in at the same time so she receives the same amount of pleasure as I do. From the breathless gasp that falls past her lips, I'm guessing I got her in the right spot.

So I do it again.

And again.

And again.

She clings to me.

Claws at my chest.

Heaves from side to side, but I keep pace, driving her closer and closer to what we both need.

"Yes, Breaker. Yes, please don't stop."

Her fingers dig into my skin, her chest arches, and her pussy tightens around my cock right before she lets out the sexiest moan I've ever heard, the sound vibrating against my heart as she comes.

"Fuck, Ophelia," I grunt as I pump a few more times. I want this euphoric feeling to last forever, I want to forever be in this state of bliss, but as she continues to clench around me, I know it's impossible as my cock swells and my orgasm rips up my back and down my legs. "Uhhhh fuck...me," I shout as I come, my hips stilling and the most heavenly feeling floating through me.

"Oh my God," Lia whispers as we both float down from bliss. Her hand falls to my hair as I press light kisses along her collarbone before lifting up to look her in the eyes.

I don't know what to do. I just...smile because there's nothing I can say other than...

I love you.

I want you forever.

I never want this moment to end.

She lightly caresses my cheek. "You are pretty stupid."

My brows narrow. "What?" Not something you expect to hear after the most mind-blowing orgasm of your life.

She chuckles. "You know, for not making a move a lot sooner."

"Oh." I laugh as well. "Trust me, I'll live with that regret for the rest of my life. I'm just grateful I have you now." I press another light kiss across her lips, and she wraps her arms around me, holding me tight.

"Are you nervous?" I ask Lia as we step up to Huxley and Lottie's front door.

"No, why should I be?"

I shake my head. "No, if anyone should be nervous, it's me. Once my brothers see us holding hands, they're never going to let me live it down that they told me long ago we belonged together. But the ribbing will be worth it."

"I think it's necessary. After this morning…very, very necessary. You prevented us from partaking in so much…joy."

"Is that what you're calling it? Joy?"

"Yes." She smiles cutely.

Well, I guess I'd call shower sex with Lia joy too. And sex on the kitchen floor. The only reason we're here, dressed, is because Huxley required my presence at brunch. Said he had news about the company. I asked him if it was okay if Lia joined, and he said it wasn't a problem. Otherwise, I'd be in my bed with Lia, naked, just reveling in her body and her sweet lips.

I ring the doorbell and lean down and press a kiss to her neck. "Did I tell you how beautiful you look in that dress?" I ask.

"Only five times," she answers.

"Just want to make sure." She chose a light yellow maxi dress with little to no back and cuts deep in the front. According to her, it's a sundress, but I can't be too sure about that, especially with the way I can see her hard nipples.

"Oh, and just so you know…" She stands on her toes and whispers, "I'm not wearing underwear."

"Lia," I groan just as the door opens.

Reign, their private chef, greets us with a warm smile. "Hey, Breaker. Everyone is in the back."

"Awesome. Thanks." I pause and clap him on the shoulder. "Please tell me JP isn't making Bloody Marys."

"Sorry, dude, I tried to offer up something else, but he was positive everyone enjoyed them."

"We don't. We really don't."

He chuckles, and with Lia's hand in mine, I walk her to the back of the house, where I spot JP, Huxley, Ryot, Lottie, Kelsey, and Myla all standing around talking.

When we appear at the wide-open sliding door, everyone's eyes fall on us and then on our connected hands.

"I fucking told you," JP says to Huxley, who rolls his eyes.

Lottie and Kelsey clap their hands while Ryot places a kiss on Myla's head.

"Tell us, tell us it's true. You're officially a couple," Lottie says.

I glance down at Lia and then back at our family and friends. I raise our hands and say, "It's official."

The girls screech while the guys dish out their *I told you so*s.

After some hugs and handshakes, the girls usher Lia away while the guys are left to make plates for them.

"So..." JP says. "I'm assuming you're a very happy man at the moment."

I put an egg taco together for Lia and nod. "Don't think I've ever been happier."

"Funny how that is; you know, you could have been happy years ago, but—"

"Dude, I don't need to hear it, trust me. I've been punishing myself enough."

"He's right, though," Huxley says while making a plate for Lottie.

"Well aware. I didn't come here to listen to you drone on about how you were right all these years. I came here to celebrate the fact that I finally feel...complete."

"Jesus, dude," JP says. "I didn't think you would get all emotional on us."

"I'm not crying, but hell, I'm really happy. I feel like everything is in place." I glance back at the girls, who are huddled, and then I pause before scooping up fruit and say, "We kissed for the first time last night and then had the most intimate sex of my life. After that, I was a goner. I'm done. I know I need nothing else in my life but her."

"Did you tell her that?" Huxley says.

"Fuck no. Not sure she's ready to hear all of that just yet, but it's been hard to keep it to myself, that's for sure. I just want to tell her how much I love her. I mean...fuck, I'd propose today if I knew she'd be open to it."

"Well, I'm glad you're practicing self-control," JP says. "That's progress."

We finish filling the plates for our girls, and then, with a mimosa in hand, we take them their food.

"Thank you," Lia says. I slip the mimosa glass into her hand and then lean down and grip her chin. I place a soft kiss across her lips only for Kelsey, Myla, and Lottie to all make cooing noises next to us. Lia smiles against my lips and then pulls away.

"You ladies have fun talking," I say.

"Oh, we will," Lottie says while wiggling her eyebrows. Yup, the conversation is probably going to revolve around Lia and me.

I walk back over to the buffet, pick up a pink plate and blue napkin, and then fill up on tacos and a mimosa, skipping JP's Bloody Marys altogether. I will not be subjecting myself to that today.

Just as I take a seat, Banner and Penn walk onto the back patio.

Penn is a former pitcher for the Chicago Bobbies. He's been through hell and back to better his life. Being out here in California and working with Ryot and Banner, he's truly been able to find solace and peace.

"Banner Bisley," Lottie shouts from where the girls are sitting. "Where is my cousin?"

And yeah, he's been supposedly trying to date Lottie and Kelsey's cousin Kenzie, but all I know about that situation is that things aren't going the way he wants them to.

Banner pauses and sighs heavily. "I knew I shouldn't have come."

"Looks like you need a Bloody Mary," JP says, standing from his chair. "I'll get you one."

"Thanks," Banner says, walking over with JP. I feel like I should warn him, but I also don't want to hear it from JP either.

"Grab some food, man," Huxley says to Penn. "Help yourself."

"Thanks," Penn says, looking almost shy as he picks up a plate.

Huxley glances at me, and while we're to ourselves, he says, "I'm really happy for you, Breaker. All teasing aside, I think she's perfect for you."

"Thank you." I glance over at her again. "I'm getting sort of itchy about making the next move, you know?"

"Why?" Huxley asks. "Just enjoy the moment."

"I keep telling myself that, but I don't know. We got together the day she broke up with Brian, and she hasn't really had time to mourn that relationship. I guess I'm just worried about what might happen if one day she wakes up and realizes that she made a mistake."

"Not going to happen," Huxley says. "You two are meant to be together. She knows that. Stop worrying and just have fun, man."

"Yeah, you're right," I say just as Penn sits down.

"I thought we weren't ever allowed to tell Huxley he's right. Something about an ego inflating?"

"And who told you that?" Huxley turns on Ryot, who has a taco halfway to his mouth.

"Not me. Talk to your brother."

I hold up my hands. "That would be the other brother. I'd never say something like that and get uninvited from Sunday brunch, which by the way, what's with the pink and blue balloons and décor?" I ask. "Trying to spice up Sunday brunch?"

"What?" Kelsey says, interrupting all of us and standing from where the girls are huddled. Her eyes connect with Huxley and then back with Lottie.

"Uh, everything okay, babe?" JP asks.

"No," Kelsey says. "Everything is not okay." And then she dissolves into tears, causing JP to drop all Bloody Mary ingredients and rush to her side.

"Kelsey, what's going on?"

Huxley stands from the table as well, and because I don't know what's happening, I stand too. Lia looks back at me, confused. I'm perplexed as well, and then Lottie starts crying.

Uhh…

Huxley pulls her into a hug immediately, coddling her into his chest. I just stand there, unsure of what to do.

After a few seconds, I ask, "Is there something I can do? Someone I can call?"

Lottie lifts away from Huxley, and they both exchange a glance before turning toward us and saying, "Welcome to our gender reveal party."

"Gender…as in…as in you're having a baby?" I ask, shocked.

"We are," Lottie says as she presses her hand to her stomach. "And Kelsey is mad because I didn't tell her until now."

"That's not why I'm mad," Kelsey says while wiping her eyes. "I'm not mad at all."

JP kisses Kelsey's hand and then says, "She's happy because we're pregnant too."

Uh, say what?

Lottie lets out a deathly scream before they both run into each other's arms and cry together, their husbands just staring at them.

I walk up to each of my brothers and offer them a hug. "Well, that would explain the blue and pink décor," I say when I release Huxley.

"It was Lottie's idea," he says and then pulls JP into a hug. "Fuck, congrats, man."

"Congrats to you," he says while they pull away.

"Jesus, I can't believe you two are going to be dads. I don't know if I should be happy or worried."

"Maybe a bit of both," JP says. "Because I'm scared shitless."

Huxley scratches the side of his face and whispers, "So am I."

I laugh out loud and clap them both on the back. "Listen, if I know one thing for sure, it's that you two were amazing big brothers, so I know you're going to be amazing dads too."

"Shit, that's touching," Ryot says and then pushes Banner. "How come you never say that kind of crap to me?"

Banner, who's holding a Bloody Mary, says, "If you were a good big brother, then I would…"

"Ouch." Penn chuckles. "That's got to hurt."

"Not a good big brother?" Ryot asks. "Who helped you get out of your…predicament—"

"Secret predicament," Banner says through clenched teeth.

"Well…" Ryot asks.

Banner rolls his eyes. "Fine, you're a good big brother. Best in all the land."

Ryot brings his hand to his chest. "That's so touching, thank you."

"Wow, you can really feel the love," Penn says, causing us all to chuckle.

After another round of congratulations and tons of hugs, Huxley and Lottie stand by the pool, ready to tell us the sex of the baby. It took Kelsey a second not to be mad at her sister for not telling her sooner, but I think the whole thing was diabolical, and I liked it. Baby reveal AND gender reveal. Now that's the way to do it.

"Are you ready for the grand reveal?" Lottie asks.

Arm around Lia, I hold her close as we all say yes.

"Huxley, you do the honors." Lottie holds her phone out, and I have no idea what's happening, but Huxley presses a button on the phone, and the pool lights up in all different colors. Instrumental music plays in the background, making a grand show of it, and then the lights start blinking. Lottie clutches Huxley tightly.

They flash blue.

Then pink.

Then blue.

Then pink and pink…and pink again just as the music crescendos and everything stops.

"It's a girl!" Lottie shouts and throws her arms around Huxley. He holds her tightly, kissing the top of her head, and…Jesus Christ…is that a tear in his eye?

No, it can't be.

Is it?

And then, lo and behold, he reaches up and rubs his eye.

Oh my God, Huxley Cane is crying.

"Is that what I think it is?" Lia says quietly.

"If you think Huxley is crying, then you're right."

"Wow, never thought I'd see the day."

"I don't think anyone did."

But hell, look at him. Look at Lottie and their excitement. It's palpable. I can only hope that one day Lia and I will be in the same position. *It would be the best future possible.*

———————

"Do you think we got to take home croissants because we're an item now?" Lia asks as I brush her hair out of her face while we lie in bed.

Once we got home from the brunch, which lasted another three hours after the baby reveal, we went straight to my apartment, where I slowly peeled off Lia's clothes and made love to her. That's how I see it—making love—because that's how I fucking feel about her.

"That's a great observation because Penn and Banner didn't get to take any home."

"Oh my God, do you really think it's a couples' thing? Are we in some sort of unofficial croissant club now?"

"From Scrabble club to croissant club, look how far we've come."

She chuckles. "Today was kind of crazy, all the announcements, all the questions."

Lying on my side so I can look at her beautiful face, I smooth my hand over her hip as I ask, "Did they ask about me?"

"Oh yeah. A lot."

"What kind of questions?"

"The basics. If we kissed, because they knew I was waiting for that, and I told them we kissed under the fireworks at Disneyland. They, of course, all thought you are the better Cane brother."

"Really?" I ask, a smile on my face.

"Yeah, but then I told them how you're just okay in bed, and they changed their minds."

I tickle her side, causing her to laugh as I say, "You did not say that."

"No, I didn't. I told them the truth, that you have the biggest dick I've ever seen and that it's almost too big, which makes sex not fun."

"Fucking liar." I tickle her again.

"Fine, fine. I told them easily the best sex I've ever had." Pleased, I lean down and press a light kiss to her lips.

"Better."

"What about me?" she asks as she strokes a strand of my hair. "Would you say that about me?"

"Seriously?" I ask. "Do you really need to ask that?"

She shrugs. "Maybe."

"Lia," I say softly as I cup her cheek. "Before you, sex was just a means to an end. There was nothing to it other than release, but with you, it's completely changed everything about me. The connection we have is so powerful that I feel like I'm in another world when I'm with you. Sex with you is unmatched."

She smiles. "Wow, you sure know how to make a girl feel good about herself."

"It's true, though. Everything is different with you. It's as if I can see better, hear better, taste better. You've brought vivid color into my life, Lia. You're the one pumping the oxygen through my veins."

"You mean that?"

"Yes," I answer.

Her eyes soften as she loops her hand to the back of my head and brings me down to her lips where she kisses me deeply, intimately, with every inch of her body. As our breath becomes ragged, she pushes me to my back and then kisses down my neck to my chest, and then down to my stomach.

She pushes the sheets down with her and exposes my erection, which she takes in her hand and starts pumping as she moves her mouth lower and lower.

"Lia," I whisper, desperately wanting her to know how she makes me feel.

She doesn't say anything. Instead, she kneels in front of me and then takes me in her mouth, where she sucks hard on the head of my dick.

A loud hiss escapes my lips as I spread my legs and make room for her. I thread my fingers through her hair as she works her mouth over my cock, swirling her tongue, bringing me to the back of her throat, and stroking her hand up and down my length until my legs quiver.

"Lia, I'm close," I say. "I want you on top of me."

She glances up at me, and I can see her wavering on what to do.

"Please," I say. "I love your mouth, but I want your pussy right now."

She smirks and then flicks her tongue on my cock a few more times before pulling away and straddling my lap.

"You ready?" I ask her.

The confident vixen takes my hand and brings it between her legs, where I feel just how aroused she is.

"Jesus, Lia," I say right before she positions my cock at her entrance and then lowers down in one smooth motion, wrapping me up in so much warmth that I nearly come right then and there. "Fuck," I shout as I clench down on my molars. "Lia, slow. I'll come too fast if you keep that up."

She smirks. She lifts up so I'm almost all the way out of her, and she slams down again, causing my balls to tighten. She's so fucking tight, so warm, so slick, it's killing me.

"Lia, seriously."

She does it again.

And again.

And I realize I have no control over the situation. She wants this moment, and I'm going to give it to her, so I drape my hand over my eyes and let her take control.

She slams down a few more times, causing my breath to be so erratic that I start to lose oxygen to my limbs. They become numb, tingly, and my need for this woman turns frantic.

"Fuck, I'm so close."

She lifts all the way off me until my cock rests against my stomach now.

"What the fuck?" I ask as she leans down and moves her tongue just on the underside, right against the head. "Fuck, Lia… Jesus, no, stop. I don't want to come on my stomach." I grind my teeth, my will slipping. "Fuck, please, I want to come inside you."

"Are you sure?" she says, her voice seductive. *She loves every second of this.*

"Yes. Give me your cunt. Now."

She reaches over to my nightstand, pulls out a condom, and then slips it on over my aching length. She flips around so her back faces me, then places me at her entrance again and lets me slide in. It feels so fucking good that I don't think anything will ever top this.

Ever.

"Spank me," she says as she slowly, and I mean fucking slowly, pulses up and down on me.

Knowing what she wants, I whack her on the ass, the sound ricocheting through the room.

"Yesss," she groans as her pussy contracts around my cock.

Fuck, she's close too.

So I spank her again, this time, on the other cheek. Then another. The whole time, she's pulsing over me, driving us both closer and closer to our climax.

I hit her again, this one harder, and she groans loud enough that I'm sure our neighbors can hear us. "It feels so good," she says as I lift and pull her so she's lying flat against my chest.

"Spread your legs more," I whisper into her ear.

And with our new position, her lying on top of me and my hands wrapped around her, my pelvis doing the work, I take her nipples between my fingers and drive hard into her.

"Oh my God, Breaker," she cries out. "That's...oh shit...I'm going—" She doesn't finish as she moans loudly, her pussy clenching around me, her orgasm rocking through her. It's the sexiest thing ever, getting to feel the waves of pleasure rippling through her. It's so sexy that after two more pumps, I stiffen under her. I bite down on her shoulder as I come as well. Everything around me goes black as my body floats through bliss. *This* is only accomplished when I'm with Lia.

When it's just her and me.

After a few seconds of catching our breaths, she rolls off me and then lies flat on the bed, where she breathes heavily.

"That was...new," she says as she gasps.

I chuckle. "Did it feel good?"

She turns toward me and rests her hand on my chest as she nods. "Yeah, it was a completely different orgasm for me. Like I felt it internally." She smiles. "I want to do that again."

I chuckle. "Okay, just give me a second. Got to, you know...recharge."

She smiles and then leans on my chest and moves her hand across my hair before pressing a gentle kiss to my lips. "I still can't believe I get to kiss you. It still feels so unreal."

"It's very much real," I say, returning the kiss. "Everything about you and me is real. The best kind of real."

Her fingers dance along my chest. "You're not going to get sick of me, are you?"

"You kidding me with that? If I haven't gotten sick of you over this last decade, I'm certain I won't get sick of you now."

"But relationship me is different."

"How so?" I ask. "You seem the same."

"I'm very clingy."

"When it's you, I love clingy."

She chuckles. "I'm also apparently very horny."

"Once again, when it's you, horny is amazing."

"And demanding, I'm going to need to hold your hand on all outings."

"I think I'll manage."

"And I'll require at least one date night a week."

"Am I only allowed one, or can I have more?"

She smirks. "You can have as many as you want."

"Good." I move my hand around to the back of her head and stare at her beautiful eyes.

Fuck...I love you, Lia.

I want to always be with you.

Nothing, and I mean absolutely nothing, will be better than you.

You're my forever.

"Why are you looking at me like that?" she asks.

"Like what?" I reply.

"I don't know...all...heart-eye like."

"Maybe because I have heart eyes when you're around."

She palms my face and laughs. "Don't be lame."

I twist her so her back is on the mattress and pin her down. "I'm never lame, but if you think I am, then maybe you should just walk away."

"Okay," she says as she attempts to get up.

"Oh fuck no." I pin her down again, causing her to laugh. "You're mine now."

And then I press my lips to her neck and kiss every inch of her body.

CHAPTER 22
LIA

"LIA," BREAKER GROANS AS I walk past him.

"What?" I ask when I set my empty coffee mug in the sink.

"You're killing me with that dress." He leans against the doorway to his kitchen, dressed in a dark green suit and white button-up dress shirt.

I'm killing him? The only reason I'm wearing this dress is because he chose to bust out that suit for work today, and it's taking everything within me not to tear into that suit before he goes to work.

So to counteract his full-frontal attack with the suit, I slipped on a sundress that I would normally never wear for a day of work from home, but you know, desperate times call for desperate measures.

Playing nonchalant, I glance down at my dress and then back up at him. "It's just a regular dress."

"That is *not* a regular dress," he says, walking up to me and running his fingers along the thin strap. "You don't normally wear dresses, so is there some special occasion I don't know about?"

"No," I answer. "Can't a girl just wear a dress and not get berated about it?"

"Am I berating you?" he asks. "I was unaware." He grabs my neck, possessively holding me and bringing me in closer. "I'm just wondering if you're trying to tempt me to stay home with you when I should be heading into the office."

"You're a grown man, Breaker. You can decide what you want to do with your life. I don't need to wear a dress to tempt you."

"Bullshit." He smiles right before he tilts my jaw up with his thumb and then kisses me so deep that I grab the lapels of his suit to keep from falling. I slip my tongue past his lips, and he groans right before pinning me against the cabinets in the kitchen. "Fuck," he says against my lips as he slips his hand under my dress and finds the lace strap of my thong. "I have to fucking go," he says as he tugs on my thong and sends it down my legs. I kick it to the side and spread my legs for him.

He slowly starts fingering me as his mouth takes control.

"Jesus, Lia. You're already so wet."

I untuck his shirt and thread my hand past his abs. "You're so hot in a suit."

"I knew you wore this dress on purpose," he says right before lifting me onto the counter. He then sheds his jacket, undoes his pants, pulls out his hard cock, and lifts my dress. He picks me up, and I loop my arms around his waist as he finds my entrance, and I fully take him inside me.

"Fuck, this will never get old," he says right before pinning me against the wall and thrusting up.

I'm so overwhelmed and caught off guard by the abrupt change that my body freely gives itself to him. I feel my body climb, especially from the way he's driving into me.

"Breaker," I whisper into his ear, which makes his entire body shiver.

"Shit, Lia. This is going to be fast." Holding me tightly, he thrusts a few more times, and I feel my orgasm breaking. I squeeze him tightly, tilt my head back where his lips fall to my neck, and as he peppers kisses along my skin, I let out a guttural moan as I come.

He pumps a few more times and then he releases me, pulls out and then turns away, pumping at his cock until he comes right there on the kitchen floor.

My face heats up from the sight of it.

His hand presses against the counter as we both catch our breath.

"Motherfucker," he whispers as I walk up to him and lightly take his cock in my hand. I stroke it a few times and then grab a wet paper towel from the kitchen and wipe everything up before helping him put himself back together.

When I'm done, he places both his hands on my cheeks and then kisses my mouth for a few moments before pulling away.

"This is going to be impossible."

"What will be impossible?" I ask.

"Leaving you to go to work," he answers. "I just want to stay here all fucking day with you…and night."

"Now who's the clingy one?"

He chuckles and sighs before pulling me into a hug. "Okay. I'll see you later."

"Okay."

He kisses me one more time before groaning and stepping away. "Bye, Lia."

"Bye, Breaker. Have a good day."

I wave, and he takes off. When the door shuts, I press my hand to my forehead and lean against the counter.

God…that was intense and oh so satisfying.

———

Breaker: How's your day so far? Mine's been pretty lame. I think I'm going to ask JP and Huxley if I can work from home from now on.

Lia: Probably not your best idea. We wouldn't get anything done.

Breaker: Not my problem.

Lia: It's your company with your brothers. It's very much your problem.

Breaker: Then I need to go on vacation. Let's go somewhere.

Lia: I'm still trying to catch up on all the work I've missed out on over the past few weeks.

Breaker: Quit your job. I'll hire you.

Lia: To be what?

Breaker: To sit on my dick. It's a very sought-after position.

Lia: Oh, is that so?

Breaker: Ehh, that didn't come out right.

Lia: Because I'd hope there isn't anyone else applying.

Breaker: You're the only one. So what do you say? I'll give you whatever compensation you want.

Lia: Appealing, but I'm afraid of the chafing. I'm going to have to pass.

Breaker: At least give it a trial run.

Lia: Sorry, but you sound too demanding. I don't think I can commit myself to such an arduous workplace environment. Pass.

Breaker: Dammit. At least come meet me for lunch.

Lia: Can't. I'm heading to the office supply store because I ran out of toner, and I have to print some documents to work on.

Breaker: So you're saying I have to wait until tonight?

Lia: You will survive.

Breaker: Barely.

Lia: Hang in there, Pickle.

Breaker: That just made me smile.

Lia: You make me smile. I'll talk to you later.

Breaker: Okay. Bye.

———————

"Excuse me, would you be able to direct me to your toner?" I ask the worker.

"Yes, aisle twelve," he answers. "On the right."

"Thank you." With a pack of felt-tip pens in hand, because I have a sick obsession, I walk down to aisle twelve and spot the toner. I take out my phone to see the note I wrote myself to know which toner to get when I see a text from Breaker.

> **Breaker:** JP just came into my office and started crying because he doesn't think he's going to be a good dad, and he's freaking the fuck out. What is happening to my brothers?

I smile and text him back quickly.

> **Lia:** Who knew babies were going to be the thing that took them down?

Once I press *send*, I go to my notes just as there is a tap on my shoulder. I turn and come face-to-face with Brian.

"Oh my God," I say, taking a step back. "Brian…uh…hi."

Wearing a suit and looking as handsome as ever, he smiles sadly while he sticks his hands in his pockets. "Hey, Lia," he says softly.

"Wow, uh…" I glance around, hoping that The Beave isn't here either. "What are you doing here?"

"My assistant quit on me, for good reason. I've been a tyrant lately, so I came here to pick up some supplies I needed."

"Oh." Awkwardly I ask, "Doesn't your office carry that stuff?"

"They do, but there are some specific things they don't carry."

"Nice," I say awkwardly. "Well, I'm just getting toner."

"And pens, I see," he says while gesturing to the pens in my hand. "You could never get enough of the felt-tip ones."

"It's an unhealthy obsession I'm okay with having."

"Could be worse, I guess." He rocks on his heels, and the awkwardness settles.

"Well, I'm just going to get back to my toner shopping." I thumb toward the shelves.

"Have dinner with me," he says quickly.

"What?" I ask.

"Dinner," he says, his pleading eyes lifting to mine. "I just… I want to talk."

"Oh." I clutch the pens tighter. "Well, Brian, I don't think that's a good idea. I'm sort of seeing someone."

"You are?" he asks, his shock quickly morphing into understanding. "Let me guess…Breaker."

Feeling so freaking guilty, I say, "Nothing happened until after you and I broke up, I swear, Brian. He never made a move on me, ever. I need you to know that."

He nods. "I believe you."

And even though he says he believes me, it doesn't lessen the guilt pumping through me because I know Breaker was such a sensitive topic for him.

"So…"

"I still want to have dinner or even just coffee," he says. "I just… Well, fuck, Lia." He tugs on his hair. "I just want to clear the air. I know you've moved on, but I think I just need some closure."

As I stare at his weathered eyes, eyes that I used to stare into dreamily, I realize, that yeah…maybe I need some closure too.

So before I can stop myself, I say, "Coffee would be fine."

"Okay. Thanks. I'll, uh, I'll text you the details and leave you to your toner purchases."

"Sounds good. Thanks, Brian."

He barely smiles and then turns away. When he's out of sight, I exhale harshly, unaware I was holding my breath.

Closure. I think he's right. In the back of my mind, I know something has been holding me back from giving myself fully to Breaker. From giving him everything he deserves. *My whole heart.* Maybe I haven't closed the chapter on Brian just yet. Although he never usurped Breaker's number-one spot in my heart—*I can see that now*—he was important to me.

Closure is always good before you start something new.

Maybe something that's forever.

———————

Lia: I'm an idiot.

I pace my bedroom while I wait for Myla to text me back. I didn't want to bother Kelsey or Lottie because they seem to be going through a lot with their pregnancies and their bumbling husbands. In the off chance that they might say something to JP and Huxley, who might say something to Breaker, I think keeping them out of the loop is smart.

My phone chimes, and I quickly read the text.

Myla: Doubtful, but tell me what's going on.

My fingers fly over my phone, texting her back as quickly as I can.

Lia: I ran into Brian at the office supply store, and he asked me to coffee. I said yes.

I hit *send* and wince.

Myla: Huh, that seems pretty idiotic. Is there a reason?
Lia: I told him I was dating Breaker, and he understood that. He said he wanted closure, and a part of me wants that too. But I feel like Breaker will freak out.
Myla: Why do you think you need closure?
Lia: At some point, I imagined I'd marry the man. Even though

things didn't end well, we still had some good times, and he
played an important role in my life. I think I owe it to us both
and to Breaker to close that chapter.

Myla: I could see that. So what's the problem?

Lia: I just want to make sure it's a valid reason. And sure, when I
saw Brian today, I thought he was handsome, but I'd NEVER,
and I mean never, even consider going back to him. Breaker
is...well, he's my forever, but when I go to say that to him, I
feel this mental block. I think that mental block is Brian.

Myla: I think you might be right. So then just tell Breaker you
need closure with Brian and go have it.

Lia: OH MY GOD! I can't tell Breaker. He would freak out. He's
already super possessive of me. If I told him I had to meet
with Brian, he'd second-guess everything, and I'm pretty sure
he'd become very insecure. I don't want to do that to him.

Myla: I know the feeling. Ryot is the same way when it comes to
me. So, if you think you need to do this to find closure so you
can freely move on with Breaker, then do it.

Lia: Yeah?

Myla: Yeah. If you truly want a fresh start with Breaker with nothing in the way, then you need to make sure you have a clear
mind. Trust me, I know from experience.

Lia: I think you're right. Okay. Thank you so much. I really appreciate it.

Myla: Anytime!

―――――――

"Where the hell are you?" Breaker says, flying through my front door.

"Back here," I say from my bedroom.

I hear him set something down, his shoes fly off, and then he jogs into my bedroom. I turn around just in time to catch him flying at me and tackling me to my bed.

His lips find my neck, my jaw, my mouth.

"Fuck, I missed you," he says while tugging at my shirt.

"Hold...hold on there," I say.

"What do you mean *hold on there*? I've been waiting all day for this." He lifts up to look me in the eyes.

"I know, I just, I have to go out tonight."

He lifts up even more. "What do you mean you have to go out? I thought I was all yours when I got back."

"Something came up, and I need to meet a friend."

"Oh." He lets me up. "Everything okay?"

"Yeah." My phone lights up on the nightstand with a text, and I quickly grab it and stuff it in the back pocket of my jeans. That has to be Brian. "Just an impromptu thing. Not sure when I'll be home."

He scratches the back of his head. "Okay. Well, should I wait to have dinner with you?"

"No, that's okay. Eat away. And don't feel like you need to hang out here. You can go back to your place if you want."

I move toward the entryway, a light sheen of sweat hitting my lower back. I just need to get out of here with minimal questions. But of course, he follows me.

"You seem uneasy. Are you sure everything is okay?" he asks.

I turn and place my hand on his chest and press a quick kiss to his lips, not letting him deepen it like I did earlier today. "Everything is great. I'll text you when I'm home."

"Okay." I turn to move toward the door, but he stops me and pulls me into his chest. "You'd tell me if something was wrong, right? Like if I did anything?" See...this is exactly why I don't want to tell him about Brian, because he would be way too insecure about it.

"You did nothing. Okay? I'll see you later." I give him one more kiss, and then I head out the door. I draw my phone from my pocket, grab the coordinates of where we're meeting up, and head straight there.

Dinner seemed like too much. Coffee was a perfect idea and gave me a quick out.

I approach the small coffee shop I've never been to before and spot Brian in the window, with two cups of coffee on the table in front of him. I'm surprised he even knows my order. Well, I guess I'll see if it's right.

I push through the glass door of the quaint coffee shop and move toward him. When he spots me, a light smile passes over his lips, but it's not the kind of smile he used to have. No longer in a suit, he's in a simple pair of jeans and a T-shirt. And his hair is messy, not styled like normal. I almost don't recognize him as I approach.

But what really catches my eye is the large white garment bag sitting on my chair.

"Hey…Brian," I say as I approach the table.

"Hey. Thanks for coming. I, uh, I brought one of your dresses. It was delivered to my mom's house. Uh, apparently, the other two will be delivered next week. I thought you'd want to take care of it. Maybe change the delivery address…"

"Oh, thank you," I say as I lift it and set it to the side. *I'll definitely be canceling the other dresses. Will I be able to get a refund?* Once I take a seat, Brian hands me the coffee.

"Got you a cappuccino, thought it would be the best choice for you."

Ah, so he doesn't know my order. Not that a coffee order would make or break a relationship, but the little things like that drove me crazy. After over a year of being together, how could he not know?

"I…I don't drink cappuccinos, Brian."

"Oh, sorry," he says, his shoulders deflating. "I guess I don't really know what you would drink."

"I think that was one of our problems," I say.

"So we're just going to jump right into this?" he asks.

"Might as well." I shrug.

"Okay." He shifts and twists his cup on the table. "So I clearly didn't know your coffee order."

"It's not just that," I say. "It's that I don't think you knew much about me at all. And I'm not sure I knew a whole lot about you either."

He nods. "I think you're right, and I'm probably to blame for that." He sighs. "I'm seeing that I've been so hell-bent on making something of myself and checking off all the boxes of what I need to do to get there that I don't think I've actually been living." He lifts his eyes to mine and says, "That day, when you walked away at the bakery, I wasn't even mad. I knew it was going to happen. I could feel the tension between us, I could feel you slipping away, and I knew there was no one to blame but myself."

"I should have tried harder too," I say.

He shakes his head. "I know you, Lia. You're just trying to be nice right now, but please, the blame deserves to be placed on me. I drove you away. I became uninterested. I wasn't...hell, I wasn't even fully in this relationship when I proposed. I just did it because my mother was pressuring me. It wasn't right for you, and it wasn't right for me."

"Would you have gone through with it if I hadn't called it off?" I ask.

He nods. "Yes. I would have, and I would have only made you more and more miserable because no way would I have ended it. I would have kept it going until you probably wouldn't have been able to take it anymore."

"Why?" I ask.

"Because my parents have made it impossible to please them. Status is so important to them that I would have done anything to maintain that."

"I can understand that. I probably would have done anything to make my parents happy, and I think that's why I went out with you too. They never wanted me to be alone. When I went to college, they were so scared that I didn't have anyone to lean on, like a sibling, so when I met Breaker, they were relieved. They knew he would always be by my side. When they passed shortly before I met you, I think I was trying to let them know that I'd be okay, if that makes sense."

"It really does," he says. He stares down at his coffee and asks, "Did you ever love me?"

I reach across the table and place my hand on his. "Of course, Brian," I say softly. "I loved you for so many reasons; I just don't think you and I were in love at the end. I think we were just going through the motions."

"We were, and I'm sorry about that."

"Don't be," I say. "I think I'd have been madder if you'd put in the effort, even though it was all a lie."

"My love for you wasn't a lie, Lia."

"I'm sorry, I said that wrong. I guess your intentions were a lie."

He glances out the window and sighs. "You know, if things were different, if I didn't have to live with this pressure, and I could be the man I truly am for you, the one you first met, I think we could have had a great life together."

"We probably could have," I say because Brian was fun at one point, but his competitive side—*his workaholic nature*—got the best of him.

He leans back in his chair and says, "Well, fuck." His eyes connect with mine. "Are you happy, Lia? With Breaker... Does he make you happy?"

I can't hold back the smile that crosses my lips. "Yes, I'm thrilled. It still doesn't feel real, but I'm happy."

"I'm glad. He's a good man, even though it might have seemed like we didn't get along. You two always had a special connection that I was very jealous of, and I'm sure that didn't help our case."

"It was hard hanging out with both of you, but that doesn't matter anymore." When he looks away, I ask, "Brian?"

"Hmm?"

"Are you going to allow yourself to be happy? Or are you always going to look for what's next in your career? What you can do to make your mother happy?"

"I'd like to say I'll find happiness one day, but I'm not sure." His eyes connect with mine. "My brain is wired differently. I have this internal need to please and to accomplish, and if I'm not doing one of those things every day, I feel itchy, out of control, like my life is falling apart. I'm not sure happiness can fall within those parameters."

"I know this isn't my place, but it might be helpful for you to talk to someone, a therapist, to help you work through those feelings. And maybe, to become stronger in yourself. I was so hurt when you didn't stand up for me in front of your mother, and on behalf of your future Mrs. Brian, can I urge you to learn how to do that?"

He smiles and grimaces in that order. "You're right. I know you are. I'm sorry I didn't do that. I need to find the courage first." His eyes connect with mine. "Maybe this conversation was the boost I needed."

I smile. "Well, I hope so."

We spend the next few minutes catching up quickly, but we never dive too deep. I don't tell him much about Breaker because I don't want to break his spirit. By the time we say bye, and I carry my wedding dress away from him, I feel the weight come off my shoulders like I did what I needed to do, and now I'm free.

I'm free to be with Breaker.

I'm free to love.

And I'm free to live the life I've always wanted with the man of my dreams.

I pull out my phone and text Myla.

Lia: Just got done with coffee. This was everything I needed. I'm ready to give my all to Breaker.

Myla: This is exactly what I wanted to hear.

CHAPTER 23
BREAKER

"ARE YOU BREATHING INTO A bag?" JP asks as I'm on the phone with him.

"YES!" I shout through the brown paper.

"Why?"

"Because I'm freaking the fuck out," I say as I pace my bedroom.

After Lia blew me off, I stood in her apartment for a few minutes, thinking that maybe she was only joking and she would come back, but when she didn't, dread started to fill my brain.

Why did she just walk out like that?

Who is she going to go see?

Why didn't she make solid plans for when she returned?

Why am I a needy little salamander of a man who requires to be next to her bouncy bosom at all times?

Fuck!

"Why are you freaking out?"

"All day, I was pining to see my girl, and when I got home, she was on her way out. Said she had to meet someone, but who the fuck is she meeting? I mean, we had plans, JP, not official, but I mean it was assumed we'd be spending every goddamn second with each other when we're not working and she's not working, and I'm not working, but she's not here because she's out somewhere and she was really fucking evasive about it, and now I'm wondering if I'm not good enough and if she found someone else that suits her fancy more."

"Okay, well…first of all, wow. Maybe take a breather for a second, dude. Your desperation is showing."

"I fucking know that it is," I say as I pace. "Dude, listen, I'm terrified, okay? I feel like we're together, but something has blocked her from fully being with me, and I know it's just a feeling, but it's there, and this little stunt has pushed me over the goddamn edge. I can't lose her."

"You're not losing her, you moron. She probably went out with a friend."

"What friend?" I ask. "Yeah, maybe I was a psycho and asked Ryot if Myla was with him, and maybe I asked Huxley, and maybe I called you to see where Kelsey was. She doesn't hang out with anyone else."

"Yup, okay, the desperation is truly thick. Maybe she had an embarrassing appointment and didn't want to talk to you about it. Maybe…I don't know. She has to get a mole removed or something."

"I have licked every inch of that woman's body. Trust me, there is nothing she needs to get removed."

"Valid, I've done the same to Kelsey, and she's perfect." He pauses for a second. "Ooo, maybe she's surprising you with something, like…a new car."

"What the fuck is this? *The Price Is Right*? She's not getting me a goddamn new car."

"Okay, yeah, but maybe it's something else, like lingerie! Now that's exciting and nothing to get your dick in a twist about."

"Yeah, I could…I could see that. Maybe she's buying me something."

"I bet that's it, buddy. She's getting the old Breaker boy a little treat. What a fucking nimrod, here you thought…" His voice trails off, and then I hear him say, "Uh, dude."

"What?" I ask.

"Question. Do you remember what Brian looks like?"

"Of course, I remember what he looks like. A punchable turd nugget, why?"

He's silent for a second and then says, "Well, I think I know where Lia is."

The hairs on the back of my neck stand to attention.

"What do you mean you know where she is?" I ask, once again that dread filling me.

"So Kelsey asked me to pick up some mozzarella from a deli that she's obsessed with, and since she's pregnant and hasn't been able to keep food down lately, I'd do just about anything to make her feel better, including driving twenty minutes to a deli to grab mozzarella."

"What the fuck does this have to do with Lia?" I nearly yell.

"Well, the deli is next to a coffee shop, and in the coffee shop window, I can see Lia...with a guy who I think is Brian."

"What?" I shout. "Take a picture. Take a goddamn picture right now."

"Isn't that a little stalker-y?"

"JP, I'm going to fucking rip your dick off if you don't take a picture right fucking now."

"Okay, fine. Jesus." He pauses for a second and then says, "I just texted you the pic."

I go to my text messages just as his comes in. I click on it frantically, and when the picture comes into view, I zoom in, and sure enough, there's Lia, her hand on Brian's as they both share a cup of coffee.

I sink onto my bed and stare at it.

"From your silence, I'm going to assume you're unwell at the moment."

That doesn't even begin to describe it.

"Why wouldn't she tell me?" I ask as I stare down at the picture. "Fuck, do you think...do you think she's getting back together with him?"

"No fucking chance," JP says. "Come on, dude. She was miserable with Brian."

"Then why the hell is she secretly meeting with him?"

"Huh, that's a great question."

"What are they doing now?" I ask. "FaceTime me. Let me see what's happening."

"Are you kidding me? Dude, I bolted immediately. I'm in the deli."

"Well, go back. Stand outside the window, watch everything, tell me everything. Are they going to hug? Kiss? Fuck, I think I'm going to throw up."

"Will you settle down? I'm already dealing with a hormonal wife. I don't need a hormonal brother as well."

"Excuse me, but when Kelsey was going out with another guy, I'm pretty sure I was fucking there for you."

"Yeah, and you were also single with nothing better to do than to soothe my aching soul. I'm trying to buy fucking mozzarella, for fuck's sake. You're asking too much of me."

"Why are you useless?" I ask while I flop back on the bed.

"Listen, I'm sure there's a logical explanation about what's going on. Why don't you just wait for her, and when she gets home, you ask her? Don't confront her. Don't blame her. Just ask her. Think you can do that?"

"Yeah, I think so," I say, taking a deep breath.

"And for the love of God, don't tell her I saw her and sent you a picture. That shit will get back to Kelsey, and she'll have my nuts." He lowers his voice. "I truly am scared, man. She's something different when pregnant."

"Wow, you make wanting a family so much less desirable."

"Currently, it's a three out of ten for me. I'd not recommend it."

"Great." I stand from my bed. "I'm going over to her place. The sooner I see her, the better."

"Remember, be cool."

"Yeah, thanks," I say before hanging up and stabbing my hand through my hair. "Fuck, I feel sick." I take a deep breath, and wearing only a pair of joggers and a white T-shirt, I walk over to her apartment, where I set my phone down on her kitchen counter and start to pace the living room.

She can't be getting back together with him, right?

There's no fucking way.

I'm tempted to stare at the picture, to analyze it until nothing is left inside me but dust and failed dreams, but I know that will do nothing for my psyche. Instead, I continue to pace and not freak myself out.

I love her.

It's plain and simple, just like that. I love her, and I won't fucking lose her. Not to Brian, not to anyone.

The elevator down the hall dings, and I shoot up off her couch, where I was attempting to meditate but doing a piss-poor job. All I ended up thinking about was the picture JP sent me and wondering why the hell she was touching him. *And why she was still with him an hour after that photo came through. She's now been gone for over two hours.*

Footsteps track down the hall and come closer and closer to her apartment until her key fits into the lock. I steal my breath, and as the door opens, sweat breaks out over my skin as her beautiful face comes into view.

When her eyes lift and spot me, she startles, clutching the giant white garment bag in her arms. "Jesus, Breaker. I didn't know you were here."

My eyes fall to the garment bag, and I know what that is...her wedding dress.

What the fuck is going on?

"Hey," I say, swallowing hard.

"Have you been here the whole time?"

"No," I say, feeling jittery. "I went back to my place to get changed, but then I came back here to wait for you."

"Oh," she says as her eyes fall to the garment bag and then back to me.

Fuck, fuck, fuck. Why is she holding that? Why isn't she kissing me? Why did she meet with Brian?

"Did you, uh...have a nice time?" I ask.

"I did," she says as she opens her coat closet and hangs the garment bag. She had a good time? With Brian? My stomach plummets as I squeeze my hands together, attempting to stop myself from doing something stupid. When she shuts the door, she looks at me and says, "Listen, we need to talk."

I'm going to vomit.

How?

How could he possibly come back into her life and Lia be okay with it? She even said it herself she didn't love him in the end. She was happy with her choice. So what changed her mind? Was it me? Did I do something wrong? I thought...well, fuck, I thought we were okay. Better than okay. I thought we were amazing.

"Do you think we could sit—"

"Don't choose him," I shout, unable to stop myself. "Please, Lia." My voice grows shaky. "Don't...don't choose him."

Her expression turns into confusion as she says, "Choose who?"

"Brian," I say. "I...fuck. JP saw you at a coffee shop with Brian, holding hands, and I know this is shitty of me to say and to put this kind of pressure on you, but please don't go back to him. Choose me. I promise I'll do whatever it takes to make you happy. Anything, just—"

"Breaker," she says, coming up and taking my hand. "I'm not getting back together with Brian."

"You're not?" I ask as a wave of relief floods through me, causing my eyes to tear up.

"No," she answers as she cups my face. "Oh my God, I'm so sorry that your mind even went there." And then she lifts onto her toes, brings my face closer, and presses a kiss to my lips. I'm so relieved that I nearly collapse.

"I need...fuck, I need to sit down," I say.

She guides me to the sofa, where I sit, and she sits next to me. I shake my head, wanting her as close as possible, and I bring her to my lap, where she straddles my legs, and I can hold on to her.

"Oh my God, were you thinking this whole time that I was getting back together with him?" she asks.

"Yes," I whisper as I rub my hands up and down her sides.

"No. I would never. Brian and I...well, I guess I should start from the beginning."

I nod. "Yeah, it might be a good idea."

She presses her hand to my chest and says, "I ran into Brian at the office supply store. It was really strange seeing him again, for obvious reasons. He was cordial and asked if we could go out to dinner." My body tightens at the thought of them sharing a meal together. "I told him I was seeing someone, and he guessed it was you. I don't know if he was happy for us, but he was happy that I was happy. Not sure where he stands with you."

"As if I give two fucks," I say.

She chuckles. "Anyway, he thought things ended abruptly and asked if we could just talk it out, find some closure. Basically, he wanted to apologize. At first, I was unsure. I told him to text me where to meet him, but after, I was uneasy about it. I was talking to Myla about whether I should go or not when I realized that it wasn't a question at all. I needed to meet up with him."

"To, uh…to see if you still had feelings for him?"

She smiles lightly. "No, Breaker, to find closure. You see, I happen to be in a relationship with someone I really care about. I wasn't giving him everything I had because this door with Brian was still open. I never truly got to close it. That's what tonight was about. Ending that chapter in my life so I can have a fresh start…with you."

More relief floods through me, and I drop my head to the back of the couch. "Jesus," I whisper. "Why didn't you just tell me that?"

"Because you would have freaked out."

"No, I wouldn't have."

She gives me a judging look before saying, "If I told you I was going to coffee with Brian, you would have flipped out. Don't even lie to me."

I glance away and mutter, "Yeah, that might have been true. But you could have told me you needed closure."

"I guess I wasn't one hundred percent positive about what I needed. But I'm glad I figured it out."

"And what do you need?" I ask.

She drags her thumb over my five o'clock shadow. "I need you, Breaker. I need us. I want us." She wets her lips. "I'm not convinced I was fully committed up until this point, and I can truly say I know what my feelings are. I know where they rest, and that's with you." She leans in and presses her forehead against mine. "I'm in love with you, Breaker, and that might be too soon to say, but that's where I'm at."

I place my hands under her shirt and hold her tightly as my chest swirls with so many fucking emotions.

She loves me.

Jesus Christ. And here I thought she was going to break up with me.

I chuckle, and she pulls away. "What's so funny?"

"Shit, sorry. I didn't mean to laugh at that. Poor timing." I let out a deep sigh. "I've wanted to tell you I love you for some time now, but I've held back because I didn't want to freak you out. And then today, I thought you were breaking up with me, but instead, you tell me you love me. I mean, fuck, I've been through the wringer."

She smiles and leans in close while playing with the collar of my shirt. "You love me?"

"Desperately," I answer. "Pathetically. To the point that I'd have no shame in following you around even if you did get back with Brian. I'm so fucking in love with you, Ophelia, that I can feel it all the way to the marrow of my bones. It's a part of me. You're a part of me."

Right when I think she's going to kiss me, she stands from my lap.

"Where are you going?" I ask, confused.

She holds her hand out, and I take it. She weaves me through her apartment to her bedroom, and then turns to face me. In one smooth motion, she lifts her shirt up and over her head.

"Fuck," I mutter as I take in her purple lace bra.

She slides her hands under my shirt as she says, "You are a part of me too, Breaker. I'm sorry it took me a second to realize that, but I'm glad I did."

"Are you saying that you're mine...forever?" I ask.

She helps me out of my shirt and nods. "Yes, I'm yours...forever."

Then she lays me down on the bed and straddles my lap. I roll her to her back and pin her to the mattress. I lower my mouth to hers and kiss her with every inch of my heart. And she returns the kiss, her mouth parting, making room for my tongue.

When I pull away and stare down into her beautiful eyes, I say, "I love you, Ophelia. So fucking much."

She smirks and says, "I love you too...Pickle."

Laughing, I bury my head in her shoulder and kiss up her neck while she settles underneath me, letting me take the lead.

Sure, do I wish I'd realized several years ago that getting together with Lia was inevitable—some might say...a long time coming? Of course. But I also realize the extraordinary bond we built over the years, and Lia might be right. I'm not sure how close we would really be if we didn't have those years to bond.

All I know is that I'm fucking happy, and my brothers will never let me live this down.

Ever.

EPILOGUE
BREAKER

"IS THIS STUPID? THIS FEELS stupid," I say as Lia is in our bedroom with Myla, changing her shirt since Myla spilled a drink on her.

"This is not stupid. This is well executed," JP says. "Now, don't fuck this up for me. I've put a lot of energy into this."

"You bought the balloons," I say.

"Uh, and I came up with the Bloody Mary spill idea—the tactic to surprise Lia. You're welcome."

He is right about that, unfortunately.

Shortly after Lia and I said the big *I love yous* to each other, we decided to give up our apartments and buy a house. It was a big decision, one we didn't take lightly. We walked through twenty-three houses until we found the perfect one...a block down from my brothers. Lia liked that we were close to Lottie and Kelsey, and I liked that Lia was finally happy with a house.

We moved in two weeks ago, and today, we're hosting Sunday brunch with some help from Reign of course. No, we didn't steal him, but we're hosting so I can propose to Lia but make it a surprise.

The plan is this: We eat, chat, have a good time, and then Myla spills a drink on Lia's shirt. Her task is to keep Lia upstairs for at least five minutes. The moment they disappeared, all hands were on deck. We moved all the premade decorations into place, along with a giant light-up sign that says, *Marry Me.*

When it came to the proposal, I thought of many ways I could do it. There was proposing at Disney, since that's where we shared our first kiss. I thought about it before we moved out of our apartments. I thought about it while playing a game of Scrabble with her, you know, to make it full circle. But when it came down to it, I knew having the support of friends and family was what I truly wanted. Plus, I wanted pictures and video, so I've put Lottie and Kelsey in charge of that.

Not to mention, I truly believe one of the main reasons Lia is with me now is because of the people around us. They helped bring us together with their advice and their gentle nudges of encouragement. Okay, full-on pointed opinions. It feels only fitting to have everyone here.

"Do you have the ring?" Huxley asks as he comes up next to me.

"Of course I have the ring," I say as I hold up my hand.

A week ago, Huxley, JP, and I picked out the ring, the exact style I know Lia will love. Three stones represent past, present, and future on a white-gold band, topping off at two carats. I considered getting something bigger, but I know she wouldn't want it. This is perfect.

"Are you nervous?"

"Yes," I say, my legs trembling beneath me. "I think she's ready for this. I mean, we bought a house together, but a part of me is still scared that she'll tell me she's not ready."

"Not going to happen," Huxley says. "She looks at you the way Lottie looks at me and the way Kelsey looks at JP. That kind of love is forever."

"Thanks," I say as he pats me on the back.

Something has happened to Huxley over the past couple of months since they announced Lottie's pregnancy. He's more sensitive and less robotic. He seems to have actual feelings now. And the only time I see the old Huxley return—the sharp, rigid Huxley—is when someone is looking at Lottie the wrong way, or he needs to put someone in their place. But this new touchy-feely guy is really throwing me off.

As for JP, well, he has become ultra annoying, clinging to me every chance he can get to stay away from what he refers to as the "she-devil," a.k.a. Kelsey. The pregnancy hormones have apparently scared JP right out of his own house. Not sure what he's talking about because she's been absolutely pleasant to me.

"Anything else we need to do?" Banner asks from the side where he oversees the music. His girlfriend, Kenzie, is right next to him, holding a confetti popper. She's really freaking funny. I've gotten to know Kenzie over the last month or so, and she's a perfect addition to the group. Quirky and odd but a whole lot of fun.

"I think we're good," I say. I glance around. "Is everyone in place?"

Kelsey and Lottie offer me a thumbs-up as they hold their phones, ready to record everything from different angles.

JP and Huxley are off to the side, holding the curtains to the backyard shut so Lia doesn't see what's going on as she walks back to the brunch.

Ryot and Penn hang out by the table with confetti poppers in hand. Which by the way, I heard Penn finally took Birdy out on a date, but he has yet to tell me how it went. I'm hoping it went well, although I know Penn has been fighting some demons, so I'm not entirely sure if there will be a second date or not.

"She's coming," Lottie whisper-shouts, pulling me to attention.

"You got this," JP says while giving me an exaggerated thumbs-up.

I steal my breath, pray that I don't pass out, and as JP and Huxley pull the curtains open, revealing Lia in the doorframe, looking confused and surprised, it's impossible to catch my next breath.

Banner plays the music, soft instrumental, while everyone else fades into the background.

Lia's eyes find mine, and they immediately begin to fill with tears.

"Oh my God," she says softly as she brings her shaky hand to her mouth. I take a step forward and hold out my hand for her to take.

She does, and as I bring her out onto the patio and in front of the lit-up *Marry Me* sign, I can't help but notice just how jittery I am as well.

"Ophelia," I say softly. "When I first met you, I thought you were everything I needed in my life. You liked all the things I liked. You made me laugh. You put me in my place. And you were so fucking beautiful that I told myself I was going to ask you out. Unfortunately for me, you were looking for a friend, not a boyfriend, and I'm glad you were because I can't imagine enduring the last decade of our lives without each other." I get down on one knee as tears fall down her cheeks. "You make me so fucking happy that I don't need anything in life but you." I take a deep breath and say, "Ophelia Fairweather-Fern, will you please be my wife?"

She nods, not even taking a second to think about it. Confetti poppers shoot into the air, our friends and family cheer, and as I stand to put the ring on her finger, an overwhelming sense of relief hits me all at once.

She's going to be mine forever.

"Oh my God, Breaker," she says right before she grips the back of my neck and brings me down for a kiss.

It's a brief kiss because she's crying and everyone is crowding around us looking for hugs, but when I look into her eyes, past her perfectly purple glasses, I know for a fact that she'll forever hold my heart, and I will forever hold hers. A long time coming? Perhaps. But every day together, every challenge we faced, every joy we shared, every game she trounced me on, made us closer than I could ever imagine two people being. I love this girl, and I'll do everything to make her life as wonderful as she is. She *will* carry knitted flowers down the aisle, and she will have daisies everywhere she wishes. I'll make every dream come true. And most of all? I can't wait to say those two additional words that join us until the end of time.

ABOUT THE AUTHOR

#1 Amazon and *USA Today* bestselling author, wife, adoptive mother, and peanut butter lover. Author of romantic comedies and contemporary romance, Meghan Quinn brings readers the perfect combination of heart, humor, and heat in every book.

Website: authormeghanquinn.com
Facebook: meghanquinnauthor
Instagram: @meghanquinnbooks